Lamb to the Slaughter

Also By The Same Author

Death is my Neighbour

Last Act of All

Past Praying For

The Trumpet Shall Sound

Night and Silence

Shades of Death

NOVELS FEATURING DI FLEMING

Cold in the Earth

The Darkness and the Deep

Lying Dead

ALINE TEMPLETON

Lamb to the Slaughter

HODDER &
STOUGHTON

First published in Great Britain in 2008 by Hodder & Stoughton
An Hachette Livre UK company

4

A CIP catalogue record for this title is available from the British Library

Hardback ISBN 978 0 340 92228 6
Trade Paperback ISBN 978 0 340 92229 3

Typeset in Plantin Light by Hewer Text UK Ltd

Printed and bound in the UK by CPI Mackays ,Chatham ME5 8TD

Hodder & Stoughton policy is to use papers that are natural, renewable and recyclable products and made from wood grown in sustainable forests. The logging and manufacturing processes are expected to conform to the environmental regulations of the country of origin.

Hodder & Stoughton Ltd
338 Euston Road
London NW1 3BH

www.hodder.co.uk

For Milena with fondest love

I

'No,' the woman said. She could feel the muscles in her neck tense into cords, and her nails dig into the palm of her hand in an effort to stop her voice from wavering. 'Whatever you say, whatever you do – no.'

She had to use both hands to set down the receiver and even then she was shaking so much that she knocked it off its stand again.

'What do you do about a dead sheep?' PC Sandy Langlands's cheerful, cherubic face was creased into worried lines as he came into the CID room at the Kirkluce headquarters of the Galloway Constabulary.

'I don't know, what do you do about a dead sheep? Just get to the punchline, Sandy – I'm busy.' DC Will Wilson was working on a tricky report at one of the computers and didn't look up.

'No, a real dead sheep.' Langlands came across to perch on a nearby desk. 'It's not very nice – pretty messy. Looks as if someone shot it, then dumped it in the courtyard of the Craft Centre. Mrs Paterson, her that has the pottery there, found it when she came in this morning and about had a fit.'

Reluctantly abandoning his report, Wilson grimaced. 'I hate Mondays. The vandals all go on a spree at the weekend and we get to clear up the mess. Whose sheep was it – any mark on the fleece?'

Langlands shook his head. 'No. Cut away, probably. And I checked – there's been no report from any of the farmers about a problem.'

'Not a lot we can do about it then, is there? Take statements to make them feel we've taken this seriously and get someone to remove the beast before the story's all round the town and everyone comes to take a look. There'll be muttering about us not stopping vandalism, but at least we can look efficient at clearing it up.'

Langlands thanked him and went away.

If only everything was as straightforward as that! Going back, frowning, to his problems, Will Wilson dismissed it from his mind.

On this windless Saturday evening, there were three swallows on the telephone wire which looped across Andrew Carmichael's garden. Only three, but next week there would be more, then more, their twittering the knell for the passing of another summer.

Sitting on the low wall that surrounded the rose garden, Andrew sighed. It seemed an alarmingly short time since he had sat here last year in the same elegiac mood, watching the swallows prepare for departure as August slipped into September.

It was still warm, but over the low Galloway hills beyond the garden wall the weakening sun was a line of fire below a sky streaked with gold, pink, purple and lilac – a good show, tonight, in full technicolor. He was something of a connoisseur of sunsets from this vantage point. How old had he been when he had watched his first one? Four, perhaps.

That was a lot of sunsets over seventy years – minus, of course, the years when he'd been posted to the Tropics. Korea, Malaya, Belize: when night fell there like a shutter coming down, feeling homesick and sometimes scared, he had hungered for the slow golden gloaming of a Scottish summer night and the sweet-pea perfume of the old blush rose which had always rambled along the wall.

It was still and silent tonight, apart from the muffled croon of a wood pigeon in one of the silver birches. Andrew tipped his face back to the last of the sunshine and words by his beloved Browning came unbidden to mind:

I am grown peaceful as old age tonight.
I regret little, I would change still less.

That wasn't true, though. He had much to regret, and old age was more of a burden than a benison when he would need so much energy for the meeting later. He was coming under pressure, severe pressure. How much easier it would be simply to give in to it! After all, it wasn't as if there weren't arguments in favour of doing just that.

But supposing he did, what about lovely, vulnerable Ellie? And Pete too – a charming fellow, but he was heading for trouble again, sadly, and Romy's job as the main breadwinner would be harder still without his own support for her studio. He knew he ought to stand firm. Ought to.

He'd never had a problem when it was just bullets that were being fired at him. Physical courage was easy; moral courage in your personal life was different and he didn't like to think about the times when he hadn't had the guts to do what he knew was right. He'd paid the price today already for what had been cowardice, pure and simple. An ugly vice in an old soldier.

He shifted uncomfortably on the wall, which seemed to have become harder over the past few minutes. The colours were fading now, turning muddy and dull, and Andrew rose a little stiffly.

He still had a military bearing, straight-backed without the chin-poking stoop of old age. The twinges of creaking joints were no more than a nuisance; he'd been lucky compared to his poor Madeleine, who had found relief from the agony of her twisted, arthritic limbs only in death last year.

He turned towards the house. Fauldburn House was a sprawling grey sandstone building, grown over the centuries from its austere Scottish Georgian beginnings to accommodate large Victorian and Edwardian families. It was far too big for him now: with no one coming to visit, there were too many rooms shut up and unused. He and Madeleine had talked about selling, but he shrank from the thought of seeing his household goods dispersed. All he wanted now was to be left in peace, which at the moment seemed a forlorn hope.

The estate that went with the house was on the western edge of the market town of Kirkluce. It had never been extensive, and land had been very advantageously sold off for housing over the years, but there was still some tenanted farmland and a courtyard with old stable buildings round about, converted now into shops as a Craft Centre.

Andrew went down the stone-flagged steps, in at the back door and along the passage by the kitchen where Annie had said she'd left a salad for him on a covered plate in the fridge. He'd fetch it later, he decided, once he'd changed out of his gardening cords and the soft cotton twill shirt that was frayed round the collar. His King's Own Scottish Borderers tie with grey flannel bags and his blazer would be more suitable to put steel into him, because no matter what he decided, battle lay ahead.

He changed, then took the silver-backed hairbrushes from his dressing-table, one in each hand, and was applying them to the springy white hair which, thank the Lord, showed no sign of deserting its post, when the doorbell rang.

He swore mildly. Someone coming round, no doubt, to bend his ear in advance of the meeting. Just as long as it wasn't Norman Gloag: he'd been tried enough by that unspeakable man and he'd reached the point where he couldn't guarantee to be civil.

He went downstairs, across the cool darkness of the entrance hall and opened the door.

'That's the last burger, Cammie.' Bill Fleming, his fair complexion flushed from the heat of the glowing charcoal, took it from the grid, stuffed it into a bun and handed it to his son Cameron.

From an elderly deckchair with sagging canvas, Bill's wife Marjory watched them lazily, putting her hand up to shield her eyes from the low sun. Cammie, at twelve, was growing fast now, so fast that she sometimes thought she could see the gap between his trainers and the hem of his jeans widen as she watched. He'd overtaken his older sister Catriona and looked set fair to top her own five foot ten by the end of the year. And she'd noticed a few more strands of grey in her chestnut crop lately – an unwelcome reminder of the passage of time.

Cammie was looking anxious as he took the burger. 'What if I'm still hungry?' he demanded.

'There's times when you aren't?' his mother said caustically, then relented. 'OK, I brought the Tin back from Granny. She was baking today, and she filled it up for us.'

'Oh good,' Cammie said indistinctly and, still chewing, headed for the kitchen and the Tin, whose contents over the years had compensated for the inability of his culinarily challenged mother to bake so much as an edible scone.

Marjory grinned at Bill, then leaned back and shut her eyes, enjoying the lingering warmth. For once she'd had a Saturday off from police work when the weather was kind, and Bill had been persuaded to leave the evening chores on the sheep farm to Rafael Cisek who, with his wife Karolina and their toddler son, had come from Poland to Scotland as soon as it became legally possible. The family was happily installed now in the farm-worker's cottage just below the Mains of Craigie farmhouse. Rafael was a good man, son of a tenant farmer himself and experienced with the young cattle Bill was now buying in to fatten for the market. Better still, Karolina, who was sweet and shy, was delighted to have a little job helping in the house while Janek, aged two, tumbled about the place after her like a puppy. Marjory could hear them now in the cottage garden, Janek shouting with glee and his parents laughing. She smiled herself at the happy sounds.

At last Marjory's personal life was running more smoothly, easing the domestic pressure on her as she coped with the professional demands of her challenging job as detective inspector with the Galloway Constabulary. Even Marjory's father, Angus Laird, now in the long twilight of dementia, was settled in a pleasant, comfortable nursing home, and his wife Janet, relieved of the stress of caring for him, was more like her old self again.

Marjory's main concern at the moment was Tam MacNee, her detective sergeant, mentor and friend, who was taking a long time to recover from the head injury he'd sustained in a vicious attack a few months before. He'd been a bad patient – 'patient' wasn't a word she'd ever associated with Tam – and he was still suffering from cruel headaches and tiredness. He had lost weight, too, and with his thin, wiry build he didn't have it to lose. The doctor had so far refused to pass him as fit for work and though Tam was all for ignoring this, she'd had to tell him that for insurance reasons he couldn't be allowed to return to his duties. She'd made the mistake of trying to console him by saying if he took it easy he'd get better quicker: Tam had always been possessed of an acid tongue and Marjory got the full benefit. He was definitely improving now, though, and she thought it was probably only a matter of a week or two more.

She was missing her friend Laura, too. Laura Harvey, a psychotherapist whose perspective on some of Marjory's problems, both personal and professional, had been invaluable in the past, had gone to London to record a TV programme based on her popular column in a Sunday broadsheet. It had been for a fortnight, originally. She had been away now for three months and Marjory had an unhappy feeling that she was unlikely ever to return. She sighed, unconsciously.

'You do realise Cammie's in there alone with the Tin?' Catriona's voice broke in on her mother's thoughts. She was curled up on a sun-lounger, idly flicking through a teen magazine, and Marjory opened her eyes again to look at her fourteen-year-old daughter. She was growing up fast and, her mother recognised with a pang, was hardly a child any longer. She had the happy combination of Bill's fair hair and blue eyes and Marjory's own long legs, quite a lot of them now exposed in skimpy shorts, but she was slightly built and looked like remaining the smallest in the family.

This evening she was wearing make-up and had changed into a bright pink crop top – a little elaborate for a family barbecue, but then she was still at the stage when she changed her clothes three times a day and of course never wore anything again after she'd had it on, however briefly. Still, it didn't matter too much now that Karolina had a firm grip on the laundry. God bless Karolina!

'Good thinking,' Bill said. 'You'd better go and prise it away from him. Bring it out here – there was a rumour of brownies.'

Cat unfolded herself and was on her way to the kitchen when the evening peace was shattered by the roar of motorbike engines, close and getting closer. Meg the collie, lying asleep on the lawn, raised her head with a growl, then jumped up and loosed a volley of barks. Cat turned and went to look over the old orchard below the house, where Marjory's hens had started cackling in fright, to the track which wound up to the farm from the main road.

'What on earth—?' Marjory exclaimed, sitting up, and Bill, who was still on his feet, went over too to peer down at the two approaching motorbikes, with their denim-clad and helmeted riders.

Cat turned pink. 'It's all right,' she said hastily. 'It's just some boys from school.'

They had pulled up by the farm gateway, taking off their helmets to reveal one close-cropped dark head and one with bleached shoulder-length hair tied back in a ponytail. The engine noise stopped and petrol fumes drifted up to mingle with the lingering smell of char-grilled meat.

'What's all this about?' Bill, eyebrows raised, turned to his wife.

'It explains the make-up and the smart top. She must have been expecting them.'

'Was she, indeed!' Bill came back and sat down heavily on the vacated lounger. 'What age do you have to be to ride a motorbike?'

'Seventeen,' Marjory said grimly.

'And she's fourteen.'

'I had noticed.'

'Well, she's not going on the back of one of those things, and that's flat.'

'You tell her. If I do it'll start World War Three.'

'Oh, I'll tell her. And I want to know a lot more about them, too.' He got up purposefully.

'Give her ten minutes, then go down and ask them up for coffee. Nicely,' Marjory suggested.

'Five.' Bill sat down again, looking at his watch.

Cat was doing a lot of laughing. They could hear the distinctive teenage giggling, high-pitched with nervous excitement, and

Marjory looked at her husband with a wry smile. 'You have to face it, Bill – your little girl is growing up, and she's bonnie. We're going to have to get used to boyfriends.'

'Not seventeen-year-old bikers. She's far too young.' He consulted his watch again.

'That's three minutes. Barely.'

'I know.' Bill got up restlessly and started collecting the ketchup-smeared plates. 'It's not going to be easy, this next stage, is it?'

'No, I don't suppose it is.' Marjory sighed. 'And I was just thinking how good it was to have things sorted out – Dad settled, and Mum so much better, and with Rafael and Karolina . . .'

'So it's your fault, is it? You ought to know better than to tempt providence like that.

'Well, that's five minutes. Seven, in fact. I'm going down.'

But just as he spoke the bikes' engines started up again and when he looked they were on their way down the drive and Cat was walking back up the slope, still smiling. Without looking at her parents, she headed for the house.

'Cat!' Bill called and the girl turned, but made no move towards him.

'Come here!'

She obeyed with obvious reluctance, the smile disappearing.

'Who was that?' he asked.

She shrugged. 'Just a couple of the guys from school.'

'Do they have names?' Marjory asked.

'Oh, so it's police questioning now, is it? Do I have a right to remain silent?'

Marjory counted to ten. Bill said mildly, 'Is there some reason why you shouldn't tell us your friends' names? Are you ashamed of them?'

The colour rose in Cat's face. ' 'Course not. Just, it's, like, my business, isn't it? All they did was look in to say hello. So shoot me!'

'If we had friends visiting and we spoke like that to you, you would have a right to be annoyed. Don't be rude, Cat.'

There was an edge to Bill's voice and Cat's eyes filled. 'Oh, if it's so important – just Dylan Burnett and Barney Kyle. So now can I go – or did you want to grill me some more?'

'Go if you want to.' Recognising a losing situation, Bill shrugged in his turn and his daughter didn't give him time to change his mind. They could hear her crying as she went back to the house.

'Hormones,' Marjory said. 'That's her going to phone her friend Jenny to tell her she's got, like, the world's cruellest parents.'

'How many years before she leaves home?' Bill was saying as Cammie emerged from the house eating a brownie.

'What was with the bikes?' he asked.

'Friends of Cat's,' Marjory said. 'Dylan Burnett and Barney Kyle.'

Cammie's eyes widened. 'They came to see Cat? Wow! They're seriously cool.'

'Oh, are they,' Bill said drily. 'What does being "seriously cool" involve?'

'Well, they've got the bikes. And they do crazy things.'

'Like what?' his mother asked him, but he didn't seem to know. Just 'everyone said' they did crazy things.

Later, as they were putting away the garden furniture, Bill said to Marjory, 'I suppose it would be unethical for you to see if there's anything on them in the files?'

Marjory laughed. 'I'm sure it is. And in answer to the question you haven't asked yet, first thing in the morning.'

Romy Kyle had arrived early at St Cerf's Church Hall in Kirkluce High Street, hired for the public meeting about the superstore which Councillor Norman Gloag had arranged – not that she was even remotely inclined to cooperate with the nasty little man. But he'd have managed to get people together and she was going to see to it that they heard the other side.

There was a lot of unease, even anger, in Kirkluce. To the traditionalists, its atmosphere was unique and precious: an old-fashioned town centre, where greengrocers and bakers and butchers served the population in the way they always had since Kirkluce had been a village, where each day you 'went for the messages' and met your friends in the High Street. A superstore would drive most of the local shops out of business.

Ranged on the other side were the working mums, who found the little Spar supermarket inadequate for their needs, allied to those for whom tradition was a dirty word and the young who longed for the excitement of change and the ready availability of seventy-five different flavours of crisps as opposed to the half-dozen on offer at the moment.

The battle-lines were drawn and the plans were being made for committees and pressure groups, but it was early days yet. It was common knowledge that Colonel Carmichael could refuse to sell the land that was needed and it would all come to nothing. Only those most directly affected, whose immediate livelihood was threatened, were ready to make trouble.

The Church Hall was a clever choice of venue. In the sober atmosphere, with the hall's dark cream and brown gloss-painted walls and splintery floor, strong passions would seem out of place. Well, Romy Kyle was prepared to do a bit of rabble-rousing, if that was what was needed.

A stocky figure in jeans and a burgundy cotton fisherman's smock, she walked down the aisle between the rows of stacking chairs, her square jaw set as she made her way purposefully towards the table where Gloag and the representative from the superstore would sit. She nodded, unsmiling, at a couple of people who had arrived even earlier and took her seat right in the middle of the front row, where Gloag couldn't pretend not to see her when she wanted to speak.

She set her well-worn leather tote bag down on the chair next to her to save it for Pete, her partner – and where the hell was he? She'd reminded him about the meeting this morning but when she got home from the Fauldburn Craft Centre he wasn't there. She and Barney had eaten alone and there was still no sign of Pete when she left. Gone to the pub, no doubt. He'd claim he hadn't noticed the time, like he always did. Romy suspected that he never wore a watch just so he had that excuse.

Why on earth had she put up with him all these years? Eight of them, last time she counted, including two when he'd been behind bars and at least wasn't giving trouble then. If she had the sense of a dim-witted amoeba, she'd have thrown the useless bugger out years ago, with his 'deals' and his 'projects' which never seemed to work out. God knew she'd thought of it often enough, yet he'd only to look at her with those dark, dark blue eyes and that crooked smile, and her resolve would crumble. Her artistic soul loved beauty, and he was beautiful.

He was also a professional conman, with the record to prove it, and Romy was his most consistent victim. She had no illusions. He didn't fool her – yet always she chose to swallow the latest lie. The only way she'd ever get rid of him was if he decided to go, and then she'd die of grief.

There were more people coming in, a steady trickle, and she half-turned in her chair to assess the strength of the opposition. There was MacLaren the butcher, with his wife and a posse of friends: he'd be happy enough to trouser what he could get and retire. And Senga Blair – her fancy goods shop had been struggling for years, and when she caught Romy's eye she quickly looked away again. That was a bad sign. It was becoming clear that Gloag had managed to pack the hall with his supporters.

Andrew Carmichael hadn't arrived yet. She hoped he wouldn't be late: she was wanting a word with him to discuss tactics. If he told them outright he wasn't prepared to sell, things could get ugly.

But Ellie Burnett had appeared. Romy waved, gesturing to her to come forward, but Ellie didn't seem to notice, making for a seat in the middle of the hall as she greeted acquaintances with her sweet, vague smile.

As the mother of a teenage son, she had to be well on in her thirties, but she looked ten years younger than that, wearing a long flowered skirt with a ruffled white cotton shirt, her fair hair all pre-Raphaelite waves and tiny ringlets round that Madonna face. She was very pale, though, and there were blue marks like bruises showing through the delicate skin under her eyes, an indication of the stress she was under. She was looking utterly exhausted too.

They were all under stress, especially since that disgusting business with the dead sheep earlier this week – intimidation from ALCO or their chums, no doubt. It was just that in some people stress didn't make you look so rose-petal fragile that men fell over themselves to pat your hand and ask tenderly how you were, like they were doing to Ellie now. But then, men always made fools of themselves over Ellie. When she did one of her folk-song nights in the Cutty Sark pub, they sat about drooling in a way that put you off your beer.

Romy's tensions showed in the deepening lines between her dark eyes and around her wide mouth; she'd accumulated a crop of angry spots on her chin, too – not a pretty sight. Unconsciously she touched them with her short, square fingers, scarred with calluses and burns from years of working with silver.

And here, at last, was Pete, chatting his way down between the chairs, scattering his famous smile like largesse to the punters as he passed. Seeing her, he waved and came to sit down, breathing beer and charming apologies at her.

'Sorry, sorry, sorry, babe,' he murmured. 'I had an idea about that project I needed to discuss with Dan and then I was late leaving him.'

'So you didn't have time for more than a couple of pints on the way home.' Romy's voice was tart.

Pete grinned, unabashed. 'You know me too well. Forgive me?'

He took her rough hand in his, stroking the back of it with his thumb, and as always at his touch, a thrill ran down her spine.

'One day I won't,' she warned.

Pete didn't even acknowledge the empty threat. 'Barney didn't want to come?'

'No, I suggested he might, considering what's at stake, but—' She shook her head.

Barney had looked at her as if she were mad. 'How can I? I'm going out on the bike with Dylan,' he said with the elaborate patience of one explaining to a small child with learning difficulties.

'You wouldn't have the bike if it wasn't for the business,' she'd pointed out, knowing she was wasting her breath. She hadn't wanted him to get it anyway, given the shocking death toll for young riders, but it was never easy to make 'no' stick where Barney was concerned. He didn't scruple to play the resentment card because she'd walked out on his father to take up with Pete, and once Dylan Burnett persuaded Ellie to get him a bike, Romy knew Barney wouldn't give up. It was smarter to stick it on the credit card at the start and save weeks of aggro.

Dylan was a bad influence – there was no doubt about

that. Well, what could you expect? His father was a showman in a funfair; Ellie had stuck with the travelling lifestyle for a couple of years but once their informal partnership broke up, such contact as Dylan had with his father had been casual at best. It was tough, being a single mother, and her worst enemy couldn't call Ellie forceful. She doted on Dylan so that he was thoroughly spoiled, so no wonder he ran wild.

Romy had been strict enough with Barney as a child, but she was worried about him now. He spent holidays with his father, and the occasional weekend, but that didn't give him the paternal discipline that a young man needed. Pete certainly wasn't about to take on the role. His attitude to Barney was detached, to say the least. Sometimes Romy suspected there was actual dislike there, though it was hard to tell with Pete.

Still, she had other, more pressing problems at the moment. She turned again to scan the hall. There were probably seventy people here now, but there was still no sign of Andrew and she felt a little lurch of disquiet. Surely he couldn't have forgotten?

Alanna Paterson appeared, panting, at her side and collapsed into a chair. She'd shut up her potter's workshop at the Craft Centre just before Romy left, but she didn't seem to have found time to change. She was still wearing clay-smeared jeans and a grubby-looking top and her grey hair was wild.

'I thought I was going to be late! I had a couple of phone calls.'

'Better late than never. Andrew hasn't arrived yet. I can't think what's happened.' Romy was starting to get nervous.

Alanna seemed surprisingly unmoved. 'Oh, I expect he'll turn up. What about Ossian – did he say if he was coming?'

'He'll probably only come if he can sit staring at Ellie. He's hardly going to be worried about losing the studio. Mummy and Daddy will write the cheque for another one,' Romy said acidly. She didn't have much time for Ossian Forbes-Graham; the oils he produced from his Craft Centre studio were beginning to be taken seriously by the art establishment in Edinburgh and even London, but it was all about image, in her opinion. He'd seen *La Bohème* once too often, probably, from the way he behaved, and he seemed to her weird and getting weirder.

'Oh well,' Alanna said, a little uncomfortably, 'everyone's got their own take on this.'

Romy gave her a sharp look. Was it possible that Alanna, too, had been got at by the enemy? And perhaps even Ellie had been made an offer she couldn't refuse? You could produce crochet work anywhere and there she was now, her head bent over some coloured wool and her fingers flashing. But Romy had so much to lose – the perfect workshop, the expensive equipment – and when Gloag had phoned to try to talk her round, she'd told him in no uncertain terms that she wouldn't drop her opposition to the project.

But Andrew – surely not Andrew too, Andrew who had been her saviour and whom she trusted as she didn't trust herself? With his background of soldier ancestors, it was hard to imagine that Andrew could do a dishonourable thing.

Yet there was Norman Gloag now, beaming as he ushered in the too smart young man from ALCO, ready with his file of rebuttals and the promises which would fool the gullible into believing that a superstore wouldn't leach the lifeblood out of the place.

And Andrew hadn't come. Romy's lips took on a curl of bitterness. There was no such thing, after all, as a man who didn't deal in lies. She despised herself for ever believing there might be.

The young man from ALCO spoke well, Ellie Burnett had to acknowledge that. He was very personable, with a soothing manner and a light touch as he talked about all the benefits a superstore would bring to Kirkluce: low prices, extended choice, employment prospects. He laid particular emphasis on the scope for part-time jobs, ideal for mums wanting to be able to pick the kiddies up from school, and for the older kids after school, 'saving for further education – or just saving Dad from having to fork out for all those cool items "everyone else" has!'. That got a responsive laugh. He was working well, and you could feel the mood of the meeting shifting in his favour.

She could see why people would like the idea of jobs for their kids. If Dylan had been doing even a few hours a week, the money would have helped, though she couldn't imagine him paying off the loan she'd taken out for his bike and she'd be too frightened of losing him even to suggest it. But at least it might have kept him busy, instead of spending all his time hanging round with Barney Kyle, who always led him into trouble.

It had got worse since he had the bike – but how could she have said no and risked alienating him? Even as it was, her heart was in her mouth every time the funfair was in the area and Dylan went off to see his dad – not that she had anything against Jason. It was only after she left him that her life had fallen apart for those dark, dark years. He was a kind man, but she had found caravan life in a small, intimate community quite simply unbearable. Now it was her constant fear that their son might choose the travelling life and never come back to her.

It was thanks to Andrew that she'd been able to indulge Dylan. 'One of your lovely, delicate flower paintings on my birthday,' he'd asked as a rent for the studio. Then, a couple of years later, he'd quietly handed her the keys to the two-bedroom flat above it, saying he couldn't let it and he'd be grateful to have someone to keep it aired: it had belonged to his father's chauffeur and it wouldn't be economic to do it up. He'd had central heating and a new bathroom and kitchen equipment put in, though, and saving the rent for 'social housing', as they called it nowadays, had made all the difference to her.

She'd been keeping her hands busy with the mechanical creation of a little bunch of blue and green crochet flowers to put on a hat, in an effort to keep her mind off other things, but now they faltered and she laid the work down in her lap.

The tiny shop in the Craft Centre where Ellie sold paintings, knick-knacks, crochet and colourful wall-hangings wasn't just her workplace. It wasn't too much to say that it had saved her life: it was her refuge, the personal space she needed if she were not to feel – well, bruised, was the only way she could think of it, by the harsh world outside. It barely washed its face: even living rent-free with such state benefits as she could claim, it was harder and harder to keep her head above water financially as Dylan got older and more expensive.

She was having to accept more singing engagements. She was very popular in the local pubs, and she liked to sing – perhaps even needed to sing, sharing the beautiful instrument God had given her for the delight of others – but it was so often an ordeal. Men looked at her as if they fantasised about possession. They always had. If she needed a reminder, Ossian was looking at her adoringly from across the hall, with his strange eyes, almost aquamarine in colour, fixed on her face.

He had come in late, and she had seen him trying to find a seat as near her as possible. He was only a boy, not a great deal older than Dylan, and he was romantic and over-sensitive, but she found it difficult to handle his fixation with her, especially when his studio was only twenty steps away from her little shop.

She'd read, in her Catholic girlhood, of some saint or other – Agnes, was it? – who had multilated herself as a deterrent to the lusts of men. Perhaps she should have done that . . .

But she daren't go there. If she wasn't careful, she'd reach the point where she yielded to the deadly longing which was still at the back of her mind: to escape, to blot out all the problems in the old way . . .

The applause startled her. She hadn't even heard what else the ALCO man had said and now he was handing over to Councillor Norman Gloag.

What was it about Gloag that so repelled her? He was ugly, of course, with a bulbous nose and flabby pouches round a fleshy mouth, but it wasn't simply that. Perhaps it was his air of invincible self-satisfaction, suggesting that whatever he wanted would happen, regardless of the wishes or needs of anyone else.

He was wearing a blue suit, expensive no doubt, but fractionally too small for his bulky frame, and the sort of club tie that was like a Freemason's handshake. It didn't mean anything to you unless you were the right sort of person.

He'd been a surveyor for years, but more recently an estate agent, when, despite properties having been bought and sold without their help for centuries, the Scots were foolish enough to be persuaded that they were necessary. Gloag had done well for himself; he knew all the Kirkluce solicitors and had what was almost a monopoly in the area. One of Ellie's friends had told her, when she sold her house, that she was sure a deal had been done behind her back. She'd got a disappointing price for it from a friend of Gloag's, but of course nothing could be proved.

Gloag was talking now. As local councillor, he should be putting the hard question which the ALCO man had so efficiently ducked: the effect of a superstore on a market town with thriving individual shops. But it was clear his only interest was to support a future planning application and discourage objections. A farmer who demanded to know what price he'd get for his milk once the superstore had strangled the local dairy was slapped down so unceremoniously that the emollient young man had to intervene, softening the rebuff with an assurance that his company used local products at a fair price 'wherever possible'. Meaningless words, of course, but there were nods of approval from the audience, apart from the farmer who walked out, turning at the door to yell, 'Blood-suckers, that's what you are – bloodsuckers!'

There was fierce applause from one small sector of the hall, where older people were sitting together, but the hostile looks directed at them from all round told their story.

Now Romy was on her feet, with bright colour burning in her cheeks, haranguing Gloag and ALCO and – unwisely – people who were stupid enough not to see how bad this would be for the town, how the atmosphere would change, how the holiday visitors who had brought trade to Kirkluce because of its good local shops would go to Castle Douglas instead, how shops would close and how, once the superstore had no rivals, the prices would rise.

Ellie winced. Romy had never been sensitive, and despite the rebellious mutters behind her seemed oblivious to the damage she was doing. Her cause was losing support with every word she uttered.

Now Romy was using the big gun. 'Anyway, Gloag, however you threaten and bully, you and your oily little sidekick there can't do a damn' thing about it. If Andrew Carmichael refuses to sell the Craft Centre, the deal collapses. And he will.'

She sat down to a chorus of booing, with only a few brave people clapping.

You wouldn't think, Ellie reflected drearily, that Gloag could look smugger than he normally did. But somehow he managed it as he smirked, 'So you say, Mrs Kyle. But perhaps some of us have noticed that Colonel Carmichael isn't here to speak for himself, which may tell us something.

'Clearly there are negotiations still ahead, but if the sale to

ALCO goes through, from the tone of this meeting I feel I would be able to assure the planning department that local opinion is in favour.'

Although there were people sitting with their hands firmly in their laps, the number applauding made it clear enough where the balance lay. Romy got up and stormed out, as Ellie gathered up her crochet and stowed it into the workbag she always carried. It had been clear right from the start that this was what would happen.

2

Had anyone expected a different outcome, except perhaps Romy Kyle? Christina Munro stumped out of the Church Hall, knowing that unless Colonel Carmichael stood his ground the battle was lost. She'd wanted to come and vote against the proposal if votes were to be counted, but there had been no need to count. The feeling of the meeting was all too obvious.

She hadn't much of a personal stake in what happened, beyond hating the changing world. Oh, everyone mocked the Fifties, when the horrors of a second world conflict had shocked people into good behaviour, but in those days you felt so safe you never even locked your door. And if youngsters were causing trouble you told the parents, who would give them a good leathering and see that it didn't happen again.

It wasn't like that today. All you could do was phone the police and if you were lucky someone would come to take a statement the next day. And you knew it wouldn't stop them, and you lived in fear all the time, being punished instead of them.

As she hurried back to where she had parked her elderly pickup, Christina, a small, stooped figure with a face where nose and chin looked set to meet eventually, glanced anxiously at her watch. One of Ellie Burnett's crocheted cloche hats – dark maroon, with a jaunty bunch of bright pink, purple and white flowers – was pulled down over her ears.

She'd taken a risk leaving the farmhouse this evening, but

it was still light and they hadn't come before until it was growing dark. She'd have time to get the donkeys into the shed and check that every door was locked before she settled down to wait fearfully with the cats and her rescue greyhound.

Sometimes she wondered what her father would say if he could see her now. When he'd died thirty years ago Wester Seton, just on the eastern edge of Kirkluce, had been a flourishing small farm. She was never sure it was true that he thought she was as good a farmer as any son would have been, but he'd said it as if he meant it, which was important. She'd never been bonny; he was the only man who'd ever loved her, but looking at the messes that the other kind of love got folks into, she reckoned she hadn't missed much.

He'd trained her well, and at first the farm prospered in her hands. But then, with all the regulations and the complicated paperwork, and the supermarkets beating down the prices, you found yourself with an operating loss and in order to go on, having to take charity – which was what she knew her father would have termed the handouts from Brussels.

There wouldn't be anyone to take over after she'd gone, anyway. She'd sold off the land gradually until there was only the house – a low, grey stone building, not really much more than a but and ben – with a couple of fields for the elderly donkeys she'd rescued from the knacker's yard and the steadings, mainly unused and now falling quietly into decay.

Christina had always prided herself on being feisty, but she was old now. Latterly her life had contracted more and more, and with this latest persecution she had begun to feel trapped and helpless. And what was the point of life as a prisoner? She was a countrywoman born and bred: she had a shotgun for herself and the animals no one else would look after if she wasn't there, and she wouldn't scruple to use it.

It would only take her minutes to get back to Wester Seton,

but the shadows were lengthening as she drove out of the car park. The rickety frame of the pickup shuddered as she floored the accelerator, disregarding the speed limit. This just could be a matter of life or death.

'And what can have happened to Uncle Andrew, then?' Fiona Farquharson wondered aloud as she left the hall with her husband.

Giles Farquharson didn't look at her. 'I don't know.'

She gave him a look of barely concealed dislike. 'It has to be a good sign that he didn't turn up. Perhaps he's changed his mind about the development after all. That ghastly Kyle woman was obviously rattled.

'You didn't go and see him this afternoon, did you?'

'No. No, I didn't.' He marched on, staring straight ahead.

'Oh – just as well, probably. You'd only have made things worse.'

'It's his decision, Fiona. There's nothing either of us can do, anyway.'

'You'd always take the easy option, of course,' she said with a sneer, but he wouldn't be drawn, lengthening his stride so that she almost had to trot to keep up.

Fiona's thin scarlet lips tightened in irritation at his feebleness, wondering yet again why she'd ever married him. But in those days, when she was a leggy blonde and he was a tall, fit young officer in the Coldstream Guards, he'd looked a good prospect, especially given his mother's benevolent and childless older brother. Now, though her own legs were admittedly sturdier than they had once been and she only remained blonde at considerable expense, he was totally unrecognisable from the wedding photos. Giles, as Fiona's mother was wont to say crisply, had run to seed; what had once been muscle was now fat and flab. The bright prospects had been dimmed by a succession of dead-end jobs, culminating in his present one as land agent for an estate about five miles to the north of Kirkluce, in the hillier countryside on the fringe of the Galloway Forest Park.

When Fiona was having a bitch session with her two closest girlfriends once, she'd said Giles's name should have been Sidam, since he was Midas in reverse: everything that he touched turned to dross. If Uncle Andrew hadn't paid the boys' school fees at Wellington, they'd have ended up at the local comp, unable to read and write. Not that you would think they could, given how seldom they contacted their parents.

Uncle Andrew's legacy was their only hope of a comfortable retirement – even a luxurious one, considering that the superstore would pay whatever it took. If he just hadn't been so damned selfish, fussing about that pathetic little Craft Centre . . . She felt deeply embittered about what she had been through, thanks to that.

'Of course, none of this mess had to happen. If you had gone to him years ago, the way I told you, and got him to put the estate in trust to avoid death duties . . .'

Her husband's face had flushed. 'There's no point in going on about it. Where did you park? I'm up the side street here.'

'In the Square,' she said, but found she was talking to herself.

The War Memorial was in the Market Square, just off the High Street, surrounded by self-important grey stone buildings which housed the council offices, the library and firms of long-established solicitors and accountants. When Fiona reached it, there was a group of the local neds and hoodies fooling about at the other side, clustered around three motorbikes with their engines running. It was a common gathering-place for them, and Fiona had wondered at the time about the wisdom of leaving the Saab there, but with so many people coming to the meeting, parking space was at a premium. She looked anxiously at the car as she reached it.

It was thankfully unscathed and, focused on the bikes and their riders, they weren't paying any attention to her either. There was a lot of laughter, jeering and pushing, then they scattered in mock terror as the motorbikes revved their engines and took off, one after the other, going far too fast and cutting the corner of the Square.

Where were the police when you needed them? Having evening classes in Human Rights, Fiona reflected acidly, which never seemed to take account of the rights of people like her not to have to share the planet with people like that.

The motorbikes shot along Kirkluce High Street, past a group standing talking just outside the Church Hall, provoking an outburst of communal tutting.

'Kill themselves, that's what they'll do,' an elderly man leaning on a stick said, glaring after them and shaking his fist.

'Sooner the better,' added his wife. 'Just as long as they don't take anyone with them.'

'Where was the Colonel tonight, then, Annie?' Another woman, after shaking her head in disapproval, returned to the main topic of conversation.

Annie Brown, a comfortable-looking woman with greying hair and clear blue eyes, shook her head too. 'When I went in at five o'clock to leave him his tea, he was out in his garden, though he was meaning to come. But I thought maybe he was kinda sweirt to go and speak out—'

Two young women, coming out together, stopped. One of them, a henna redhead with a steel ring through her eyebrow and several more along the side of one ear, said aggressively, 'What's he got to be reluctant about? See him? He can screw the whole deal, right there, and none of us able to do a thing about it. It's not right – it's high time this dump joined the twenty-first century and had some real shops.'

Annie squared up to her. 'If you wonder why he wasn't keen to come, it's because of the likes of you. He's a good man, the Colonel, and there's plenty of us don't want to see the High Street just a row of charity shops and folk who've been there years put out of business. We maybe don't make as much noise about it as you lot, but we've a right to our opinion too.'

'You tell them, Annie,' the old man quavered. 'That's the trouble with you young ones nowadays – want it all your own way.'

The girl sneered. 'You're living on borrowed time, Granddad. Get on with it – move aside and make room for the future.'

Her friend giggled and they strutted off, well pleased with the shocked silence left behind them.

'Well!' Annie said, recovering herself. 'What those young besoms need is a good skelping.'

'We'll come and visit you when you get the jail for assault,' someone assured her, and raised a laugh.

'Might as well laugh,' the old man said morosely. 'There's not a muckle lot we can do about it anyway.'

Tam MacNee pulled off the sweater with the elaborate dartboard motif, lovingly knitted by his wife Bunty for his evenings out with the Cutty Sark Warlocks darts team. It was out of keeping with his usual style – black leather jacket, jeans, white T-shirt – but it had been a labour of love on her part and he wouldn't hurt her feelings by failing to wear it, even if she wasn't there to see. Bunty was the rock on which his life was built, a buxom, pleasant-faced woman with a heart as generous as her hips, and he adored her.

Anyway, the sweater had become a sort of talisman for the

whole of the team from the Cutty Sark and had probably got more credit for the Warlocks' victories over the years than had Tam's own skill with the arrows. It hadn't worked tonight though: his first night back after his injury, and he'd even missed the board a couple of times.

His team-mates were overly supportive, cheering extravagantly anything that could possibly qualify as a good shot. Worse still, their opponents, the Toreadors from the Black Bull, were ready to make allowances, one of them even beginning an offer not to count a particularly wild shot, an attempt which ended in a sharp 'Ow! Whad'ya do that for?' as a Warlock's foot made contact with his shin.

Tam was in a black mood as he sat down with his pint afterwards, deliberately pushing his way through the crowded bar to a chair in a corner at the back of the big room. If there was one thing he couldn't take, it was pity. Even when it came disguised as kindness, he recognised it with a curling lip. Marjory had tried it more than once and he'd had to be – well, what he termed straight, but Bunty, when he'd repeated it to her, had called downright rude. Women! Can't take a telling, then get all hurt when you repeat it.

It had been a punishing spell. His work was the focus of his life, and though at first the struggle towards recovery had been a job in itself, now that he was feeling better the lack of occupation had been driving him demented, to say nothing of what that did to Bunty. Only another couple of weeks or so, the doctor had promised, but he'd said that before to buy him off and Tam wasn't holding his breath.

Staring morosely into his glass, he didn't hear the team captain say quietly, 'If he's feeling thon way, better just let him be.' But before long Tam perversely began to resent his isolation, and was on the point of swallowing his beer as well as his pride and using his empty glass as an excuse to rejoin the party, when a little stir of activity indicated the arrival of the folk-singer.

Tam brightened. He liked Ellie Burnett's voice. They all did, and as a bonus she was a wee smasher. Every man's head turned as she made her way to the stool at the back where a microphone had been set up, near to where Tam was sitting. She shook her head at the offers of drinks that pursued her, sat down, tuned her guitar and without introduction began to sing.

She had a surprising voice for someone with her slight frame, a honeyed contralto with an earthy tone to it. Her repertoire was undemanding jazz, Scots ballads, Bob Dylan classics. She began with Gershwin's 'Summer Time' – a favourite with Tam. The caressing voice wove its magic; he could feel the tension in his neck and shoulders beginning to ease, and the sadistic monster which now inhabited a corner of his brain, and had been stirring, quietened down again.

Conversation gradually started up once more, though at a lower level so that she could still be heard; there was a smattering of applause when Ellie finished. After a sip of water from the glass on the table at her side she went on into 'O whistle and I'll come to ye, my lad', another of Tam's favourites. Anything at all written by his idol, Rabbie Burns, was a favourite with Tam.

Watching idly, he became aware of a young man sitting opposite, beside the table nearest to the singer. He had pulled his chair towards her and away from it, turning his back on its other occupants who were chatting and laughing, though quietly enough. It was the extraordinary intensity of his unwavering gaze that attracted Tam's attention.

He was a striking-looking lad, pale-skinned with a mop of light brown hair flopping forward over his brow. His eyes were a vivid light blue, and the way they were locked on

Ellie's face must, Tam thought with slight professional unease, be making the woman uncomfortable, however used she might be to punters who thought stripping her with their eyes wasn't assault. Bastards!

Tam had a well-hidden romantic streak, and she had an air of vulnerability that made you want to protect her, to go out and duff up a dragon or two if necessary, or maybe just tell that wee nyaff to move along now and not embarrass the lady.

She finished that song, and another, then set down the guitar to catch her breath. Immediately the lad was on his feet, going over to her.

'You snare my soul with your songs,' Tam heard him say. 'You set me ablaze.'

Ellie smiled faintly; she knew him, obviously, and seemed to be treating his extravagance with a kind of weary indulgence. But he reached out to take her hand, then, when she moved it away, grabbed her wrist in a sudden movement. Ellie said nothing, seeming reluctant to make any sort of fuss, but she was twisting her wrist to try to break his hold. He didn't let her go.

Just as Tam was getting up to see to it that he did, another man brushed past him: a man in his late thirties, perhaps, wearing jeans and a short-sleeved shirt which exposed well-muscled arms. The pub was crowded but a passage opened in front of him as he reached Ellie's side, attracting a few curious glances.

'Evening, Ossian,' he said. 'I don't think Ellie likes you holding her arm.'

The younger man flushed scarlet, then dropped his grip with a look of hatred at the speaker. From where he was sitting, Tam could see a red pressure ring on Ellie's pale skin where his hand had been, but her face was expressionless and she didn't rub it, as if she was afraid that might provoke a scene.

'That's better,' her protector said. 'But you've hurt her, Ossian. Don't do it again.' He reached out and took Ellie's arm himself, rubbing it gently. He had big, powerful hands, but his touch was delicate.

Ossian looked at the mark on her wrist. His eyes filled. 'I wouldn't hurt you, Ellie, you know that,' he cried. 'I'm sorry, I'm sorry! I just wanted you to listen to me, that was all. Oh God, you're bruised! I want to die!'

The little drama was beginning to attract attention. Ellie said hastily, 'It's all right, Ossian. Don't worry, Johnny, I'm not hurt.'

She looked, Tam thought, as if she would have liked to pull her arm away from him too, but she waited until he let it go with a final pat, then picked up her guitar.

'I'm going to do my next song now. People are waiting, and I'm being paid for this.'

Ossian, his face still crimson, shouldered his way to the door. As he passed Tam, he was on the point of bursting into tears. Tam grinned, unfeelingly. Humiliation was good for the gallus young, who thought that if you'd enough cheek you could have whatever you wanted. It was a small revenge for the roaring boys whose gallus days were, sadly, over.

Johnny had stood his ground. 'Just been chatting to Dylan,' he said, and Tam saw Ellie's face change.

'What was he doing?' Her anxiety was obvious.

'Oh, not a lot. He and Barney and some of the other guys were just hanging out in the Square.'

Ellie's eyes were on his face. 'They weren't planning to do anything stupid, were they? There's been complaints—'

'No, no,' he said soothingly. 'They're good lads. They're young – it was just a bit of fun anyway – hysterical old bat—'

'She's not—' Ellie began, then, seeing the landlord looking pointedly at her, said, 'I've got to do my next song.'

'Fine.' He turned to move away. 'We can chat later. See you after.'

He took up his position by the bar, a little distance away, and she launched into 'Blowin' in the Wind', a little hesitantly.

Tam had a clear view of him now; short, curly dark hair, dark eyes, designer stubble and a face that gave no clue as to what he was thinking. And he'd seen him before – not in a professional context, just seen him before. But where was it? There was nothing wrong with Tam's powers of observation, but his retrieval system wasn't as good as it used to be.

He was worrying away at it when a hand grasped his shoulder.

'Come on, Tam, stop brooding, man! If you think you can put the blame on being injured because you can't hit the side of a bus, think again. You're out of practice, that's all, you idle bugger. And if you're sitting there indulging an old man's fantasies about Ellie, I'll clype on you to Bunty, and she'll show you what a sore head's really like. Rejoin the human race, and I'll even buy you a drink.'

'I know you, you crafty sod,' Tam said as he got up. 'We'll reach the bar, and then it'll be "You pay and I'll fumble."'

As he followed his friend to the bar, the memory came back: that was Johnny Black, who'd come to Kirkluce fairly recently to work in a motorbike business. Tam had even gone in himself once, to lust after a Harley Davidson that was on display. Only the 'mid-life crisis' mockery that he'd get from colleagues, and the thought of Bunty's anxiety which would be bravely but inadequately concealed, had stopped him falling for the illusion that youth was something you could buy with money.

Greatly cheered, he accepted a dram. Maybe his hand–eye coordination really would improve with practice, and it gave him a good excuse for a few more evenings at the Cutty Sark.

* * *

It was the dog that heard them first. It was an elegant creature, a honey-coloured greyhound with a coat soft as cashmere and eyes outlined in black like Cleopatra's. It stiffened and sat up from the rug where it had been lying at Christina Munro's feet, a low growl rumbling in its throat.

The old woman's stomach lurched. She had been listening to the radio; she turned down the volume, and now she could hear it too – the distant whine of motorbike engines. The black and white cat which had been purring in her lap jumped down, affronted by her sudden movement, and glared round, tail twitching. A tortoiseshell in a basket beside the kitchen stove raised its head lazily, while another cat, asleep on a cushioned chair, opened one eye.

Christina's eyes went nervously to the door, though she knew she had locked and bolted it when she came in. She had secured the shutters then too, blotting out what was left of the daylight, so for some while the kitchen, where she spent most of her time now, had been in darkness, apart from the lamp by her chair. She had to fight the temptation to switch it off and pretend there was no one in; it might feel safer, but who knew what they might do if they felt there was no one to witness their actions?

Anyway, she told herself, it was only noise and a bit of minor damage. They'd broken some old flower-pots and churned up her vegetable patch, but she didn't think they'd actually harm her. At least, she had to hope they wouldn't. The police seemed to know who they were, and they'd had a word, they told her, with thc parents and with the boys themselves, so that should put a stop to it. Christina knew it wasn't polite when she laughed in their faces.

The bikes were roaring up the farm track now. The noise was deafening, and led by the tortoiseshell, the cats, one after another, shot under the dresser. The greyhound, shivering, came to press itself against her side and she stroked its velvety ears soothingly, though she suspected that all she was doing was communicating her own fear. Her heart was banging in her narrow chest.

Now they were in the yard. Through the chinks in the shutters she could see their headlights flickering as they began their usual roaring circuits of the farmhouse and the yard. Even above the engine noise Christina could hear their whoops and hollering.

Wearily, she reached for the phone and dialled 999. She gave her message, admitted that no one was hurt and that as far as she knew no particular harm was being done, and received the bland assurance that someone would attend as soon as available.

She heard a crash, somewhere at the back of the farmhouse. What had they found to damage now? Or had someone come to grief? She was always afraid that one of the speeding bikes would lose its grip on the rounded cobbles of the backyard, and she feared their fury if one of them got hurt.

Apparently not. They were coming towards the front again, stopping just outside her door, talking and laughing.

Bang! Bang! Bang! She leaped to her feet in fright and the dog, startled, began to bark – high, terrified yaps. They were bashing at all three windows round the kitchen. They'd never done that before, and though with the sturdy shutters bolted in place she didn't think they could break in even if they broke the glass, it told her that their attacks were getting bolder. They were shouting now too, taunts, threats, obscenities, challenging her to 'come out and give us a laugh'.

Opening the door, confronting them, getting it over with was a real temptation. The police knew about them so they wouldn't actually harm her, would they, and maybe once they'd got what they wanted, abused her to her face, seen her alarm, they'd lose interest and leave it at that.

But bullies didn't. Bullies who got their way went on and

on, getting worse and worse, high on the excitement of their cruelty. And if ever she came out, it would be more dangerous not to, the next time.

There was no point in telling them she'd called the police. She wasn't sure she could shout loudly enough to make herself heard, and anyway these thugs knew as well as she did that the polis wouldn't appear till long after they'd made their escape. She'd only make a fool of herself if she tried.

Her legs were giving way. She collapsed back into her chair and the dog came to lay its head on her knee, the pleading eyes begging for protection.

And at last, the banging stopped. The bikes drove off and the engine noise dwindled away into the distance. The room was suddenly very, very quiet, the only sound the muted voices from the radio. Shakily Christina got up, and with the dog closer than a shadow at her side she went to draw back the bolts and open the door.

Outside it was quite dark now. Over the low, rolling hills which rose beyond her land the moon had come up, a waning half-moon, and in the starry sky darker clouds were drifting across. There had been a heavy shower earlier and she could still smell rain on the rising wind, though for the moment at least it had gone off. In the old barn she could hear the three donkeys moving restlessly but the steel bar with its sturdy padlock was still in place across the double doors. The grass in front of the house was badly churned up, but she could live with that. It had never been what you could call a lawn anyway.

When she went round to the back, the yard was awash where they had overturned the rain-butt, which explained the crash. With some difficulty she got it set up and back in its place, then continued her round of inspection. No broken windows, no other damage that she could see.

She'd got off lightly – this time, at least.

* * *

The rain started again, whispering through the leaves of the old mulberry tree in the middle of the gravel turning-circle in front of Fauldburn House. The black front door was standing open and Andrew Carmichael lay on the doorstep, his eyes wide open and sightless, with a gaping hole blown in his chest.

3

Norman Gloag sliced a careful triangle off his fried potato scone, speared it along with a piece of bacon, dipped the forkful into the yolk of his fried egg and conveyed it to his mouth.

Sunday breakfast was his favourite meal. On Sundays he always insisted they ate in the dining-room of their modern villa – 'the ultimate in distinctive living' – instead of the family room off the luxury kitchen, 'boasting integrated appliances'. As pater familias he enjoyed presiding over the only meals the family ate together, when he could instil what he called 'proper values' over the inadequate meals his wife unenthusiastically provided.

A fry-up was the high point of her culinary activities, but in the frigid atmosphere this morning he found himself chewing and swallowing without pleasure.

His wife Maureen, at the other end of the black glass and chrome table, was still in her dressing-gown, a slovenly habit, as he had told her often enough, and it wasn't as if the dressing-gown was even particularly clean, marked as it was with old coffee stains that hadn't quite washed out. She was engrossed in the medical page of the *Sunday Post*.

His daughters, eleven-year-old Cara and Denise, sixteen going on thirty, were respectively eating Chocolate Krispies and drinking a virulently pink slimming milk shake. Where his son Gordon should have been, a cream upholstered dining-chair stood empty. Its emptiness seemed mocking, and Gloag could feel himself starting to lose his temper.

He was scowling as he addressed Denise. 'Ask your mother where Gordon is.'

Denise, leafing through the magazine section of the *Sunday Mail*, paid no attention.

Maureen, a small, wiry woman with the sort of neat features which, while pretty enough in youth, sharpen unbecomingly in dissatisfied middle age, took a cigarette from the packet that lay on the table, lit it, and took a drag before she said, 'Tell your father he's in bed.'

Gloag addressed the table at large, his face red with anger. 'Oh, he is, is he? Well, he needn't think, if he chooses to come home at one in the morning, that he can make up for it by lying in bed all day. Denise, go and waken your brother.'

Denise raised her eyes only to roll them, and went back to her magazine.

'I'll go, Dad,' Cara piped up eagerly. 'I'll tell him you're mad at him and he's to get up now.'

Gloag looked with approval at his youngest. She was the one most like him in appearance, a sturdy, round-faced child who so far at least seemed to have escaped the attitude of insolent indifference which had been fostered in her siblings by their mother's attitude.

As Cara left the room, Maureen looked up from her newspaper and said, 'Tell your father he's a bloody idiot. That's bound to cause trouble.'

Gloag glared at his wife. 'Tell your mother that if she didn't encourage Gordon to behave badly—'

With a sudden movement Denise pushed her chair back and stood up. 'You two are pathetic. Tragic, really. Stop trying to use me in your stupid games. I'm going to my room, so you'll have to shut it, won't you? Or behave like adults – as if!'

As her daughter stormed off, Maureen too stood up, stubbed out the cigarette and walked out. Gloag heard her go to the kitchen and shut the door; then there was the sound of Cara hurrying down the stairs.

'He called me a fat pig!' she said as she opened the door. 'And he used the f-word.' She gave a few token sobs, but as she went on, 'And he won't get up. He just turned over and went back to sleep. I told him he's in B-I-G trouble,' satisfaction banished any tears.

Gloag felt suddenly very tired. It had been, as Maureen had not hesitated to point out, a bad decision, one that was going to cost him. 'That's all right, Cara,' he said heavily. 'Now, why don't you clear the rest of the table and take it through to the kitchen, like a good girl.'

Cara pouted. 'I haven't finished my breakfast.' She sat down again, helped herself to a piece of toast and spread it lavishly with Nutella.

Her father looked down at his own congealing plateful without appetite. It was all Maureen's fault, of course. Women nowadays believed that because they went out to work it gave them the right to spend their earnings in any way they chose, even when it should involve a family decision. And he'd made it quite plain what this decision was: no motorbike. The two youths in Kirkluce who had them already weren't the types that Norman Gloag's son should be associating with, and Maureen's deciding to buy one for Gordon, in full knowledge of her husband's opposition, had been an act of pure spite.

Even by their standards the row which had followed a humiliating visit from the police had been on an epic scale. They hadn't spoken since, and Gloag's attempt to assert his paternal authority by confiscating the bike had failed. His son had the nerve to tell him that since his mother had paid for it, it was up to her.

Last night, Gordon had ignored the rule that he was to be

back by midnight, and this morning, in the grip of temper, his father had put himself in a position where his bluff could be called. Where was he to go from here? He could hardly go upstairs and eject him physically from his bed. Gordon was bigger than he was now.

Cara had at last finished and under protest ('Why shouldn't Denise do it?') began to clear the table. Gloomily, Gloag collected up his own plate, cup and saucer and handed them to her.

But, he told himself, he wouldn't have to put up with it for ever. He had had enough of Maureen's sluttish habits and her constant undermining of his authority with his children. He'd even caught her laughing with them behind his back the other day – that came close to being the last straw. He'd have gone for a divorce years ago, but he'd no doubt she'd fight like a cat to get every penny off him that she could, and he'd no fancy for living in penury.

But all being well – and all did seem to be going well, after all – he reckoned he'd done enough to ensure that the superstore deal would go ahead. Then there would be money, a lot of money, coming his way, money which meant he could readily afford to buy his freedom. The words 'irretrievable breakdown of marriage' had begun to sound very appealing.

As she came into the Kirkluce headquarters of the Galloway Constabulary at half-past nine on Sunday morning, Marjory Fleming was pleased to see that the officer on duty at the desk was Sergeant Jock Naismith. A bulky, good-natured man, he'd been her sarge when she joined the force as a probationer, more years ago than she cared to remember, and no one knew more about what went on in this patch than he did.

There was no one in the waiting area. 'Quiet night, sarge?' Fleming asked hopefully.

Naismith, glad of some distraction, leaned forward on his

elbows. 'Not bad. Road accident, couple of people hurt, but nothing that won't mend, from the sound of it. The usual drunk and disorderlies but we've no one for free bed and breakfast.'

'That's what I like to hear.' She hesitated. 'Jock – a strictly personal enquiry. Do you know anything about two boys called Barney Kyle and Dylan Burnett? The only background I have is that they've got motorbikes and they're at Kirkluce Academy.'

'Ah! Funny you should ask that.'

Fleming's heart sank. 'Got form, have they?'

'Not exactly. There's a wifie with that farm just out of the town on the Newton Stewart road that's been having problems with them. She phoned in last night again, seemingly – 999 call – but when we could send a car they'd scarpered, of course, and all she'd to show for it was a water-butt they'd turned over. They seem just to have been buzzing round the house, winding her up. Young limbs of Satan, I've no doubt, but we've only her word without much in the way of corroboration, so there's not a lot we can do. A couple of the lads went round last time to speak to the parents, but it obviously didn't do much good.'

Norman Gloag's son, it appeared, was involved as well. Fleming knew Councillor Gloag – who didn't, when he made it his business to feature in every edition of the *Galloway Globe*? – but she didn't know the two women from the Craft Centre.

'Fathers?' she asked.

'Don't know about Burnett. Kyle's mother has a toy boy with a record for fraud.'

Fleming groaned. 'They don't sound exactly the chums you'd choose for your fourteen-year-old daughter, do they?'

'Fourteen – Cat?' Naismith was startled. 'Dearie me – I mind when you were on maternity leave and came in to show her off. Bawled the place down, and you were that embarrassed!'

'Let's just hope she's not planning to embarrass me all over again,' her mother said darkly. 'Thanks anyway, Jock.

'So – looks like a quiet enough day, then, does it? I've a bit of paper to shift, but I'm hoping to get away home for my Sunday lunch.'

Naismith shook his head. 'Lassie, have you learned nothing at all, all these years? You're tempting fate with a remark like yon.'

Laughing, she left him and headed for the stairs.

It was almost midday when Dylan Burnett, bleary-eyed and still wearing his night attire of grey T-shirt and boxers, came into the kitchen/living-room of the flat above Ellie's shop. His long hair, fair anyway and bleached blonder still, was tousled from sleep.

His mother, getting ready to go down and open the shop, turned and smiled. 'You know, with your hair all mussed up like that, you look almost the way you did as a toddler,' she said, with fond inaccuracy. 'Want some breakfast?'

Dylan yawned, scratching his armpit. 'Just coffee. We'd a bit of a night of it, last night. Ended up at Johnny's. He's seriously cool.'

Ellie turned away. 'You'd better have something to eat,' she urged, switching on the kettle. 'There's bacon – do you want me to make you a butty?'

He indicated revulsion. 'Look, I said just coffee. You going to open up the shop?' Hopefully, that would get her out of his hair so he could come to in peace.

'In a minute. There's tourists still around and even if there's only a few come to the Craft Centre there's the chance of sales.'

The kettle was boiling and she spooned Nescafé into a

mug inscribed 'Fauldburn Craft Centre'. There were another fifty in boxes downstairs: they hadn't been a big seller.

Dylan took the coffee from her and slumped at the table, adding four heaped sugars from a rather ugly pottery bowl. He stirred, sipped and shuddered.

'God, I'm feeling rough today!' he said, then regretted it when he saw his mother's anxious expression. She bugged him about everything – the things he did, the people he hung out with, the amount he drank, the dangers of drugs – as if he didn't know, having lived through a time when she'd been permanently out of it. He scowled as she said, 'What all did you do last night?'

'Not a lot.'

'You've not been bothering Miss Munro again, have you?'

Dylan gave her a sidelong look but didn't answer. Ellie waited a moment, then gave up. She put the crochet she'd been working on into her bag to take down to the shop and went to the drawer where she kept the float. He stiffened, watching her under his thick blond eyelashes, but though she froze for a second when she saw what was left, she said nothing. She usually said nothing, which made him feel a bit guilty sometimes, but Barney would sneer if he hadn't enough for a few beers.

'Saw you with Johnny last night,' he said, changing the subject.

Ellie didn't turn round. 'Did you? We just had a chat after I was singing in the pub, that's all.'

'You two should get it together. That'd be ace.' It was weird that Johnny fancied an old bag like his mother, but Dylan had said last night he'd put in a good word. Anyway, if Johnny was around it might get her off Dylan's back. And he'd make sure, too, that she stayed – well, OK.

His mother still didn't turn round, staring out of one of the small windows into the courtyard below. 'Aren't you happy the way we are, with just the two of us? It's good, isn't it?'

Dylan said uncomfortably, 'Oh, sure. But get real – a year, couple of years, and I'll be off. You've got your old age to think of and you'd be all right with Johnny. He's a man of his word.'

It wasn't his own phrase, of course, and when his mother turned there was an odd expression on her face. 'Did he tell you to say that?'

'Well, kind of. It's true anyway. And it'd be better for me having a man around.'

'I – see.'

He wasn't in the habit of noticing his mother much, but there was something in her voice which made him glance at her sharply. She been all stressed out about this superstore stuff and she was looking awful, scrawny and pale, with black circles round her eyes like she hadn't slept. Now her eyes were swimming too.

Time she got real, he thought with irritation. He didn't want to have to spend his life hanging round in this dump of a town where there wasn't even any decent clubbing, just to keep an eye on his mum. He didn't answer when she picked up her bag and said, 'I'm just going. You know where to find me if you want anything.'

Dylan watched her going out, then shrugged. He got up and went over to the fridge. A bacon butty might hit the spot after all.

The morning service at St Cerf's had just finished and the congregation was slowly dispersing, pausing in little gossipy groups before they went home to the Sunday roast.

Annie Brown was the last to leave, collecting the church flowers to be distributed to sick and suffering members. As she emerged, the minister – a nice enough laddie, in her view, but just a wee thing inclined to those awful silly new hymns

– who had been dutifully shaking hands with his flock as they left, was waiting for her.

'Is Colonel Carmichael away, Annie, do you know?' he asked. 'He was down to read the lessons this morning, and it's not like him not to tell me if he can't make it.'

'He maybe forgot,' Annie suggested, but her concern showed in her face. 'Mind, he wasn't at the meeting last night either. He's not getting any younger. I'll away round and see if he's all right.'

'Would you like me to come?' he offered. 'The beadle will lock up. If you wait a minute while I take off my robes—'

'Och no,' Annie said. 'He'd not want a fuss made, if he's just got himself in a bit of a mixter-maxter over the dates.'

'Well, let me know if there's anything I can do.'

Annie nodded, then, still clutching her flowers, she hurried off down the High Street with her heart racing uncomfortably. She knew the Colonel wasn't away. He'd said he'd be at the meeting but hadn't appeared, and now he hadn't come to do his reading. She'd never known him let someone down without warning.

Kirkluce was very quiet. The Spar shop was open, with a few cars parked in front and one or two people coming out with their Sunday newspapers, but all the other shops lining the wide High Street with its spreading plane trees were closed. Some of the gift shops would maybe open this afternoon, but once the last of the summer visitors had gone, the Sabbath calm would descend. Anxious as she was, the thought occurred to Annie as she jog-trotted past the Craft Centre next to Fauldburn House that if the superstore came, other shops would need to open in self-defence and this precious, peaceful day would become just the same as all the others.

When she reached the Fauldburn drive, she was out of breath, with the beginnings of a stitch in her side, and she slowed to a walk. The drive seemed longer than usual this morning, stretching ahead of her to the central circle with the mulberry tree which concealed the front of the house.

As Annie rounded it, she saw him immediately, half-in, half-out of the front door, a crumpled figure, lying on his back. She stopped in dismay, the tears springing to her eyes. How long had he lain there? He'd been fine last night, when she took in his tea.

He'd changed out of the old gardening clothes he'd been wearing then, and from his blazer and tie it looked as if he'd maybe been on his way to the meeting and had a heart attack. And no wonder, with all the strain they'd put him under, one way and another! Hot anger dried the tears as she trotted across the gravel.

It was only as Annie got closer that she saw the dark, bloody hole torn in his blazer pocket. She gave a cry of disbelief, of horror, and for a moment her head swam. She dropped the flowers she was holding and took a few, faltering steps closer and knelt down beside him, not noticing the puddle which soaked through her Sunday skirt. His eyes were wide open. It was horrible, that blank, glassy gaze.

Annie took a sobbing breath. Fetch help. It was the only coherent thought in her head, though it was plain enough that the Colonel was far beyond the reach of human aid. She staggered to her feet and began to run unsteadily back down the drive.

There was a sudden stream of traffic as Romy Kyle waited crossly to turn into the Craft Centre. She was in a filthy mood, largely thanks to drowning her sorrows in a bottle of cheap plonk, after Pete had gone out to escape her ranting on about Andrew Carmichael, Norman Gloag and the entire global management of ALCO, with particular reference to the slime bucket they had sent to the meeting.

She was still muttering as she drove in. The Craft Centre,

sympathetically converted from the old stable buildings of Fauldburn House, was entered through a pretty grey stone arch, and when it was warm enough and the small coffee shop had its tables outside in the cobbled centre courtyard, it had an almost continental air.

Romy parked in front of the double doors of one of the old storage sheds. There had been plans that this would be converted into another unit to add to Ossian Forbes-Graham's studio, Ellie's shop, Alanna Paterson's pottery and the coffee shop, but that wasn't going to happen now, was it?

She unlocked the door into her workshop and as the alarm system buzzed, keyed in the code, then pulled back the steel shutters covering doors and windows. With the value of the stuff she had to keep here, her insurance policy demanded the highest level of security.

It was painted white throughout with a black tiled floor, and in the shop area to the front the soft gleam of silver was the only touch of colour. There was a cabinet which held a display of silver jewellery bought in from other silversmiths, and she fetched a few samples of her own work from the built-in safe – a couple of bowls, an austerely elegant candlestick, a few irregularly shaped coffers – and set them in the individual boxed shelves attached to one wall.

She wasn't really interested in the shop. While it did provide a showcase to exhibit her skill, it was mainly a token gesture. Her real income came from the commission pieces – extremely expensive and sought-after – and what the shop brought in from passing trade was negligible. Her only reason for opening at all today was that she might as well, since she badly needed time in her workshop. She'd been recklessly agreeing to every commission offered, over these last uncertain weeks, to try to build up a financial cushion before the axe fell. Anyway, she loved her work – the silky feel of the silver under her hands, the joy of working with all her heart and soul to produce something perfect. And she loved her workshop.

As she hung up her jacket, Romy looked unhappily round at the curved work bench with the leather skin below for collecting any shavings of silver that fell as she worked, at the rolling mill, at the cabinet with the compressor and the blowtorch, black-enamelled inside so that you could see the colour of the flame as you worked, at the extraction fan, at the tool racks and the guillotine and the presses, at the elegant lighting for the showroom . . .

How much was all this stuff worth? Twenty thousand? The security, she knew, had cost at least three, and Andrew certainly hadn't got that back in rent. The Craft Centre had been his baby, his contribution to the amenities of the town, and if it was a sort of charity, so what? Artists had always had wealthy patrons, and the man was loaded. He'd be even more loaded if he'd agreed to this deal.

Guilt, she suspected, would mean that she'd be offered the equipment at a bargain basement price or even free, given luck and his guilty conscience, but still there would be setting-up costs which would need a bank loan. Unless, of course, Pete's latest get-rich-quick scheme actually worked, unlike all the others. She wouldn't be holding her breath. There was certain to be a spell when she couldn't work, and what were they to live on meantime?

Bugger Andrew! He didn't need ALCO's money. There would have been unpleasantness, OK, but all he had to do was stand firm and it would blow over. She'd had half a mind to go in and slag him off for cowardice, but it would be crazy to offend him as long as there was a chance of him refusing to sell. Not that she'd much hope of that now.

Romy took a thin round of Britannia silver from the safe in the workshop at the back. From a file, she fetched a drawing, just to remind herself of the design – a simple, exquisite silver bowl with an elliptical rim – then pinned it to a stand in front of her and started work.

She had just paused for a breather when Ossian Forbes-Graham came running into the cobbled yard. It was unusual to see him hurrying: he affected a languid, Byronic style, and Romy's attitude to his highly acclaimed oils was that they were emperor's-new-clothes paintings, involving minimal time, minimal skill and a helluva lot of bullshit.

He was heading for Ellie's shop – where else? – but Romy was curious enough to walk to her shop window to watch. From its position in the left-hand corner of the square facing the entrance, she could look across to Ellie's shop, first on the right as you came in.

She couldn't see Ellie herself. She'd be working in the cosy corner at the back, no doubt, on some woolly creation of the sort that gave kitsch a bad name, or one of her twee paintings of dear little daisies and buttercups. Confident of her own artistic brilliance, Romy was merciless in her judgement of others.

Ossian hadn't even shut the door. He was imparting information of some kind, something which brought Ellie from the back of the shop towards him. Even at this distance, Romy could see that she was staring at him, her body rigid.

Something was going on. Romy flung open the door and marched across the cobblestones. As she reached the other side, she heard Ossian saying earnestly, 'But don't worry, Ellie. Whatever happens now, you'll be all right. I'll look after you. There's stable yard on our estate – my parents could do a brilliant conversion—'

Ellie's face was an expressionless mask. 'Just get out and leave me alone, would you?'

With uncharacteristic forcefulness, she pushed the young man, still protesting, out of the shop, followed him out, locked the door behind her and headed for her upstairs flat.

Unashamedly, Romy stared after her as the door was slammed shut, almost in his face. 'What was all *that* about?' she demanded.

'Andrew Carmichael's dead. He's been shot.' Ossian was very flushed, his bright blue eyes glittering.

'*Shot!* But why on earth—' Romy broke off. 'Oh yes,' she said grimly, 'to stop him turning down ALCO's offer.'

'Or to stop him agreeing to it. Depends what he was going to do.' But Ossian seemed almost indifferent to the point he had made. 'The thing is, Ellie's upset – really upset! You saw her. But she won't let me comfort her,' he said wildly. 'She needs me to look after her, only she won't accept it.'

'You heard what she said – leave her alone,' Romy advised brutally. 'She's made it pretty plain. You won't get anywhere trying to force yourself on her now – or, if you want my frank opinion, any other time.'

He turned, his eyes narrowed. 'She was having a thing with him, wasn't she? It wasn't her fault – I suppose she needed the money.'

Romy was startled. 'I never heard that!'

'You haven't watched her like I have. But it'll all be different now. She needs help, and I can help her. Once she's got over the shock, you'll see.'

He walked away, leaving Romy feeling shocked herself. What the hell would happen now?

The news went round the Cutty Sark like wildfire. Tam MacNee, given leave for once to come to the pub on a Sunday since it was, as he pointed out, an important part of his rehabilitation, was one of the first to hear.

There was no doubt about it, his aim at the darts board was improving. He'd taken a quid off one of the locals who'd heard about his loss of form and was keen to take advantage, and Tam's victory cheered him out of all proportion to the scale of his winnings. He was trying to entice his opponent into another game when the ripple of rumour began spreading.

Tam wasn't sure who started it, but whenever it reached him he switched into operational mode, watching faces. He noticed the young man with the strange eyes, whom he'd seen last night pestering pretty Ellie Burnett, making a sharp exit. Apart from that, responses seemed to be entirely as you would expect: shock, expressions of dismay, extravagant theories and sensationalist pleasure disguised by head-shaking. Standard reactions.

He considered phoning Bunty, then decided against it. What was a marital disagreement and a dried-out roast against the chance of getting himself back into the game? He finished his pint and headed out towards the Galloway Constabulary Headquarters.

'I – see. Right. Right.' DI Marjory Fleming set the receiver on its stand and put her hands to her head, trying to take it all in.

A murder. The shooting, here in Kirkluce, just along the road there, of someone she knew, a prominent local figure, on a quiet Sunday. Well, probably from the sound of it, a quiet Saturday.

She grabbed a pad and started scribbling. She'd have to summon her front-line team, but Tam, she reflected with a sinking heart, wouldn't be one of them. She was all too aware of how much she had relied on him in the past. He was still paying for his perceptiveness on their last case.

She'd call in Tansy Kerr, Andy – now Detective Sergeant – Macdonald, and Will Wilson. Andy, the oldest of them, was only thirty-four.

So? They were able and enthusiastic. It was just that it made Fleming herself feel old, very old, and hideously responsible. What she said went, nowadays, and sometimes she longed for a voice that would greet one of her pronouncements with, 'You're kidding!' then add, 'ma'am,' in Tam's old piss-taking way. If she was absolutely sure she was right, she'd never had any problem slapping him down; if she wasn't sure, it would make her think again.

She'd better get on with it, anyway. The new police surgeon had arrived at the scene, and she'd better go and butter him up. They weren't easy to come by these days. She gave her instructions, then was just picking up her big leather shoulder bag when the knock came at the door.

'Come!' she said impatiently, then, when the door opened, 'Tam! Goodness – this is a surprise visit. I was – I was hoping to get back home for my mother's Sunday lunch.' It wasn't exactly a lie.

Tam wasn't on the strength just now, and it would be quite wrong to fill him in on a case which even her Superintendent, Donald Bailey – out on the golf course at present – hadn't heard about yet. She put down her bag again and said, 'Sit down! What can I do for you?' as if she had all the time in the world for stray callers.

'Oh, I'm not wanting to hold you back.'

There was a look in his eye that made her uneasy. 'No, no,' she protested.

'Just for a wee minute, then. I wouldn't want you to keep the corpse waiting.'

'How the hell did you know that?'

Satisfied at her blank astonishment, MacNee grinned as he tapped his nose. 'That's for me to know and you to guess. What's happened?'

'You probably know more than I do,' Fleming said tartly. 'I suppose the local grapevine was on to it at the same time as the call came in to us – if not before. What have you heard?'

'Colonel Carmichael, him that could put the kibosh on the

new superstore if it took his fancy, has been gunned down on his doorstep in broad daylight, most likely by the boss of ALCO, who is in the Mafia. Or possibly in a Russian syndicate that's hired a hit man. Then there's them that's saying someone local took a pop at him because he'd changed his mind about not selling. Though it might have been someone who wanted him to change his mind, and he hadn't. So what's the real story?'

'He's been shot,' Fleming said simply. 'That's all I know. And Jamie Rutherford, the new police doctor, is there already, so I'd better be on my way.'

'Rutherford? He'll probably say nothing's allowed to happen till the body's had a few weeks' sick leave. That's what he said to me, with about as much justification.'

'I can understand you're fed up, but he's only doing what's best for you,' she pointed out. 'Now, I'd better go—'

'Is that all you're going to tell me?' MacNee demanded.

'Tam, you know perfectly well I can't let you get involved.' Then, seeing his crestfallen expression, she relented. 'Oh well, you'll hear this in the street anyway. He was lying there overnight, certainly, and most probably before the supermarket meeting last night. But it depends what the pathologist can tell us, obviously.

'Cheer up! You could be signed off any day now and the minute you are, I'll welcome you back with a whoop and a holler.'

'Can't see it. Bunty's got to that bloody doctor, somehow.'

'Then he's probably right. Don't hurry it, and you'll get properly well sooner.'

'Oh, right! Spend all my time at the darts board, when this is going on! Guaranteed to make me relaxed and happy.' His tone was mutinous.

Fleming's voice sharpened. 'Tam, I can't bring you in on the official investigation. End of discussion.'

He conceded that, then, brightening, he said, 'Not *officially*, no. But it could be useful, not having to thumb through the rule book every time I asked a question—'

'Don't even think of it!' She was horrified.

'No, no. Of course not. Just my wee joke,' he said soothingly. Then he left, smiling his notoriously alarming gap-tooth grin.

There was no point in arguing, but the thought of a maverick Tam made her blood run cold.

4

'Pull!' Fiona Farquharson, in heather-mix tweed trousers and a green quilted jacket over her Aran sweater, swung her shotgun as the clay disc came over, fast and low, and blasted it to pieces.

It was a fine day, with only the lightest breeze and wispy clouds high in a sky of softest blue. The heather was still in bloom and the scent of vegetation, damp after the night's rain, was strong in the warmth of the sun. The Forbes-Graham estate was a modest one, but the acres of moorland, set aside for the grouse before the bird all but disappeared, made a beautiful upland setting for the clay-pigeon shoot which now produced a very respectable income. In the distance, the drone of motorbike engines indicated another money-making activity.

Flushed with triumph, Fiona took off her ear-muffs and turned round.

'Shot, Fiona! Good girl!' Murdoch Forbes-Graham applauded, then turned to the score-keeper. 'How are we doing? Good, good. Now, Giles, you'll be on next. Don't go letting the side down again.'

Giles Farquharson looked at his beaming wife unhappily. Fiona had always been a better shot than he was and today he wasn't on form anyway. Being invited to a scrappy buffet lunch by Deirdre Forbes-Graham – not renowned for her cuisine – didn't make it a pleasurable social occasion, when it was perfectly clear you'd been invited only as the hired hand, to make sure that the traps operated smoothly and that the two other invitation teams were suitable impressed. And preferably beaten, too. Murdoch Forbes-Graham liked to win.

Not that spending his free day at home would have been relaxing. Fiona had been on and on at him, and with everything going round and round in his head he'd hardly slept last night. Not that it was easy to get a good night's kip even at the best of times, the way Fiona snored.

The other teams had taken their turn – one success, one failure – and Giles gloomily loaded his gun and stepped up to the stand. Murdoch, a heavily built man with jowls and a weather-beaten face, raised a silver hip-flask to his employee. 'Good luck! It's a Driven Pheasant – should be simple enough. Don't screw up, now. We only need a few more points, and we'll have them by the short and curlies.'

Giles pulled the mufflers over his ears, raised the shotgun to his shoulder and shouted, 'Pull!' Just as he did so, the mobile phone in his pocket vibrated, he tensed up and the clay sailed by, unscathed, to bury itself in a clump of whins. He broke his gun, pulled off his ear-muffs, and took the phone out of his pocket.

'Sorry about that,' he muttered. 'Had to leave it on in case there was a problem with the traps.'

Murdoch was swearing, his face redder than ever.

'For goodness' sake, Giles,' Fiona snapped, 'why didn't you have the sense to switch it off when you went to take your shot?'

He ignored her, walking out of earshot to take the call.

'Bloody idiot!' Murdoch snorted. 'Still – another few rounds to go. We'll get the bastards yet.'

He turned to Wilfrid Vernor-Miles, roped in from a neighbouring estate as a good gun, who was standing grinning broadly with a Purdey broken over his arm. 'Wilf, old man, there's a Bolting Rabbit coming up, OK? Nothing in your trousers beyond the usual equipment, have you? And you've got that under control, I trust? On you go, then.'

Wilfrid, sturdy in plus-fours, gave a hearty laugh as he loaded his shotgun. He was just stepping up to the stand to wait his turn when Giles came back, a strange look on his face.

'Hold it, Wilf!' Murdoch snapped. 'Don't want to lose another point because Giles is wandering round like a sick sheep. What's the matter, man?'

Fiona looked at him sharply. 'Giles – something wrong?'

He was finding it difficult to frame the words. 'It's my uncle. It's Andrew. He's been shot. Dead.'

The report of the shotgun fired by one of the other team made them all jump. Fiona put her hand to her heart dramatically.

'Uncle Andrew – dead? How – how absolutely awful!'

Giles looked at her bleakly. Behind the surprise, behind the expression of shock, he could see calculation. It was news Fiona had been anticipating for years and perhaps now, at last, she would get what she had been waiting for.

Dr Rutherford, squatting beside Andrew Carmichael's body in a position which made Marjory Fleming's hamstrings ache just looking at it, straightened up with the offensive ease of the fit and youthful as she approached. He was wearing jeans and a pale blue polo shirt and he was tall – six foot two or three, Fleming guessed – with light brown hair very neatly cut. It was a solemn occasion, of course, but even so she thought he looked a serious young man, with his narrow, sensitive face.

He was coming down the drive to meet her, holding out his hand and smiling. He had a very pleasant smile.

'Sorry about the clothes. They asked me to come at once. You must be DI Fleming. I've heard a lot about you.'

'I've heard about you too, mostly from Tam MacNee.' She shook hands. 'But I didn't believe much of it.'

His mouth twitched. 'I'm grateful!'

'I can only hope you've done the same for me. Anyway, thanks so much for taking this on. It's not the most congenial of jobs, but it's very necessary and much appreciated.'

Rutherford shrugged. 'Compared to hospital work, what I do now is a doddle. And it's all part of being in a community, isn't it, which was what made me apply for the job here in the first place.'

Fleming liked that. She'd heard a lot of good things about the new young doctor; her mother was a great fan and this certainly confirmed her belief in Janet's good judgement. 'I'm glad that's the way you see it,' she said warmly.

They walked on up the drive to the house. Fleming had never been to Fauldburn before and she looked now at the frontage of the pleasant, sprawling family house, built of grey sandstone and softened by a Virginia creeper which was starting to take on its fiery autumn colours.

There was a lot of activity, with uniformed officers now marking off the area with blue and white tape. She nodded to the sergeant in charge, but she was startled to see, lying on the gravel, two bunches of flowers, white chrysanthemums and lilies.

'A bit premature for that sort of thing,' she said sharply, then, raising her voice, 'What's going on here? Has no one sealed the site?'

A uniformed constable hurried forward, a clipboard in his hand. 'Just going down to do that, ma'am.'

She took it from him. 'Who else have you logged?' The sheet was blank. 'Not good enough, constable. I can see at least five officers, the doctor and myself. And where did the flowers come from? I take it this wasn't a little floral tribute you picked up on the way here?' She handed back the clipboard.

The young man flushed to the tips of his rather prominent ears. 'Sorry, ma'am. The flowers were there when we arrived.'

'I see. Well, record those names now, get yourself to the end of the drive and see to it that there are no unauthorised visitors to the site.' She turned away, and then on an afterthought turned back. 'And that includes DS MacNee, if he appears. He's on sick leave at the moment so he has to be treated as a civilian.'

Rutherford had been waiting a short distance away. 'Sorry about that,' she said as she rejoined him.

'Not at all,' he responded politely, but she thought he was eying her a little warily. It was always hard for civilians to understand that in running an operation, sweetness and light didn't feature.

'How much can you tell me?' she asked, walking over to where Andrew Carmichael's body lay. It was the first time she had been confronted with a murder victim she had known in life and she hoped she would be able to view it with professional impassivity. She hadn't known him well, but she'd had the impression of a decent man, very much of his age and class. He'd served as a Justice of the Peace for a time too, with a reputation for being firm and fair, if a little too inclined to believe a sob story.

Carmichael's blank face, skin waxy in death and eyes fixed in an empty stare, gave no indication of the violence that had torn the gaping hole in the breast pocket of his blazer, displaying torn and bloody flesh. His head was resting on the floor of the vestibule, its blue, yellow and red encaustic tiles and a brilliantly polished brass door-sill seeming incongruously cheerful, like an ill-judged stage-set.

Fleming had often thought that death scenes looked unreal and it was a relief to find that she could feel the same sense of detachment about this one, as she listened to what the doctor was telling her.

It was the first time he had attended at a murder scene; he was tentative and, Fleming thought, a little shaken by the experience. In any case, the police doctor's examination was a cursory one, though it would be interesting to know what his impressions were.

'I want to stress that I'm no expert,' Rutherford said earnestly. 'Anything I can say would be guesswork more than anything.'

'Believe me, detectives understand all about guesswork. Carry on.'

'From the face, I'd say he didn't know what hit him. No time to register pain, or surprise, even. Opens the door, then bang! A full-on shot, and he dropped where he was standing. From a shotgun, obviously.' He pointed to the filigree of holes in the blazer and shirt which indicated the scatter of pellets.

'If you're ever looking for a job in the CID, I could put in a word for you. So – he came right out on to the doorstep, presumably, then staggered backwards and fell.' Fleming was thinking aloud. 'Someone he knew? Someone he wouldn't be alarmed to see carrying a gun? Or possibly someone he didn't see immediately, someone who'd perhaps concealed himself behind one of the bushes, then stepped out?' She looked at the shrubbery which extended on either side of the front door. 'Certainly plenty to choose from.

'Any guess about time of death? I know, I know–' she raised her hand as he opened his mouth to protest '– the pathologist will do all the tests, but that takes time and any indication you can give would be helpful.'

Rutherford thought for a moment. 'For a start, the jacket, where he was sheltered by the porch, is dry but the trousers are damp. I haven't turned him over – I know you'll need photos – but if the ground below is dry it will give you some idea. I seem to remember it was raining at one stage yesterday evening.

'When I took on this job I did a bit of reading to brush up on my pathology. When I checked just now there were still some signs of flexibility in the hands and feet. It takes around twelve hours for rigor mortis to be fully established, as a rule of thumb, and a few more before it starts to wear off again. So twelve hours takes you back to midnight, more or less, then another five or six . . . Early evening, maybe, or could be a bit later. Best I can do.'

Fleming was impressed. 'You obviously studied to some purpose. That's very helpful as a basic framework, anyway.'

At the sound of footsteps on the gravel, they both turned and Fleming said, 'Oh, good. That's the first of my team arriving now.' She went to meet them.

Andy Macdonald was smart in a Sunday suit, and Tansy Kerr, famous in the CID for her unorthodox approach to plain clothes, was looking surprisingly respectable in a fitted white shirt over jeans which were neither distressed nor so long that the hems were frayed from dragging on the ground. Her hair, usually tinted at least one alarming shade if not more, was a soft ash-blonde: it had produced a bit of leg-pulling from the lads about losing her nerve, but she'd developed an enigmatic smile to go with the new hairstyle and was using it a lot recently.

'Unless there's anything else, doctor, I don't think we need to keep you any longer,' Fleming said. She could see the photographer arriving, and the fewer people there were to clutter the place up, the better.

Rutherford nodded gravely, said goodbye and disappeared down the drive. Tansy Kerr swivelled to watch him go.

'Wow! He's all that and a bag of chips, isn't he?' she said approvingly. 'Maybe I might throw a sickie next week and catch a piece of the action.'

'There'll be no leave of any sort till this one's cleared up,' Fleming said tartly.

Kerr straightened her face. 'Sorry, boss. Just a joke.'

'Yes, I know. But—' She caught a look between the two young detectives and hastily said, 'Oh, never mind.' It was unreasonable to be irritated, she knew that. Jokes came with the job, even, or perhaps particularly, in gruesome situations, but these days living with yoof culture at work as well as at home was a bit of a strain.

'I haven't got much to go on as yet. The first person to talk to is someone called Annie Brown. His housekeeper, I think – she found the body. I jotted down the address—'

'I know where she stays,' Macdonald volunteered. 'She's a friend of my Auntie Irene's – her that has the coffee shop in the Craft Centre. There's been a lot of feeling, of course, with this superstore business.'

'Superstore? Oh, that's right. There was a public meeting about it last night, wasn't there?' Fleming had given the rights and wrongs of it little thought, only reflecting secretly and guiltily that it wouldn't do any harm to have a better class of ready-meal available than the Spar supermarket could offer, without having to drive miles to stock up.

'There was quite a bit of aggro, apparently. Some people are set to lose their businesses and there's others ready to make a fortune out of it, my auntie says. Councillor Norman Gloag, for a start – he's saying he's no axe to grind, but everyone knows he'll be given the company's business if it gets the go-ahead. And of course it all depended on Andrew Carmichael agreeing to sell the Craft Centre. My auntie said he was going to refuse and there'd be a lot of people upset about that.'

'Your auntie seems to be the fount of all wisdom.' Fleming was amused. 'You'd better go and see her once you've talked to Annie Brown.

'There should be uniforms out knocking on doors by now so we'll have quite a bit more information by mid-afternoon.

I'll have to wait here for the pathology team, but I'll be in my office after that. Was there any sign of Will?'

'Will's out sailing with one of his mates today,' Kerr said.

'Right – it's up to the two of you, then. Follow your noses if there's anything interesting.

'And one last thing – Tam's been in to see me already. And much as I miss him, much as I'd like to have him in on this, he hasn't been signed off so he can't come back to work yet. He's threatening to go freelance, but for his own good, not to mention ours, he's got to be stopped. Understood?'

As they walked back down the drive, Kerr looked up at Macdonald. 'Oh, sure! Easy! Will you tell him, or will I?'

'You tell him. He wouldn't hit a woman,' Macdonald said simply.

Norman Gloag walked out of the house and slammed the door. His hands were not quite steady as he fumbled in his pocket for his car keys. Shouting at his son had done nothing except make him look foolish, but he had been provoked, coming into the kitchen to find Maureen cooking bacon for Gordon when it was clearly understood that if you didn't turn up for breakfast, you missed it.

It had ended with Gordon saying, 'It's sad, really, what a boring old fart you are,' and strolling out of the kitchen.

Gloag was going out to give his car its Sunday wash when he saw it. There, right across the whole of the driver's side of the BMW, scratched in the gleaming metallic blue paintwork, was – well, an obscenity. Directed at him. By name.

For a moment, he couldn't move. Then he stormed back into the house and went to the kitchen. He wasn't talking to Maureen, of course, but you couldn't launch into a furious tirade when you were alone.

She was sitting at the table with a cup of coffee and another fag in her mouth, wearing an air of indifference, but when he at last ran out of steam with an announcement that he was just going to phone the police, she did speak. 'It was probably Gordon and his pals. Won't do your public image any good if your son's arrested for doing that to his dad, will it?'

Tam MacNee drove up the pot-holed track which led to Christina Munro's farmhouse with mixed feelings about his mission. He knew perfectly well that it was pointless, but on the other hand it was getting him out of the house when Bunty's sister, her that was married to the bank manager, was bringing her husband to tea, and the pair of them always got his dander up. Last time she'd said, with ill-concealed satisfaction, 'You'll just have to face it, Tam – you'll never be the same again.'

So having to go to Wester Seton and listen to the old biddy rabbiting on about the wickedness of the younger generation, then make meaningless soothing noises, was a small price to pay, especially since it would give him a chance on the way home to pop into the Salutation Bar, frequented by officers from the Kirkluce HQ.

Anyway, Bunty had insisted that he went. She and Christina both belonged to the bunny-huggers sisterhood, always taking on animal down-and-outs that no one with any sense would allow over the threshold.

The whole place was neglected. The farm was situated on rising ground, quite exposed and bare, and it could never have been really prosperous. The farmhouse was no more than a run-down cottage, and as Tam parked in the yard he noted there were slates missing from the roof and weeds growing up between the cobbles. There was some elderly farm equipment rusting away in long grass and the house itself, with its weathered paintwork and all the downstairs shutters closed even on this bright afternoon, looked abandoned. As he got out, three donkeys, browsing an adjacent field, looked up, and one came towards him, exposing pale gums and large yellow teeth in a series of brays.

A shutter opened cautiously and MacNee caught a glimpse of a face behind it. Then it closed again and a moment later he heard the rattle of bolts and Christina Munro opened the door, a tiny, stooped figure in a crocheted hat, wearing a blue jersey with pulled threads and grey trousers which were much too big for her.

'Bunty said you'd be, so you better come in. Not that there's any point.'

It wasn't what you'd call a gracious welcome, even if she was right. Tam followed her in, feeling aggrieved. It was very dark, coming in from the sunshine, and he blinked as his eyes adjusted. There were a couple of low-wattage lamps on, and a fire was burning in the meagre grate of a black-leaded kitchen range. He hadn't seen one of those for years.

'You'll be wanting a cuppa, I suppose. You can sit down there.'

She indicated a chair opposite the one she obviously sat in herself, which had cushions, a multi-coloured crochet rug and a tortoiseshell cat sitting on the arm. Tam obediently took his place while she went to push a kettle by the side of the range on to a hotplate where it at once began singing. The cat jumped down with a glare of indignation and took up a position under the kitchen table, its tail twitching.

There were a couple of other cats around and a greyhound, too, a pretty creature, which stood watchfully beside its mistress, but after a moment, when Tam held out his hand, it came over to lay a trusting head on his knee.

Christina cackled. 'Oh, they know a soft tumphy when they see one!'

Affronted at the suggestion, Tam stopped stroking and the

dog, with a reproachful look, went to lie down in front of the fire.

The kitchen, he thought, looking about, could have gone straight on the telly for one of these dreary Scottish kailyard dramas he never watched: chipped stone sink, a meat safe instead of a fridge, an opening on to a pantry with thick slate slabs for shelves, a rough wooden table covered with a green checked oilcloth. The flowered linoleum on the floor looked like the most recent addition to the decor and he reckoned that had probably been laid in the Fifties.

Christina was producing some tired-looking biscuits from a faded tin marked 'Peek Frean's Fancy Selection'.

'No, no, nothing for me,' Tam said hastily. 'A cup of tea'll do fine – milk and three sugars. I've just had one of Bunty's Sunday lunches and you know her – not happy till you can barely stand.'

She didn't respond to the pleasantry, scooping tea from a caddy with a Coronation picture of the Queen on it into a brown pot which had been warming by the range. *Well, be like that*, he thought, irritated, but then, as she started pouring on the boiling water, some of it missed the pot and splashed, hissing, on to the range. Suddenly he realised that her hands were shaking badly – in fact, her whole body was shaking.

He didn't think it was a physical disability. The woman was in a highly nervous state. As Tam got up to take the thick china mug she had filled, he said gently, 'Tell me what's been happening.'

When Bunty had told him what she knew, he'd pointed out it was just the usual stuff – neds mucking about. Difficult to handle, when there wasn't real damage done, but usually you could reckon they'd get tired of it and move on. Apart from a slap on the wrist and a word with the parents, there wasn't a lot the police could do, except threaten an ASBO – for what that was worth.

But as Christina talked, he began to be alarmed. This was nasty stuff, calculated to intimidate, and it was having a dangerous effect. As the old woman talked on, in her quavering voice, of her fears for her animals more than herself, he found himself unable to reassure her. Certainly he didn't think she was in physical danger personally – the police knew who they were and they would know that they'd be picked up immediately if she came to any harm. But the donkeys, for instance—

And she was talking wildly. How could she let the poor beasts be persecuted? She was their protector, she had a duty. Suddenly, Tam noticed the shotgun propped on the wall beside the door, and he broke into what she was saying.

'Here, have you a licence for that thing?'

Christina followed his eyes. ' 'Course I do. I've aye had a licence.'

'It should be locked up,' he said firmly. 'Have you a secure cupboard?'

She jerked her head. 'There's one through the house there.'

'That's where it should be, then.' He went over and picked it up, noting with some alarm that it was loaded. He broke the gun and shook out the cartridges into his hand. 'Through here?'

With a bad grace, Christina led the way and opened the door to show him into another darkened room. Flicking on the light switch, Tam saw a dingy farm office, a desk piled with yellowing paperwork and shelves stacked with drums and packets of farm supplies, thick with dust. A sack of animal feed was open in one corner and the air was heavy with its fusty smell.

The built-in cupboard looked secure enough, fitted with steel-lever locks – about the most modern things in the house, Tam reckoned. There was a small, ancient safe under the desk and Christina, bending with difficulty, turned the dial on the outside, opened it and took out keys. He could see there were cartridges stocked there as well.

'That's good security,' he approved. 'Excellent, in fact. But not if the gun's standing in your front room.'

The door to the cupboard wasn't locked and she looked at him expressionlessly as he opened it. The cupboard was empty. 'This is the only gun you have?'

'Only need one. I go out shooting rabbits for the cats' supper.'

It was a reasonable enough thing to say, but somehow he didn't find it reassuring. Tam set the gun inside, locked the door again and handed the keys to Christina, but she made no move to return them to the safe. 'Shall I put them back for you?' he offered.

'I'll put them back after. Once you've gone. I'm not telling anyone the combination.'

He could hardly insist. They went back into the kitchen, but she didn't ask him to sit down to finish his tea. She stood pointedly near the door, not actually holding it open but making it perfectly plain that she expected him to go.

'Look, Christina,' he said awkwardly, 'I know you're having a hard time. It's not fair, and there's nothing I'd like better than to give those wee toerags a lesson they'd never forget. But it's not like that nowadays. I can't act outside the law, and neither can you.'

'So you can't do anything either. Never thought you could.' Her stance was defiant, but she was still shaking. The dog, which had silently appeared again at her side, gave a little whine and nudged her; her hand went down automatically to fondle its head.

'I'll get the police to go and lean on them a bit heavier this time,' he promised.

She laughed at that. 'Oh, that'll sort it, right enough. And next time they're going to be worse.'

The terrible thing was, Tam couldn't deny it. She was holding open the door now and he had no choice but to leave. On the threshold he turned.

'Christina, what I'm saying is, don't take matters into your own hands. There was a farmer in the south who tried that and it ended in a tragedy and him in jail.'

She was silent for a moment, and then she said, 'Aye. Well, I expect he thought it was worth it. They wouldn't go back there in a hurry, would they?

'Oh, I know the law, Tam MacNee. In my day we were brought up to respect it. Just a pity we're the only ones that do and folks like me are left sick with terror – sick to my stomach – the whole time.'

She shut the door on him, but not before he had seen the tears in the fierce old eyes.

Tam drove back to Kirkluce in a very thoughtful mood. It was an alarming situation, and perhaps he ought to report it and have Christina's gun licence revoked. But in truth, while he thought she might fire the gun as a warning – which would, of course, cause trouble enough since neds always knew their rights and wouldn't hesitate to report it – he didn't believe for a moment that she would deliberately injure anyone, except perhaps herself. And it probably gave her some feeling of security. If she felt totally helpless she might, at her age, simply die of fear, and how would he feel then?

No, he wasn't going to mention taking the licence. But he would pop into HQ and have a word with the desk sergeant, say they needed to send someone round again to those little sods to spell out that if it happened again it would be more than just a warning. Threaten to pursue the case and ask for confiscation of the motorbikes – that might do it.

And if he was in the station anyway, surely someone would tell him what was going on.

* * *

'And then she just walks straight past me, into her bedroom, like she was a zombie or something. I go, "What's wrong, then?" but she didn't say anything. Ossian Forbes-Graham and Romy were there, down in the courtyard, so I went down and they told me what had happened.'

The roar and whine of Formula One engines were almost drowning out Dylan's agitated recital. Johnny Black, just back from organising a motocross event at the Forbes-Graham estate, was lounging with a beer on the sofa in the front room of the flat which occupied the space above the showroom on the High Street and the repair workshop and yard at the back, watching TV. He picked up the remote control and killed the sound.

'Carmichael's been shot? Do they know who did it?'

Dylan shrugged. 'Don't think so. There's police cars and all sorts at the house now.

'Listen, do you want to come round and talk to my mum? It's really, like, weird the way she's acting. Ossian was wanting to come in and speak to her but when I go to ask, she's just sitting on the bed and doesn't say anything. And when I say would I just bring him up, then, she starts shaking her head and going, "No, no, no, no," on and on. It's like I said – weird.'

'Don't blame her,' Johnny said. 'I'd go, "No, no, no," too, if you were going to land Ossian on me.'

His reaction was in itself calming, and Dylan's laugh was one of relief. 'Yeah, you could be right. He's a real tosser. So – what about Mum?'

Johnny paused for a moment. 'Look – she's had bad news, poor girl. The old guy was good to her, wasn't he? She'll be upset, need time to get over the shock.

'Tell you what. You make her a cup of tea and take it in to her – women like that. You can do sympathetic, can't you? Oh no, I forgot – you're a teenager.'

Dylan grinned. 'I can fake it.'

'Then say, would she like me to come round. I don't want to push in where I'm not wanted, but if she says yes, give me a bell and I'll be there.'

'Thanks, Johnny. That's cool.'

Feeling a burden lifted, Dylan went back along the High Street to the Craft Centre.

Kirkluce was a typical Scottish market town, with shops, pubs and a couple of take-aways lining the main street and one or two side streets as well; the slate-roofed houses were grey stone or white harling, though occasionally a more adventurous householder challenged the monochromatic townscape with a daringly pink, green or even, unwisely, purple paint job. On Sunday, though, the town was dead. There was a local saying that if you'd become a nudist and wanted to keep it quiet, walk down Kirkluce High Street on a Sunday afternoon.

But a group of people had gathered outside Fauldburn House, just beyond the door to the Craft Centre, and Dylan walked on to join them. There wasn't anything to see, except some blue-and-white tape and a bored-looking constable at the entrance to the drive. After a moment, when nothing happened, he went back into the courtyard.

There was no sign of Ossian now, though he could see Romy working in her studio. He went upstairs and let himself into the flat.

'Mum!' he called, but there was no answer. Following Johnny's advice, he put on the kettle, fetched a mug and raked around for a herbal tea-bag. She liked those; it would show he was being sympathetic and understanding.

He didn't get it, really, though. So the old bloke had been good to her, OK, but he'd have been popping his clogs soon anyway, wouldn't he? Dylan could go along with her being stressed out about maybe losing the shop and the flat now the Colonel wasn't there to stop it being sold – he felt a bit edgy about that himself – but even so . . . Still, if Johnny thought a cup of tea was the answer, he'd give it a go.

With the mug in his hand, he went along to his mother's bedroom and tapped on the door. There was no answer, and when he went in it was like she hadn't moved at all. Her face was blank and she was staring out of the window, but he reckoned she wasn't looking at anything.

'Here, Mum,' he said awkwardly, 'brought you some tea. Peppermint. You like that.'

She turned her head and for a moment there was a flicker of animation. 'Thanks, that's kind. You're a good boy.'

She took a sip and he went on, 'I saw Johnny. He said, would you like him to come round? It'd be good for you to talk to him, Mum—'

The blank look came back to her face. 'No,' she said. She jumped up, letting go of the mug as if she were unaware it was in her hand, and it fell to the floor, spreading a pool of the hot, pale liquid on the carpet. 'Leave me alone! Leave me alone!'

Baffled and scared, Dylan retreated.

5

Marjory Fleming was less than pleased, when she came back to the station after seeing the pathologist, to find Tam MacNee at the desk, talking to Jock Naismith.

She did not try to hide her irritation. 'Tam! What are you doing, back here again?'

Out of the corner of her eye she could see Naismith suppressing a smile. MacNee turned an innocent face to her and put his hand to his heart.

'Mine,' he declared, 'is "*an honest heart, that's free frae a' intended fraud or guile*". How could you think I'd try and get in on the case, with you telling me I was banned?'

'Can't imagine,' Fleming said crisply. 'So – what *are* you doing here?'

'I'm a concerned member of the public, come to share information useful to the police, just like I'm supposed to.' He spoke with some dignity. 'And I'm entitled to be treated with due respect and maybe even given a wee cuppie tea.'

Exasperated, she turned to Naismith. 'What's all this about?'

It was MacNee who replied, more soberly. 'It's not really a joking matter. I was away seeing Christina Munro today – her that's being hit on by those neds on motorbikes – and if you ask me it's a nasty situation.'

Fleming's annoyance evaporated. 'Burnett and Kyle?'

MacNee looked surprised at her tone. 'That's right. And Councillor Gloag's son too, Jock tells me. Och, they're just doing the intermittent harassment bit – we know all about that. But she's an old woman all by herself and they're leaning on her. She's reached the dangerous end of scared. She could take a heart attack and drop dead – either that or she'll take the gun she's got for potting rabbits and use it.'

'And these are Cat's latest school chums!' Fleming said hollowly. 'No chance we can arrange for them to be committed for detention, preferably tomorrow?'

'Yesterday would be better,' MacNee said.

'Jock, we'll have to get on to that, come down heavy. But frankly, we can't spare the manpower right now. All this today has left us seriously overstretched and everything else has to take second place.'

'Any leads on that?' MacNee's question was elaborately casual, fooling no one.

'Mr MacNee,' Fleming said formally, 'thank you so much for your public-spirited action in reporting to Sergeant Naismith a matter of legitimate concern. Your cooperation is much appreciated. There is the door. Goodbye.

'And Jock, may I remind you that Mr MacNee is, as he explained, a member of the public and as such not party to the internal details of a police investigation.'

As she headed for the stairs, Naismith shook his head. 'Aye, she's a hard woman, Big Marge.'

'She is that,' MacNee agreed solemnly. 'Lucky you told me all that before she told you not to.'

With a wink, he sauntered out, his hands in the pockets of his jeans, whistling '*Will Ye No' Come Back Again?*' which, even if it hadn't been penned by the Great Man himself, seemed suited to the occasion.

It wasn't often that Pete Spencer could be found in the bedroom he shared with Romy, working at the table which served as a desk, on a Sunday afternoon. In fact, even on weekdays he spent as little time there as he could. His skills were people skills and you couldn't exert them alone, pushing paper. Figures resolutely refused to be charmed.

And however you looked at these, they came out the same way. He put his head in his hands and groaned.

Finding Dan Simpson, a local lad, but one with a background as a broker on the London Stock Exchange, had seemed an amazing piece of luck. It had given credibility to his own idea of setting up an Investment Club, and there had been no need to say, in the glossy prospectus they produced, that Dan had come back home under a cloud, any more than to mention Pete's own chequered past. It didn't do to dwell on unfortunate misunderstandings and it wasn't as if they hadn't both suffered for them. Dan had a boring job on the Forbes-Graham estate, and Pete himself hadn't enjoyed the success a man of his talents deserved.

They'd worked out the investor profile they wanted with great care. The younger female pensioner, sixties and early seventies, preferably widowed: everyone knew that, whatever the bleeding hearts said, pensioners were the ones with money. And greedy with it; they got a taste for exotic holidays and cruising and it didn't come cheap.

They weren't the internet generation, and in any case, as Dan pointed out, the fraud squad had officers whose job it was to trawl the sites, and if there was one thing that mattered to Pete more than money, it was not going back inside. It was still a vivid and terrifying memory; sometimes he woke at night sweating and crying out.

Pete was good at chatting up the ladies in that age group. They liked his cheeky charm, and he had an instinctive understanding of the buttons to press. They were familiar with women's book groups, so a Ladies' Investment Club was a reassuring idea. Explaining to them that insiders in the business world, like Dan, all knew how to get a proper return on their money at the expense of ordinary folk, played neatly to an existing prejudice. He cautioned them that, though of course they were welcome to get their friends to join (a natural female instinct), he couldn't pay them commission since it would be illegal – a masterstroke, that, suggesting strict attention to the law – but as founder members they would be in Tier One, entitled to a yearly bonus once there were enough members to form a larger Tier Two, which converted them into supremely effective recruiting agents. Then, of course, he had taken care to give the usual caveats about the stock market going down as well as up, but not until he had seen the pound signs flashing in their eyes and knew they wouldn't listen.

One day it would unravel, without a doubt. Dan had an exit plan: if they were lucky, the market would have one of its periodic crashes, and the alarmist stories in the newspapers would mean that the failure of the Ladies' Investment Club was explicable, if unfortunate. And if it got awkward, by then Dan and Pete would have the money in the offshore account to allow them to disappear quietly to some pleasant haven, preferably one with no extradition treaties.

Pete looked grimly at the figures in front of him. There certainly wasn't enough for that yet. Not by a long way.

It was his own fault. He had made a stupid misjudgement, one he should have been able to foresee. He'd said nothing to Dan about it, though. He hoped he'd done enough to stop it all coming out in the most disastrous way, but he couldn't be sure: if they came after you, it would be every man for himself, and Pete didn't plan to be the one left holding the baby.

Recently he'd been seriously contemplating leaving Romy anyway. In his indolent, easy-going way he'd been happy enough; her support meant he could dabble in this and that, always hoping for the big break, rather than getting a steady job. But recently, as her son had grown older, his comfort had been eroded.

He'd more or less been able to ignore Barney when he was young, but increasingly the boy was intruding on his personal space, sneering and making veiled comments about Pete's past. He was nosy, too; Pete had recently caught him going through the papers on his desk. Then there was his constant rowing with his mother – Pete hated arguments, especially when Romy kept trying to draw him in. And to add to all that, Barney was getting very expensive.

The motorbike was a case in point. Romy had ignored Pete's objections: she felt guilty about walking out on her marriage and Barney was skilled at rubbing her nose in it. Pete could almost admire his talent for manipulation, but not when it impacted on his own lifestyle.

He'd tried to persuade Romy to talk to Gloag about compensation from ALCO but, pig-headed as usual, she wouldn't listen. A few thousand in their joint account might have given him the escape route he was beginning to think might be necessary. At the moment, if he needed to get out quick, all he had was a credit card, and that wasn't very far off its limit.

Pete was trapped here, just waiting to see what would happen. He felt sick at the thought of all that might go wrong.

'Right. The information we have so far: I'll summarise.'

Macdonald, Kerr and now Will Wilson too, with his face still glowing from the salt sea air, had gathered in Fleming's office. She had switched the phone to voicemail; it had been ringing constantly and, after three interruptions in the five minutes since the meeting started, it was all she could do, though it would mean a lot of time working through the messages later.

Fleming glanced down at her notes. 'Carmichael was shot with a shotgun at fairly close range, less than ten feet, they think. If it was closer than that, there may be powder residue on the clothes, but there'll be the usual long wait for lab tests. The wad of the cartridge went straight to the heart and there was also a peppering of pellets. At that distance the shot would have needed no particular skill.

'He died instantly. The estimated time of death is between five, when Annie Brown saw him, and eight last night when the rain started. It looks as if he was dead by then since the ground underneath the body was dry.

'That's supported by the lack of footprint evidence, which is unfortunate, but there's apparently visible disturbance of the soil and broken twigs in the bushes to the left of the front door, so it looks as if someone rang the bell and hid, then when Carmichael came out to see if anyone was there, stepped out in front of him and shot him. If we have a suspect they'll be able to do analysis of the shoes, of course, to match up with the samples they've taken of soil and gravel.

'Annie Brown claimed that he'd been planning to attend the superstore meeting in St Cerf's Hall, and what he was wearing – blazer and regimental tie – supports that. There was also food untouched in the fridge which looked as if it was meant for his supper. The meeting started at six-thirty so we're focusing on the earlier time, at least initially.

'That's about it. What have you got for me?'

Kerr picked up the notebook she had laid on the desk and flipped it open. 'Andy and I split up. Seemed better use of manpower at this stage.

'I went to see Annie. She's in quite a state, but dead keen to get whoever did this to "the Colonel" locked up. She'd reckoned he'd be at the meeting, but she didn't fall over backwards when he never appeared. He'd been under a lot of pressure because if he refused to sell the Craft Centre, the deal wouldn't go through.

'He'd been worried about the effect on the community – a laird complex, if you ask me –' Kerr sniffed, 'and he'd been subsidising the Craft Centre too. Patron of the Arts – saw himself as Kirkluce's answer to the Medici family, no doubt.'

Wilson was grinning, but Macdonald protested, 'Come on! My auntie says he was a nice man – old school, but always ready to help if you'd a problem. Too soft for his own good, she reckoned.'

Kerr was unabashed. 'That's class guilt. And people like your auntie and Annie still have the servant mentality – my granny was in service when she was a girl and she still goes on about "the Family" – Miss Mary this and Master Charlie that.'

'Come on, Tansy, we're not here to discuss your social hang-ups,' Fleming said firmly. 'Save it for the pub and stick to the point. Anything else?'

'Sorry, boss. That sort of thing just gets right up my nose.' She turned over a page. 'Anyway, Annie thought he was ace. His wife died recently, an invalid for a good while and a cantankerous old besom, as far as I could make out, but the sainted Colonel was wonderful with her.

'And he'd no children so now the whole thing will go to the nephew, Annie says, Giles Farquharson – daft name – and she's no time for him. He and his wife Fiona – what else? – have been round every ten minutes, trying to push him into selling up to ALCO. Out for the pickings, jackals round a lion, according to her. Been watching too many David Attenborough programmes.

'I think that's about it.' She shut the notebook.

'Why did Annie go round to see him this morning?' Macdonald asked. He'd been scribbling notes and frowning in concentration, Fleming was pleased to see – shaping up quite well, was DS Macdonald. She wasn't so sure about Wilson; he was sitting back in his chair, as if not having been involved at the start meant that this wasn't much to do with him.

'Carmichael hadn't turned up to read the lessons at church,' Kerr said, 'so the alarm bells rang. Oh, and she'd been taking church flowers to give to someone housebound – dropped them on the gravel, she said.'

'I was wondering about that!' Fleming exclaimed. 'Thought it might have been some sort of kinky tribute left by the killer. Good to have it cleared up. Thanks, Tansy. Any questions? Will? You've got a lot to catch up with.'

It was a pointed remark, but it didn't lodge in its target. Wilson shook his head. 'Nothing too complicated there. I reckon I'm up to speed.'

'If you're sure.' Fleming let a pause develop, then when he didn't speak nodded to Andy.

'There seem to be two opposite theories going the rounds – he was killed because he wouldn't sell the Craft Centre, or else he was killed because he would. I thought getting my aunt to explain the set-up there was a useful starting-point. Do you know the layout?'

'Looked in years ago, when it opened,' Fleming said. 'I'm not really in the market for the stuff they sell and I never have time for coffee.'

'Ellie Burnett seems to be the most favoured tenant. She's got a nice wee flat as well as the shop and the rumour is she doesn't pay much for it. The Colonel, my auntie says, has a soft spot for her.' He paused. 'Well, I've seen her singing down the pub, and you would, wouldn't you?

'Romy Kyle's been the one leading the opposition to selling. He did up the workshop for her, no expense spared, so she's a lot to lose – quite a temper too, by all accounts. Then there's Ossian Forbes-Graham – successful painter, has indulgent parents with an estate a few miles away. It's a second marriage; there's a stepsister who runs a riding school somewhere, but Ossian's the apple of their eye.

'Seemingly he's besotted about Ellie. Saw her performing

so took the unit when it came up for rent last year – there was a bookbinder before who moved out. The only other one is Alanna Paterson, who makes pottery, but she's not young and seemingly isn't too bothered about losing the shop. The other three are desperate it shouldn't be sold, for one reason and another.'

'And what about your auntie? She'll have a problem too, won't she?' It was the first question Will Wilson had asked. There was an edge to it, and Fleming looked at him sharply.

'Not really.' Macdonald's voice was determinedly level. 'She's sixty in a couple of months and she's giving up. Booked a world cruise already. And just to make sure, I checked where she was last night, and she and my uncle were on a theatre trip to Glasgow with the Rotary Club. Left at four, got back after midnight. All right?'

'Hey, hey!' Wilson said, putting his hands up. 'It was a reasonable question.'

'Sure it was,' Macdonald said. 'And you got a reasonable answer.'

Fleming looked from one to the other. She said nothing, at the top of her voice, and it was Wilson who began to shift in his seat first.

'Sorry. I was out of order.'

'Let's put that to one side – for the time being.' It wouldn't do him any harm to sweat. 'So, Andy – anything else?'

'She said that Romy was absolutely convinced that Carmichael would refuse to sell, but she wasn't so sure herself. There was a stack of money involved, and there was a lot of people leaning on him. Councillor Gloag, for one, who seems to have his fingers in the pie right up to the elbow.'

'Annie mentioned him too,' Kerr added. She had been, Fleming thought, uncharacteristically silent during the exchanges between Wilson and Macdonald. 'And I'm not sure she was totally convinced about him saying no either.'

'That's what my aunt said. Hated upsetting people. Liked a quiet life.'

'So to sum up: what emerges is two distinct camps, one of which has a motive if he'd decided to sell, and the other if he decided not to sell. Well, it leaves the field wide open, anyway.

'Does that cover it, then? There's door-to-door stuff going on, and I've asked for a printout of all the shotgun licence holders in the area. I'll be drawing up an action plan for the briefing tomorrow – eight-thirty sharp.'

Fleming looked after them thoughtfully as they went out. Why was it that, no sooner had one personnel problem resolved itself, another appeared?

Wilson and Macdonald had seemed to be on good enough terms, until Macdonald's promotion. Will had always been a bit of a golden boy, good-looking with his blond curly hair and ready smile, and a competent officer. Andy had fewer years of service, but Will had been slower to take his sergeant's exams – a home which had three kids under six wasn't the ideal place for studying – and he couldn't expect to achieve seniority without the necessary piece of paper.

Tansy and Tam had usually worked together, a good team which formed a solid heart to any enquiry. Now Tansy worked mainly with Will, she seemed to have changed, somehow – a bit more chip-on-the-shoulder, a bit less supportive. Or was Fleming only imagining that?

She had rather more pressing worries than Tansy's attitude problem or Will Wilson's nose being out of joint. Fleming looked hopelessly at the flashing light on her phone, the papers on her desk and, when she opened her email, the messages clicking up one after another. She'd be lucky to get home before midnight, at this rate.

* * *

Like a spider sitting watchfully in a corner of its web, waiting for an unsuspecting fly, Tam MacNee sat at one end of the bar counter in the Salutation. It was a less civilised pub than the Cutty Sark, with the sort of wooden floors that weren't a design statement and a thickened atmosphere from the fire that burned in a central grate open to the two long rooms on either side, but it was the nearest port of call for officers going off duty and desperate for a drink after a trying day.

There was no sign of any of them yet, though, and it was well past five o'clock. MacNee was on to his second pint, and his afternoon pass from Bunty would be running out soon. The pub was quiet anyway, and though the drinkers had been blethering on about the murder, no one had anything new to say and now the conversation was being recycled for the third time. MacNee looked at his watch again gloomily.

When the door swung open and PC Sandy Langlands appeared, MacNee brightened immediately. If he could have chosen someone for his purposes, it would have been Sandy: cheerful, open, trusting, like a Labrador puppy. He particularly liked the 'trusting' bit. It would never occur to Sandy that Tam MacNee should be denied information, just because he was away from his work for a wee while. And surely Big Marge couldn't yet have got round absolutely everyone with her directive?

'Sandy! Good to see you, man!' Tam greeted him, smiling broadly. 'What'll it be?'

The smile, the enthusiasm and the unaccustomed generosity all combined to alarm his victim. 'What are you after, Tam?' Sandy asked suspiciously.

It was sad to see such an innocent nature corrupted by cynicism. 'Just your company, that's all. Sit down and give us your craik.'

Gingerly, Langlands took a stool at the bar and accepted his offer.

'Pint of Special here, Donnie,' MacNee called to the barman. 'Now, what's been going on today? Bit of a shock, something like this within spitting distance of the station, eh?'

'Right enough. Not what you expect in a douce place like Kirkluce.' Langlands's pint arrived and he raised it. 'Cheers, Tam! I'm needing this – thirsty work, asking people questions.'

'Been out on the knocker, have you?' Tam could sympathise. 'Tough to go on looking interested when they've nothing to tell you.'

'At length,' Langlands said with feeling. 'I was working the houses opposite Fauldburn House and not one of them had actually seen anything, but they were all wanting to tell me why it had happened.'

This was a distinctly poor return on MacNee's investment. 'And what did they reckon the motive was?'

Langlands took a reflective pull at his pint. 'You could say there were three categories. One lot think it's because he was going to block the supermarket. There's the ones that think it was because he was going to sell to the supermarket, and then there's the idea that it's nothing to do with the supermarket, that it's a crazed gunman with no reason at all, and we're all going to die.'

MacNee raised his eyebrows. 'A lot of them think that?'

Langlands grinned. 'Only one, but she was noisy.'

'Anyone mentioning names?'

'Apart from sinister forces sent by the ALCO bosses, there's the nephew who'll clean up, Giles Farquharson, you know? He was mentioned once or twice by the first lot, and Councillor Gloag featured too. Then Romy Kyle from the Craft Centre – she's been shooting her mouth off about stopping it, apparently. Didn't give us anything to go on, though.'

'Mmm. Not much to show for an afternoon's work. Any of the other lads have better luck?'

Langlands shrugged. 'Haven't heard. I was first back, but no one I spoke to on the way round had come up with anything better.

'But listen, how are you doing yourself, Tam? You're looking fine. We could do with you back at work, I can tell you that, specially now.'

MacNee had a pleasurable minute or two slagging off Dr Rutherford, then, full of the injustices done to him, was just about to embark on a diatribe about the ridiculous position Big Marge had taken when he realised he would be giving himself away. He stopped just in time, and after that the conversation faltered. Langlands hadn't finished his drink, but it was getting late and it looked as if the orange had been squeezed dry.

MacNee drained his pint and stood up. 'I'll need to be getting back. Good to see you, Sandy. And watch out for that crazed gunman.'

'Aye, I'll do that,' Langlands promised. Then he added thoughtfully, 'Mind you, it was a funny thing about that dead sheep.'

Christina Munro had fallen asleep in her chair by the fire. When she woke with a start, it was nearly midnight.

So they likely weren't coming tonight. Sometimes there was a week or more between their visits. She got up painfully and hobbled to the door to let the dog out. It slipped past her like a shadow and disappeared in the darkness.

It was a fine, chilly night, with a hard silver moon, and in the blackness of the sky the stars were glittering pinpoints, so thick and so numerous they almost seemed to be bearing down on her. How could she, just one wee tiny speck of dust, matter in the grand scheme of the whole universe?

She shivered and whistled to the dog. It came bounding in and she shut the door and locked it, then slid across the four solid bolts she had recently and roughly installed. Before she switched off the lights and went to bed, she glanced to make sure that the reloaded shotgun was propped up on the wall beside the door.

6

Ossian Forbes-Graham surfaced dreamily, still not quite sure if he was awake or not. The sickly-sweet smell of last night's spliff hung in the air and pictures and shapes still drifted behind his closed eyelids.

His bedroom was a turret room on one corner of the red sandstone, Scottish baronial Ravenshill House. It was a Victorian monstrosity, too big to be comfortable and too small to be seriously grand, bought by his grandfather, a man with a small business and large aspirations. Ossian's father, having sold the business advantageously, now viewed it as ancestral property.

Ossian opened his eyes and the comforting dream-world slipped away to be replaced by the churning anxiety which was more and more often taking possession of him now. He sat bolt upright and pulled open the top drawer of the chest by his bed, knowing it was useless; he'd stocked up when he went to the pub the other night, but he'd smoked all he had.

His hands went to his mouth, first one, then the other, nibbling desperately at his nails, already bitten to the quick. He began tearing off the tiny, ragged ends of skin round about them, drawing blood. It took a considerable effort of will to stop himself and get out of bed.

He padded across the bare, whitewashed floor. The walls had the same soft, powdery finish, and they too were bare apart from an unframed mirror over the black cast-iron Victorian fireplace. The white furniture consisted of a bedside chest, a wooden chair, and the bed itself, made up with white bedlinen. The only colour came from a jumble of paints, brushes and used palettes in one corner, beside an easel on which was propped a blank canvas.

He went to stand in front of it, oppressed by its silent reproach. Once, he'd seen the whole room as a sort of composition to show up the explosion of colour he laid on his canvases. Now he felt blank himself, as if the colour had been leached out of him, as if he was white like his white room, his white canvas. Invisible, even.

Ellie. Ellie. Ellie. It was only when he was with Ellie that he felt alive. If he had Ellie, he knew he could paint again. But that she wouldn't let him touch her, wouldn't let him near her, even, left him an unpitied victim to his inner torment. She was an incubus, a vampire, sucking away his soul. Sometimes he hated her. Or loved her. One or the other. How did you tell which was which?

A jar on the floor by the easel held turpentine, stained muddy red from the steeping brushes used in the last painting Ossian had done, weeks ago now. In a sudden fit of rage he picked it up and hurled it against the fireplace. It shattered, and the pool of liquid spread across the hearth.

The noise seemed to bring him to his senses. Ossian shuddered, then shook his head as if to clear it. He dared not go on like this. If he did, the strings he used to make the Ossian puppet work would snap, and he would fall apart.

He stared at his reflection in the frameless mirror. He looked strange and wild, his dark hair disordered and his light blue eyes glittering. Deliberately, he slapped his face, once, twice on either side, so that red marks showed on his pale skin. He went to one of the turret windows and threw it open, taking deep gasps of the cool, early-morning air.

It was hardly light yet. No one would be about. An icy

shower and a long cold walk would shock him back to being normal. At least, as normal as he ever was now.

But first, he had to clear up the mess he had made. If his mother saw it she'd make him go and see the doctor.

'Dead sheep?' Fleming said blankly. 'What are you talking about, Sandy?'

There was a worried frown on PC Langlands's usually cheery countenance. 'I know it sounds a bit daft, boss. But I was talking to Tam MacNee down the pub last night and he said it was something I should tell you as soon as possible.'

Fleming had notes for what she had to say at the morning briefing lying on her desk; now, as she said, 'I see. Out with it, then, Sandy,' she was writing in block capitals across the top, 'Warning about Tam'.

'It probably never reached your desk, boss. It was last week – not quite sure which day, but it'll be logged.' He told her what had happened. 'Sergeant Bruce and me went out to it, and it looked like it'd been shot, all bloody.'

'Shot? Shot somewhere else, then dumped, or shot there in the yard?'

Langlands looked blank. 'Couldn't say, boss. Linda and me checked it out but no one knew anything about it.'

'What sort of wound – a shotgun wound?'

'I'd guess maybe a shotgun – it was in a real mess, anyway. But I don't know much about that kind of thing. Sorry – we maybe should have checked,' he said uncomfortably. 'But there's a Mrs Kyle has a shop there, she thought it was a threat because they were against the superstore. Didn't give us anything to go on, though.'

Fleming was scribbling notes. 'So what happened to the sheep, then?'

He had nothing to offer on that either. 'We just reported

it and they got it removed. There was a story in the local paper – you maybe saw it?'

Fleming shook her head. 'Life's too short to worry about what they think we've done wrong this week. Did the paper take a photo?'

Langlands shook his head. 'It had been taken away before they got there. Don't know what happened to it.'

It was frustrating, if understandable. 'Sent to the knacker's yard, most likely. Was there a lot of talk in the town?'

'A bit. But everyone just reckoned the neds had been at it again.'

'Mmm,' she said glumly. 'Who did you report to?'

'I spoke to DC Wilson, but he said there wasn't a lot to be done unless there was more to go on. There wasn't any brand to show where it came from.'

Fleming frowned, then sighed. 'Not much you could do on that basis, I suppose. OK, Sandy. Could you see that I get copies of the statements you and Linda took? Thanks.'

As he left, she was frowning and tapping her finger on a front tooth, an unconscious habit she had when concentrating. Could it be some form of intimidation, or was it just irrelevant, unpleasant vandalism? It wasn't unknown for animals to be attacked, though that tended to be with airguns, and from what Langlands had said about messiness, it sounded like a shotgun right enough.

Fleming glanced down at her desk, where she now had a printout of the list of licences. Bill's name was there, along with that of pretty much every farmer in the district, and when you added those who quite legitimately wanted them for what were termed 'rural pursuits', it ran to pages. Gun laws in Scotland had been tightened since the tragedy at the school in Dunblane, but even so you couldn't stop people shooting pheasants or rabbits or even clay-pigeons, come to that.

Will Wilson had been involved, so he might have some light to shed on it. She wanted to talk to him anyway; she'd seen what happened when antagonisms developed within the CID, and without being heavy-handed, she was keen to sort him out before things went too far. She picked up the phone.

While she waited for him to arrive, she prepared notes for the briefing. It was much too early yet to decide on a direction for the enquiry, but as a starting-point she recorded the names of people so far involved: the occupants of the Craft Centre units; the nephew who stood to inherit, since it would be foolish to overlook the straightforward motive in the maze of complications; Councillor Gloag, whose name had surfaced in several reports from the door-to-door enquiry teams. But in addition a good number of local people had strong views one way or the other, and there were a couple of other shops directly affected by the superstore proposals, now also on her crowded desk somewhere. She scrabbled papers aside, looking for them: it would be instructive to find out whether the owners it involved were for or against the development.

She found the plans and spread them out. There was a little fancy goods shop that would go, but it belonged to Senga Blair who must be at least sixty-five, with stock that reflected her age. A lavish offer from ALCO would probably be an answer to prayer as far as she was concerned.

The other shop affected was much bigger, with a sizeable yard at the back, owned by George MacLaren, the butcher. He was a major customer for Bill, and for the first time Fleming felt a chill of unease. By selling out, MacLaren would stand to gain a great deal of money, and she knew what happened to farms that lost their local outlets and had to sell to the supermarkets instead: they were beaten down on price until they were actually losing money on what they produced. They had some friends in the Borders who'd been forced to sell up because of this, and they were far from the only ones.

Bill, characteristically, hadn't so much as mentioned the threat, at least in her hearing. He'd often enough told her he'd a philosophical objection to worrying about things that might never happen, and she hadn't until now given the supermarket more than the most casual consideration.

Wilson's arrival brought an end to her troubled thoughts. He was looking a little awkward, which was all to the good after his behaviour yesterday, but she went straight to the question of the dead sheep.

He was annoyed not to have thought of it first. 'It happened last Monday. I should have picked up on that, boss. Sorry. I didn't make the connection.'

'There may not be one,' Fleming pointed out. 'It's interesting, though. Sandy Langlands gave me the bare facts, but perhaps you could talk to Linda Bruce? She might have noticed more about the nature of the wound, for instance—'

Wilson was shaking his head. 'I can tell you that right now. She didn't look. Felt a bit squeamish, I think.'

Disappointed, Fleming said acidly, 'Needs a spell on Traffic – that would sort her out. Anyway, keep that in mind when you're doing interviews today – put on a bit more pressure than Sandy and Linda did at the time, see if anyone can come up with anything to give us a lead.

'I'll give out details at the briefing, but I'll be wanting you, Andy and Tansy as a task force. I'm hoping Tam may be allowed back soon, but until then we'll be understrength and under pressure. It will mean working as a particularly close team.' She looked at him with a half-smile. 'OK?'

Wilson coloured. 'Yes, of course. Er – sorry about yesterday.'

'Is there a problem?'

'No, not really.' He sighed. 'Just – well, there's a few things not going well at the moment.'

'Anything you'd like to talk about?'

'Nothing right now. Got to work it out for myself, but thanks anyway.'

'Fine. But Will,' and there was just the slightest edge to her tone now, 'I'd like to think you'd bring it to me if you're in some difficulty before it affects the team.'

He promised, smiling, and left. He wasn't a bad lad, Fleming reflected, just perhaps having to come to terms with reality when a rather raffish charm wasn't enough.

The dead sheep, though. She went back to that. Except that it had happened last Monday, Wilson hadn't really had anything to add to what she knew already. She didn't know what to think, and was left wondering uncomfortably if Tam had seen something in it that she hadn't.

'Well?' Fiona Farquharson demanded from the table in the corner of the smart 'farmhouse' kitchen where she was finishing her breakfast coffee, as her husband came back into the room. 'What did he say?'

Giles was looking even worse than he usually did this morning. His heavy face had a greyish tinge beneath its tracery of broken veins, and the bags under his eyes were puffy and reddened. She'd had a disturbed night herself, not helped by him tossing and turning and switching on the light to see what time it was.

He'd wanted to go to work as usual this morning, but Fiona had insisted he stay to phone Uncle Andrew's lawyer. 'Anyway, you'll have to go along to the house. You ought to be there as next of kin, to keep an eye on what the police are doing.

'And don't say Murdoch won't like you taking the time off. You won't have to put up with his demands for much longer.'

Giles had been reluctant. 'People will think—' he began, but she hadn't let him finish.

'Don't be ridiculous, Giles. That's your problem, always trying to duck your responsibilities. You're going to have to make it clear from the very start that you're in charge, and that you're not going to pay attention to what people think. There's going to be opposition, and you'll have to be prepared for it. The sooner you get in touch with ALCO the better. You don't want them thinking there's a problem and deciding to go elsewhere.'

Eventually he had allowed himself to be driven to the phone. Now, as he came in, she saw the set of his shoulders with a twinge of alarm. Surely a man who had been told his long-awaited ship had come into harbour at last would look a little more cheerful?

'Well?' she said again.

Giles came over to the table and sat down heavily before he replied. 'He was non-committal. Said he'd be ready to give us the details of the will shortly.'

For just a moment, her confidence was shaken. Then she said scornfully, 'Lawyers! They're all the same. Won't have bothered to look for the deed box, and then he'll call us in and charge £100 for his time.'

'Probably.' It was all he said, but Fiona looked at him sharply.

'Giles, after all this, there isn't something else you're not telling me, is there?'

Her voice had risen. He said hastily, 'No, no, of course not. It's just that we shouldn't go counting our chickens. You can't be sure what's in a will until you see it.'

Reassured, she laughed. 'You're always such a pessimist, Giles! For heaven's sake, your mother told you years ago that you were Uncle Andrew's heir. And it's obvious – who else? Oh, I'm not saying there won't be legacies for people like Annie Brown and maybe even that sly little Ellie Burnett, but he would know what's appropriate. And with the money from ALCO we can afford to be generous.'

'I know, I know.'

He still looked gloomy, but that was just Giles. 'Right then,' she said briskly, getting up and stacking the dishes to clear the table. 'You get on over to Fauldburn now. And while you're there, you could take a look at the bedrooms. I haven't been upstairs for years and I can't remember if there's a dressing-room off Andrew's bedroom that could be converted into a bathroom for us.'

Johnny Black put a notice on the door of the motorcycle showroom which said unhelpfully, 'Back in ten minutes' without giving a time.

He hadn't had a phone call summoning him to Ellie's side. He hadn't altogether expected it, and he was prepared for that. He wasn't giving up.

He'd tried phoning her earlier, but she wasn't answering and there wasn't even an answerphone to talk to. Still, there was just a chance that despite everything, she might have opened up her shop this morning. If he could only find an opportunity to talk to her properly, he believed she'd come round – but how could you talk to a closed door?

At least he had Dylan on his side. Dylan could see the advantages for Ellie, and for himself too. She still thought of him as a child; he was a young man, and Johnny heartily endorsed his view that it was time his mother got a life. That was where Johnny came in, and if she couldn't see that yet – well, she was the woman he wanted and he'd just go steadily on until he had convinced her.

When he reached the Craft Centre, Ellie's shop was shut up and empty. He paused in front of it, considering his next move. After what Dylan had said last night, she was hardly likely to respond to a knock on the door of the flat, and the boy would be at school.

If Dylan hadn't locked it when he left, Johnny reckoned

he might risk going up and taking her by surprise, to get her to listen and allow herself to be calmed and reassured. Why not? What, at this stage, did he have to lose?

The door to the flat was painted white, with panes of clear glass in the upper half. Johnny peered through, but could see nothing beyond a cream-painted staircase. His hand was on the handle when an aggressive voice spoke behind him.

'You needn't try to get in. It's locked.'

Johnny spun round. Ossian Forbes-Graham, scowling, stood behind him like a dog guarding a bone which was out of its reach, determined to see to it that no rival would reach it either.

Johnny surveyed him. 'So you've tried it yourself, then?'

Thrown on the defensive, Ossian stammered, 'I – I knocked first. Then I thought perhaps she needed help—'

'From *you*?' The scorn in the word stung like a lash.

His face crimson, Ossian cried, 'Yes, from me! I understand her. We're both artists. What would she have in common with a grease monkey?'

'You wouldn't begin to know.' Johnny was angry now too. 'Go back and play with your paintbox. Women prefer men to children, hadn't you noticed?'

Breathing fast, Ossian took an ineffectual swing at him. Johnny parried it without difficulty, catching his arm and twisting it up behind his back. 'Stupid little sod,' he snarled.

'That's enough! Break it up!'

A man had just sauntered into the courtyard, a man wearing jeans and a black leather jacket. He was smaller than either of them, thin and wiry, but there was something about him that made Johnny feel it wiser to loose his hold. Forbes-Graham sprang away from him, rubbing his arm and still glaring.

'Who the hell do you think you are?' Johnny demanded.

The man had his hands in the pockets of his jeans, meeting Johnny's belligerence with a cold stare. 'MacNee.'

Suddenly, Johnny recognised him. 'I saw you in the pub on Saturday night. And you were in the shop, looking at the Harley. You're a copper, aren't you?'

'If you're a policeman,' Ossian interrupted, 'I want him charged with assault. You saw what he was doing.'

MacNee gave him a sardonic look. 'It's the polis decides who's charged, laddie, and anyway I'm off duty. What's it all about?'

Like the schoolboy he wasn't far from being, Ossian looked down and muttered, 'Nothing.'

Johnny said smoothly, 'A misunderstanding. We were both concerned about Ellie Burnett. She's not answering the phone or the door and she's been very upset about Colonel Carmichael's death. Maybe you could gain entry, see she's all right—'

'And maybe I couldn't. Like I said, I'm off duty, and maybe the lady's not wanting to be squabbled over by the two of you. I'd advise you both to leave her alone before she makes a complaint about harassment – and I can promise you that would be taken a lot more seriously.'

For just a moment the two men held their ground, then, shrugging, Johnny left. Ossian, after lingering for a moment to emphasise his rival's retreat from the field of battle, went back to his studio, to watch from the window for any sign of Ellie appearing.

MacNee continued with his interrupted programme. He'd timed this visit carefully. The officers on the case, he reckoned, would be tied up in a briefing at the moment, which gave him a window of opportunity of rather less than an hour. He wasn't going to go knocking on doors and waving the warrant card he wasn't, at the moment, entitled to use. That would be asking for a further suspension and he wasn't daft. But there was nothing that said you couldn't walk into a public place, like a shop, for instance, and have a wee chat with the owner.

A delicious smell was wafting from the coffee shop, and MacNee could see someone at the back putting a tray in an oven. But it wasn't open yet, and there was a light on in the shop next door, which had a window display of rather solid brown and cream pottery, as well as in the silversmith's opposite, where a display of silver gleamed under blue-white spotlights.

The pottery shop was nearer. As MacNee opened the door, a bell jangled and the woman reading a newspaper which was lying on the counter looked up. It was hard to say what age she was, though she was certainly well over fifty; she had shaggy grey hair cut in a heavy fringe, thick, gold-rimmed spectacles and a lumpish figure. There was no sign that she had been working that morning, but the beige jacket she was wearing over a rust-brown dress of indeterminate shape was daubed with smears of clay.

'Morning!' she greeted him. 'You're an early bird!'

'Oh, I'm the wee boy for getting the worms.' MacNee winked at her, then glanced around the shop. 'Some nice stuff you've got here,' he said insincerely, pointing to an earth-coloured bowl. She smiled complacently.

The paper she was reading was folded to an inner page, to a short item headed, 'Man found shot'. He jerked his thumb towards it. 'Nasty business, that.'

The woman shuddered. 'Can't bear to think about it. Poor man.'

'Was he someone you knew?'

'Och yes! I kent him fine – he was in and out of here all the time, him being the landlord. Always took an interest, and one of my best customers too. He'd a coffee set of mine and seemingly they'd an awful lot of breakages. He was for ever replacing them.'

The mugs she indicated didn't look to MacNee the sort of thing you'd expect to find gracing the drawing-room coffee table in a house like Fauldburn. Was there a stash of clumsy mugs in a cellar somewhere, a testament to the Colonel's acts of patronage?

'Sounds as if you liked him, then?'

'Everyone liked the Colonel. It's an awful shame.'

'Someone didn't,' MacNee pointed out.

'I suppose so.' Then she stopped, her round blue eyes, magnified by her glasses, wide with suspicion. 'Here, you're not one of thae reporters, are you? I'm not wanting to be all over the front page.'

'No, no,' MacNee soothed her. 'I'm a policeman – Tam MacNee. I'm off work at the moment, but I've an awful curious nature. Can't help being interested, but it's all unofficial. You can say what you like, and it'll not go any further.'

She smiled, reassured. 'Nice to meet you, Tam. Alanna – Alanna Paterson. Well, don't say I said this because Romy would go daft, but he should just have agreed to sell up and none of this would have happened.'

'And you'd have been jake with that? You've a nice wee set-up here.'

Alanna glanced round at the potter's wheel, the airing shelves with drying pots, and the kiln which, to MacNee's admittedly inexperienced eyes, looked state-of-the-art, then said, a little uncomfortably, 'Oh, it was nothing but the best for the Colonel. But I'm not getting any younger and I'm needing to think about the future. ALCO was ready to be very generous with compensation, but of course Romy wouldn't hear of it. I'm not sure about Ellie – keeps her cards very close to her chest, does our Ellie, but if you ask me the Colonel wouldn't sell if she didn't want him to.'

MacNee cocked an eyebrow. 'Close, were they?'

'Oh, I wouldn't like to go spreading gossip,' Alanna said

hastily. 'It was just that he seemed to dote on her. She has quite a way with her, has Ellie.'

Sensing a certain dryness in her tone, MacNee curbed his enthusiasm as he agreed. 'So do you reckon he was definitely going to refuse to sell?'

'That's what I thought,' she said, then stopped. 'There'd be a few people wouldn't take it lying down if he'd changed his mind,' she said slowly.

'Like—?' MacNee prompted, but that was a step too far.

She backtracked. 'Och, I'm sure he didn't. He wasn't one to go telling lies and he'd said to us not to worry, we'd be staying on.'

'So there'd be others keen to see the back of him, then.'

'Oh, plenty of them!' She was much more prepared to be frank about this. 'That Gloag, for a start – we all know he's taking backhanders to get it through planning. And I never had much time for the Colonel's nephew and that stuck-up wife of his. We'll know the difference with Giles Farquharson as the landlord, I can tell you that. Even if the Centre's still going, none of us'll be here, with what he'll put the rents up to.'

'Where does he live?' MacNee asked innocently.

'He's land agent for Ossian Forbes-Graham's father, up at the back there, about five miles away, between New Luce and Carsriggan. They've a wee estate at Ravenshill, and they do motocross and shooting and stuff that he manages for them. But it's just one of the lodges they live in, and that doesn't suit Lady Muck. They were desperate for the Colonel to sell so when he died they'd come into the big house and all that money too.'

That suggested a very satisfactory new angle. MacNee changed the subject. 'I heard you'd problems with a dead sheep a wee while ago?'

The round eyes widened and she put her hand to her chest,

as if the very thought gave her palpitations. 'Gave me nightmares, I'll tell you that! It's not nice, is it – poor beast, all bloody, just lying there,' she gestured. 'Well, you know how it is with sheep – I've been out walking on the hills and seen one lying dead sometimes, and I thought at first it had just daundered in and died, or been hit by a car, maybe, but when I looked – well, I about had a heart attack!'

'Do you think it had been shot on the spot?'

She shook her head. 'No, no. Ellie was in all evening and she said she never heard a thing. It must have been shot somewhere else and dumped here. Romy said it was ALCO trying to scare us off, but . . .' She hesitated. 'I'm not sure. It was just kind of – weird. What my grandson would call random.'

Then another thought struck her. 'Here – you don't think maybe whoever did it went on and killed the Colonel? They'd have to be mad, going round shooting like that—'

'No, no,' MacNee said hastily. If Marjory heard he'd started a rumour that there was a crazy loose with a shotgun, he'd find himself back in uniform when he returned to work. 'More likely just some kid mucking about and dumping it so the farmer wouldn't find out.'

'I'd like to think that, right enough,' she said dubiously.

Out of the corner of his eye, MacNee caught movement – two people entering the courtyard. Tansy Kerr – with a smart new hairdo – and Will Wilson. Damn. Big Marge must have kept the briefing short. Luckily, they were heading for Ossian Forbes-Graham's studio on the other side.

'I'll need to be going,' he said.

'Oh – you won't say what I told you, now, will you?'

He grinned. 'If you won't tell them –' he jerked his head – 'I was here.'

'That's a promise.'

He slipped quietly out of the shop and, walking close to

the wall, left the courtyard, congratulating himself that he hadn't been spotted.

'What's MacNee up to?' Will Wilson said to Tansy Kerr as he opened the door of Ossian Forbes-Graham's studio.

'Don't ask,' Kerr said darkly. 'There are some things it's better not to know.'

7

Annie Brown sat in what she had always thought of as 'her' kitchen in Fauldburn House. It looked a bit old-fashioned to her way of thinking, with a china sink and a dresser and chests of drawers and tables instead of the proper fitments, like she had in her own semi. Where the old range would have been there was a great big dark blue Aga; the tiles round about it were bonny enough, with wee blue ships and windmills on them, but it was a shame they were a bit old-looking. From Holland, Mrs Carmichael said they were, but she'd have been better with new ones that were easy to keep clean. Still, it was comfortable to work in and a nice sunny room too, with big windows looking out to the garden.

But it didn't feel like Annie's kitchen now. The police were wandering in and out, opening drawers as if they owned the place. She hadn't been happy, the way they were going through the Colonel's stuff, not just his papers but personal things too, and his clothes, even his underwear. Not that there was anything to be ashamed of; the Colonel was most particular and Annie looked after his laundry herself. They'd find no greying whites here!

It didn't seem right, though. They'd fetched her to let them into the house, then suggested she went home again, but she wasn't having that. Leave them with the run of the place, not knowing what sort of mess they'd make – or what might mysteriously disappear? You couldn't trust anyone these days.

She'd suggested contacting Mr Giles for permission – she

knew her place, and knew too what Mrs Giles would say if she overstepped the mark. But they'd waved a piece of paper at her and said it was the law, and she couldn't argue with that.

Anyway, she'd no time for the Farquharsons. Once this was over she'd put in her notice. She'd have no problem getting another job; there were plenty folk had tried to get her away from Fauldburn before now, but she'd never have left the Colonel. After Mrs Carmichael became really disabled, they'd got very close.

He'd never said a word out of turn about his wife, and neither had she, but Mrs Carmichael hadn't been what you could call easy-going – and right enough the poor soul had a lot of pain. But there were two kinds of invalid, the kind that wanted to make the best of it and be as little trouble as possible, and the other kind. Mrs Carmichael was the other kind. No one but Annie knew what the Colonel had had to put up with, or how he'd always managed somehow to be kind and cheerful. There didn't seem to be gentlemen like that around nowadays.

Tears welled up and Annie left the kitchen, heading for the garden door. If she was going to cry, she didn't want to do it in front of the fat policeman who was rummaging in one of her kitchen drawers and looking at her with open curiosity.

It was peaceful out here at least. The Colonel had loved his garden and there was always something in bloom. She walked slowly up the steps to the rose garden, dabbing at her eyes with a hankie, and sat down on the low wall surrounding it. She'd often seen him there of late, taking a breather from gardening in his old tweeds, enjoying the perfume of his late roses.

There was a real hint of autumn in the air today. Some yellow leaves had drifted down into the flower beds and there were a good few swallows gathering on the telephone wire. They'd be going soon.

Annie let herself have a little cry. There had been a lot of little cries since yesterday, partly for the Colonel and partly for the passing of the years which, she realised looking back, had been happy ones. How did you never notice you were happy until afterwards, when it was too late? And this wasn't only going to mean change for her. Now the Colonel was dead, Mr Giles would be all ready to sign on the dotted line with ALCO and that would be the end of it.

Absorbed in her unhappy thoughts, she didn't hear the young man approaching, and it was only when he cleared his throat that she looked round. He wasn't in uniform but he was obviously a policeman.

Her eyes were blurred and she scrubbed at them with her hankie. 'Sorry.'

'Not at all,' he said. 'This must be very hard for you.' He held out a card in a plastic wallet. 'DS Macdonald.'

That must mean he was a detective. He was quite tall, solidly built, with dark hair cut so close to his head that it looked like fuzzy felt. Annie liked the look of him; he'd nice brown eyes and quite a thoughtful expression.

She blew her nose hard and put her hankie away. 'What are you wanting? If you're needing tea, there's plenty stuff in the kitchen. I could make some for you—' She stood up.

He smiled. 'That's a good offer – I'll maybe take you up on it later. But that wasn't what I wanted to ask you.' She saw now that he had a couple of photographs, which he held out to her. 'Do you recognise these? We found them in a drawer beside Colonel Carmichael's bed.'

Annie took them. They were of different sizes: one was in a large folder with the name of a photographer in London on the outside, but the other was a black-and-white snapshot, yellowed with age and slightly curled at the edges.

She looked at that one first, holding it flat between her thumbs. It had been taken in foreign parts, clearly, since there was what looked like a big rubber plant growing in the background and a shrub with foreign-looking flowers behind where the woman was standing.

The woman was foreign too. Coloured, Annie thought carefully. That was what you were meant to say instead of black – or was it the other way round? It was hard to keep track, if you wanted to do the right thing. Anyway, the woman wasn't black. This one was more light brown. It wasn't a good photo but she was young and small and sweet-faced, as far as Annie could tell, and she was wearing a long straight skirt with a sort of draped blouse on top – silk, Annie thought, peering closer.

DS Macdonald was waiting patiently. She shook her head. 'I don't know who that would be. I never saw it before.'

'Not even in the drawer?'

'I only looked after the Colonel's washing. I'd never go looking among his personal things.'

There was a reproach in her voice and Macdonald said hastily, 'No, no, of course not. What about the other one?'

She opened the folder. This one was quite different. It was a studio portrait and the man had been professionally posed, smiling confidently at the camera. He was wearing what she could see was an expensive suit, with a tie in discreet colours. He had smooth, coffee-coloured skin and deep brown eyes with just a slight tilt to them and thick, glossy dark hair, well shaped. Annie reckoned he was in his early twenties. She reckoned, too, from the set of his jaw, that this could be a very determined young man, despite the smile.

'Any idea?' Macdonald asked hopefully.

She shook her head. 'Well, I know the Colonel was out abroad when he was in the army. Maybe they're friends of his. But that's all I can think of. I'm sorry.' She was sorry, too. He seemed a nice laddie and she hated to disappoint him.

He took the pictures back. 'Never mind, it's probably not important. Now, if you really meant it about the tea . . .'

'I have the CC with me, Marjory. He wants you to brief him directly on Colonel Carmichael's murder. Perhaps you can join us now?'

Recognising an order, DI Fleming said, 'I'll be right up, Donald.'

Setting down the phone, she opened the drawer where she kept a mirror, a comb and lipstick. Being summoned to the Chief Constable's presence was never a comfortable experience. Not that Menzies was a difficult boss – in fact, swapping notes with officers in other forces often made her realise she had reason to be thankful.

He had an office here in the Kirkluce HQ but he was away so much on administrative and even political business that his visits to it were irregular and usually fleeting. Superintendent Donald Bailey reported to him; Menzies had always seemed content to leave the job on the ground to the people doing it, and so far at least the Galloway force had been spared the micromanagement from on high which so often meant trying to reconcile two entirely opposite courses of action.

It made Fleming uneasy that Menzies seemed to be interesting himself so directly in the present case, but of course Carmichael was a figure in the community and Menzies had probably known him socially. It would add to the pressure on her, especially when she had as yet so little to go on. Normally your starting-point would be the deceased's personal circle, then the professional one. But Carmichael's power to determine the future for Kirkluce, and the fortune of a vast number of interested parties, changed the dynamic – though, of course, you couldn't ignore the personal dimension either.

Superintendent Bailey, always punctiliously polite, got to his feet as she came into the room, and after a momentary hesitation, the Chief Constable did the same. Fleming had to suppress a smile: well trained in gender politics, she could read his mind. Political correctness decreed that treating a female officer in any way differently from a male one was an Issue. Since neither Menzies nor Bailey would have stood up for a man . . .

She smiled, said thank you and sat down. The two men did likewise, Menzies with a definite air of relief.

Bailey had ceded his desk to his superior and moved a chair to sit at his side. 'Colonel Carmichael's death – the CC is anxious to know the details, Marjory.'

'Of course, sir.'

Menzies was a tall, distinguished-looking man with iron-grey hair; he was, she happened to know, forty-eight. Bailey always looked smart and professional, but beside his immaculate chief wearing a uniform that was clearly tailor-made, he looked almost scruffy.

'The Colonel is a great loss to the community,' Menzies was saying. 'He gave sterling service as a Justice, and – in confidence, of course – he was being considered for the next Lord Lieutenant. And always a great supporter of the police force.

'I have to confess to a personal interest too. His wife was my wife's cousin and she has been much distressed by this, as indeed have I.'

'I'm sorry, sir. Perhaps it would be best if I simply outlined the situation as we know it at present? And of course I can arrange to copy reports to you.'

'Good.' He sat back in his chair, his grey eyes fixed on her face. 'Carry on, then.'

Fleming ran through the sequence of events, and went on to outline the plan of action: questioning interested parties, reviewing CCTV footage, fingertip search on site, and the usual legwork. Then, after a moment's hesitation, she mentioned the dead sheep.

The two men had listened in silence. Now they both spoke at once.

'Is this relevant, Marjory?' Bailey asked sternly.

'Same kind of gun used?' That was Menzies.

Fleming would have preferred to be answering the superintendent's question, but she knew which took precedence. 'It seems possible, from the sound of it, though we can't definitely state that it was shot, unfortunately. We'd had no report of a missing animal, it had no identifying brand, there was nothing from witnesses—'

'Yes, yes, inspector,' Menzies said irritably, 'but surely we found out what caused the injury?'

Fleming swallowed. 'It wasn't thought to be worth initiating further action at the time. With the budget constraints, ordering ballistic tests seemed excessive, for a sheep no one had claimed.'

That was inspired, if untrue. It hadn't crossed anyone's mind that anything was called for, beyond disposing of the carcass and calming the natives, but it was the sort of language her bosses understood.

'I can see that,' Menzies conceded. 'And no evidence as to the nature of the wound?'

'It was very messy, according to the constable who saw it, but I'm afraid that's all I can tell you.'

'Pity. Could have been useful.'

But it was Bailey who seemed more alive to the implications. 'Surely we can just take this as yet another example of the sort of mindless brutality which is so sadly prevalent nowadays? Otherwise, what we're suggesting is someone taking shots at random – a sniper, in fact, with escalating ambitions.'

Menzies recoiled. 'Oh, surely not! If there is a connection, perhaps a practice shot to . . .' He didn't finish his sentence.

Fleming's face had shown no emotion, but her stomach lurched at the very thought. She said hastily, 'I think we should remember that there were perfectly logical reasons for killing Colonel Carmichael. And after all, there's a sporadic problem with that type of vandalism.'

She got heartfelt support for that and she went on, 'I haven't as yet had the ballistics report, of course, but I'm not sure how much help it will be. It's not as if it was a rifle making distinctive grooves on a bullet, so it's likely the best they can do is identify the gauge and so on. But for a start, I've ordered checks on all the firearms registered in the area. There haven't been any reports of stolen guns, but it would be as well to check that none of them are missing.'

Menzies nodded agreement. 'Right, right. But that's quite a tall order. What about manpower?'

'We'll be at full stretch. I'd like more, of course, but just at the moment we can work on overtime without importing officers. Save that for later, if we need it.'

'I'll be happy to authorise any support you might need.' Menzies glanced at Bailey. 'Anything else? No? That's about it, then. Thank you, Marjory.'

'Sir.' She was on her way to the door when he added, 'By the way, how's MacNee? Back at work, is he?'

'Not yet, I'm afraid. He's fretting at the bit, but the doctor seems very cautious.'

'Wise, I'm sure. But you'll miss him, with a case like this on your hands.'

'Oh yes,' Fleming said hollowly. 'I miss him.'

* * *

'What sort of party would you be thinking of bringing?' the bored young man, who had introduced himself as Danny Simpson, asked him.

Three? Twenty? MacNee hadn't a clue what was normal. Clay-pigeon-shooting, for some reason, hadn't been on the curriculum at his inner-city Glasgow comp. Six seemed plausible.

'Six,' he said, and was relieved to see the man nod.

They were standing in an old stone building, once a barn and now set up as an office. As the talk ranged over traps, skeets, stands, dropping ducks and bolting rabbits, MacNee's eyes began to glaze over. He'd had this clever plan for getting access to Giles Farquharson, only to be told by Simpson that he hadn't turned up today; his uncle was that guy who'd got himself shot.

'What about guns?' MacNee asked. 'Would we have to bring our own?'

'We can provide guns. Cost you, though.'

'Right. I'm not a shooting man myself – can I have a look at what I'd be using?'

'No problem. We'd have to give you tuition, of course – health and safety and all that.' Simpson took a bunch of keys out of a drawer in the counter, then led the way to a door at the opposite end of the room, a stout door, MacNee noted with a professional eye, with a security keypad on the wall beside it. MacNee watched him tap in the code, able to see clearly what the numbers were. He'd have liked to know how often it was changed, but he didn't want the man to go thinking he was there to case the joint.

The door opened on to a windowless store, with three steel gun-lockers on one wall. 'Looks as if you've quite an armoury here,' MacNee remarked.

'Any time you want to start the revolution, this is where to come.' Simpson unlocked one cupboard and took out an over-and-under Remington 12-bore.

MacNee admired it, put it awkwardly to his shoulder and saw his companion smile. 'You'll need a bit of tuition before we let you loose with that, mate!'

He lowered it again, saying meekly, 'Certainly will,' just as if he hadn't done basic firearms training. 'Looks a nice piece of equipment, that.'

Simpson took the gun from MacNee, put it back in the cupboard and locked it again. 'We get a lot of corporate business and people expect decent stock.'

They went back to the reception area, MacNee now satisfied that while they had good security, they had a casual attitude to codes and keys. With his mission accomplished, the sooner he stopped wasting his time here the better. He cut across the sales pitch that was still going on. 'So how much? That's what I need to know, to tell my pals.'

When the price was disclosed, MacNee sucked his teeth in horror. 'Oh, I doubt they'd never go for anything like that! I think I'm just wasting your time, laddie.'

'That's all right.' The brief animation the young man had shown while demonstrating the gun was once more replaced by a bored expression and his tone indicated that this only confirmed his already jaundiced view of life.

Ossian Forbes-Graham didn't seem to know where he'd been at what time on Saturday night. 'Around,' he said vaguely. 'I don't wear a watch.'

His studio here, too, had been painted white, though the floor was natural wood. There was a comfortable-looking white leather chair near the window, but apart from that all it contained was painting equipment and half-a-dozen abstract canvases on the walls. Two were huge, taking up most of the space on the back wall, and there were four of varying sizes and shapes on the others.

Not exactly a commercial concern, Tansy Kerr thought,

looking round. She quite liked the artworks, in fact, though she wasn't entirely sure why. They didn't look like anything in particular, just great sweeps of paint, mostly in reds and oranges, but you could somehow feel a sort of energy coming off them. She couldn't see any sign of work in progress.

The artist himself was definitely flaky, but quite fit in a manic sort of way, with those very striking blue eyes.

Wilson was prodding him. 'Do you have definite opening hours?'

Ossian looked at him pityingly. 'You really don't understand art, do you? You stop when you've finished something, not because of what it says on some clock.'

'Working on something at the moment?' Wilson's tone was casual, but there was nothing casual about the question.

He succeeded in his objective. Ossian had the sort of clear, pale skin which colours easily and Kerr saw a red flush rise as he said defensively, 'Not – not at the moment.'

'What on earth do you do all day, then?' She hadn't entirely meant to ask that question; it had just popped out, and she was unprepared for his response.

He put his hands to his face and groaned. His nails, she noticed, were ragged and bitten. 'I think. I think, all the time. I do nothing *but* think.' He looked up and glared at her. 'Do you ever think? Really think?'

Taken aback, she didn't know what to say. Wilson stepped in. 'We think all the time too, sir. And what we're thinking at the moment is that it would be a great help to us if you could manage to focus on the events of Saturday night when, you may recall, a man was brutally murdered.'

Ossian looked positively shocked, as if such a confrontational approach was new to him.

'For a start,' Wilson went on, 'had the other shops closed before you left?'

'Ellie's had.' The response was immediate. 'Once she'd gone, there wasn't any point in staying.'

Wilson and Kerr exchanged glances. 'Why not?' Kerr said more gently.

'Because—' Ossian stopped. He had been standing in an almost hunched position; now he stood up straight, almost as if he were pulling himself up on a string. When he spoke again he sounded, if not quite normal, certainly a lot less weird.

'You could say I see Ellie as my muse, if you like. I've been struggling with my painting and I look to her for inspiration. And if she's not there—'

Kerr looked across to Ellie Burnett's shop, directly opposite. 'You mean, you just sit here all day watching her?' She wasn't exactly into artistic muses but she knew all about stalking.

He looked away. 'Sort of.'

'And is she quite happy with this?' Wilson's voice had an edge to it.

'She's my friend! She understands – she's an artist too.'

'Hmm. We'll leave that – for the moment. So, after Ellie went home, you shut up shop?'

'She didn't go to the flat. She left the Centre.' He seemed to be remembering now. 'But by the time I left and went out into the street I couldn't see her.'

'And then?' Wilson had taken over the questioning.

'I walked, I expect, hoping I'd bump into her. Then I went to the meeting. I knew she'd be there, and singing in the pub afterwards.'

'Where did you walk?'

Ossian was impatient. 'How would I know? I just – walked, probably. As you do.'

'You didn't go home to—' Wilson glanced down at his notebook. 'Ravenshill?'

'*I don't know*. I told you. Ask my mother if it's so important. She'll probably remember.'

Wilson made a note of that. 'And you don't know what time Ellie closed her shop?'

'I told you, no.'

'Or where she went when she left?'

'*No!*' Then he hesitated. 'I wondered if she'd gone to see Black.' He spat out the name.

'Is that Black who works in the motorbike shop in the High Street?'

'Yes.' Ossian's eyes narrowed. 'If you ask me, he's got some sort of hold over her.'

Again, Kerr caught Wilson's eye. 'A hold? Really? What sort of hold would that be?'

'He must have! Why else would she so much as want to talk to someone like him?' His voice had started to get wilder again. 'He's a – a nothing, just a mechanic, poor white trash! Ellie's an artist. She couldn't want to have anything to do with him, she couldn't!'

'Phew!' Wilson said as they left. 'Lucky to get out of there before he started foaming at the mouth and biting people.'

'Spoiled,' Kerr said tersely. 'And a raving snob. People like that bring me out in a rash. We'd better go and see Ellie. See if he scares her as much as he'd scare me, if I was in her shoes.'

They set off across the square. Ellie's shop was obviously shut, but they knocked on the door leading to the flat above. There was no answer.

They tried again, and Wilson called out, 'Ms Burnett! It's the police. Could we have a word?'

There was still no response. 'Maybe she's out,' he suggested.

'Maybe she's just not answering, but we can hardly knock the door down, can we? Someone can try again later.' Kerr rubbed the back of her neck. 'Anyway, don't let's stand here any longer. Forbes-Graham's eyes are boring a hole in my back.'

'There's still the potter and the silversmith to see, not to mention Andy's auntie. Let's do the others first and go there at coffee time. I can smell baking.'

Still thinking about the photographs, DS Andy Macdonald walked back down the drive of Fauldburn House. He couldn't help wondering who the sharp-looking guy in the photo was, but that might be a mystery that would remain unsolved.

They hadn't found anything else of interest in the house so far. The Colonel's life seemed to be just as you would expect it to be, though they'd need to speak to the accountant and the lawyer later, just to check the details.

Giles Farquharson had turned up as Macdonald was tucking into some of Annie's oatie biscuits. He'd felt that having a mouthful of buttery crumbs put him at something of a disadvantage, but Farquharson seemed to be in such a state of nervous tension that he didn't even notice. Macdonald had scheduled an interview with the Farquharsons for the afternoon, and Giles, twitching visibly, agreed that he and his wife would be there.

He didn't seem to know why he'd come, asking vaguely if everything was all right, a question which in the circumstances was a little hard to answer. When shown the photographs he'd glanced at them, then said blankly that he'd no idea except that his aunt and uncle might have had some foreign friends. He bumbled round for a bit before muttering something about his wife and a bathroom and heading upstairs, leaving Annie rolling her eyes in a pantomime of disapproval. He had left, still looking awkward, shortly afterwards.

Macdonald's next assignment was an interview with Norman Gloag. He'd been told, when he made the appointment, that Councillor Gloag was a very busy man but naturally his civic duty would take precedence over other demands on his time. Macdonald had struggled to sound appropriately grateful, instead of saying that too damn right it would.

He had arranged for the most recent addition to Kirkluce CID to join him, DC Ewan Campbell, a quiet, red-headed lad from Oban. Despite his ancestral hostility to any member of Clan Campbell, Macdonald had to admit his new colleague was shaping up all right though he wasn't talkative – which was an understatement on a par with describing the Great Wall of China as a drystone dyke.

When he arrived, Campbell was waiting on the pavement outside the Gloag residence. The house was in a small development of luxury villas, with price tags which had caused headshaking and a prediction that they'd stand empty long enough, but not one house was still unsold and judging by the cars parked outside – second cars mostly, at that – their purchase hadn't exactly cleaned anyone out.

Campbell greeted him with his usual silent nod and Macdonald rang the bell. It had a Westminster chime, which stopped disappointingly short of striking the hour.

A woman, middle-aged and discontented-looking, wearing tracksuit bottoms and an orange V-neck T-shirt, answered it. 'He's got someone with him. But I'm to tell you to come in anyway.'

She led them across the hall to a door at the back, opened it without knocking and stood aside to let them enter unannounced before shutting it behind them with a definite slam.

There was a desk in one corner of the room, but there were two men sitting in chairs around a coffee table in front of a living-gas fire. Macdonald recognised Councillor Gloag, who had made it his business to be recognisable to anyone in his local constituency. The other he didn't know, a stocky man wearing a green tweed suit, with grey hair and what Macdonald had heard described as an expensive complexion. They were drinking coffee, though the proximity of a bottle of whisky suggested that more had been added to it than the traditional milk and sugar.

The two officers displayed their warrant cards and introduced themselves. Gloag made no move to get up, merely waving them towards two vacant seats.

'I'm Norman Gloag, as I'm sure you know,' he said. 'This is my friend Mr Vernor-Miles. He's just called in to discuss this most distressing event. I trust you are proceeding towards a speedy resolution? It would be most unfortunate, most, if uncertainty prevailed for any length of time.'

Macdonald could feel his hackles rising, but said only, 'We are doing all we can to avoid that, sir. Now, perhaps—'

Wilfrid Vernor-Miles leaned forward. 'I hope your superiors understand the urgency of this.' He had a smooth, plummy, upper-class voice. A surprising chum for Gloag, Macdonald thought, as he went on, 'ALCO is, it goes without saying, extremely keen to establish a business here, *extremely* keen. And Kirkluce, of course, will benefit hugely from increased amenity and trade.'

That wasn't what Macdonald's auntie thought, which wasn't to say the man was necessarily wrong. 'But—?' he prompted.

Vernor-Miles jabbed his finger in Macdonald's direction. 'But! Exactly!' he cried. 'If this should become a long-drawn-out scandal, which in some way reflected badly on the company, I would certainly think that the fear of adverse publicity would lead the board to reconsider.'

It was clear that this had not formed part of his discussion with Gloag. The other man looked at him, aghast. 'I'd no idea that was a possibility! Surely they couldn't – not after all that's been done, Wilf—'

'I'm very much afraid they might,' Vernor-Miles said gravely. 'I have influence, of course, and I shall use it in Kirkluce's interest, but clearly I can't speak for the others.'

Macdonald stepped in. 'Perhaps you could explain your position, Mr Vernor-Miles?'

'Of course. I'm a non-executive director for ALCO. I have a background in business but now my work is mainly consultancy. I have an estate in the area, over towards Kirkcowan, and it was I who suggested Kirkluce, with its central position on the main Dumfries–Stranraer road, as an ideal site for our next superstore. And naturally, my first step was to sound out Norman here, who has his finger on the pulse.'

He smiled at Gloag as he paid him the compliment, but the man was clearly too upset at what had just emerged to acknowledge it.

'It is a wonderful opportunity for Kirkluce, and one which we simply cannot afford to lose. Wilf—'

'Interesting as this conversation is,' Macdonald cut in, 'you will understand that we are under considerable time pressure and I am here to get the answers to some routine questions.'

'Of course, of course. I do apologise,' Vernor-Miles said urbanely.

Gloag snapped, 'Get on with it then!'

Macdonald saw that Campbell had quietly produced his notebook. He never missed a trick – maybe it would be better if the rest of them said less and listened more. It might make interviews a bit tricky, though, with your suspect having to guess what you were thinking.

He went on, 'You first, Mr Vernor-Miles, and then perhaps you could leave us to talk to Councillor Gloag. I'm sure you will have other calls on your time.'

'Indeed. How can I help you?'

'First of all, have you any information that might be useful to us concerning the murder of Colonel Carmichael?'

'I'm afraid not. If I had, you can be sure I would have contacted you immediately.' Vernor-Miles's expression was suitably grave.

'What were your movements on Saturday afternoon and evening?'

'Ah, that's very straightforward. ALCO was sending down one of their PR johnnies from London – excellent fellow – to address the public meeting. I had occasion to stay in Glasgow the night before so I offered to pick him up from the airport and drive him down here. I did that, then took him home to have a quick shower and change before the meeting, which I attended. Afterwards, I gave him and Norman dinner at the hotel where he was staying. Then drove home.'

'Thank you, sir. That's very clear. Did you know the Colonel?'

'We met occasionally at drinks parties, but he wasn't a personal friend. And the poor chap was very tied latterly with his wife – invalid, you know. Hadn't set eyes on him for a long time, but he always seemed a pleasant fellow, even though he was causing us a few problems. But Norman here was confident he'd come good, weren't you, Norman?'

Gloag said heartily, 'Absolutely. A few more visits, and I reckon we'd have had it in the bag.'

Macdonald noted with interest that despite the assertive tone, there was a line of sweat on the man's upper lip. Had he been rather less sure of his ability to deliver than he would like ALCO to think? He had a strong suspicion that, at the very least, Gloag had not shed many tears over the Colonel's passing, especially since, according to his auntie, Giles Farquharson would be signing the deal before his uncle's body was cold. Which left the interesting question – what exactly did Gloag stand to gain?

'Were you on a retainer from ALCO, councillor?' he asked bluntly.

Gloag looked shocked. 'Of course not! I am The People's Representative – that would constitute corruption! I trust that accusation arose from ignorance rather than malice, sergeant.'

'I can assure you there was nothing of that nature.' Vernor-Miles, too, looked horrified. 'ALCO does not do business that way. Norman works solely in the interests of the people of Kirkluce.'

And if you believe that, you'll believe anything, Macdonald added silently. 'Thank you, Mr Vernor-Miles. I think that's probably all for the moment.'

'I'll leave you, then.' Vernor-Miles got up. 'I've a lot of phone calls to make. Try to calm down the nervous nellies on the board!'

He winked at Gloag as he left. Gloag returned a sickly smile, but he didn't look a happy man.

'Now, councillor,' Macdonald said.

'Bit disappointing, that,' Will Wilson said to Tansy Kerr as they left the little coffee shop in the Fauldburn Craft Centre where, after they had spoken to Romy Kyle and Alanna Paterson, Andy Macdonald's auntie had more or less force-fed them with home-made scones.

'The scones were definitely the high point,' Kerr agreed. 'After hearing theories about what might have happened three times over, I'd had enough.'

'You've left out the sermon from Kyle with the text, "Thou shalt not prefer a superstore to the work of my hands."'

'She is good, though – you have to give her that. If I could have afforded it, I'd have bought out the shop.'

'Mmm.' Wilson was only half-listening. 'There was one thing she said, though. You know when I asked her if she thought the Colonel could have changed his mind about selling to ALCO? She said she'd be surprised if he would do anything to upset Ellie. And Alanna sort of hinted that too. What was that about?'

'I've never seen the woman, but men obviously fancy her rotten. There are two of them panting after her – the guy from the bike shop and of course our present representative of the inbred aristocracy.'

Her tone was bitter, very personal. Wilson turned to look at her and pulled a rueful face. 'Hey, hey! What's this? I thought you told me you were over him. Finally. Absolutely.'

Kerr crimsoned, stretching out her hand to take his. 'I am, Will,' she protested. 'Just, like, totally over him. I never want to see him again. I told you. You showed me how false the whole thing had been – remember?' She smiled up at him.

Wilson smiled too, squeezed her hand, then with a quick look round to see that they were unobserved, kissed the tip of her nose. 'I'm seriously glad about that. Listen, it's ten past one. How about we drive out of town, find a wee quiet pub for lunch?'

She hesitated. 'Do you think we should? Oh well, why not? Let's live dangerously.'

'That's my girl,' Wilson said approvingly as they headed back to the car.

8

Councillor Gloag was not having a happy morning. He had said, several times, 'Surely it isn't necessary,' and, 'I take exception to that suggestion,' as well as, 'I would remind you, sergeant, that I am an elected representative of the people of Kirkluce.'

DC Campbell had remained silent. DS Macdonald had remained imperturbably polite, but inexorable. 'So, if I may summarise what you have said, just so DC Campbell can prepare a statement for you to sign. You have done whatever you can to promote the ALCO development because you see this as being what the majority in Kirkluce wants. Though there is a sizeable minority opposed, you feel their concerns are needless. You were working on Colonel Carmichael to agree, having already had assurances from the planning authorities that they are disposed to look favourably on the application.'

Gloag inclined his head. 'That is correct.'

'You said to Mr Vernor-Miles that you were sure that Colonel Carmichael would agree when it came to it. Why?'

Macdonald watched with clinical interest as thc man shifted in his seat. 'Well, the Colonel could see, naturally, that it was in his interests, and also the will of the community. I was able to assure him that any worries were absolutely groundless.'

'You see,' Macdonald said pleasantly, 'we have several statements to the effect that the Colonel remained totally opposed to the development.'

Gloag didn't meet his eyes. 'His decision wasn't exactly going to be popular in all quarters, so it's hardly surprising that he wouldn't want to tell them before it was a done deal.'

'Ah yes. Now, speaking of deals, was there some arrangement—?'

Gloag erupted into artificial indignation. 'I thought we had already put to rest that scurrilous suggestion! Mr Vernor-Miles himself pointed out how ridiculous—'

'We've been told you're to be handling all the property transactions.'

It was DC Campbell who spoke. He had a soft, West Coast voice, but it was almost as if he had shouted. Both men stared at him.

'Well – er – that's – er – there is no definite—' Gloag spluttered. 'Any – any formal negotiation would – would have to be conducted after decisions had been taken.' But he was unlucky that he sweated so readily.

Recovering from his surprise, since this had indeed been only a scurrilous rumour circulating in the town, Macdonald said, 'But are we to assume that there is a clear understanding?'

'Not at all,' Gloag said with dignity, making a recovery himself. 'It would hardly be out of order for ALCO to give their business to local services as far as possible – one of their policies, incidentally, which made me believe that they would be good news for Kirkluce. But I can assure you there has been nothing improper about their approach.'

'As I'm sure we'd find Mr Vernor-Miles can confirm.' It was so transparent it was almost funny. Almost. 'Right,' Macdonald went on, 'I think that's all quite clear. Again, to summarise: your movements. You were here, at home, from four o'clock onwards on Saturday afternoon, until you left for the meeting. But your wife and family were out – is that correct?'

'Correct.'

'And I see, from our records, that you have a shotgun?'

Gloag sprang up. 'Sergeant, this is outrageous! Of course I am entirely supportive of the police in their investigation, but the juxtaposition of these two questions—'

Macdonald looked at him blandly. 'I'm sorry, sir, I assure you there was no significance. I was working through the standard questions we are obliged to ask. Of course, if this is a sensitive area for you . . .'

A faint smile flickered on DC Campbell's face as he bent over his notebook.

'No, no, of course not,' Gloag said, calming himself with an effort and sitting down again. 'I have a properly licensed shotgun for sporting purposes – pheasant shoots and so on. I take it there can be no problem with that?'

'No indeed. Perhaps we could see where it is kept?'

'If you must,' Gloag said stiffly. 'It's secured in a gun-locker. I keep the ammunition separate, of course, as I am required to do.'

The two men followed him through to the back of the house, where they inspected the cupboard and the gun and Macdonald pronounced himself satisfied, 'for the time being'.

They were on their way out when Gloag said aggressively, 'There is another, unrelated matter I wish to raise with you, sergeant.'

Macdonald braced himself. The man was down, but he wasn't out; they bred them tough in the local council, what with punch-ups between the opposing parties every other Wednesday. 'Oh yes?' he said, crossing his arms, unconsciously creating a barrier between them.

'As The People's Representative, I am most concerned – *most* concerned, about the activities of the local youth. My own son, Gordon, has, I freely admit, not always been wise in his choice of companions, but of course he is young and the glamour of rebellion is hard to resist, as I daresay you remember yourselves?'

The blank faces of the two officers suggested memories only of a blameless youth, but Gloag went on, 'There are two young men who are – I use this word with great reluctance – a pernicious influence: Barney Kyle and Dylan Burnett. Of course, neither of them has had the benefit of a strong paternal influence, as Gordon has, and I feel the police would do well to take an interest in their activities. Only the other day, I myself had damage done to my car and I have reason to believe that Burnett and Kyle were involved. Of course, this is not an official complaint – their mothers have problems enough as it is – but I would like to see action taken before they draw more innocent young people into anti-social behaviour. This, you understand, is only a word to the wise.'

They were luckily at the front door, since Macdonald was uncertain how much more of this oleaginous performance he would be able to take without throwing up. 'I've noted your concern, sir, and will pass it on. Thank you for your time.'

As he and Campbell walked back down the path, Macdonald said, 'That was a good call, suddenly asking him about handling the properties. It was the question that really got him rattled.'

Campbell didn't look at him, or smile. 'Can't stand canting bastards,' was all he said.

Tam MacNee was feeling tired as he drove back into Kirkluce. He was feeling angry about feeling tired: what the hell had he done today to make him feel tired, except talk to a couple of people? And he had the beginnings of a headache as well.

He pulled off the road to take two – no, three of his painkillers. If his headache developed fully, he'd have no alternative but to go home and go to bed, and then Bunty would phone and tell the doctor and he'd be off for another six weeks.

The black depression he'd had to fight ever since his injury was descending again. Perhaps he'd never get back. The waters would close and they'd all forget about him, except to say, 'Poor old Tam – real bummer, wasn't it?' occasionally. No doubt even now Marjory was assembling a team to operate without him. And even if he did return, could he be sure he'd be able to contribute as once he had?

Leaning his head back and shutting his eyes as he waited for the painkillers to take effect, he tried to sort what he'd heard this morning into some sort of order. He hadn't been able to take notes, but then in the past he'd only done that because it was the procedure. He wasn't in the habit of referring to them.

Now, the thoughts swirling in his mind were incoherent, indefinite. They weren't organised, suggesting a way forward, and for a moment he felt panic. He had to fight it. That was something he simply couldn't afford.

'It's always like this, remember?' He spoke out loud in defiance of the self he refused to recognise, the self that all his life had told him he was somehow less than the people around him, that he always had something to prove, the self that had got it all its own way, these last painful months. 'At this stage, you'd just be taking in what people told you, not trying to come to conclusions. You hear what they say and see what comes to the surface later.' Rutherford would probably shove him in the funny farm if he heard him talking to himself like this, but it was more convincing when you said it out loud.

What the rest of the CID would be doing was no different from what he'd done so far. They'd be listening, thinking, then discussing the next stage – which was, of course, where they had the advantage. They shared a pool of knowledge and they could get access to whatever they wanted. Tam was denied that.

It was a challenge, though, and he liked challenges. He hadn't quite seen it as a competition before, but if he'd been put out of the team . . . He began to feel better.

Kyle had a shop, and so did Ossian Forbes-Graham and Johnny Black, even. Ellie Burnett too, once she opened it again. And he wondered if Marjory had thought of talking to the butcher, who stood to make a huge amount from selling his property, and Senga Blair, come to that. There was nothing to stop him having a chat over the counter, even if as far as Senga was concerned, he doubted whether she could lift a shotgun, let alone knew how to fire one.

He'd have problems getting at Giles Farquharson, though. He stood to benefit most directly, which had to put him right up there as a suspect – especially if he believed his uncle was about to refuse ALCO's offer and lose him hundreds of thousands. But Tam couldn't march up to the front door and ask for a chat, and he could hardly pretend to be interested in paint-balling or motocross next.

Probably his best bet was to drop in on Annie Brown. She'd been one of their neighbours when he and Bunty were first married, before they'd moved to the larger villa which gave Bunty scope for her mission to mother anything with four legs or, even more often, with three – a mission he'd never questioned since he knew the heartache of childlessness which had prompted it.

Annie was a good soul and she'd been fond of the Colonel. It would be no more than a neighbourly act to drop in and see how she was. And Annie would know all there was to know about Farquharson's relationship with his uncle.

Tam was feeling better. He sat up. Home first for lunch, then he'd tell Bunty he planned to have a good long walk. She and the doctor were keen on good walks. She'd probably insist he took a couple of their present lodgers with him, but fortunately dogs weren't in a position to clype and tell her they'd been shut up in the car for most of the afternoon.

He'd drop in at MacLaren's and Blair's shops, then pay a visit to Annie. That was a good, clear plan of action. Nothing wrong with his brain.

And he'd finish off by dropping in at the Salutation. Even if he couldn't find a colleague prepared to defy Big Marge, the local grapevine would no doubt be able to tell him everything the police had been doing today. He drove off with a lighter heart.

Romy Kyle, with her ear protectors on and her back to the door, was hammering with a wooden mallet at the edge of a round of Britannia silver which was on its way to becoming a beaker. She didn't hear her partner approaching, and only realised with a start that he was there when he came into her line of vision.

'Well,' she said, pulling the headpiece down to hang round her neck, 'this is an unexpected honour. Something wrong?'

She couldn't remember the last time Pete had come to the workshop. Perhaps seeing her skill made him feel inadequate or something, but there wasn't a lot she could do about that.

He came over to her, tipped her chin up and kissed her on the mouth and, as always, she couldn't help responding. She could be clear-minded about Pete when he wasn't there, touching her, but the physical side of their life together, she often thought, was actually addictive, blotting out everything else.

He released her slowly, then smiled down at her. 'You do worry about me, don't you? No, there's nothing wrong. Just thought I'd pop in and say hi.' He picked up a silver bracelet from the counter display and fiddled with it, draping it over his wrist to admire the effect, without looking at her.

Romy's heart sank. This wasn't normal – what the hell had he been up to this time? 'Hi, then,' she said warily, picking up a cloth and needlessly polishing the piece she had been beating.

'Had the police round then, have you?' Pete asked with elaborate casualness. 'I was in a shop and someone there was saying they'd seen them coming in.' He'd put down the bracelet and picked up a dangly earring now and was squinting in the small mirror on the counter as he held it up to his ear.

'That's right. Just going through the motions – did I know anything, which I don't; did I suspect anyone, which I do – that sod Gloag or one of his pals; what were my own movements—?'

'What did you say?' he interrupted.

'What did you expect me to say?' She had a cold feeling in the pit of her stomach. 'I told them I was here till I went home to make supper.'

'Did you say anything about me?'

'They didn't ask me anything about you, Pete, if that's what's bothering you. I said Barney was at home but I didn't say you weren't.'

'So you could say I was,' he said eagerly. 'That you just hadn't thought to mention it.'

'I could. But it wouldn't be true.' Romy put down what she was holding. 'Pete, look at me. What's this about?'

'Nothing,' he said vehemently. 'Nothing at all. Except that I know how their minds work. First thing they'll do, they'll go to the files, see who's got a record. Saves time, you see, if they can lean on some poor bastard, scare them into a confession. I just don't want to be the poor bastard they pick on.'

'You're paranoid,' Romy said flatly, relief surging through her. She'd been afraid it really was something serious and she knew that whatever it was, whatever it cost her, she would still have protected him. 'Listen, love – there isn't a reason in the world for them to suspect you. You were caught in a silly scam, but you've kept your nose clean since and there's never been a question of violence. I should think the only time you've even held a shotgun was when Danny took you to shoot clays that time.'

'For God's sake, don't tell them that!' he cried. 'That would be all they'd need.'

Romy picked up the silver round again. 'You're just being stupid now. Look, I've got work to do.' She was just about to replace her ear protectors when she stopped. 'There isn't anything to connect you to Andrew, is there – I mean, apart from this place?'

'Of course not. I'm probably just being paranoid, like you said.' He gave her a big, confident smile. 'I'll get out of your hair, then. But you'll watch what you say to the filth, won't you?'

She grunted, settling the ear-muffs in place again. He went out, but she didn't immediately go back to her work. Her lovely Pete, charming, feckless and amiable, would never have harmed Andrew, of course he wouldn't. She had to believe that, even if it left her with questions she wasn't sure she wanted answered.

'Do you suppose someone actually designed that, or did someone just get a Lego set with real bricks for Christmas one year?' Tansy Kerr viewed the Scottish baronial front of Ravenshill House with some amazement.

'If they did, it was something they dreamed after a heavy supper,' Will Wilson agreed as they parked on the gravel square outside the front door. 'Nice view, though.'

The house stood on rising ground and beyond the mature trees in the parkland in front, moorland stretched to forest-clad hills. In front of the mullioned windows to the left of the imposing entrance, a sculpture group showed a stag having its throat torn out by three leaping hounds.

Wilson pointed. 'Nice thing to look at when you open the curtains in the morning.'

Kerr shuddered. 'No wonder Ossian's weird. What do you reckon the parents are like?' They walked into the ornamented stone porch, then she pulled a brass bell-handle and heard a clanging somewhere inside.

The heavy wooden door was opened quite promptly by a man who, while his appearance fitted perfectly with his surroundings, looked a most unlikely father for the Byronic Ossian. Murdoch Forbes-Graham had iron-grey hair, the reddened face of a man who spent much of his time outdoors, and a paunch and jowls which suggested more time enthusiastically spent with a decanter of vintage port after a hearty dinner.

'Yes?' He looked from one to the other without enthusiasm.

Wilson showed his warrant card. 'DCs Wilson and Kerr. May we have a word, sir?'

'Ah, is it to do with this most unfortunate Carmichael affair? You'd better come in, then. I'll call my wife.'

The hall was cavernous, with a positive forest of stags' antlers on the walls. At the foot of an oppressively carved staircase a huge, moth-eaten stuffed bear reared up in a threatening pose. Forbes-Graham, cupping his hands round his mouth, shouted up, 'Deirdre!' There was a muffled response and he called again, 'In the morning room!' then, turning to the officers, said, 'This way.'

As they followed him across the polished parquet floor, Kerr reflected that a son like Ossian must be a considerable disappointment to a man like this, who would surely prefer a rugger-bugger type. Like Rory Douglas, whom she'd vowed never to think of again. And she didn't, not much. Not now. She stole a sideways glance at Will.

The morning room was at the back of the house, with low windows looking out over an expanse of smooth green lawn. It had a massive oak mantelpiece with a high brass fender topped with green leather cushioning you could sit on and the furnishing of the room was conventional – two sofas facing each other across a huge tapestried stool piled with back numbers of *Country Life* and *Scottish Field*, as well as books you would need a small crane to lift, with covers featuring houses and gardens so lush and inviting that they classed as property porn.

What was astonishing, though, was the pictures on the walls. There were no representations of stags at bay here, nor improbably purple mountains with a Highland cow or three, and not even a mounted salmon in a glass case. What hung on the walls was modern, three huge artworks which Kerr had no difficulty in recognising as produced by Ossian.

Forbes-Graham saw she was looking at them. 'My son's work,' he said with unmistakable pride. 'Do you like them?'

Kerr was able to say, quite truthfully, that she did, and he beamed. 'Ossian is a seriously talented artist, internationally recognised. Do you know what his most recent paintings sell for?'

He mentioned a figure which sent Kerr's eyebrows shooting up almost into her hair. Perhaps that explained the man's admiration for his son – money would talk, where he was concerned.

A woman came into the room. She was wearing what Kerr thought of as wispy clothes, layers of soft blue fabric and a couple of scarves that fluttered when she moved in a way which somehow made her edges look blurred. She had greying fair hair, worn long, and with her good bone structure and a softer version of Ossian's blue eyes she must once have been a very pretty woman, though middle age had slackened and wrinkled her pale, fine skin. She drifted across to settle on one of the sofas; Forbes-Graham took his place beside her and she waved the detectives to the sofa opposite.

As Wilson made the introductions, Kerr studied the pair with some interest. They were older than you might expect Ossian's parents to be – had someone said this was a second marriage? – and hers were evidently the dominant genes when it came to their son. From the way her husband deferred to her, Kerr wondered whether she was the stronger character too, despite her delicate appearance.

Forbes-Graham was looking at her fondly. 'It's my wife who is the artistic one, obviously. I'm just a simple farmer.'

Deirdre looked up at him from under her lashes, smiling. 'If it weren't for the practical people, artists couldn't flourish, could they?'

It was a flirtatious performance. She clearly had her husband wrapped round her little finger.

Wilson was taking the lead in questioning. Kerr didn't mind; it seemed natural, somehow, and she took out her notebook and discreetly began scribbling.

'We have obviously spoken to your son about the events of last Saturday, as one of Colonel Carmichael's tenants—'

Forbes-Graham bristled immediately. 'And what is that supposed to mean?'

'Nothing at all, sir. Entirely routine. He was unable to recall precisely what his movements were on Saturday—'

'This is a disgrace! Are you suggesting that my son has to account for his movements—?'

His wife put a thin, blue-veined hand on his knee. 'Darling,' she said so gently that he was immediately quelled, 'you're making it sound as if Ossian might have something to hide. Which of course he doesn't.'

She turned a charming smile on the detectives and as her husband subsided, muttering, 'Of course. Sorry,' Kerr was suddenly reminded of something she'd read in a magazine once: 'Any woman can manage a clever man, but it takes a very clever woman to manage a fool.' Deirdre Forbes-Graham might be a very clever woman.

Now she was saying to Wilson, 'Tell me what it is that my son's told you that you don't believe.' She made a charming joke of it, and Wilson smiled back.

'No, no,' he protested. 'It's nothing like that.'

Isn't it? Kerr gave him a dagger look: Will was just a bit too susceptible to feminine charm – but perhaps she didn't want to go there.

He didn't notice. 'It's only that he didn't remember his movements clearly on Saturday, after he left the Craft Centre. He thought he might have come home—'

'Might have!' Deirdre gave a silvery laugh. 'That really is Ossian all over. Of course he did! I can't tell you exactly when he left, but it was to go to the meeting about the superstore – those dreadful people!' She wrinkled her nose in distaste. 'When he came in, he popped his head round the door of my studio to say hello. I'm an artist too, but in a very small way.'

'I wouldn't say that,' Forbes-Graham protested, and she rewarded him with another smile.

'I know, darling, but that's because you're very sweetly biased and a complete philistine.'

Oh, clever, Kerr thought. A pat on the head and a kick back into the gutter in a oner. She stepped in.

'Mrs Forbes-Graham, we're looking for a precise time,' she said, earning herself a venomous look.

'Artists are notoriously vague about time, I'm afraid. But I should think we could work it out if you give me the time Ossian left the studio.'

Sure she could! 'The thing is,' Kerr said quickly before Wilson had a chance to oblige with the information, 'he wasn't absolutely clear about that. We may find someone who saw him leave, but after that he mentioned taking a walk.'

'I – see.' Deirdre frowned. 'So what is the time-frame you're interested in?'

It was blatant enough even for Wilson to see what she was up to. 'I'm afraid that's not something we can tell you at this stage,' he said stiffly. 'It would help if you could give us your recollection, as precisely as possible.'

She thought for a moment. 'It's always hard to be sure one is thinking of the right day – Saturday, not Friday or Thursday. But I'm fairly sure it would have been somewhere around half-past four or five that he came back. Would that fit with the information you have?'

If not, I can always change it – that was the implication. Wilson ignored her. 'Mr Forbes-Graham, did you see your son on Saturday, late afternoon?'

The man was visibly uncomfortable. 'I'm not sure I can recall, exactly—'

Deirdre gave another tinkling laugh. 'Oh, my love, your memory! Of course you do! You were up checking the arrangements for the clay-pigeon shoot on Sunday and when you came back Ossian was just having a bite to eat in the kitchen before he went out to the meeting. Remember now?'

Her tone was playful but Kerr noticed that her hands were restlessly plucking at the fringe of one of her scarves.

'Oh – oh yes, that's right.' Forbes-Graham gamely followed her lead. 'The clay-pigeon shoot – had some chaps coming next day and there was a query about the stands.' He was clearly on firmer ground now. 'Young Simpson phoned. He couldn't find Giles, so I had to pop up myself.'

'And then you came back, when Ossian was just finishing his sandwich,' Deirdre prompted him again.

'I said that, didn't I?' He was starting to sound defensive.

Quit while you're ahead, Kerr thought, and Deirdre seemed to have worked that out for herself. She got up. 'If there isn't anything else—?'

The officers rose too. Wilson said, 'Thank you for your help, Mrs Forbes-Graham. All right, Tansy?'

She nodded, then, looking up at one of the paintings, said innocently, 'Is your son working on something at the moment, Mr Forbes-Graham?'

He was clearly pleased that the conversation had turned. 'He's having a bit of a problem just now, for some reason. Very up and down, is Ossian – painting like a demon for a while, half the night, sometimes, and barely sleeping. Then of course he's so worn out he gets depressed and can hardly get out of bed. Worries me a bit, to tell the truth.'

Deirdre intervened. 'My husband finds it very hard to understand the artistic temperament. All we artists are volatile – never sure when inspiration will strike again. It's perfectly normal.'

She stepped forward and somehow Kerr and Wilson found themselves wafted inexorably out of the front door.

'No alibi,' Kerr said quietly as they reached the car. 'And she's desperate to cover up for him, for some reason. Why? We're just asking routine questions.'

Getting into the driver's seat, Wilson agreed. 'I tell you something. I read a book where someone had manic depression. Sounded like Forbes-Graham.'

'Off his trolley?'

'Tansy, using words like that gets you sent on a course. Don't you know anything?' But he was grinning as he drove away. 'He's not what you'd call a stable personality, that's for sure.'

'Hmm.' Kerr digested that. 'I think, if I was Ellie Burnett,' she said slowly, 'I'd be pretty careful about locking my door at night.'

Fleming was restless. She had read such reports as had reached her and summarised them for her report, she had attended the autopsy on the Colonel's body, she had briefed the Procurator Fiscal, she had even started her policy book, recording her decisions and the rationale behind them, so that someone with the benefit of hindsight could go through them later and say how stupid they had been. She could, of course, make a start on assessing budgetary implications but that was so profoundly unappetising that it could wait.

She was suffering, as she sometimes did, from nostalgia for the days when she would have been out there, doing the tedious, boring job in the perpetual hope that the next routine interview would produce the breakthrough, whether it was petty crime you were talking about, or murder.

Nothing so far had emerged that would justify a personal follow-up from the Senior Investigating Officer, but sitting at her desk waiting patiently had never been Fleming's style. If Tam had been around, she'd have called him in for a brainstorming session, but if she tried that with her present team, they'd be off like bloodhounds, following up on her random thoughts.

Was it something you had to adjust to as you got older – becoming the generation that should know all the answers, even if you didn't? Learn to make pompous pronouncements, as Donald Bailey did, since they were less dangerous than off-the-cuff suggestions which wouldn't be subjected to proper scrutiny? She wasn't ready to do that, not for a long time yet.

OK, so she enjoyed power. If you looked at it closely, everyone did, from the two-year-old winding up his mother by refusing to open his mouth for the Brussels sprouts, to granny playing games about who would get the Clarice Cliff tea set once she was gone. Trouble came when the balance of power shifted – look at parents and teenagers. Take Cat, for example, starting to assert her independence – but she didn't want to think about that.

Fleming's problem at the moment, though, was not losing

power, but finding herself with more than she wanted. It was fine to be able to direct operations, to decide when and where to take a hand, to reap the benefit of others doing the more boring parts of the job. But now it felt as if what she had was the power to fall flat on her face because no one would pose the awkward questions she hadn't thought of herself.

Andy Macdonald would have to learn to challenge her, when necessary. He was no fool, and he wasn't lacking in courage either. In that last, most painful murder enquiry, he'd dared to offend his Super, risking his own promotion.

Fleming suspected, though, that he was personally more in awe of her than he was of Bailey. She knew her reputation for having, as her mother would say, 'a tongue that could clip cloots', and there were several officers who could display the shredded rags of their self-esteem in support of the accuracy of that assessment.

To be realistic, she wasn't going to change. That was how she ran her team and Andy would have to learn to be a big brave boy.

Restlessly, she shifted the papers on her desk. She'd be as well to tackle the budget now. She hadn't any excuse, and wouldn't have, at least until Macdonald, Kerr and Wilson reported back, which wouldn't be until much later. She turned reluctantly to her computer and opened a new file.

When the phone rang, she picked it up with unusual enthusiasm. 'Fleming.'

She listened, then said blankly, '*Who* did you say?'

9

'It's awful good of you to come, Tam,' Annie Brown welcomed him as she took him through to the immaculately neat front room of her semi. 'There's not many people would think about how I'd feel, losing the Colonel, but it's been twenty-five years I've worked for him – that's longer than I had with my husband, God rest him!'

Tam MacNee followed sheepishly, making embarrassed noises. She insisted on fetching him tea and a slice of her fruit cake and sat down, ready to talk for as long as he would listen about the loss that was obviously a genuine bereavement. And her gratitude for his 'kindness' would make it harder for him to push the conversation the way he wanted it to go.

The Colonel's devoted care of his arthritis-crippled wife was Annie's starting-point, and she favoured MacNee with a rather more robust description of Mrs Carmichael than she had given Macdonald that morning: 'Oh, the woman was a right besom! The man was a saint.'

MacNee was cynical about saints. In his experience, a man behaving that way likely had either a very wealthy wife or a guilty conscience, or both, but he knew better than to say it.

'Have you had the police round?' he asked instead, and was treated to a report on their activities more exhaustive than any that would reach Big Marge's desk. He smiled inwardly. He might be out of the official loop, but he had his spies.

The photos of the foreigners she described seemed a

mildly interesting irrelevance, but her description of Giles Farquharson's odd behaviour left him feeling frustrated. That demanded follow-up, and no doubt Andy Mac was even now probing all the sore places, while MacNee didn't even have a plan for how to get a word with the man. As Annie talked on about the shortcomings of the future owners of Fauldburn, MacNee found his mind wandering.

He'd spoken already to Senga Blair and George MacLaren. Senga was desperate to sell, right enough, but she was even frailer than MacNee had remembered, and she was a gentle soul anyway. George was a jolly, open-faced man in his late fifties, whose jokey asides made waiting in the often lengthy queue a positive entertainment. He was forthright in answer to MacNee's innocent question, as he purchased three chump chops, which Bunty would be most surprised to receive.

'It's win-win, as far as I'm concerned. If it falls through I go on doing a job I like fine – I'm not past it yet. If it goes ahead, I can retire a few years early and start taking those Caribbean cruises the wife's set her heart on. Don't mind much either way – but I tell you, it's as well that Herself doesn't know one end of a shotgun from the other!' He had roared with laughter and turned to his next customer. 'There you are, my dear – this steak's tender as a woman's heart. So maybe you'd prefer a pound of sausages?'

It was hard to imagine George gunning someone down for the sake of an early start to the Caribbean cruises.

The 'Highlights of the Colonel's Virtuous Life Over the Last Twenty-five Years' recital was still going on. MacNee was beginning to rehearse tactful escape techniques when Annie said something that did catch his attention.

'I wouldn't tell anyone else this, Tam – to be honest, I don't like looking a fool. But you've been that kind, letting me blether on, and this just shows how the Colonel always looked after me.

'I've a wee bit money put by and I've a friend over Stranraer way that's in this Ladies' Investment Club. They put in money and get it invested by these fellows who know the ropes, and I'm not getting much on my savings account. I've two wee grandsons and I want them to get something worthwhile, once I'm away.

'So this lad came and talked to me a couple of weeks ago – Pete Spencer, you know, him that lives with Romy Kyle from the Craft Centre? Real nice, he was, and nothing too much trouble, explained everything so I could understand and it seemed fine, so I got out five thousand pounds from the bank and gave it to him.'

'A lot of money,' MacNee said gravely.

'It is and all! I'd only meant it to be a thousand, but it looked that good, and it was for the boys . . .' Annie sighed. 'I was talking to the Colonel next day and said what I'd done, and he said he didn't like the sound of it. It was maybe all right, but then he told me Pete had been jailed for confidence tricks before – not in a gossipy way, mind, just because I should know, with so much money involved. He said it was the law that I could change my mind. He had a word with Pete for me, and right enough when I asked I got my money back.

'Now, how many employers would do that for a stupid woman who'd only herself to blame?'

MacNee agreed that indeed, the Colonel's halo shone even more brightly after this disclosure, but it wasn't the man's imminent beatification that was foremost in his mind as he made his excuses and left.

Fiona Farquharson was in the kitchen of the Ravenshill factor's house, preparing the evening meal. She prided herself on her cooking and she had a nice little business doing shooting lunches and so on: nothing too elaborate for her clientele, just tasty traditional fare, but today she was wondering whether making a proper supper was worth her while. Neither she nor Giles had done much damage to the veal and ham pie at lunchtime.

After his visit to Fauldburn, all he'd said was that the police were coming to interview them this afternoon, and somehow that took away her appetite. Of course, as she'd emphasised to him, this was merely routine, with him being the heir and obviously in the picture, and anyway they'd got it all covered. Just as long as he didn't blow it. She did wish she could be sure he wouldn't. He'd only to do as he was told.

But when the phone rang, and Giles, who'd been driving her demented by hanging round her kitchen, jumped as if he'd been jabbed with a cattle prod and went to take the call in the study, the possibilities which intrusively presented themselves left her in an unfamiliar state of nervous confusion. The call might be no more than everyday routine, it could be the call Fiona had been awaiting for years, which would make everything worthwhile, or it could be – disaster.

She couldn't possibly have held her breath for the whole of the lengthy phone call, but it felt like that. And when Giles came back, she knew that the first two possibilities were out. He had been looking dreadful when he went out, but now he looked as if he was about to face a firing squad.

Fiona's heart started thumping and her head seemed to be floating. 'What? What, Giles?'

'That was the lawyer. I'm not the principal legatee. Fifty thousand, that's all.'

'Fifty thousand!' It was derisory, a pittance! So everything she had done had been wasted, pointless. All she had to look forward to now was the present dreary existence, kow-towing to the Forbes-Grahams to keep Giles's job, living in this – this *hovel* – she cast a disparaging glance round the kitchen, fitted with cupboards from MFI, for heaven's sake! – and on into an even more restricted old age. With Giles.

Anger surged through her. 'That deceitful, cheating bastard!' she screamed. 'All those years, dancing attendance, being charming – "Yes, Uncle Andrew, no, Uncle Andrew" – and for this? He must have lied to your mother all along. So who gets it? If it's that Burnett woman, we must contest it – undue influence. He was probably bonking her. Is it her?'

Giles sat down heavily on one of the kitchen chairs. 'He wouldn't tell me. We'll get details later.'

The young man who came into DI Fleming's office was a little above medium height, with small hands and feet. He was wearing what was clearly an expensive casual shirt with what was equally clearly a cashmere sweater draped over his shoulders and he had dark brown hair and eyes with a slight oriental tilt. He held out a business card in a slim brown hand with a heavy gold chain at the wrist.

'Zachariah – Zack Salaman,' he said.

'DI Marjory Fleming. Do sit down, Mr Salaman.' Fleming took the card and indicated a chair, trying to conceal her astonishment.

'I've no doubt this may have come as something of a surprise to those who knew my grandfather.' He had an English voice and he was very composed; he did not smile and the eyes which were assessing her coolly were very shrewd.

'I'm sorry, Mr Salaman,' she said. 'I'm afraid we had no idea that Colonel Carmichael had children at all, never mind a grandchild.'

'No one did.' He smiled now, a formal smile which showed teeth so perfect they had to be a triumph of orthodontics. 'I felt it was incumbent upon me to get in touch, as his next of kin. Do you want to put your questions to me, inspector, or would you rather I simply told you the background?'

'That might be best.' Listening to this supremely confident young man might give her time to collect her thoughts and have the right questions ready to ask when he'd finished.

'I was born in London. My father is Malay, my mother is half Malay, half English – I'm sorry, Scots,' he corrected himself, smiling. 'They met in Kuala Lumpur where he was an investment banker in DBS Malaysia and later transferred to London.

'My mother knew little of her origins, except that a major in the King's Own Scottish Borderers, who had been serving in the then Malaya, was her father. She had a difficult life. Her mother's pregnancy was a disgrace and her family disowned them, though they were well provided for financially through an allowance sent via lawyers. A condition of receiving it was that they made no attempt to get in touch.

'My grandmother wouldn't have tried. She accepted the situation – indeed, never even told my mother the father's name – and died in her fifties. My mother, after she married, wrote to the lawyers and said there was no further need for maintenance payments, but she would value the chance to know more about her father. This was refused.'

Fleming could see anger in the tension of his position in the chair. This was a very proud young man; he didn't find it easy to accept that to his mother's family, on both sides, he was a non-person. Who would?

'She didn't pursue it. I never knew my grandmother; I only discovered this story relatively recently. And unlike my mother, I wasn't prepared to leave it there.'

Fleming interrupted. 'What do you do yourself?'

'I am a corporate lawyer.'

She might have guessed. 'So – go on. What steps did you take?'

'The obvious ones, of course. I repeated my requests to the lawyers in Kuala Lumpur through a professional contact, and was able to find the firm of London solicitors who dealt with it. They were, unfortunately, entirely unhelpful. The extent of their indiscretion was that payments came to them through another solicitor whose name they were not prepared to divulge.'

He would, Fleming thought, make it quite difficult to refuse. She rather hoped not to have to come up against him: lawyers were tricky at the best of times, and someone in his profession in London would be top-flight.

'So I took it from the other end. I employed a firm of international private detectives who didn't find it difficult to narrow the field. I then employed a firm in Glasgow and with fairly precise dates and locations, it wasn't very difficult to come up with Colonel Carmichael's name and address.'

Fleming had a brief moment of sympathy for the Colonel, suddenly exposed to this fierce young man's attention. 'How long ago was this?'

'I set it in train six, seven months ago, perhaps.'

'And you met him at that time? Here?'

'No, at my hotel in Glasgow, a bit later, once I had considered the matter thoroughly and then made contact to arrange a time convenient to us both.'

'So is this your first visit to Kirkluce?'

The young man hesitated. 'No,' he said at last. 'I came last week. I felt it was time to have a look at the place, but I didn't visit my grandfather.'

For the first time, she was seeing signs of unease. Even a fool would realise that this was a significant admission in a murder enquiry, and Salaman was far from being a fool. He hadn't tried lying, or even evasion; there were too many other ways the police might get this information.

'When you met, what was his reaction?'

'You won't believe this, of course. It all sounds too convenient.' Again, he gave that chilly smile. 'But he seemed – pleased.'

'He was ready to acknowledge you?'

'Not – not quite.'

Fleming raised her eyebrows. The man opposite her looked as if he was in his mid-twenties; professionally he might be formidable but when it came to the sensitive matter of human relationships he was little more than a child. Cruelly she asked, with synthetic surprise, 'Not quite? When he was so delighted to find he had a grandson?'

Colour rose in his face. 'He had quite a lot to straighten out first. He explained that he had severed contact with my grandmother to "spare his wife".' There was a flash of anger as he said that, swiftly concealed. 'He has a nephew, someone who expects to inherit, and he felt it was only fair to prepare him before he acknowledged me openly, as he was planning to do. As is only right.' He had obviously prepared his defence.

'And did your grandfather tell you about the offer from ALCO?'

Salaman shifted in his seat. 'I – heard.'

'You have a contact in Kirkluce?' It had been reported in the local press, of course, but that wasn't what you'd say if you'd read it.

'I – yes.'

'Who?'

His face went very still. 'I don't think that's relevant, inspector.'

There was little point in pressing him on that, for the moment at least. Fleming went on, 'The offer was worth a huge amount of money, of course. Were you aware that Colonel Carmichael was considering refusing?'

'It was my grandfather's decision. Nothing to do with me.' He was definitely uncomfortable now.

'Did you discuss it with him? Express your opinion, as his heir?'

'Why should I?'

Neat answer. Not quite a lie; half-truths were always easier. She wasn't ready to let him off the hook yet, though. 'But you must have an opinion?'

Salaman met her eyes squarely. 'Sentimentality is no way to do business. But as I said, it was entirely my grandfather's decision.'

The consistent use of the family term was revealing. Fleming changed her tone. 'He was greatly respected, your grandfather.'

His expression was hard to read. She had hoped for signs of pleasure, interest even, but he said only, 'I'm sure.'

Time to drop it and move on. 'I'm afraid there are routine questions I must ask you,' she said carefully.

'I understand that.' Salaman's eyes were wary.

'Where were you last Saturday, when Colonel Carmichael was killed?'

'Fortunately, that's very straightforward.' He relaxed, which rather suggested to Fleming that she'd missed something. 'I was celebrating a particularly good legal victory at Rules in London with some friends. I can supply you with their names, if you like.'

'If we need that we'll come back to you. I'm grateful to you for being so frank. It's been most helpful. Are you going back to London, or staying in the area?'

'I'm staying at the Gracemount House Hotel for a few days. There's some business to be taken care of.'

No doubt there would be some interesting conversations to have with ALCO, Fleming thought as she wrote down the name of the country house hotel.

'Thank you. I would be grateful if you would tell me if you are planning to leave the area. Now, I think I only need one more thing for now – the name of the private detective you used to trace Colonel Carmichael, please.'

The shutters came down so fast she almost heard them

rattle. Salaman got up. 'I have been, as you said yourself, anxious to cooperate in any way I can, but I see this as a privacy issue. You have my card – I know you will contact me if I can be of further assistance.'

Then he was gone and Fleming found herself staring at a closed door.

Walking along the High Street, Tam MacNee paused to consider his next move. He was keen to talk to Ellie Burnett – somehow he had the sense that there was a lot of stuff going on there – but from what he'd seen this morning, she wouldn't be in her shop today. It was too early to go to the Salutation in the hope of finding someone with a proper sense of loyalty to an old pal, and anyway Bunty was starting to get suspicious about his sudden interest in taking long walks. It would make sense to go home now, then after his tea he could use the excuse that he was needing to practise his hand–eye coordination at the darts board. She'd swallowed that before.

He had stopped, he realised suddenly, just outside the motorcycle showroom. School must be out; there were several boys and two or three girls looking at the gleaming monsters on display, talking and laughing. From behind the counter Johnny Black was watching them indulgently. It had clearly become some sort of meeting-place for the young, and given the pester-power of teenagers, it probably made commercial sense as well.

It occurred to MacNee that among them might well be the little sods currently making Christina Munro's life a living hell. No one would have had time to follow up on that officially, with all that was going on today, and on an impulse he opened the door, untroubled by scruples about claiming an official status he didn't currently possess.

He walked up to the counter, where four youths were

clustered, talking to Black. There was another man beside him: Danny Simpson, from Ravenshill. That was a bit unfortunate, but MacNee wasn't going to turn back now.

'Afternoon,' he said to Black. 'Are Barney Kyle, Dylan Burnett and Gordon Gloag in here?'

'Who wants to know?' The speaker was a stocky, square-faced boy with close-cropped dark brown hair, dark brown eyes and a mouth fixed in what looked like a permanent sneer. He was a big lad, three or four inches taller than MacNee himself.

Tam swivelled, looked at him, then turned back to Black, raising his eyebrows pointedly.

'Barney, Gordon, Dylan,' the man said hastily, indicating three out of the four round the counter. 'Just watch it, fellas – Mr MacNee's a policeman.'

Danny Simpson looked startled. As MacNee confronted them, the fourth member of the bunch slid away to join the safety of a larger group round the big Harley Davidson at the front of the showroom, and a leggy, fair-haired girl detached herself from it and slipped unobtrusively from the shop.

With the shrewdness born of long experience, MacNee eyed the group in front of him. The spotty, pasty-faced one at the back, Gloag, was clearly a hanger-on. He'd positioned himself behind the other two, with a telling distance between him and Burnett, who was at Kyle's shoulder. Burnett was slight, with a blond ponytail and something of his mother's delicacy of feature, and though he was trying to look defiant, the nervous movements of his eyes told a different story.

Kyle was different. Kyle had a strong, square-jawed face, with five-o'clock shadow showing under his swarthy skin. He was good-looking, though, with heavily lashed dark eyes, and he was smiling insolently, his elbows still on the counter. The leader, definitely, with Burnett as his henchman.

'What do you want with us, anyway?' Kyle demanded.

MacNee didn't reply. He stared directly at him until the pause became so uncomfortable that even Black, behind the counter, was shifting uneasily.

With affected indifference, Kyle straightened up. 'If you've nothing to say to us, I'll just—' He made to move away.

'You won't "just" anything,' MacNee said flatly. 'You'll stand there and listen till I choose to stop.'

There was nothing, absolutely nothing, to stop them all laughing and walking away, except MacNee's absolute conviction that they wouldn't. The extent of Kyle's defiance was to shove his hands in his pockets; the others were watching the policeman warily.

'You've been warned about victimising an old lady who lives alone at Wester Seton, but you haven't stopped.'

'Us?' Burnett said, plucking up courage. 'Case of mistaken identity, that's all.'

MacNee looked at him with a dead stare until Burnett's eyes dropped. 'Finished? Listen, and listen good.

'Know what happens when you push people too far? They snap. Farmers have shotguns. A kid got himself killed that way a while back. If the lady snaps, and uses hers, OK, she'll be jailed, but you'll be dead.

'Think about it. If you can think. You're in line for ASBOs as it is and we'll be watching every step you take. One breach, and you'll find yourselves banged up as first offenders. Only seeing as there aren't enough places and you're low-grade trash, it'd probably be Barlinnie.' He smiled unpleasantly. 'Oh, they like sweet young unspoiled lads like you in Bar L.'

There was an absolute hush in the showroom. Even the kids at a distance were staring in shock, and MacNee was pleased to see that Gloag, at least, had gone pale. Burnett was chewing his lip, but Kyle, though lacking the nerve to take him on, had an expression of sullen impassivity. MacNee was unsurprised to hear, just as he walked out and closed the door behind him, Kyle squeal, 'Oooh, I'm scared!' and the burst of nervous laughter which followed.

Kyle, plainly, was the ringleader. Burnett, cocky though he might be, was too flimsy to go against what he decreed. Gloag just might have been frightened enough to make an excuse and drop out the next time. There was, unfortunately, little doubt in MacNee's mind that there would be a next time. With some discomfort he reflected that he probably hadn't done much good. He could only hope he hadn't done any actual harm.

Just as he was leaving, he saw a sleek, black Mercedes sports coupé park on the opposite side of the road and a very smart young man get out. He looked as if he might be Chinese or something, or half-something, maybe. There were a couple of Chinese restaurants in Kirkluce but they certainly weren't making the sort of money that bought you cars like that, and MacNee glanced over his shoulder in idle interest as the man crossed the road and went into the showroom MacNee had just left.

He'd spotted the Harley Davidson, maybe. It had looked like becoming a permanent fixture, so Black would be pleased at the prospect of a sale, MacNee thought as he walked home.

'It was mostly flannel, I reckon. But according to them, they were together at Ravenshill until they went in separate cars to the meeting. Then afterwards they went straight home,' DS Macdonald said, reporting to DI Fleming on the interview with the Farquharsons.

'So . . . ?' Fleming prompted, to see what he would say.

'I know – why did they need to take both cars? Young Campbell was on to it like a shot. Says almost nothing, then throws in a grenade with the pin out. Farquharson said, "*I* drove in to the meeting," not we, and Campbell suddenly went, "So where was your wife then?" And he blurted out that she was following in her car. If looks could kill, she'd be downstairs right now on a murder rap.

'I asked if they had separate things to do, but she faced me down. Looked me straight in the eye and said they drove in convoy there and back – produced some guff about neither of them liking being driven. She's tough, that one.'

'Good follow-up from both of you, there,' Fleming said approvingly. 'With what they had to gain from Carmichael's death, they have to be firmly in the picture, and if she really was trying to fake an alibi, you have to ask why. Anyway, the CCTV footage will tell us if they're lying. We'll need the registration numbers of both cars—'

Smugly, Macdonald said, 'Got them already. I've passed them on.'

'OK, you are today's winner of the big badge that says "My inspector's thrilled skinny with me." But tell me, how were they looking when you arrived?'

'Sorry?'

'Happy? Sad? Scared – I mean, more scared than people usually are when you and Campbell start in on them?'

Macdonald thought about it. 'Hard to say, exactly. Not happy. He looked as if he hadn't slept for a week. She wasn't so bad – hadn't slept for three days, say.'

'They were stressed?'

'You could say.'

'It could have had something to do with the Colonel's grandson.'

Macdonald was startled. 'Grandson? He didn't even have children.'

'That's what you think, but it's a pardonable error. His wife was under the same impression.' She filled him in on the story of Zack Salaman.

'That fits!' He told her about the photographs. 'He must have given him the one of himself, I suppose.'

'Maybe so he could recognise him when they met,' Fleming suggested.

'Right. So where do we go from here?' Macdonald asked.

'You tell me.' Fleming sat back in her chair. 'Play your hunches, Andy. Should we be going all out after the Farquharsons?'

He thought about it, then shook his head. 'Too early to say that. Too many other loose ends. I'd want to pick up on Salaman as well – after all, he has a grudge motive on top of a financial one.

'We ought to trace the detective – you said he clammed up on that. If he's reluctant to say who it is, there may be a reason for it. Some fairly dubious firms operate in Glasgow. This is where we need Tam. He's the only one of us who can use the Old Pals Act to get an inside track.'

Fleming grimaced. 'I know. But we haven't got him at the moment, for good medical reasons, and I've warned you about leaving him out of it. Just go through the official channels, Andy – you'll get the information perfectly well that way.'

'No problem.' Macdonald hesitated. 'Can I ask, has anything else come in?'

'Of course you can ask! This is teamwork. You've got your stripe, you need to be more assertive. You have to pin me down about anything you need to know. Tell me when you think I'm wrong. I'm a pussycat, really.'

He couldn't quite conceal his sceptical look, and she laughed. 'OK, I'm not exactly a pussycat, but when I take a swipe, it's rarely fatal.

'Anyway, you wanted to know what else we'd got. Will and Tansy reckon Ossian Forbes-Graham is losing it rapidly and his mother will do anything to protect him. Tansy thinks he's stalking Ellie Burnett; Will reckons it's weirder than that.

'From the door-to-doors, nothing much. They talked to George MacLaren and Senga Blair since money's involved there, but—' Fleming shrugged. 'My bet is that we can forget about them.

'There are a number whose livelihood's going to be affected if it goes through – bakers, greengrocers, not to mention the workforce with jobs at risk, and it doesn't do to underestimate that in a community like this where there's not a lot of alternative employment. Then there's the suppliers too. Farmers, for instance, who know a superstore will cut their throats. And yes, that means Bill among a load of others. They're all having to be interviewed.' She sighed. 'There's going to be enough material to keep me tethered to my desk for days.

'So we have to talk priorities. What's the first angle we take?'

'I'd go after the Farquharsons,' Macdonald said. 'It's a good, straightforward motive. Not sure I'd buy someone like a farmer or a shopkeeper actually killing to protect a future market – certainly at this stage in the proceedings.'

'Right – run with that. May even do a spot of legwork there myself – I think I'm beginning to go stir-crazy. And you sometimes see things clearer when you're out there. Anything else?'

Macdonald shook his head. 'OK if I go off now? Oh, there's just one thing – Ewan Campbell's doing well. He's got a nice line in unsettling questions. Maybe we could include him in task force discussions?'

'That ever I should see the day when a Macdonald had a good word to say for a Campbell,' she mocked him.

'Ha, ha!'

Fleming was pleased by his scathing tone, even if he did look faintly scared once he'd said it. She slapped her wrist. 'Sorry. I know racist jokes aren't funny,' and saw him grin.

'Good work, Andy. We're not going to finger someone overnight, but I feel we're getting somewhere. Thanks.'

Fleming turned back to the reports she was preparing for Bailey and Menzies. Andy Mac was shaping up well, and it sounded as if the taciturn Campbell was an asset too.

It was half-past eight when Marjory Fleming left the Kirkluce HQ to head for home. Her mind was still on the case, though, as she drove past the entrance to the square round the war memorial.

There was a gathering of youngsters there, with a couple of motorbikes at the heart of the group. She frowned, remembering what Tam had said yesterday morning about the persecution of Christina Munro. It was really a matter for the uniforms, but Tam's uncharacteristic anxiety nagged at her and she stopped, backed into a side street and drove past again, more slowly this time.

Even if some of them were wearing the dreaded hoodies, they weren't committing a crime except the usual one of being young. She remembered, with a touch of envy, just how it had felt. She recognised a few of them, decent kids, just 'hanging out', with a lot of horseplay, the boys pushing and the girls giggling. No change there, then.

There was one girl standing talking to the bikers, a slim girl, laughing and tossing her fair hair flirtatiously. A girl who looked hideously familiar.

Transfixed, Marjory drove on mechanically. She knew where Cat was. Didn't all conscientious mothers know where their children were? She was having supper with her grandmother, then going to a netball practice, after which her friend Jenny's mother, who passed Mains of Craigie on the way home, would drop her at the road end.

Cat Fleming wasn't at a netball practice. Cat's mother made an illegal U-turn, drove back and turned into the square. She drew up alongside the motorbikes, leaned across to open the passenger door and said tersely to her startled daughter, 'Get in.'

Her face flaming and her eyes filling with angry tears, Cat complied. As they drove off, Marjory could see the others begin to laugh.

Cat, sinking down in her seat, saw them too. 'You deliberately humiliated me!' she cried.

'Fasten your seat belt. Yes. You lied to us. And the boys you were talking to are on their way to having a police record.'

'So put me under arrest, why don't you?'

Breathing deeply, Marjory turned out into the main road, making herself look both ways with extra care, since in her present frame of mind she might miss a ten-ton truck bearing down on her at ninety miles an hour.

'I'm willing to listen to a grovelling apology. Otherwise, it might be a good idea to say nothing until I've discussed with your father where we go from here.'

In cold silence, they drove out to Mains of Craigie.

10

'Enjoy your fish, Mr Salaman?' the waiter asked, stopping by the table where a young man was dining alone. Like he cared; this place was dying on its feet.

The dining-room of the country house hotel, painted in a historically authentic but oppressive deep red, was all but empty. Of the thirty tables with their crisp white cloths, shining glasses and deep red carnations, only three were occupied. Retired couples were at the other two, carrying on desultory conversations in muted, middle-class voices.

Zack Salaman looked down at his plate, an oblong plate with flared edges, on which there remained most of a sea bass, still resting on a pile of indeterminate greenish vegetables and surrounded by a pattern of drizzled balsamic vinegar. 'As you see,' he said coldly. 'My compliments to the chef.'

Sarcastic bastard! Keeping his face studiously blank, the waiter removed the plate. 'Thank you, sir. I'll pass that on. Shall I bring you the dessert menu?'

Salaman shuddered visibly. 'No. Coffee. Black.' Then he said, 'On second thoughts, perhaps not. Is there a decent Italian restaurant in Kirkluce?'

The waiter was tempted to suggest the chippie in Market Street which had a fine line in deep-fried pizza, but he needed the job for another few weeks. 'I couldn't say, I'm afraid.'

'Is there a night porter?' Salaman asked.

'Not in that sense, sir. There is a key with your room key –

there.' He gestured towards the bunch of keys lying on the table.

'Of course. I should have guessed from everything else. Perhaps you could ask your manager some time precisely how this could be described as a luxury hotel?'

He walked out. The waiter shrugged, and moved on to the nearby table where one of the elderly couples was looking on disapprovingly. The lady, with greying curls and a plump, kindly face, had finished every scrap of her Death by Chocolate in Three Variations.

'That,' she said, in ringing tones, 'was absolutely delicious!' Then, as Salaman reached the door she added, sotto voce, 'Foreign, of course. So I suppose you have to make allowances.'

Tam MacNee had soaked up local gossip until he felt saturated. And if they didn't let him back to work soon, he'd find himself with a drink problem as well as everything else.

He'd had no joy at the Salutation. He'd gone home early for his tea, then Bunty had wanted to bend his ear about her youngest sister – a sparky girl, and the only one of her family Tam had any time for – who was enjoying her youth rather too enthusiastically. By the time he'd given her the benefit of his considered advice ('Och, the lassie's fine! Leave her alone.') and walked back to the pub, there wasn't an officer around. Since the Salutation's only real attraction was its proximity to the Kirkluce HQ, he drank up and left for the more congenial Cutty Sark.

He could always count on finding a few of his cronies there, but by this stage, they were reacting as if the murder investigation was one of those reality shows Bunty liked and Tam couldn't stand: life, in his experience, was hard enough without deliberately making it worse – and if suffering was your thing, why not just follow Ayr United?

It was a waste of time, even if it was doing wonders for his aim at the darts board. He'd just decided to finish up his pint and go home to get Brownie points from Bunty for having an early night, when the door opened and to his surprise and delight, Andy Macdonald, normally a Salutation man, appeared.

'Andy!' MacNee hailed him. 'You're a stranger! What's yours? I'm buying.'

From the expression on the other sergeant's face, MacNee could see that Andy Mac's sole reason for being here was a suspicion that Tam would have the Salutation staked out. He was hovering uncomfortably just inside the door.

'I only looked in to see if Tansy was here,' he said unconvincingly. 'She mentioned she was going out for a drink this evening – I'd maybe better—'

'She's not here. I am. Pint?'

Feebly, Macdonald agreed. MacNee drained his glass and ordered two pints of Special.

'Look, there's that wee table by the window come free. You go and sit down and I'll bring them over.'

With a resigned shrug, Macdonald complied, but as MacNee brought the drinks to the table, he got his retaliation in first. 'You're looking at me as if you're a cat and I'm a mouse with a wee label round my neck saying, "Enjoy!". Well, forget it. I've had my orders. You're not in on this until you've a piece of paper signed by the doctor. It's for your own good – and God help me if Big Marge passes and sees me fraternising with the enemy.'

MacNee sat down and took a sip of his beer, with exaggerated dignity, before answering. 'Boot's on the other foot, the way I see it.'

Macdonald looked at him narrowly. 'You mean, you think you know something we don't know?'

'I never said you were stupid.'

'And so you're wanting something in exchange?'

'Do I look like Santa Claus? What about it?'

Macdonald was always cautious. 'How do you know we don't know about what you know anyway?'

'Oh, I know.' MacNee sounded smug.

'But I don't.' Macdonald was stubborn, too.

MacNee eyed him with considerable irritation. 'Take my word for it – this is something you won't even have considered. There's only three people know the facts, and one of them's dead. And I probably know most of what you could tell me anyway – half an hour at the bar's enough to find out everything the polis have done today.'

'Oh, not quite everything. Not nearly everything, in fact.' It was Macdonald's turn to look smug.

MacNee's resolve to play it cool snapped. 'Let's cut the cackle. If I can point you in a direction you hadn't thought of, will you tell me what's going on?'

'Big Marge will—'

'Have your guts for garters. I know. But she's not going to find out. You're just going to come up with this brilliant new angle, suggested by a source you're not prepared to disclose. OK?'

'I suppose so.' Macdonald shook his head helplessly. 'But you go first.'

'I'll trust you.' MacNee told him what Annie Brown had said about Pete Spencer's little operation, and Macdonald pursed his lips in a silent whistle. 'That certainly didn't come our way. And he's got form, hasn't he? If the Colonel was planning to shop him, he'd have a powerful reason for wanting him out the way. I'll make a point of seeing him tomorrow.'

'Good. Now it's your turn. I want to know about Farquharson. He's the obvious suspect. There's his uncle all set to refuse an offer of serious money, and with him being the heir—'

'Ah, but is he?'

'He isn't?' MacNee was startled. 'It's been left to a cat-and-dog home, has it? Or, wait a minute – Ellie Burnett? There was a suggestion of a bit of the hochmagandy going on with the two of them—'

'Guess again.' Macdonald was enjoying himself now, but MacNee gave him a look which made him say hastily, 'All right, all right. The heir's his grandson, Zack Salaman – a Malaysian corporate lawyer working in London. The Colonel had a bit on the side when he was serving out there in the Fifties.'

'A *grandson*? Malaysian? So that would explain the photos!' MacNee exclaimed. Well, well – the Colonel's halo was fairly slipping.

Macdonald looked at him with respect. 'How the hell did you know about the photos? You're good, I'll give you that.'

MacNee tapped his nose. 'I have my sources. So, I guess he'd be the lad I saw going into the motorbike showroom this afternoon. Very slick, driving a top-of-the-range Mercedes.'

'The showroom – Johnny Black. I wonder . . .' Frowning, Macdonald broke off.

'Go on,' MacNee urged him. 'We're getting somewhere now.'

'We know Salaman employed a private detective from Glasgow to track down his grandfather, and he met the Colonel less than six months ago. He has a contact in Kirkluce, but he wasn't willing to say who it was, or give us the detective's name. Very touchy about it, the boss said.

'I seem to remember Black was new to the area when I went into the showroom one day, and I know when that was, because it was just after my thirtieth birthday in March.'

MacNee grinned sardonically. 'Checking out the Harley Davidson, were you? Feeling your youth slipping away? Terrible thing, old age.'

'You should know. But someone living in London wouldn't

be thinking about buying a bike up here. So why would Salaman be going in there, unless it was Black who was still working for him?'

' "Working"?' MacNee raised his eyebrows.

'Salaman has what sounds like a rock-solid alibi for Saturday night.'

'Hmm. It would have to be worth Black's while, though, to throw up a business in Glasgow. Otherwise, why hang around here?'

'Exactly. It's a nothing job in the showroom – though of course he's got a workshop there and someone said he helps run the motocross at Ravenshill as well. We could be on to something here, Tam!'

MacNee was frowning. 'There's just one thing,' he said slowly. 'Ellie Burnett. I keep thinking she's in this, somewhere. Have you seen her doing her singing slot here in the pub?'

'Sure. Hasn't everyone?'

'There's something about her gets to you. And this morning, when I went to the Craft Centre – oh, only as a customer, that's all,' he put in, in response to Macdonald's quizzical look, 'Black and Ossian Forbes-Graham were having a stramash about her. And I saw Black with her when she was singing here on Saturday night. If he'd come down on the job for Salaman, and fancied her . . .'

'You believe in love, Tam, do you?' Macdonald, heart-whole as yet, looked at him with some amusement.

There were not many people who had seen Tam MacNee look embarrassed, but it wasn't a question he'd ever been asked before and he was an honest man. 'Yeah, suppose so,' was all he said. Then, 'Bloody hell!'

His voice was drowned out by the roar of two motorbikes, racing along the High Street. As the roar faded, Macdonald said, 'Where are Traffic when you need them? They'll kill themselves – or someone else!'

MacNee was on his feet. 'I think that's trouble, and I think it's partly down to me – at least, if they're going where I think they are. Where's your car, Andy?'

'Round at my flat. Ten minutes, if we hurry. But—'

'Never mind "but". It's nearer than mine. I'll explain – I want to catch them at it, before there's a disaster.'

Dylan Burnett hadn't wanted to come tonight. He really envied Gordon Gloag, who could say that his father would kill him if there was any more trouble. Dylan didn't even know where the funfair was at the moment, and anyway Jason Jamison wasn't the type to come the heavy, given his own attitude to the polis.

Barney had been, like, mental since this afternoon. He couldn't take anyone dissing him, and there, in front of a dozen of the other kids, a wee man half his size had made the three of them look rubbish. He'd scared them all, Barney too, even if he was trying to cover it up.

But the minute he'd gone, Barney'd started acting like it had just been a joke. Then he said, 'I'd been kind of thinking we might hang out there tonight. Say hi to the old bag. She's probably missing us. OK, dudes?'

That was when Gordon had said his piece and Dylan saw Barney sneer, and heard a whisper and a titter from one of the girls. So what could he do but look cool and say, 'Sure, I'm safe.'

Later, though, he'd tried to tell Barney he was crazy. 'That guy will get us locked up and throw away the key.'

Barney's lip curled again. 'Feart, are you? Away home to your mammy.'

'No,' Dylan protested. 'Just, maybe, wait a bit, till he's forgotten—'

'Look.' Barney's voice was elaborately patient. 'Let's use some smarts here. He'll think he's scared us off, OK? In a few days, he might reckon we'd try it on again, that we'll think he's forgotten, like you said. He won't expect it tonight. We make this the last visit, and we make it good. It's a no-brainer. So they guess it's us? Guess isn't proof, when we're long gone.'

Dylan had been worried enough to persist. 'So she describes us—'

'With helmets on? Do us a favour. There's plenty guys have bikes – bet she can't recognise the make, even. And it's all round that we're up for it. You want to be the one who's chicken?'

Why hadn't Dylan said, 'You go yourself, if you like'? Sometimes he got the feeling Barney needed someone tagging on behind to feel comfortable, and if he didn't agree it wouldn't happen. But somehow he hadn't. Barney always called the shots.

Dylan had gone home feeling a bit sick. He was scared what he'd find there too, but when he let himself into the flat his mother was in the living-room kitchen, looking sort of white and rigid, but she'd asked him what he wanted for supper, in almost the normal way. Then suddenly she said, 'I was wondering if we could maybe find out where your dad is just now. You could go and spend some time with him.'

Dylan stared at her. She'd never said that before, had always tried to find reasons why he shouldn't go, even when it wasn't term-time, like it was now.

'Why?' he asked blankly.

A little colour came into Ellie's cheeks. 'Maybe you need a man around, like you said yourself. I'm not happy about what you've been doing, you and Barney Kyle.'

He knew she'd blamed Barney for the police coming round. Barney's mother blamed Dylan. They'd had a good snigger about mothers.

'Barney's OK,' he said defensively, then an idea struck him. 'Here! Is this about you and Johnny? You trying to get rid of me, because I'll be in the way? I wouldn't, I guarantee. He's cool.'

Ellie turned away. 'That's – that's nothing to do with it. I just wish – oh, what's the use?' She sounded very tired as she went to fetch a packet of beef burgers from the freezer. 'Do you want chips?'

'Just a bun. I'm going out again.'

'Where? What are you going to do?'

Sullenly he said, 'Just hang out in the square, with the other kids.'

His mother's eyes fixed on him as though they might pierce a window into his thoughts. He shifted in his seat and she said sharply, 'You're not going out to Christina Munro's again, are you?'

' 'Course not,' he muttered, but he knew he'd gone red.

She went very still. Then she said, 'As if everything isn't terrible enough, you're going to end up in jail—'

It was an uncomfortable echo of what the policeman had said. Dylan pushed his chair back. 'Forget the burgers. I'm not hungry now,' he said over his shoulder, and left.

He'd gone to the chippie and now, here they were, waiting for the right moment to go, as Barney saw it. He'd been there ahead of Dylan and was sitting astride his bike now, doing the gallus bit to a couple of admiring girls.

Dylan didn't feel gallus. Being wild, bold and cheeky didn't square with having a dry mouth and a sinking feeling inside. It was a bad moment when Cat Fleming's mother appeared and dragged her away – everyone knew Cat's mum was in the polis – but Barney said she wouldn't drop them in it. 'She never tells her mum anything,' he said, and Dylan found he believed him.

'Right?' Barney said, revving his engine, and 'Right,' Dylan replied, putting on his helmet, and then they were off, to a chorus of mocking cheers.

The speed alone was exciting, and the looks of alarm, too, from passers-by as they tore down the High Street, along to Wester Seton which was just outside the thirty-mile limit. He got scared himself when he swung a bit too recklessly on to the farm track and the bike wobbled, but he saved himself and, with Barney ahead, covered the short distance up to the farm rather more slowly.

As before, the greyhound heard them first. Christina Munro had allowed herself to become absorbed in a play about the Second World War on the radio: after a trouble-free night, and Tam MacNee's visit, she had begun to hope that perhaps they had been discouraged, that her turn had passed and some other poor soul was now their victim.

Hearing the sound of the engines herself, as they came up the short farm track from the main road, was a bitter blow.

And they were bolder this time. This time, they began by banging on every window and every door. She cowered inside, so paralysed by fear that she could not even reassure the shivering, whimpering dog.

With a roar of engines, they circled the house, once, twice. Then they stopped. That was worse, because with the windows shuttered she had no idea where they were or what they were doing.

After that the banging outside started. Christina could tell, from the direction of the sound that they were attacking the barn where she had shut up the donkeys for their protection. She could hear the donkeys start to move restlessly, then to whicker, then one of them brayed in alarm. Then another, again and again. Christina wanted to cover her ears, not hear what was happening to these creatures, so ill-treated before they came under her protection.

Protection? What sort of protection was this? She owed it to them, innocent, helpless creatures. What did it matter to her what happened now? Her life was all but over. Surely, with nothing to lose, she could show the merest fraction of the courage of her own contemporaries, the young men who had offered their lives to protect the weak and helpless.

Christina walked to the door where her loaded shotgun stood and picked it up. With trembling, twisted fingers she turned the lock, pulled back the bolts and flung open the door.

Dylan was enjoying himself now. It gave you a real buzz to know that behind the shutters the old bag was cowering, afraid to show her face, even if a tiny bit of you felt ashamed. They both banged on the windows and doors, then Dylan, high on the adrenalin of violence, looked round to see what else they could do. Find a stone, maybe, to break windows – just a couple, as a reminder . . .

But Barney had other ideas. He'd pushed up his visor and Dylan could see an evil grin on his face as he brought out a solid wooden mallet from one of the panniers. He swung the mallet round his head. 'Nicked this from my mum's workshop. Come on!'

He ran across the yard to the barn, Dylan close behind. It had two great doors, fastened by a metal bar and a serious-looking padlock, but round the side there was a window, low down, blocked with half-a-dozen stout slats of wood. Beyond, you could see the shapes of the donkeys shifting uneasily.

'Stand back!' Barney shouted, swinging the mallet in an arc, to hit the slats. One splintered, and a donkey whinnied, starting back from it, then began braying in fright.

The next blow knocked one slat out completely and the other donkeys, terrified too, joined in – a fine sound! Barney was laughing so hard he didn't hear, as Dylan did, the shaking voice shouting, 'Get back from there or I shoot!'

Dylan swung round. The door to the cottage had opened and the old bag herself was standing there, wearing a crocheted hat which he recognised as one of his mother's making. Her eyes were wild, she was shaking, and she was holding a shotgun. She looked completely crazy.

Dylan swore. Then he yelled, 'Barney, for God's sake, stop! She's got a gun. Let's get out of here!'

He didn't wait for his friend. He sprinted past her, threw himself on to his bike and heard the sound of a shot just as he took off, as if all the devils in hell were after him, chancing his neck on the rough surface. He made it safely to the road, but didn't stop till he was round the next bend, almost at the thirty-mile limit. His heart pounding, he cut his engine, waiting for Barney to catch up. Then he stiffened. Was that another shot?

She wouldn't really have fired *at* them, of course. Not in cold blood. She'd have been firing into the air, just as a threat, to scare them off. And she'd done that, all right. Barney could suit himself, but Dylan was never setting foot in the place again.

Maybe Barney hadn't been as scared as he was, and had taken the farm road more slowly than Dylan had. At least, he hoped to God that was why he hadn't appeared.

Still shaking, Christina Munro went back into the house. There was a half-bottle of brandy in one of the cupboards; she fetched it, and a tumbler. As she poured in a couple of inches, the bottle clinked on the edge of the glass, and her teeth knocked against it too as she took a mouthful, then another, grimacing at the fierceness of the cheap spirit. She sat down on the edge of her chair and emptied the glass. The dog, which had stayed inside, trotted across to sit pressed against her leg and she stroked its soft fur absent-mindedly.

Warmth was running through her now. She hadn't shut

the door and outside, apart from the still restless movements of the donkeys, all was quiet. She went to check on them again; they were alarmed, not hurt, and she spoke to them soothingly before she came back in and closed her door. She didn't lock it. Then she folded back the window shutters, and evening light flooded the room. That was better.

The radio play was still going on, with the sounds of gunfire and men's voices, shouting orders. She'd probably lost the thread by now, but she went back to her chair to listen anyway.

Still not quite sure what he was doing there, DS Andy Macdonald drove out of Kirkluce, MacNee silent and tense at his side. He'd asked, of course, what was going on and Tam had explained about the neds who were persecuting Christina Munro, but he hadn't been very explicit.

Macdonald was just slowing down to turn into Wester Seton when a motorbike erupted out of the entrance in front of him. He swore, wrenching the steering wheel to the left; the bike braked, swerved across the road and wobbled sideways, throwing its rider on to a grassy bank.

Macdonald and MacNee were out of the car before the bike's wheels had stopped spinning. The rider, looking to be unhurt, sat up as they approached and took off his helmet. He was ashen with shock.

MacNee looked at him with some distaste. 'Not very clever, Burnett. What are you doing here? And where's your pal Kyle?'

The boy seemed hardly able to speak. Then, 'Help!' he said, bizarrely.

The policemen glanced at each other. 'What's wrong, son?' Macdonald said more gently.

'It's – it's Barney. There.' Dylan pointed up the track. 'It's – horrible—' He began to shudder uncontrollably.

Macdonald took off, MacNee at his heels. Just a few yards

short of the main road, another motorbike had toppled, part of it pinning down a helmeted figure lying on its side in a pool of blood. Macdonald was aware of MacNee's voice muttering, 'Please God this is an accident,' as they reached it. Macdonald lifted the bike off and dumped it to one side.

The helmet was still on, but this was Barney Kyle, presumably. From the front there was no sign of injury, apart from foam-flecked blood at the corner of his mouth. The back—

There was a hole in the back of his denim jacket towards the left-hand side, and the wound beneath was still pumping bright red arterial blood.

'He's alive,' MacNee said sharply, grabbing his mobile from his pocket and dialling 999. 'Ambulance. This is police. Top priority,' he snapped, then impatiently gave details.

'Twenty minutes,' he said, switching it off. 'That's the best they can offer.'

Macdonald was kneeling at the boy's side. 'Five would probably be too late anyway. Nothing we can do.' He stood up, his cream chinos bloodied to the knees. The two men watched, helpless, as life ebbed away.

MacNee was one of the hardest men Andy Macdonald knew, but his face was green. 'Phone the boss,' he said. 'I think I'm to blame for this.' Then he turned to the side of the track and vomited into the hedgerow.

11

Fiona Farquharson had been in a state of silent rage ever since the lawyer's phone call that afternoon. It showed in the way she banged the pots together on the stove, and she'd chipped a Nigella Lawson bowl, one of a set Andrew had given her last Christmas when she'd rather have had a bottle of Chanel No. 5. She just might throw the bowl at Giles when he deigned to come home.

The quiche was past its best. The ones she'd cooked to be cut into cocktail-sized squares for the Forbes-Grahams' party tomorrow night had been taken out long ago. Of course, she and Giles could have had theirs cold, but there was a vindictive satisfaction in producing it dry and overcooked, with the subtext that he had forced her to suffer by his lack of consideration. It would also give her an excuse for refusing to eat. She wasn't hungry, couldn't imagine feeling hungry ever again. She was so filled with rage there was barely room to breathe, let alone eat.

Fiona's eyes were glittering dangerously when Giles appeared at last. 'Where the hell have you been?' she screamed as the back door opened.

He was looking dishevelled, with dirty streaks on his face and mud caking his trousers. 'Some bullocks got out from the field on the road, and the stockman and I had a helluva job rounding them up,' he said tiredly. 'I need a drink – you want one?'

'You'd better have your supper first,' she said with deliberate cruelty. 'It's pretty much ruined already. And why didn't you let me know? You do have a mobile phone.'

For once Giles stood his ground. 'If it's spoiled already, it can wait while I have a drink. And anyway, I came in to tell you what had happened and your car wasn't there. Where were *you*?'

He had managed to wrong-foot her. Fiona snapped back, 'Where do you think? Taking Gemma back home, of course. She came out like she always does to help me prepare for the Forbes-Grahams' party tomorrow – I suppose you do remember I told you? The sort of thing that I'm going to have to do as long as I can stagger to the stove. Thanks to Andrew Carmichael.'

She spat out the name, but Giles didn't even seem to hear. He went to the cupboard where the whisky was kept and filled a tumbler. He had drunk half of it before he even sat down.

An ambulance and two patrol cars had arrived at Wester Seton by the time Fleming got there, blocking the entrance to the farm track. She parked on the main road, behind a car she recognised as Macdonald's. It was almost completely dark and the cars' headlights were trained on a green sheet covering something on the ground. Two paramedics were talking to DS Macdonald; as she approached, she heard him say, 'You can't move him. This is a murder scene.'

A uniformed officer came towards her, a neat man with a dapper moustache, and she recognised Sergeant Christie from the station at Newton Stewart. 'Evening, ma'am,' he said gravely. 'I'm afraid we have a tragedy here.'

Fleming had had dealings with Christie before. He was pompous, but a conscientious officer who, if lacking in imagination, could be relied on to do everything by the book – a useful attribute, in such circumstances.

'I'm not clear exactly what's happened. Brief me.'

'The farmer's Christina Munro. Elderly lady, something of a recluse, as I understand it. A group of youths has been subjecting her to a campaign of intimidation.'

'Yes,' Fleming said hollowly. 'I heard about that.' And she hadn't done anything about it at the time, hadn't seen it as a priority in comparison with the murder investigation.

'Tonight, apparently, two of them came back, and she seems to have had a brainstorm and gone after them with a shotgun. The victim is Barney Kyle – shot in the back as he was riding away on his bike. The other lad, Dylan Burnett – he's in the car over there with a woman constable.'

'Unhurt?'

'He's in shock, seemingly, but otherwise he's all right. Luckier than he deserves to be.'

'We can be thankful for that, at least.' Fleming was suffering a fair degree of shock herself. She had been told only that a youth had died, in suspicious circumstances; to discover that, like Andrew Carmichael, he had been gunned down was horrifying. And the worst of it was that perhaps it could have been prevented.

Was she to assume that it was at Christina's hands that Carmichael too had met his death? Presumably, though a motive wasn't immediately obvious. No doubt one would appear when they looked into it. Could Christina, in her youth, have been another of the Colonel's extra-marital interests, say? They must be much of an age.

'Where is she now?' Fleming asked.

'In her cottage. My constable and one from the other car are with her now; I think DS Macdonald has told her to stay there for questioning.'

'He seems to be finished with the paramedics now. I'll go and have a word with him. Thanks, sergeant.'

She set off, shielding her eyes with her hands as she stepped into the glare of the headlights. She didn't see Tam MacNee until he spoke at her side.

'Boss.'

She spun round. 'Tam? What the hell are you doing here?' She was angry; if he'd heard something was going on, and followed the cars, she'd flay him alive. Or suspend him for a week, after he was cleared to come back.

'I wanted to speak to you before you went in there. I've something I need to say.'

He was very serious, disquietingly so. 'Get it over with, then,' she said with some unease.

'This needn't have happened. I told you I was worried about what Christina might do.'

'I remember. You passed it on, and it wasn't your responsibility after that, Tam. You're on sick leave, remember.'

'Oh, like I haven't noticed? But what I didn't report was that when I visited her she'd a loaded gun parked by her door. Going out to pot rabbits for the cats' tea, she said, but she was half-daft with fear, maybe dangerous, even. I should have taken it off her then – or,' he corrected himself, 'if you're going to nitpick, said what I'd seen and had someone else take it off her. But I never thought she'd do anything more than fire it over their heads to scare them, and to tell you straight, I thought it wouldn't do the little bastards any harm to get a fright. If she felt she was totally helpless, she could have taken a coronary next time they tried it on and she didn't deserve that.'

Fleming was silent for a moment. Then she said, 'So you should have reported what you saw, but as I said at the time, Tam, you were acting in a private capacity. No one expects the public to police the gun laws.'

'There's more.'

'More?' she asked bleakly.

'This afternoon I went into Johnny Black's motorbike showroom, where there were a load of school kids hanging around. Burnett and Kyle and Gloag were there, and I said I was police and gave them laldie. Warned them that farmers have guns and scared folk sometimes go crazy. I reckoned I'd put the frighteners on Gloag and Burnett, but Kyle's a different type – could just have taken it as a challenge. I was in the pub having a drink with Andy Mac when I saw the two bikes go tearing along the High Street and I thought if we caught them at it we'd be able to get them in court. We arrived just as Burnett had found out what had happened and was on his way for help.'

'I – see. And there were a lot of people around who heard you?'

'Black and a guy called Dan Simpson were in the showroom as well as a lot of bairns I didn't really register.'

'Even so, we can hope it won't be a problem – at least, not an official one. What you feel yourself – well, that's something else.

'I'm feeling guilty too, that I didn't move on the whole thing sooner, but hindsight's a wonderful thing. Anyway,' she said decisively, 'there's no time to wallow in guilt. Give one of the uniforms a modified statement – no need to mention more than that you were worried about the situation – and try to forget about it. What's done is done.'

She knew, as she walked away from him, that it was small comfort. There could be trouble, and they both knew it. And while she didn't have time to wallow in guilt, Tam at the moment had all the time in the world.

Christina Munro looked very tiny and frail, sitting on a wooden kitchen chair beside two officers in their body armour gilets. They hadn't known what they were coming to, except that it was a shooting, and calling, 'Come out with your hands on your head!' through a megaphone at a safe distance while they waited for backup from an armed response unit was an entirely new and distinctly alarming experience. When the little old lady appeared, too arthritic to get her hands higher than her ears, tension had evaporated in snorts of stifled laughter. She had pointed to a shotgun, standing behind the door. Later, DS Macdonald had cautiously checked that the safety catch was on, then wrapped it for testing.

She'd admitted that she'd fired it, almost gleefully. 'I only fired in the air,' she said. 'Just to scare them, that was all.'

They could smell the drink on her breath. DS Macdonald had told them to sit with her, listen to anything she had to say, but not ask any questions until he came back. The old biddy had sat in tranquil silence, stroking a cat that had jumped up on to her knee. It was all a bit surreal.

The officers stood up when DI Fleming appeared, with DS Macdonald behind her. Christina looked up. 'I know I'm in trouble,' she said defiantly. 'I shouldn't have done it. But I'm not sorry.'

Without making any response, Fleming looked at her, then looked round the room at the cats, one on the woman's knee, one curled up in a chair and one watching from the top of the dresser with an air of interested detachment. A very pretty greyhound had taken up its post at the old woman's side.

Fleming turned. 'Caution her and take her in,' she said. 'And see to it that someone takes care of the animals. I'll see her at headquarters later.'

'See someone takes care of the animals!' Andy Macdonald said bitterly to Tam MacNee, when Christina Munro had been taken off in one of the patrol cars. 'All very well for her to say that. Where am I expected to find someone, this time of night?'

MacNee, waiting to give his statement when someone was free to take it, looked round with an experienced eye. 'The cats'll be fine till the morning, then you can call in animal welfare. The dog—' He hesitated.

It was standing by the door, where it had last seen its mistress, tail tucked in between its legs, every line of its body drooping.

'It's a bonny dog.' Macdonald clicked his fingers. 'Here, boy,' he said, but the animal didn't seem to hear him.

'Poor beast,' MacNee said. 'I don't even know its name. I'd better see if it's on the collar.'

As he approached, the dog turned its head, and then, perhaps recognising a former acquaintance, twitched the very tip of its tail. When MacNee stroked it, and turned the collar to see if there was identification, it leaned into him, as if grateful for the contact.

'It's taken to you, Tam,' Macdonald said, amused.

'Dogs take to anyone they think'll give them food,' he said gruffly, but he went on stroking its narrow head. 'Och, I'll take him back to Bunty. She's used to strays.'

'Put it in my car and I'll give you both a lift home when we're finished up here. I'll need to get back to the boss – that's the pathology team arriving now.'

Macdonald went out, leaving MacNee in the kitchen feeling useless and excluded, alone with the unhappy dog and his own wretched thoughts.

'Suppose you tell me exactly what happened, Christina,' Fleming said gently to the old woman sitting on the other side of the table in the stark impersonality of the interview room. Andy Macdonald had gone through the formalities for the video recording, and been told her full name – Christina Margaret Munro – her address, and her age, seventy-six.

She was still wearing the maroon crocheted hat and its incongruously cheerful flowers quivered as she shook her head in a movement of denial.

'They said something about murder,' she said. 'I didn't kill anyone.'

Fleming and Macdonald exchanged glances, the thought occurring to both of them that it might be safer to have a medical check before proceeding. 'I want to be quite sure that you understood the caution, Christina. We can pause here, if there's a problem.'

That got a surprisingly spirited response. ' 'Course I *understood*,' she said fiercely. 'I may be old but I'm not stupid.'

'No, no,' Fleming said hastily.

'It's just it doesn't make any sense. Who's dead? If someone's dead, it's nothing to do with me.' Her voice was querulous.

'Suppose you tell me exactly what happened this evening,' Fleming said again.

Christina gave a shuddering sigh. 'It all started a while ago,' she began. As she detailed a history of persecution by Kyle and his friends, Fleming, at least, began to feel uncomfortable. The six hours of questioning before a suspect was entitled to have access to a lawyer was vital to their conviction rate, but usually it was a teeth-pulling operation to get information. Now, Christina was freely making admissions which any lawyer would have warned her were most unwise. A jury might have sympathy for what she had suffered, but shooting in the back a seventeen-year-old who was riding away on his bike wasn't self-defence.

'It was because of the donkeys,' she said, at last reaching the events of the evening. 'They were attacking the donkeys' barn – at least one of them was.'

'Kyle?' Macdonald asked.

'I didn't know who they were. They both had helmets on. And the donkeys were screaming. They're old, they've had hard lives. The only comfort they've had is since I took them in.' Her voice was fierce. 'If those savages got to them, they were going to hurt them, and I had to protect them from that.'

'How did you know they would hurt them?' Fleming asked.

Christina stopped for a second. 'I – I suppose I didn't *know*. But they were the worst they'd ever been this time, more violent, and I knew if they didn't do it this time, they would the next. So I fetched my gun.'

Fleming hated to ask the next question. 'Was it loaded?'

'Yes. I'd decided what I was going to do, next time they came. I had it right by the door.'

Admission of premeditation. Fleming could almost hear Macdonald groan. He was a decent man: Will Wilson, or Tansy even, might not have felt the burden of the woman's naive disclosures quite so much. She certainly felt it herself and it was all she could do to ask the next question.

'So, when they came, and you felt the donkeys were threatened, you went out with your gun?'

Christina nodded.

'And what happened then?'

'I warned the one who was attacking the barn to stand back. The other one shouted something, then he ran past me and went off on his bike. The one at the barn paid no attention until I fired the gun into the air. Then he turned – he was scared. Served him right,' she said with satisfaction. 'He ran away and got on his bike. Then I went back inside.'

Macdonald said gently, 'Christina, had you been drinking?'

She looked, as she would have said herself, black affronted. 'Drinking? Me? A wee sherry at the New Year, that's all I ever take. But I've brandy in the house for medicinal purposes, and I was that shaken up I had some, after.'

Fleming knew she had to say it. As a police officer, she had little sympathy with the view that the perpetrator should be given more consideration than the victim, but the words almost stuck in her throat as she said, 'After you'd killed him?'

Christina looked at her pityingly. 'How could I have killed him? I fired up in the air, he was wearing one of those helmet things. Even if it had hit him coming down, it wouldn't have done him any harm.'

'Did you fire the other barrel?' Fleming asked.

'No. I just fired once. That was all. I don't know what this is about. I'm an old woman – it's all very confusing.'

Abruptly, the inspector got up. 'DI Fleming is terminating the interview at this point. Stay where you are, Christina.' Macdonald switched off the tape and followed her out.

'What do you make of that?' she demanded.

'You tell me, boss.'

Fleming sighed. 'I suppose I have to. My job, not yours. She's admitted to motive, means, opportunity – is there some way it could have been a freak accident?' Then, seeing Macdonald's expression, she said, 'No, no, of course it couldn't. I know that. It was a direct shot, at comparatively close range, they told me, but given that he was alive when you and Tam found him—' She broke off, frowning.

'How come you and Tam were together? You know what I said—'

'No, no,' Macdonald said hastily. 'We both happened to be in the Cutty Sark when Tam heard the bikes going along the High Street and as he didn't have his own car, he thought mine would be nearer. That's all.'

Fleming was far from certain that it was all, but this was hardly the moment to pursue it. 'Where do we go from here?' she said.

'Question her for another five hours, charge her or let her go on police bail,' Macdonald said promptly, and got an acid look from his boss.

'I didn't ask what you would write if that was an exam question. I mean, what is your opinion as to which of these options we should pursue? It's all right, it's my decision. But I want to know what you think. One or the other. Just like that.'

She knew she was pushing him further than he wanted to go. But Andy Mac had to grow up; if he was going anywhere – and she had a feeling that he might – he had to learn about putting his neck on the block.

'I'd let her go on an undertaking to appear,' he said at last. 'I don't believe she killed someone, in cold blood, or that she's going to do a runner.'

'I don't either,' she said heavily. 'I'm going to play down the loaded gun and charge her with culpable homicide not murder, but I'm going to lock her up. And yes, that's a political decision. A young man has been killed. I know how the community will feel, and if she's to be bailed, I want it to be the Sheriff who decides. I'll hate doing it, but that's the job.

'But before we do that, we're going to ask her about the Colonel's death.'

Macdonald was startled. 'You don't think – oh well, I suppose . . .'

'Exactly. Two shootings barely a mile apart. What else can you think? You can't judge by appearances – who'd have guessed the Colonel would have an illegitimate Malaysian grandson? Maybe there was something between him and Christina at one time.'

'Hard to imagine, her looking like that,' Macdonald said with the merciless judgement of youth.

'She might have been pretty when she was young. Age does cruel things,' Fleming said, conscious of a slight defensiveness in her tone.

Macdonald was oblivious. 'Pretty? You think? So – back to some more self-incriminatory statements. Her brief will be tearing his hair out when he sees what she's said.'

When PC Sandy Langlands and Sergeant Linda Bruce arrived at Barney Kyle's home and rang the doorbell, there was no answer, though there was a light on behind the drawn curtains of an upstairs room. Langlands pressed the bell again, but there was still no response.

'I reckon someone's in there,' Bruce said. 'I thought maybe the curtain moved.'

'I'll try again.' He leaned on the bell this time, then banged on the door.

'Mrs Kyle!' Bruce shouted. 'Police. We need to speak to you urgently.'

That got no reaction either. The two officers retreated down the path and stood looking up at the window.

'Where do we go from here?' Bruce said helplessly.

'We can't exactly kick in the door then say, "Sorry about the damage, your son's dead,"' Langlands pointed out.

'Maybe I was wrong about the curtain. She could be out – she's hardly likely to refuse to open the door to the police.'

'Maybe. So – where would she be? The neighbours might know.'

The house next door was in darkness, but two doors along lights were on downstairs and the door was answered immediately by a young woman who looked at them first with alarm, then when they said they were trying to contact Mrs Kyle, with lively curiosity.

'Oh, if she's not in she's probably down at her workshop in the Craft Centre. She often works late. Is – is there something wrong?'

Langlands didn't answer. 'We'll try there. Thanks for your help, madam – sorry to disturb you.' They went back to the patrol car.

As he drove away, Bruce burst out, 'I really hate this kind of assignment! And I'd braced myself – now I'll have to get psyched up all over again.'

'I've never had to do it – tell someone their kid's dead,' Langlands admitted.

'Happens more often to female officers. Suppose they think

a woman being there will help somehow – as if anything could.'

'What do you say?'

'Make it quick, make it clear. Get the news out first, leave the sorries and the sympathy till after when it doesn't matter what you say, because they won't hear it anyway.'

It had come on to rain now, a dreary, persistent drizzling, and Langlands switched on the wipers as they drove in silence to the Craft Centre. There were lights showing behind the curtains of an upper flat above a shop to the right, but the shops themselves were in darkness, apart from the unit opposite the entrance, which was brilliantly lit so that the woman inside looked almost as if she were working in a stage-set. She had her back to them, sitting working at the bench that ran along the back of the shop.

They paused, watching her for a second. 'Look at her,' Bruce said. 'We know, she doesn't, that her world is about to fall apart. You're seeing the last happy moments of that poor woman's life.' She took a deep breath, then knocked on the door.

Romy Kyle jumped at the sound and looked over her shoulder, startled. As she saw the uniforms, a frown came over her face.

She put down what she had been working with and strode across to unlock the door. 'All right,' she said grimly. 'Hit me with it – what's Barney been doing now?'

It was shortly after midnight that the phone rang in Johnny Black's flat. He had been watching a late night film; he turned down the volume and picked it up.

He listened to the voice at the other end. 'I'll come round now,' he said. 'Don't worry – it'll be all right, I promise you. I'm on my way.'

* * *

It was only as Marjory Fleming drove home that the full impact of what had happened hit her. She hadn't had time before, her mind too full of procedure, and checks and questions to be asked and answered for there to be space for feelings.

A lad had died. Officers had gone to a house and told a mother that her son was dead. As a parent, you didn't dare to think about it. You had to put it out of your mind, because there was no way of arming yourself against what would follow.

And this particular boy had been a friend of Cat's, a friend who was undesirable in her parents' eyes, which of course made him particularly glamorous. That was natural enough. Marjory could remember her own defiant attempts to wind her father up, and she and Bill had assured each other that the phase would pass.

This changed everything. You never forgot the first time a friend your age died and you were forced to accept that youth and immortality were not inextricably linked after all. Cat would be stricken. She would need her mother's comfort, but would she accept it when only this evening – was that really just a few hours ago? – Marjory had spelled out her disapproval?

She'd have to be told in the morning, before she went to school. Marjory would do it herself, answer her questions honestly and try to help, but she was too analytical to believe she was likely to succeed. At least Cat had Bill and Janet, and Marjory would just have to accept rejection as the price she had to pay for being who she was and doing what she did.

And there was the worry about Tam, too. He had overstepped the mark, as Marjory had feared all along that he would. If he'd merely failed to report his concerns about Christina Munro's gun, it would never have come out, but after what he'd said to the kids in the afternoon – while claiming to be acting as a police officer – it might well emerge, and if it did a massive damage-limitation exercise would be called for.

She could only hope it would succeed. She hoped, too, that her uncomfortable doubts about Christina Munro were unjustified. She hoped that Bailey, the Chief Constable and the press wouldn't make her difficult life more difficult, after this second death. And she hoped – oh, how she hoped – that her problems with Cat wouldn't sour their relationship for ever.

So many hopes! And there was a cold, cynical voice inside her head, mocking the folly of optimism.

Romy Kyle had no idea of the passing of time. She sat on the stool behind the counter, her elbows on the surface and her chin propped on her hands, staring out into the darkness. It was raining hard now and the plate-glass window looked as if it was veiled in the tears she couldn't shed.

They hadn't stayed long. They'd told her what had happened and seemed almost alarmed by her calm questioning. 'Suspicious circumstances', they had called it, but it wasn't hard to see what had happened. If she'd read it in the newspaper she'd just have said they were asking for trouble and the poor woman had been driven beyond endurance. As it was, she felt such overpowering anger that she could barely ask what had happened to Dylan and Gordon. Gordon hadn't been there, it seemed; Dylan had escaped unhurt.

Dylan would. If it wasn't for Dylan – oh, she knew Barney looked like the leader, but she was his mother – oh God, she *had been* his mother, and if Dylan hadn't egged him on, Barney wouldn't have done it. Oh yes, she blamed Dylan, with that feckless mother of his. Ellie had just better not come with her sympathy, that was all, or she'd get more than she bargained for.

The police had offered to take her home, or fetch someone for her – her partner, a doctor, someone from Victim Support. The woman, looking at the little kitchen area at the back of the shop, had even offered to make tea, as if this was an appropriate response to tragedy. It was funny in a sick sort of way, and she knew they'd been disconcerted by her evident amusement. Romy had got rid of them by promising she'd call her partner.

She hadn't. Pete didn't really like Barney. Well, come to that she didn't much like him herself, the way he'd been lately. She loved him, though, loved him right to the core of her being. She thought of all the Barneys of the past – the tiny, furious baby who'd made her life a haze of exhaustion for months, the feisty toddler with his sudden wild affection, the bright, cheeky ten-year-old, the teenager who was going through the difficult stage— He'd never emerge from that now. Romy could have saved her breath, nagging at him to think about his future. He wasn't going to have one. Her throat was aching so that she could hardly swallow. She couldn't sit here all night; she'd better get herself home and break the news to Pete. How would he take it? Pete wasn't good with emotional demands.

With meticulous care, she checked that everything had been switched off – burning the place down wouldn't help – and put the silver she had been working with back in the safe. She set the alarm, put off the lights and went back to her car.

The wind had got up too now, and as she turned on to the main road, out of the shelter of the buildings, she could feel the car being buffeted by the squalls of rain. The anger had drained away and she felt cold, numb. Perhaps when she saw Pete, when he held out his arms to her, the tears would come, and that would relieve the pain in her neck and throat, which was radiating into her shoulders now.

It wasn't far. She drew up outside the house, which was in darkness. She looked at the dashboard clock: half-past two. Pete would be asleep, but she'd have to wake him. She needed him. She had started to shake and it took her three goes to get the key into the lock on the front door.

Romy stumbled up the stairs in the silent house. She didn't glance towards Barney's room, though the door was half-open on the chaos of carelessly discarded clothes and belongings. She wanted to be able to tell Pete what had happened before she fell apart. A tearing sob escaped her as she opened the door.

The room was dark, but in the light from the landing she could see that the bed was empty and that it hadn't been slept in. 'Pete!' she called, then screamed, 'Pete!' There was no answer, and Romy didn't need the wardrobe standing open to reveal the empty hangers to know that Pete had gone.

12

'Councillor Gloag says he would appreciate a word, ma'am.'

DI Fleming put the hand that wasn't holding the phone to her aching head. 'Tell him I'm tied up at the moment, will you? Give him my apologies—'

'I don't think I can, ma'am.' The Force Civilian Assistant's voice had the despairing tone of one caught between the upper and the nether millstones. 'He's – very insistent.'

'I see.' Fleming chewed her lip. Gloag was a man it was dangerous to ignore. 'Get someone to show him up, then.'

It hadn't been a good morning so far, and it looked set to get worse. She hadn't got to bed till two, and had slept so badly that getting up before six had been a positive pleasure. It was a dull morning, with a clay-coloured sky and the hills opposite the farmhouse grey with low cloud. She plodded down to the orchard through the puddles from last night's rain and released the grumbling, fussing hens, then realised with dismay there was one missing. Bill must have forgotten to count them in when he shut them up last night, and after Marjory had given them their mash she walked around, looking, and sure enough found feathers and the traces of a struggle in the mud. She hated foxes – nasty, sly, skulking beasts who would kill even when they had no need for food, but because they were cutesy had sentimental townies fighting for their animal rights. You didn't hear a lot about rights for rats, did you?

Things didn't improve. Marjory had to leave early for work, but she wanted to tell Cat herself what had happened, even if it meant waking her. Cat had been resentful at being disturbed, but as she heard the news, her eyes widened and filled. When her mother said, 'I'm so sorry, Cat – this is awful,' and tried to put her arms round her, Cat had flung herself face down in her pillow. Between sobs, she had thrown muffled accusations: 'Expect you're glad – you thought they were rubbish – probably give her a medal – no, *don't*!'

She had wriggled away from the hand her mother had tried to put on her heaving shoulders and Marjory found Bill at her side, shaking his head. She'd given up and gone downstairs, knowing she was only making matters worse. Attempting consolation, he'd suggested that by this evening Cat would be seeing it differently, but in the face of Marjory's withering 'Oh yeah?' agreed that there might be a problem.

Now she had a meeting with Bailey and Menzies scheduled at ten to discuss developments and a press statement to prepare, which it looked likely she would have to deliver. She had a morning briefing to do before that, and a post-mortem to attend afterwards. A difficult conversation with Gloag, The People's Representative, was about as welcome as gastro-enteritis.

The uniformed constable who had escorted Gloag up to her office said, in a studiously neutral voice, 'Councillor Gloag has some points he wishes to raise with you, ma'am,' and ushered him in.

Fleming rose and went over to shake hands. 'Councillor Gloag. Do take a seat.'

She took her own place behind the desk but before he could say anything she said, 'As you will appreciate, I have very little time to spare this morning. I have a meeting in ten minutes so perhaps we can deal with this as quickly as possible.'

Gloag's narrow mouth pursed disapprovingly. 'I trust you understand, inspector, that I am not here in any *private* capacity. I am here as The People's Representative and I trust that concerns I may wish to raise on their behalf will not be simply brushed out of the way for the sake of going to a *meeting*.' He said it as another person might have said 'taking a long lunch break'.

'Then we'd better not waste any time, sir,' she said sweetly. 'What are these concerns?'

Gloag settled back in his chair with an air of satisfaction. 'First of all, I want to know exactly what stage this investigation has reached, with this new atrocity.'

'We are pursuing several active lines of enquiry.'

He waited for her to go on; when she didn't, he said, 'That's hardly what I'd call information, inspector.'

'I'm afraid it's all I'm at liberty to give at the moment.'

He seemed almost incredulous. 'But I have explained to you – the public has a right to know! What steps are you taking? Is Miss Munro being charged with both murders, or is everyone still under some sort of cloud of suspicion? Even I, myself, was all but accused of involvement by one of your subordinates.'

He was curiously insistent in his demands. Why, Fleming wondered, was he so keen to know what the police were up to? She said blandly, 'I'm sure that was merely a misunderstanding. There are routine questions which our officers are obliged to ask.'

'Leaving that to one side, for the moment, you haven't answered my question. Has Miss Munro been charged?'

'I'm afraid I am not at liberty to discuss that.' She could go on blocking indefinitely.

Gloag wasn't pleased. His eyes narrowed. 'I'm not at all impressed by stonewalling, inspector, as I shall not hesitate to say, both to your superiors and to the press.

'But there is a much more serious matter I have to raise. I understand from my son Gordon that one of your sergeants suggested to the boys yesterday afternoon that Ms Munro might well attempt to shoot them. If he knew of this, and took no action, it is a very serious matter indeed.'

He wasn't wrong there. Fleming's stomach lurched, but she managed not to show her dismay. 'I'm afraid I can't say anything until I have looked into it. As far as I know, there was no officer who was detailed to speak to them yesterday – though, of course, there was a record of problems.'

Gloag waved away that point. 'Irrelevant. I had also, I may say, warned the detectives who interviewed me that Kyle and Burnett were heading for trouble, and were a pernicious influence on others, but I assume they took no action. Most fortunately, my son came and told me that he had no wish to get involved with this latest stupid prank and would be staying at home rather than going with them—'

'You mean,' Fleming interjected, 'that you knew another visit to Wester Seton was planned – and did nothing to stop it? Like warning the police, for instance?'

She managed to look shocked, and saw Gloag falter. His piggy eyes, which had been boring into her, slid away and he licked his lips. 'Well, that's to say – I had no evidence – and of course they might have changed their minds.'

'We would have been happy to take precautionary action. Especially since it might have averted tragedy. This is most unfortunate – most,' Fleming said gravely, and saw Gloag squirm. As she went on, 'And apart from anything else, I feel that the public would be astonished to learn that in your position you were not concerned to stop the persecution of an elderly lady,' she saw a fine film of sweat appear on his forehead.

'I – I think I may have given a false impression. By the time Gordon told me about this, it would have been too late.'

'I see. Well, we shall be talking to him, of course.' She got to her feet. 'I'm afraid I must get to my meeting.'

'Of course, of course.' Gloag got up. 'And I trust you understand that my only motive for coming in this morning was concern for the public interest. Nothing personal at all.'

'We all have our jobs to do, and I'm sure we understand each other.'

'Of course, of course. Nothing but the fullest support.'

The way he took his leave was almost obsequious. Fleming was fairly certain he wasn't about to go and make trouble with the press; the great advantage about dealing with politicians was that they understood delicate blackmail. And he'd been surprisingly sensitive once she'd picked up on his own prior knowledge.

She wasn't under any illusions, though. The business with Tam was a ticking time bomb.

Tam MacNee was in a grim mood as he walked up the forestry track, bending into a brisk wind, the greyhound a slim shadow at his side. He'd had to bring it with him. He tended to prefer cats to dogs – there was something about their independent, to-hell-with-you attitude that spoke to him – but when he'd been going out of the door, the animal had shown such signs of distress that he'd felt he couldn't leave it: removed from its mistress, it had obviously decided that Tam represented security. He'd made token protests, but there was no doubt it was flattering, and he kind of liked having the beast with him. He'd tried throwing a stick for it, but this was ignored with a pained dignity which made him feel positively embarrassed at being so uncouth.

The early cloud had cleared and now it was a bright, breezy morning with just a slight autumnal edge to the air. Though Tam had never been exactly what you'd call the outdoor type, in these last difficult months when he'd needed to get out of the house he'd sometimes come here, up to Glentrool, to one of the rough tracks between the towering pines, where the only background sound was their branches creaking and muttering in the wind and maybe a wee burn blethering to itself. It had sometimes helped him put things in perspective, but today it wasn't working. However you looked at it, whatever the boss might have said, he knew that his part in the disaster was likely to come out, sooner or later. And then what? He simply didn't know.

Christina Munro – how could she have fired directly into the back of a youth who was running away? Fear and pressure, of course, made people do strange things. But gunning Andrew Carmichael down on his doorstep . . . Why, just for a start? She wasn't one of the farmers who could be driven out of business by the superstore deal going through – she'd sold up her stock long ago – and she wasn't, as far as he knew, close to any who did. So whether Carmichael was planning to sell or wasn't, it couldn't have mattered to her either way.

Fleming would have the lads out today, digging for a motive: going through Christina's papers, asking for telephone records, comparing with what they had already from Fauldburn House. If it were him, he'd go straight to Annie Brown. Would someone think of that, he wondered. Maybe he'd go anyway. He'd be wise to keep his head down, but there was nothing to stop him going for another chat with his old neighbour. He'd go off his head if there was nothing to do but wait.

If Christina hadn't killed the Colonel, it had to mean there was a second person out there who was also prepared to shoot to kill. He could have understood it better if the Colonel's death had happened after she'd shot Kyle: someone with a grudge might have taken the opportunity to get rid of the man in the hope that the two deaths would be bracketed together.

Tam had never taken much interest in guns. He was as

fond of a roast pheasant as the next man, but he'd always been uncomfortable with the notion of getting pleasure out of killing a living creature. Not that he'd been exactly inundated with invitations to join the local shoots – for some strange reason!

Until now, apart from the occasional suicide, gun crime hadn't featured on their patch, and ballistics wasn't something he'd had to swot up. He did know, though, that being able to identify a particular shotgun was highly unlikely. Calling in all the shotguns on the register wouldn't get them anywhere, which was probably lucky, considering how many there must be in this rural area.

If any were missing, of course, that would be interesting. Tam had seen for himself that security standards at the Ravenshill clay-pigeon shoot were lax: a check-up there might be useful. He couldn't go back, though. Dan Simpson had been in the motorbike showroom when Tam had been daft enough to stick his nose in.

Anyway, if someone else had killed the Colonel, they couldn't know Christina was going to shoot Kyle. So you were left with Christina having killed both of them, or a very odd coincidence. The gloom, which had lifted as he speculated, descended again.

There was something else, though, something niggling at the back of his mind that he couldn't quite place. He tried not to blame his injury; plenty of times in the past, when there had been nothing wrong with his head, he'd struggled to track down a passing thought. Even so—

A rabbit suddenly shot across the path. Tam had almost forgotten about the greyhound, walking daintily at his side; suddenly, there was a flash of movement and covering the ground in huge, graceful leaps like a startled deer, the dog was off in pursuit.

Just as Tam was wondering what he would do with a

freshly slain rabbit, the dog returned to his side, mercifully with nothing in its jaws. It was presumably used to its electric quarry disappearing, but Tam thought he sensed a faint embarrassment.

'Never mind, son,' he said, stroking the narrow, intelligent head. 'We all make mistakes.'

'Ossian!' she called. 'Is that you?'

There was no reply, only the sound of footsteps running up the stairs, and then, somewhere above, a door slamming.

Deirdre Forbes-Graham got up from her easel in the room she called her studio at the back of the first floor of the house. It was more, perhaps, a boudoir than a workroom, furnished with pretty, scaled-down, feminine furniture – an Edwardian *bonheur de jour*, a neat button-backed chair – and the elaborately carved easel holding the watercolour she was working on at the moment had been designed for a Victorian lady who shared Deirdre's hobby. The half-finished painting, in common with others framed on the walls or propped up ready for framing, showed misty hills and obligingly romantic trees; the scenic postcard she was copying lay on the nearby table, along with the elegant box of expensive paints.

Deirdre went to the door and out into the hall. 'Ossian!' she called again up the stairs, but there was no answer. She heard, to her alarm, a muffled crash.

She was worried about her son – very worried. An artistic temperament was all very well – indeed, she'd encouraged it, revelled in her son's mercurial talent and later in his success. The launch of his London exhibition, a sell-out, had been the proudest moment of her life.

But the way he had been behaving recently was alarming. He certainly wasn't painting and, as far as she could tell, he'd hardly eaten these last few days. She'd barely seen him; he spent all his time either at the Fauldburn studio or in his bedroom, which had always been forbidden territory to the rest of the household without due notice and permission.

It was that woman, Deirdre knew it was – a predatory harpy, driving her poor boy insane, and almost old enough to be his mother. Oh, how she wished she had never introduced them! She'd been taking in some of her pictures, which Ellie sold in the shop along with her own insipid flower sketches, and on that ill-fated day, Ossian had been with her.

She'd never forget his reaction. He'd stared at her with his mouth half-open, like some idiot child. Deirdre had been positively embarrassed! The next thing she knew, Ossian had been going to hear her sing at a pub, and then he announced he was going to rent the vacant unit in the Craft Centre, to have a permanent showcase for his paintings while he worked. Though it hadn't exactly been productive, had it?

It was almost getting to the point where she'd have to go and talk to Ellie herself, persuade her to leave her son alone. Or have Murdoch speak to her, buy her off if necessary. That would be wiser. Ossian would react badly and it would be better if he hadn't turned against his mother – for his own sake, of course.

That was another crash from upstairs. Respect for his privacy was one thing, dangerous neglect was another. Something should be done.

'Murdoch!' she called hopefully, but got no answer to that either. He must be out; he'd said at breakfast there was a corporate booking for a clay-pigeon shoot on Friday so he was probably at the office sorting things out with Dan.

Deirdre hesitated. Ossian could be so hurtful if, with the best of intentions, you did the wrong thing. But supposing there was something terribly wrong, supposing he did something desperate . . .

Fear lent wings to her feet. She ran upstairs, knocked on

his door, then, receiving no answer, took a deep breath and opened it.

The room looked as if it had been ransacked. Palettes and brushes were strewn about, a bare canvas had been slashed, the easel overturned, the pristine white of the walls daubed with red like blood. In the centre of the devastation, Ossian lay on his bed, very still, very white.

For a second Deirdre's heart stopped. Then she saw that his eyes were open and silent tears were spilling down his cheeks.

'Ossian! Darling, what is it?' She stumbled towards him, took his limp hand. For what seemed a very long time, he said nothing, then he turned his head slowly to look at her.

'He's moved in with her,' he said. 'She's let him move in with her. What am I to do?'

Deirdre felt a profound sense of relief. 'Dearest, these things happen. She's so much older than you – you would be a boy to her. A friend – that's how she would see you, and you can go on being friends . . .'

As if she hadn't spoken, he said, 'I'm very tried. I want to go to sleep now.' He shut his eyes.

Deirdre stood back. Tears still seeped from under his eyelids but as she watched his breathing became deeper and in five minutes he was, she was sure, soundly asleep.

That wasn't natural. She went downstairs, feeling hollow inside. She'd refused to believe that Ossian was in need of treatment, but perhaps it wouldn't do any harm to arrange for him to see Dr Rutherford anyway.

'Christina Munro flatly denies both murders,' Fleming said. Detectives and uniformed officers had assembled for the briefing in the incident room with its board showing photographs of Carmichael's body and the front garden at Fauldburn, and sketches and diagrams showing where traces of his assailant had been found and the angle of the shot. Rows of chairs had been set out between the computer stations.

'She admits that she fired her shotgun, a .410 Browning,' Fleming went on, 'but insists that this was harmlessly into the air. However, we charged her last night with culpable homicide and the fiscal is going along with that. She was detained overnight, but her brief will no doubt ask for bail when she appears in court this morning, and my guess is that with the Human Rights presumption in favour, she'll get it.

'The SOCOs are up there this morning and they'll no doubt find a cartridge and pellets that will be able to give us more idea about what happened.'

'Are we assuming it was one shot rather than two?' Will Wilson asked. He was sitting with Tansy Kerr and Andy Macdonald in the otherwise empty front row of chairs, police officers having the same attitude as schoolchildren to the merits of being safely at the back.

'Don't know. She said she only fired one; Burnett thought he heard two shots, but he was pretty much in shock last night so I'm not sure how far we can rely on that. We'll have to wait till they've checked her gun. The autopsy is later this morning so I'll have more detailed info for you after that.

'Now, I want a team in her house this morning, looking for any possible connection with Carmichael, and some of you will be checking the papers we've taken from Fauldburn House already. Dig out a few locals in their seventies who might have heard of a relationship between them, and anyone else you can think of who's well up in the local background – your auntie, Andy, perhaps?'

'Trawls for gossip like a Spanish fishing-boat – nothing escapes,' he agreed cheerfully. Then, more soberly, he said, 'But there's nothing to say definitely that the Colonel wasn't shot by someone else, is there, boss?'

Fleming could see that he, like her, was having difficulty in reconciling the personality of the woman they had interviewed last night with the ruthless killer of two people.

'Absolutely. It's only that I don't like coincidences – but they do occur. We could be wrong-footed if we go making assumptions, so I don't want the other enquiries scaled down until we have much more definite information. So there's follow-up work on what came in yesterday and of course formal statements from the people most closely involved. Details on the board. Any questions?'

There were a few, but nothing complicated, and she was able to send them all off a few minutes later. She asked Wilson, Kerr, Macdonald and, after a momentary hesitation, Ewan Campbell to stay behind.

A faint look of surprise crossed Campbell's face, but he came to join the others in the front row.

Fleming perched on the edge of one of the desks. 'OK. Thoughts?'

There was a brief silence, then Wilson said, 'Supposing she's right. Supposing the shot she fired didn't hit him. Could there have been someone else around? After rabbits, say, and getting Barney accidentally?'

'Seems unlikely, with the noise those kids would be making. There wouldn't be a rabbit for miles.' Fleming didn't notice the annoyance on Wilson's face as she dismissed the suggestion. 'Could Christina have seen him lying there from the house? I didn't think to check the sightlines last night.'

Macdonald shook his head. 'I doubt it. It's not a long drive but he was down near the road and there's a slope in it. There's bushes and scrub right down both sides too.'

'Maybe someone could have hidden there deliberately. Waiting for him.' It always seemed surprising when Campbell spoke, and they waited for him to go on. He didn't.

Fleming considered that. It was certainly more plausible

than Wilson's oblivious poacher. 'They'll be able to tell us the angle of the shot, and perhaps where it happened, though of course he could have ridden on for some yards before he fell off. But that would presuppose someone had a motive – and if we exclude coincidence, a motive to kill two people who, on the face of it, have no connection.

'Anyway, the picture will become a lot clearer after the post-mortem. Meantime, it's the usual thing – keep an open mind. OK? Know what you're doing today?'

Wilson said, 'Tansy and I are going to talk to Dylan Burnett and Gordon Gloag at the school. We thought we'd get the names of some of the kids who were with them last night, before they went to Wester Seton, and have a chat with them, just to get the full picture.'

'Yes,' Fleming said uncomfortably. 'My daughter was one of them, so I daresay you should talk to her. And the other thing you should know – in strictest confidence – is that Tam MacNee went into the motorbike showroom yesterday and tried to warn off the boys by more or less telling them Munro had a gun and might take a pot at them.'

There was a stunned silence. 'Did he *know* she would?' Kerr asked, horrified.

'Of course not. But he did think she might fire a shot over their heads to scare them – she had a loaded shotgun beside her door, and he wanted to stop them going so she wouldn't be tempted to use it.'

'If that comes out, we've got serious problems,' Macdonald said.

'Norman Gloag was sabre-rattling, but I've stalled him, if only for the moment.' She told them of the weapon he had inadvertently put in her hand. 'He got seriously twitchy and claimed he only heard when it would have been too late. Quiz Gordon about the timing, and if there's a discrepancy, go and lean on Gloag – that might hold him off for a bit longer.'

Fleming glanced at her watch. 'I'll have to go. I've a meeting with Menzies and Bailey. Incidentally, I shan't tell them about Tam until I have to, so see it doesn't leak out.

'Andy, are you and Ewan set up for today?'

'Plenty to do, boss,' Macdonald assured her, and she hurried out.

Romy Kyle had cried herself to sleep and woke with a start, her eyes sticky and every limb feeling as if it was weighted down. She was still wearing the clothes she had on last night. The other side of the bed was empty and the house was utterly silent. She swung herself slowly out of bed, then sat on the edge with her elbows on her knees, pushing her hands through her hair, shivering as the memories flooded back.

Barney was dead. Pete had gone. She didn't know what to do, and here she wasn't talking about the rest of her life. She was talking about the next five minutes. There didn't seem any reason why she shouldn't sit here with her head in her hands for days.

But the police would be coming, no doubt. She probably stank; her clothes were crumpled and sweaty. She got up stiffly, peeling them off and dropping them on the floor as she headed for the bathroom. She stood under the shower for what felt like a long time, though it could have been five minutes or half an hour. She didn't know. Time had gone funny this morning.

Dressing was unexpectedly complicated. She kept crumpling as shafts of pain hit her, and though she sobbed, no tears came, as if she had used them all up last night. She couldn't think clearly enough to separate grief for her son from grief for her lost lover; she was enveloped in a huge, obliterating cloud of anguish.

At last she got herself downstairs, to stand in the kitchen staring at the kettle as if she had never seen it before. She switched it on at last and made tea, though she didn't like it much. Tea was what you had for shock, tea with sugar in it. That was what the policewoman had tried to give her last night, and somehow then, when she could still think clearly, she'd thought it was funny.

She stirred sugar into her mug, though, and sat down, collapsed, really, on a kitchen chair, and sipped it tentatively. She shuddered in disgust – she didn't take sugar in anything – but she made herself drink it.

It did work, in a way. It forced her to get up and make herself a cup of coffee to take away the taste, and gradually her mind began to clear.

Romy had always told herself that if Pete left her, she'd die of misery – a Country and Western emotion, she realised now, in the consuming agony of losing Barney. She'd been permanently pissed off with him lately. He was a right little sod. He'd met his death because he'd been victimising an elderly woman. But whatever he had done, he was *hers*, formed in her body, part of herself for ever. She had been mutilated by his death.

Perhaps it was just as well Pete wasn't here. She knew he had problems with Barney and she'd have known that, somewhere at the back of his mind, was the thought, 'That's one way to solve the problem.' And when it showed – as it would, because Pete was far too self-centred to be any good at concealment – she'd have thrown him out anyway.

But why had he gone? Why last night? Had he heard about it while she was sitting in the studio staring into darkness – darkness in more ways than one? Pete didn't do deep emotion: like the banal motto on a sundial, he recorded only the sunny hours, and blotted out the rest.

The woman from Victim Support arrived just as she finished her coffee. Oh, she was well-meaning enough, but Romy had never been one to suffer fools gladly and she took a positive pleasure in telling her that she was just going into the Craft Centre where she had a lot of work waiting to be done. They could find her there when they wanted her to identify the body.

The woman would have to learn not to show quite so plainly that she was horrified, if she was to be any good.

13

Gordon Gloag was not a prepossessing young man. His couch potato's pallor was in striking contrast to the bright red blotches of acne, his mouth seemed to be permanently half-open and he was unlucky enough to have inherited his father's small, deep-set eyes. Put a baseball cap back to front on his head and he wouldn't even need make-up to go on the box as Kevin the Teenager, Tansy Kerr thought as she took her seat on one of the beige leather chairs in the Gloags' lounge.

This morning he was noticeably shaken, though the look he gave his father when Gloag Senior explained that he had taken the day off to support his son in his time of need, was not one of gratitude.

'We were hoping to have a word with you, Gordon,' Wilson explained.

'If you're up for it,' Kerr added. 'You must be feeling pretty bad this morning. You and Barney and Dylan were good mates, weren't you?'

The youth gulped. 'Yeah. What happened – it was gross.'

Kerr got out her notebook. 'Maybe you could talk us through yesterday afternoon and evening?' She turned to Gloag. 'If you don't mind—'

Gloag glared at her. 'I have absolutely no intention of leaving you alone with my son. I have had recent personal experience of police questioning, and a most unpleasant experience it was. Gordon is in no fit state to guard his words, as it is clearly wise to do, with the police state that now seems to be operating in this country.

'If you wish to hear what he can tell you about yesterday's tragic events, I know he will be as anxious to cooperate as I am myself. But I shall be present throughout.'

'Mr Gloag, your son is not a minor,' Wilson was beginning, when Gordon interrupted him.

'For God's sake, Dad, leave me alone! I don't need you fussing round me like I was six years old.'

'Gordon, you don't realise—'

'Yes I sodding do.' His son got up and turned to Wilson. 'Probably be easier if I just came with you to the police station. Get *him* out of my hair.' He jerked his head towards his father, then added with a sneer, 'That'll give the neighbours something to talk about.'

As a threat, it seemed a trivial one to Kerr, but since his son's intervention Gloag had been visibly uneasy. 'No, no,' he said in now placatory tones. 'No need for that – of course not, son. By all means, do the interview by yourself. But I want to have a word with you first, if the officers would excuse us for a minute?'

Kerr and Wilson looked at each other, but before they had time to get to their feet, Gordon burst out, 'I've had enough, OK? I'll say what I want, not what you want me to say. You've told me already and I'm not going to do it, right?'

Gloag went pale. 'That's nonsense, of course it is – a misunderstanding. These youngsters, you know!' He was trying to laugh it off, but there were beads of sweat on his upper lip. 'They never listen, then they complain when they've got the wrong end of the stick.'

Wilson got up and went to hold open the door. 'I'm sure we can sort all this out, once we've had a word with Gordon alone.'

Very masterful, Kerr thought admiringly – she liked masterful

– as Gloag, still protesting but impotent, allowed himself to be ushered out.

'Parents, eh?' Kerr winked at the boy, who sat down again, looking acutely uncomfortable.

'He's something else,' he muttered. He was still looking towards the door as Wilson came back. 'You realise he'll be standing out there, listening?'

Wilson shrugged. 'So what did he want you to tell us, then?'

Gordon made to speak, then stopped. 'It's – like, difficult.'

Kerr eyed him shrewdly. 'He's still your dad, right? You don't want to drop him in it.'

'Yeah. He's a boring old fart—' He directed this towards the door, raising his voice, then went on, 'But . . .'

'The thing is,' Kerr said, 'adults often get their knickers in a twist over something daft, like what the neighbours will think. Yeah?

'Well, where we're coming from is only that we want to know anything you can tell us about what happened to Barney. We need every scrap of information because in a court there's clever lawyers paid to do their best to rubbish our case. Look, you don't think your dad killed Barney, do you?'

' 'Course not.'

'Nothing else matters to us. So just tell us straight exactly what happened yesterday.'

After only the briefest hesitation, Gordon nodded. He addressed himself to Kerr and she saw Wilson quietly taking out a notebook so that she wouldn't have to break eye contact. He really was brilliant. As well as good-looking, and not a toffee-nosed snob . . . But she shouldn't be thinking about that now.

She listened to the story of MacNee's intervention, trying not to wince. The man was an idiot – this was going to be a right mess!

Gordon was going on, 'He scared me, you know?'

Oh, she knew. MacNee had scared many better men than Gordon Gloag in his time.

'But Barney's been – kind of crazy, lately. He really hated this guy that's shacked up with his mother, always going on about him, and it was getting to him so he was, like, taking it out on everyone else. Him and Dylan, they thought they were totally cool, so Dylan was OK but they kind of made me feel I only got to tag along because I had a bike. To be honest, I'd had it up to here with them.'

Interesting that he'd thought this through – the boy wasn't as dumb as he looked. 'So you'd all been out to Wester Seton a few times before?' she prompted him gently. When he showed signs of alarm, she said hastily, 'Oh, don't worry. What you did before is nothing to do with us, and this isn't a formal statement anyway. When they come to take that, you don't need to say more than that last night it was suggested to you that you went there and you refused – if that's what happened?'

'Yeah. Like I said, I was scared after what your guy said in the afternoon. And anyway, if I got in real trouble my mum would take the bike away. She warned me, and the only reason she didn't do it last time was because she knew that letting me keep it would wind Dad up.'

'So when you came home . . . ?'

Gordon looked down. 'Well . . . it had been a bit heavy after some damage got done to Dad's car. I reckoned it might get me in good if I told him what the others were planning to do, and that I'd said no.' His lip curled. 'He likes people who clype – my sister Cara's his favourite and she's always telling tales.'

'And did it work?' Kerr asked.

'Yeah. He was dead chuffed – said I could order pizza instead of having supper.' He grinned. 'Mum was well pissed off – she'd got stuff ready.'

So, as Big Marge had said, Gloag had known about the plan in time to put a stop to it, if he'd chosen. Useful. Kerr moved on. 'So you were just at home with your family for the rest of the evening?'

'Well, Dad was out at a meeting or back at the office or something – he usually is.'

Wilson, who had left the questioning entirely to Kerr, looked up from his notes. 'So what was it your father wanted you to say that wasn't true?'

The male voice was more carrying than Kerr's. As a red flush evened out Gordon's complexion and he said gruffly, 'Don't suppose it matters much,' there was a peremptory knock on the door and Norman Gloag reappeared.

'Finished grilling my son?' he said aggressively. 'I have your headmaster on the phone, Gordon – he'd like to speak to you.' He held out a cordless phone.

Pulling a horrified face, Gordon accepted it and went out. Kerr didn't need to look at Wilson to know that he was thinking the same as she was: who had instigated that call?

'That's very timely, Mr Gloag,' Wilson said smoothly. 'There are a few questions we have for you too.'

There were hours and hours of this stuff. Could there be anything more boring than checking out CCTV footage with poor definition, and trying to spot something significant when no one had given you any real idea of what 'significant' might be?

The woman constable stifled a yawn. Kirkluce High Street wasn't exciting at the best of times and with the starting-point being after the shops shut on Saturday it wasn't even busy. Spotting one of her pals heading for the pub had been one of the highlights.

When a possible car passed, you had to stop the tape and check for the registrations of a couple of cars she'd been told to look out for, that had claimed to be driving in convoy – and here was one of these big 4× 4s, a Land Rover Discovery, coming along the High Street at definitely over the speed limit, heading in the direction of Fauldburn House. That looked promising. She checked the number. Yes, it was one they'd been specifically told to look out for. Result! She squinted at the figures at the bottom of the screen – 17.45 – and made a note.

They'd said to watch out for another car, a Saab, which had been claimed to be driving in convoy with the Discovery, but it certainly wasn't there. A little later one did appear, coming straight along the High Street, but when she paused the tape the number was wrong. With a sigh, she went on.

It was after six o'clock when more people started appearing on the street. St Cerf's Church Hall, where the meeting about the superstore had been held, was out of range, but people were gathering and heading in that direction. Personally, she thought having one would be a big improvement, but her mum and dad were dead against it, said people would lose their jobs and stuff.

There was another Saab. It was pulling out from the side road that led out of the town to the north, and this time the number was right. She jotted down the time, 18.12. Some convoy! The Discovery had arrived a good twenty-five minutes earlier.

She started the film again. The car turned off into the memorial square and she transferred to the camera that covered it. A woman got out of the car, locked up and walked back to the High Street, then off as if she might be heading for the meeting. You couldn't see what she did after that, since it was only the central area of the town that was covered by cameras.

Having found the cars, there wasn't much else of interest. People she didn't recognise went to and fro along the High

Street, then when groups began appearing, which suggested the superstore meeting had finished, she spotted the woman who'd got out of the Saab walking along with a man. They separated at the turning into the Market Square and he walked along, out of range. Switching to the other camera, she could see a few of the local neds hanging about, not doing anything in particular as the woman got into her car and drove back the way she had come. Not long after that the Discovery appeared, then turned up into the side road too.

A little later, three motorbikes came out of the square and went off at speed along the High Street; an old man shook his fist after them. She skipped through the evening footage as Kirkluce went about its usual Saturday evening activities of visiting pubs and takeaways and having the odd scuffle. A police car arrived and disgorged two of the lads to break up a group of young men. Her friend came out of the pub, a little unsteady on her feet, with a man; she paused the tape to take a good look at him, then pulled a face.

It didn't take long after that to reach the point in the Sunday morning tape when the ambulance and police cars started arriving, and she could stop. She sat back in her chair, stretching to relieve cramped muscles. She hadn't seen anything she could recognise as significant, and it was a hell of a long time to have spent, just for two car numbers.

'I'm going to take the boss at her word and follow up on the Carmichael investigation,' DS Macdonald said as he drove with DC Campbell towards Romy Kyle's house. 'OK, coincidences are uncomfortable, but I just can't see that old biddy gunning the Colonel down on his doorstep, and anyway, I've got an idea I want to check out.

'If you're asking me what happened with the boy,' he went on, though Ewan Campbell showed no signs of doing any such thing, 'Christina was in such a state she didn't know what she was doing. Fired her warning shot, right, then swung round and loosed off another that hit him in the back. Didn't even know she'd done it. And I reckon Big Marge thinks the same.

'So I'm leaving Christina out of it when it comes to the Colonel. We're going to follow up on Mrs Kyle's partner.'

He glanced at his silent companion. He'd been used in the past to working with Will or sometimes Tansy, neither of whom was ever short of an opinion, but now they always chose to work together if possible – and that was a whole other problem, though there wasn't a lot he could do about it. It had taken time to adjust to Ewan, who never spoke until he'd something to say worth listening to, but now Macdonald had got accustomed to conducting what was more or less an audible internal monologue. He had even learned to recognise Campbell's amusement when he made a joke – a sort of twitch around the mouth. A smile was the equivalent of another person falling to the floor and beating their fists on the carpet in paroxysms of mirth.

He went on, 'I got a tip from Tam MacNee that Pete Spencer's been running a scam, and the Colonel found out. We'll have to get on to the fraud angle later – he's got previous for that already – but I'd like to know exactly what Spencer was doing, late on Saturday afternoon. He might have reckoned Carmichael would shop him.

'It's a bit delicate to go in and come the heavy, of course, with Mrs Kyle's son just dead, but I'd guess she's out of it at the moment, sedated or whatever, and we'll have a chance to get him on his own without being accused of a hobnailed boots job. Victim Support'll probably be round anyway.'

He had driven into a street of council houses, and was looking at the numbers.

'Twenty-three. There.' Campbell pointed. With an exaggerated start, Macdonald said, 'God, what a fright you gave me! I'd forgotten anyone was there,' and saw the faint flicker of amusement cross Campbell's face. 'Go on, spoil yourself,' he urged as he parked the car. 'Have a guffaw.'

'Not funny enough,' Campbell said, and Macdonald had to admit that he was, as usual, perfectly accurate.

The entrance to the house was at the side, facing the front door of the next house over a wooden fence. As Campbell rang the bell, Macdonald was aware of someone watching them from a side window opposite, and a moment later the front door opened.

An old woman, stooped and bespectacled, with sharp features and a down-turned mouth, appeared. 'Police, are you? She's out,' she croaked. 'Went off in the car a wee while ago. Awful, this, isn't it?' Her ghoulish enjoyment was obvious as she hobbled over to the fence and leaned on it.

'Of course he was a real tearaway, that laddie, him with his bike and all, a right young limmer. Born to trouble, like the sparks fly upwards. I've said it before, and I'll say it again.'

Macdonald had no doubt that she would too, at regular intervals, to anyone who stood still long enough. 'In fact, it's Mr Spencer I was wanting to see. He's out as well, is he?'

She settled her elbows more comfortably on the fence. 'Not just out – gone, by what I saw.'

'Gone?' Macdonald was startled. 'How do you know?'

'Saw him last night. I was in my bed, and then I heard two of your folk banging on the door, but he didn't answer, did he? Then a wee while later, here's himself off out with suitcases and away in the car. And he's not come back.'

'Perhaps he was going away on business,' Macdonald suggested lamely.

'Oh, fine ham and haddie!' she scoffed. 'Away on business, with three suitcases in the middle of the night! I know a moonlight flit when I see one. You mark my words, laddie, there's funny business going on there.'

He couldn't argue with that. 'Do you know where Mrs Kyle is likely to be, then?'

She admitted, reluctantly, that she didn't know. 'You'd think she'd be at home, grieving, like a decent soul, but that one's a law unto herself. Try the Craft Centre, maybe.'

'Thanks, you've been very helpful,' he said, and saw her smirk.

'I've always been neighbourly. If you're a community, you take an interest, don't you?'

As they got back into the car, Macdonald said, 'That's "neighbourly" as defined in Communist East Germany. How'd you like to have that one living next door?' He didn't really expect a reply and he didn't get one. 'We'd better try and find Mrs Kyle. There *could* be some perfectly reasonable explanation.'

'Done a runner,' Campbell said. 'Thought we were on to him, which we are.' Macdonald could only agree.

Tam MacNee got back to the car. There was a brisk breeze blowing now and his face was glowing, but his depression hadn't lifted. Even supposing Rutherford said he could get back to work when he saw him tomorrow, he could see himself being suspended pending an investigation.

As he opened the door for the dog, he said out loud, 'Well, pal, as Rabbie says, I'll just have to "*jouk beneath misfortune's blows/As best I may*."'

The dog glanced up at him as if trying to understand, then jumped in obediently. He slammed the door and got in himself. As he did so, unbidden, the thought he had been groping for popped into his head.

He realised why he didn't believe that locking up Christina Munro was the answer to their problems.

* * *

Johnny Black crossed the courtyard from Ellie Burnett's flat to Romy Kyle's workshop. He knocked before trying the door: she hadn't locked it.

Romy heard the knock, but she didn't turn her head. She was sitting at the counter, holding a silver beaker she had been rolling between her hands for the last half-hour, her eyes blank.

He came to stand in her line of sight. 'Romy? Romy, I'm really sorry.'

A sigh juddered through her. 'Yes,' she said dully. 'So am I.'

'Ellie would have come, but she's – well, a bit upset. I said I would convey her condolences.' He glanced over his shoulder, and following his eyes Romy saw Ellie standing at one of the windows of her flat, looking across.

'Condolences!' Romy gave a bitter smile. 'My, what a fancy word.'

'Sorry. I don't know what to say. She'd probably have come but – well, to be honest, she wasn't sure you'd want to see her.'

'Since her son's alive and mine's dead? Yes, she's right. I don't want to see her. Just tell her to keep away from me.

'She didn't like Barney. She blamed him for getting Dylan into trouble. Well, I blamed Dylan – tell her that, will you? If he hadn't been there, always egging Barney on, this wouldn't have happened.' Tears came to her eyes.

Black put out his hand to cover one of hers; she pulled it away. She didn't like him: what had he come for, except to see her suffering as if she was a freak in a circus?

'Shouldn't you be at home, with Pete?' he was saying.

She gave a short laugh. 'Oh, Pete? He's gone. Smelled trouble on the way and left last night. Good riddance.'

Black looked startled. 'Gone? Why? Where's he gone?'

What the hell right did he have to barge in here, asking questions? 'You're not helping. I want you to go.'

'Of course.' He backed away. At the door he turned. 'I – I feel responsible myself. If I hadn't sold him the bike . . .'

'*You* feel responsible! How do you think I feel – I paid for it. Now bugger off and leave me alone.'

As Macdonald parked the car at the Craft Centre, his mobile phone went.

'Tam!' he said without warmth. 'I'm kind of tied up.' Then, after listening to the voice at the other end, 'Dead sheep!' he said blankly. Then, 'Oh yes. Right. Right. I hear what you're saying. I've the odd doubt myself.'

He saw Campbell looking at him enquiringly but took a certain malicious pleasure in not offering the information. The man had a tongue in his head; he could just learn to give it a bit more exercise.

Dylan Burnett, with speakers in his ears, was slumped at the table in the living-room/kitchen. He hadn't finished the bowl of cereal in front of him. He wasn't feeling hungry this morning.

When the police brought him back last night, he'd been in a pretty bad state, scared out of his mind. He'd thought his mum would go mental when she heard what had happened, but when she saw him she'd gone straight to phone Johnny, which was the best thing she could have done. He'd kept her calm, and Dylan felt safer as well.

He'd stayed the night. Dylan had wanted them to get together, but it was kinda embarrassing this morning – his mum looked sort of awkward, with Johnny sitting there at the breakfast table. Still, they'd get used to it; Johnny'd said he was going back to his flat to get some stuff, so he was obviously staying on for a bit.

That was Johnny coming back now, from talking to Barney's mum after he saw her coming in to go to the shop. Ellie wouldn't go, though Dylan kind of thought maybe she should, and Johnny'd obviously thought so too because he'd said he'd make her excuses.

'I passed on your sympathy. And my own. Can't say she was very receptive,' he said as he came in.

Ellie looked at Johnny, but didn't comment. Dylan asked, 'Is – is she, like, bad?'

'Yes,' Johnny said heavily. 'She's pretty bad, I think. Awful that this should happen, when it could have been prevented.'

Ellie winced. Dylan, with a hollow feeling inside, muttered, 'If we hadn't gone there, do you mean? I didn't want to go. It was Barney.' His eyes were stinging and he rubbed them.

'No, I wasn't meaning that – you were just kids, just mucking about. There were other factors. The copper told you yesterday that they knew the old girl had a gun – if they'd taken it off her, it wouldn't have happened. Not like that.'

'What's going to happen now?' Dylan had been worrying about that, too. 'Am I going to be in trouble?'

Johnny pulled a face. 'Doubt it. They didn't exactly beat you up when they brought you back here last night. In the circumstances they won't want to push it.'

'They kept asking me, though. And I couldn't think straight.'

'You can't blame them for being keen to know everything you could tell them. Once it was spelled out that you needed your bed, they were fine.'

'Can you stay with me when they come to take the statement today?' It was like having your dad around, though Dylan's dad had never given him the feeling of security he got from Johnny.

'If you like. It's up to you.'

'What about your work?' Ellie put in. 'Won't you have to go and open up the showroom?'

Black smiled at her. 'Don't worry, sweetheart. I spoke to the owner earlier. He agreed that in the circumstances we should close for a day or two as a mark of respect. This time of year we don't do much business anyway.

'I'll tell you an odd thing, though,' he was going on, when his mobile rang.

'Oh. Mr Salaman! Yes. That's right. Look, I'll give you the background. Hang on a moment, if you would, sir – I'm going to take this in another room . . .'

As he went out, Ellie got up. 'I'm just going to make a cup of coffee. Do you want one?'

Dylan shook his head. He could tell she was trying to make out like everything was normal but it wasn't really working.

'I was wondering if you'd like to take a break and go and stay with your father for a bit?' she said. 'Get away from it all, take your mind off things?'

She'd tried that on him before and he wondered suddenly if this was what had been in her mind all along – that she'd get rid of him, now Johnny had moved in? He'd got fed up with her clucking round him all the time but the thought of rejection made him feel cold all over.

'I've got my mates here,' he said flatly. 'What would I want to go away for?'

'Oh, just for a while. I'm not banishing you or anything!' She laughed unconvincingly.

'Sounds like it to me,' he said sourly as the door opened and Johnny came back in.

'That was our Cupid, Ellie!' He was smiling, but she didn't smile back. He went over to her and put his arm round her shoulders. 'Come on, love – I know it's difficult, but everything's going to be all right now, I promise you!'

'Johnny,' Dylan burst out, 'do you want rid of me, now you and Mum are – well, together?'

He frowned. 'Rid of you? Of course not! What do you mean?'

'Mum wants me to go and stay with Dad.'

Johnny looked questioningly into Ellie's face.

She pulled away from him. 'I – I just thought, with all this going on, a bit of a change, take his mind off it . . .'

'Oh, Ellie!' He shook his head at her foolishness. 'It's all right, you know. Nothing's going to happen to him, here with us.

'Dylan, your mum's been scared silly and it's her instinct to protect you. Sending you away to keep you safe is understandable, but you could just as easily be knocked down crossing the road, couldn't you? It's up to you, lad – but I like having you around the place.'

It was a relief to hear him say that. 'I'm not going, then.' Dylan added, a little awkwardly, 'And I'm cool – you know, with you two.'

'Fine,' Ellie said tonelessly.

DI Fleming had her mobile phone clamped to her ear as she stood in the corridor outside the room where Barney Kyle's body lay on a steel trolley. 'I don't care what he's doing, or where he is. You've got to find the fiscal. I have to speak to him urgently.'

14

It was quarter past twelve when Tam MacNee drove back into Kirkluce, casting a frustrated glance at the Craft Centre as he passed. There were questions needing answers, but he couldn't as much as try to get them. Even talking to Annie was maybe pushing his luck, but she was a loyal soul: she'd never let on if he said he was operating on the quiet.

He wanted to quiz her about Christina. It was the wanton cruelty of killing the sheep which had prompted his subconscious belief in her innocence: how could someone so devoted to animals kill the poor beast as a gesture – and anyway, how could a little old lady manhandle the carcass? On the other hand, you had to remember that she'd been a farmer all her life and presumably had developed the knack of heaving sheep around, and of course there still was no proof that the animal actually was directly connected to their cases. If Annie had a story to tell about some long ago relationship between Christina and the Colonel, he might have to revise his opinion.

Annie greeted him with enthusiasm. 'You're just the man I want to see, Tam,' she said as she took him into the sitting-room, then bent to rake up the fire in the little grate to a blaze. 'What's going on? Christina Munro – I don't believe it!'

She was looking a great deal better than the last time he saw her. There was nothing like a sensation for cheering people up.

'You probably know more than I do, Annie. I'm still not back at my work, and I've to be careful not to get in trouble for poking my nose in. So I've not been here, if anyone asks you.'

'I'll never let cheep,' Annie promised. 'But Tam, is it right about Christina – not just that she killed the laddie, but the Colonel too?'

'You tell me.' MacNee settled back in the chair by the fire. 'Did she know him at all?'

Annie shook her head vigorously. 'I'd swear she didn't. She never came near the house any time I was there, and certainly he never mentioned her. She doesn't go about much. I only know her because when my mother was alive she used to come round for a cuppa sometimes – they were at the school together.'

Annie was going to be a bit sensitive about his next question, what with the Colonel's reputation having taken a wee bit of a dent recently. 'Could there have been anything – well, between her and the Colonel?' That was his best offer where tact was concerned.

Annie stared at him incredulously. 'Her – and the *Colonel*! Don't be daft. Oh, I know fine what you're thinking about – him and that foreign lady – but that was different. He was a young soldier away from home, fighting and not knowing if he was going to die any moment. It was maybe wrong, but you couldn't blame him.'

So the halo was still intact. 'What about when they were young? Before he was married, even?'

She pursed her lips. 'I don't like to cry someone down, but Christina was never bonny, even in the old school photos, and my mother always said she wasn't sociable either. And with the Colonel being sent away to school, and then Sandhurst – how would he even have known her?'

'It's what I'd have thought myself, Annie,' MacNee said

with satisfaction. 'Thanks – that's what I wanted to know.' He got up.

'Here!' Annie protested. 'You're never away without telling me what's going on?'

'No use asking me. I don't know any more than you've heard on the street. I won't have an inside track till I'm back to work.' At least the second statement was true.

She looked at him shrewdly. 'Aye. And I ken fine what'll happen then – you'll say you're not allowed to tell me. Och, away you go!'

'Thanks,' DI Fleming said, her voice flat. 'I'm sure you did all you could. I'll speak to you later.'

She'd known it would be a close call, and it hadn't worked out in her favour. For once the security service had been efficient and Christina Munro had been collected from custody and delivered to the court promptly. She had been charged with culpable homicide and had made no plea or declaration: the case had been ordained for further examination. The fiscal had resisted bail, but taking into account the circumstances – an elderly woman and a first offender unlikely to repeat the offence – as well as the guidelines on granting bail wherever possible, the Sheriff had allowed it. Christina would even now be on her way home.

Earlier, when Fleming had first arrived at the morgue, the pathologist had greeted her cheerfully. 'Well, good news! You won't have the report from ballistics yet, of course, and I doubt if even they will be able to swear the shots were fired from the same gun, but what I've taken out of the wounds is identical.'

It was good news, certainly, but it meant that her gut reaction about Christina Munro – and Andy Mac's too, she rather thought – had been wrong. Oh, she'd been wrong before, of course, but surprisingly often her gut had been right.

'I can tell you that the gun was loaded with buckshot, and though I couldn't be sure, my money would be on a 12-bore—'

'What did you say?' Fleming said sharply. '12-bore?'

The man looked surprised. 'Weren't you expecting that?'

'Not a .410?'

'Definitely not.'

'You couldn't be wrong about that?' Then, as the man looked offended, she added hastily, 'It's just that the gun we've recovered is a .410.'

He went across to the trolley beside the body which was still covered by a green sheet and picked up a steel bowl where a small, bloodied mass of fibre lay. 'The shots were both fired at close range, so the wadding was embedded in the wound. See this? The way it's constructed, it peels back on impact to form four "petals", look. If it had been from a .410 cartridge, there would only have been three.'

He was going on to explain the other differences but she barely heard him, struggling to assimilate the news. Christina Munro's gun couldn't have fired the shot. The house had been searched and there was no other gun. So she hadn't killed Barney, and she hadn't killed the Colonel, but any minute now she was going to be charged with culpable homicide, on Fleming's say-so.

'Excuse me,' she had said to the surprised pathologist. 'I'll have to get hold of the fiscal. You get started on the autopsy – I'll be with you in a minute.'

But she'd failed. And now, she would have to go back in and watch as the grisly procedures were carried out to tell her what she knew already: that Barney Kyle had been shot dead by a person unknown.

'They're all singing from the same hymn sheet, aren't they?' Will Wilson said to Tansy Kerr. 'Dylan, the school kids – hey,

Big Marge's daughter's quite fit, isn't she? Sulky, though – bet she's a bit of a handful!'

'She's fourteen,' Kerr said. 'Girls are always horrific at fourteen.'

'But look how they improve later.' Smiling, Wilson moved up closer to her on the bench seat.

They had driven the twelve miles to Newton Stewart to find a pub where they weren't likely to run into anyone who knew them. Having a sandwich and a Coke – a Diet Coke, in Tansy's case – wasn't exactly compromising, but going to such lengths to avoid their colleagues so they didn't have to be careful all the time certainly was. They hadn't had lunch in the canteen for weeks now, ever since – it – started, and they'd hardly gone to the same pub twice in case they got recognised as regulars.

Kerr was starting to get nervous. She hadn't wanted to come so far today and now she said, 'Will, they're going to start talking about us if we're not careful.'

He took her hand, stroking the back of it with his thumb. 'Nonsense! Everyone always thinks other people are interested in what they do, but in fact most of us are so caught up in our own lives we don't even notice.'

'I only hope you're right.'

' 'Course I am.' He pulled her closer and turned her face so that he could kiss her.

'Oh, Will . . .' As always, she melted, returning his kiss, then said wistfully, 'But I do so hate all this secret stuff. Where are we headed, Will?'

He made a rueful face. 'Headed? I don't know, love. We're happy just now, aren't we? And that's all that matters.'

Kerr wasn't at all sure that was true, but she agreed anyway. What else could she say? They had stumbled from comradeship into love and they'd made themselves a little, perfect, secret world, but he was the one who would have the big decisions to make and it was still early days. Before you broke up a marriage, even if it was one like this that was dead already, you had to be absolutely sure you were doing the right thing, for the sake of the children. She shied away from the thought of the children.

Wilson, with just a hint of impatience, was changing the subject. 'So what do you reckon? Dylan was pretty definite about there being two shots so I think we can assume he was right. Did she think she was firing over his head and got the angle wrong – hit Barney square in the back?'

'A tragic accident? But of course, you suggested that this morning – an accident with a poacher,' she reminded him helpfully.

'That was top-of-the-head stuff,' Wilson said stiffly, frowning. 'I didn't mean it as a serious suggestion – just thinking aloud who else might be around with a shotgun.'

She could have kicked herself for lack of tact. She remembered now that the boss had rubbished it at the time, and Will had been miffed, especially when Ewan Campbell's idea of an ambush had been taken seriously. She went on hastily, 'Absolutely. So what about the Colonel? Another accident?' Not that she thought for a moment it could be, but he would enjoy telling her why not.

'Hardly!' Wilson, restored to good humour, flicked her nose. 'Do keep up! How could she accidentally shoot someone at their own front door like that? No, you'd have to suppose that unless a connection emerges – and I'd put money on that it doesn't – the whole Munro business is a complete irrelevance. It's the sort of accident that's just waiting to happen, now you can't take neds like Kyle and Burnett round the back and explain the law to them in the only language they understand.

'It's different with the Colonel. There's plenty people might want him dead.'

'Ossian Forbes-Graham, for a start. If he thought the old geyser was having it away with the wondrous Ellie, he'd gun him down without a second thought. They're all inbred, his class, and he's barking.'

There was bitterness there, and Wilson looked quizzical. 'Not still thinking about your rugger-bugger, are you, Tansy?'

'Of course not,' she protested. 'It's nothing to do with that. I just think it stands out a mile. And I'll tell you something – if I were Ellie Burnett, I'd be paying for protection.'

As she spoke, her mobile phone rang; a moment later, so did Wilson's. He got up and walked away to take his call as she answered hers.

They both finished at the same time. 'Well!' they said simultaneously as he came back to the table.

'Back to HQ, immediately?' Kerr said.

'What's that about? Someone confessed?'

'Better step on it going back, or they'll start wondering what took us so long, when we're supposed to be in Kirkluce.' She was edgy.

Wilson gave her an exasperated look. 'We were in the middle of talking to someone, right? No one's going to put a stopwatch on us anyway.'

Fleming was frowning. 'Where are Will and Tansy? I gave instructions that they were to be told to drop everything and come straight back. It shouldn't have taken twenty minutes.

'What were they doing?'

Campbell, as usual, said nothing as Macdonald shifted uncomfortably in his seat. 'Interviewing the Gloags and Dylan Burnett, I think. Plus talking to some of the kids at school.'

'Were they in the canteen at lunchtime?'

'No.'

Fleming's unease about Wilson deepened. Could there, she wondered suddenly, be something going on there? That would be all she needed. But Will, with three kids under six – and even if he would, surely Tansy wouldn't . . .

She drummed her fingers on the desk. 'I'm reluctant to start, and then have to recap the whole thing for them. I'll give them three minutes.'

She'd had to go through it all once already for the superintendent's benefit. When she'd briefed Bailey and the Chief Constable this morning, she'd stressed that there was absolutely no proof as yet of a connection between the two murders, but though they had nodded gravely, she'd sensed she wasn't taking them with her. Menzies had only stayed ten minutes, then gone off to Glasgow to catch a flight to London, and she'd heard him say to Bailey, 'Sounds as if you've got this wrapped up, once you sort out the details. My wife will be pleased – she's been most distressed about poor Andrew.'

So Bailey had been at first incredulous – 'You don't mean to tell me she couldn't have killed the boy, even by accident?' – then agitated. 'I've had the CC's wife on the phone thanking me for clearing it up so efficiently,' he said.

'Then she was seriously premature,' Fleming said tartly. 'It certainly didn't come from me. You heard what I said this morning.'

'Yes, yes,' Bailey said testily. 'But where do we go from here, Marjory?'

'You'll be the first to know, Donald, once I know myself.' She got up. 'I've this and that to do. Like prepare a statement for the press officer.'

He went pale. 'Oh God, Marjory, the press—'

But she hadn't waited to hear his lamentations. 'Haven't time to go through that,' she'd said – but now here she was, wasting that precious commodity on two junior officers who needed a good kicking.

'I suppose we'd better get on with this,' she was saying, as there was a knock on the door and Wilson and Kerr appeared, she looking flustered and he, after a glance at her face, sullen.

'Didn't you get the message to return immediately?'

'Yes, of course,' Wilson said, with a glance at Kerr which Fleming interpreted as a warning to let him do the talking.

'So? What kept you?'

'I'm sorry. We were talking to someone and I didn't quite realise you meant us to break off in the middle of an interview.'

Kerr's eyes were lowered and her arms folded. Fleming was all but certain this wasn't true. She pressed him. 'Useful interview?'

'Sadly not. A member of the public stopped us and said he'd information about the murders, but what he meant was he had theories.'

'And you couldn't have cut him short?'

Wilson was looking at her very directly, his eyes wide and innocent. 'We did. Once we realised.'

Now she knew he was lying, but today she didn't have the luxury of time to deal with it. 'I'll leave it there – for the present,' she said coldly. 'Sit down.'

Kerr slid into a seat with obvious relief; Wilson took a moment to greet the other two men before he took his place. Fleming recognised it as a small gesture of defiance, but wasn't unwise enough to be drawn.

'We've had very unexpected results from the autopsy,' she began, and saw the astonishment in their faces as she told them.

'You mean,' Kerr said at last, 'that there really was someone hiding in the bushes, like Ewan suggested?'

'Seems so. From the angle of the shot, it looks as if it was fired at fairly short range from behind and to Kyle's right. Incidentally, the pathologist also thinks it likely the trauma was such that he would have collapsed almost instantly, though given the momentum of the bike he's not prepared to state categorically that he couldn't have been carried on. Anyway, I've asked the SOCOs to do a focused search in that area of the farm track.

'The other thing is that the gun that shot them both had been loaded with buckshot. You wouldn't use that for ordinary rough shooting, or shooting at clays. It's what you'd need to bring down a deer, say, which suggests the killer had his targets in mind when he bought the ammunition. But what is there to link the Colonel and Barney Kyle?'

'And a dead sheep,' Macdonald said.

Fleming was startled. 'Dead sheep? Oh, of course. I'd forgotten the dead sheep.'

'So had I, to be honest, until—' Macdonald stopped.

'Until?' Fleming prompted.

'Until – until I – er, remembered,' he finished lamely.

She gave him a look of exasperation. What was wrong with them all? Was lying contagious? 'Anyway, the dead sheep. We don't know, of course, how it was shot – or that it definitely had been shot, even. But in the peculiar circumstances of finding it dumped in the Craft Centre . . . You'd have to say it doesn't sound like run-of-the-mill animal cruelty for kicks.

'So what are we to make of that – someone shooting a sheep, an elderly man and a young tearaway? What's the connection between those three?' She looked round them questioningly.

There was a moment's silence, then Campbell said, 'Could be random. You know, a sniper, like they get in America.'

Fleming looked at him in horror. 'Don't say that!' she begged. 'Don't even think that, outside this room! Can you imagine the effect on the public, if they think someone's wandering around, ready to pick them off when they go out to the shops for their messages?'

'You'd have to say there's something in that,' Wilson said

thoughtfully. 'There's a weird feeling about this whole thing. Especially the sheep.'

'Let's leave the sheep out of it for the moment,' Fleming said desperately. 'Focus on Carmichael and the boy. Someone wanted rid of them both. Is it about the first murder – the boy, say, witnessing something incriminating? Is there something we don't know about that unites them? Or has someone killed two people who separately have given him reason to want them dead? Let's have some focused thinking here.'

Macdonald sat up. 'Pete Spencer – he's done a runner. He lives with Romy Kyle, but she doesn't know where he is or what's happened – she was in her workshop last night and he was gone when she got home. He wouldn't open the door when our lads went round there to break the news, and the neighbour says he left with suitcases in the middle of the night.'

Suddenly everyone was sitting up. Fleming's heart lifted. 'So he had a very direct connection with the boy—'

'And Colonel Carmichael had found out about a financial scam he'd been running. He'd form, had served time for it – he might have been prepared to take drastic action to stop that happening again.'

They were all excited now. Kerr said, 'And Gordon Gloag said that Barney really hated Pete – went on about it. And—'

Wilson interrupted eagerly. 'If there was aggro with the boy, once he'd had to bump off Carmichael, he might have thought he was as well to be hanged for a sheep as for a lamb.'

'A dead sheep,' Macdonald quipped.

Only Campbell didn't smile. 'I don't see why he'd want to kill the sheep, though. It was sort of like a warning, you'd say.'

'Right,' Kerr said. 'So it was a warning. Carmichael owned

the Craft Centre, so this was him saying, "Don't shop me, or else." '

Campbell was dogged. 'But why wouldn't he put it in the garden at Fauldburn House instead? The Colonel might never see it at the Craft Centre.'

An uneasy feeling stirred in Fleming. Why, indeed? And how could you be sure that Carmichael's immediate reaction after a threat like that wouldn't be to come straight to the police with the story? But the man had fled, after all . . .

She fought down her misgivings. 'We'll get out an All Points Bulletin. He may be gone already, but it's the best we can do. Will, you look after that. Tansy, get the number of his car and run it past the ferry companies. Ewan, find someone to swear out a warrant for Mrs Kyle's house and whenever it comes through I want you and Andy to go over there. Best contact Victim Support to be on hand as well, though – don't forget that Mrs Kyle's just lost her son, and this is going to make things very much worse. And there's the CCTV footage too – Tansy, once you've got the registration number, get that organised to see if it tells us anything about Spencer's movements at the significant time.

'And, it goes without saying, any brilliant initiative you come up with yourselves.' She smiled. 'OK, that's it.'

They got up to go, and Fleming was activating her computer when the thought struck her. 'Andy,' she called after him, 'where did this information about Spencer's scam come from?'

He came back with obvious reluctance and Fleming could see his Adam's apple moving up and down. 'Er – a tip-off.'

'A CHIS?' She gave him a hard stare. She didn't think for a minute it had come from what was now known as a Covert Human Intelligence Source, and she could see him squirming.

'Umm – you could say.'

Tam MacNee, no doubt. But she let it go. There are some things it is simply better not to know.

'Fine. Thanks, Andy.'

'What happens now, boss – to Christina Munro, I mean?'

Fleming pulled a face. 'The timing's up to the fiscal. The complaint will be reduced to culpable and reckless discharge of a firearm, so it'll be heard in the Sheriff Court instead of the High Court and it's a summary offence so there won't even be a jury. She'll probably plead guilty, and if the Sheriff's in a benevolent mood, given an early plea, the background and the fact that she had a night on remand, she'll only get a slap on the wrist.'

'To be honest, I'm glad about that,' Macdonald said, 'Oh, you can't have old ladies loosing off guns when they feel like it, but the neds have it all their own way these days.'

'This one didn't,' Fleming said soberly. Then, prompted by a niggling doubt, she went on, 'Andy, what's your feeling about Spencer?'

He shook his head. 'Don't know the man, boss.'

'I'll tell you what makes me uncomfortable. Three things, actually. One – OK, making a run for it is suspicious, but it's also seriously dumb. It's like fixing up a great neon sign saying "Guilty" and pointing it at your head.'

'See what you mean. Conmen aren't usually stupid. You'd think he'd have brazened it out.'

'Right. And two – why would the police coming to the door have spooked him? He'd have known they'd be coming to break the news to Romy. It's more the reaction of someone who thinks they're at the door because the game's up.'

Macdonald was much struck by this. 'That's right! I didn't think of it that way.'

It was a little like having a conversation with herself. Andy Mac was sound enough, with his own strengths as a detective, but he'd never have the flair for picking up connections and discrepancies that had made Tam invaluable on occasions like this.

She realised Macdonald was looking at her and she said hastily, 'Sorry, thanks, Andy, that's all.'

'You said there was a third thing?'

'Oh – oh yes.' She didn't like thinking about this one. 'It was Ewan's comment. As you said, he's got a knack of putting his finger on the problem. Why the dead sheep? You don't think we really do have a sniper, do you?'

Macdonald laughed. 'No, I don't. This is Kirkluce, not the American Mid-West. And Spencer may just have gone because he reckoned he could get clean away, and was scared that once the investigation started we'd finger him and he'd be trapped.'

'It's a good thought. Thanks, Andy.'

He left, and she went back to the computer to work out a press statement. She'd have to discuss with Bailey how much she told them. It was tempting to give them the usual line about on-going enquiries, at least until the homicide charge against Munro was officially dropped, but once you put out an APB it could easily leak. It could leak from within, too; she was painfully aware that there was an officer – or more than one, even – who had in the past done a line in tip-offs to the press.

She could only hope they'd pick up Spencer soon. It wasn't as easy as you'd think to disappear. If you weren't to leave a money trail, you needed to get your hands on cash and it sounded as if he'd left on the spur of the moment. He'd have a credit card, most likely, and if he used it they'd catch up with him before long.

'Cheers!' Pete Spencer lifted a pint of Guinness to his lips. 'You've got a bargain there. Goes like a bird.' He reached over to an adjoining bar stool and opened a bulging briefcase which was lying on it. 'Here you are – log book, MOT, insurance . . .'

The cheerful, round-faced Irishman sitting on his other side raised his glass too. 'Good deal for the both of us, so it is.' He handed over a thick wad of notes.

'Thanks. Gives me a bit of spending money!'

'Where are you off to?'

'North Africa. Taking Ryanair this afternoon.' Spencer looked at his watch. 'In fact, I'd better not hang about. Just finish this, then away to the sun.'

'Some boys have all the luck.' The Irishman looked out of the pub window. 'It's come on to rain again.'

'Is this not just what you call "a fine soft day"?' Spencer suggested, then drained his glass and held out his hand. 'Pleasure meeting you. Good luck.'

The Irishman took it. 'And the same to yourself, now. Happy landings.'

15

'Andy!'

DS Macdonald was heading for the CID room when Sergeant Jock Naismith hailed him. 'I've been looking for you!'

'Been with the boss. What's the problem?'

'Christina Munro's kicking up stink. She's out on bail and she'd been told the animal protection people were looking after her livestock, but when she got back the dog wasn't there and they didn't know anything about it. She's in a fine state. You were up there last night, weren't you? Do you know anything about it – one of these retired greyhounds?'

'It's OK, Jock. Tam MacNee took it home with him. I'll call him and get him to take it back.'

'Tam went up there last night? He's a brave man.' Naismith was impressed. 'Big Marge'll do her nut if she finds out.'

'She knows already. He'd sort of an excuse, but he'll be a bit more careful now about getting involved.'

Naismith gave him a cynical look. 'Pull the other one, laddie – it plays "Flower of Scotland",' he said as he walked away.

Macdonald took out his mobile and speed-dialled MacNee's. 'Tam? Andy here. It's about the dog. They've bailed Christina Munro and she's wanting it back.'

There was, he thought, a disappointed silence. 'I suppose she is,' MacNee said at last. 'Och well, I'll take him up to her this afternoon. I'd got sort of used to the beast, though. Cut above the rubbish Bunty usually drags home.'

'Maybe you should get a dog of your own,' Macdonald suggested, tongue-in-cheek.

'Me? You're kidding. Bunty's menagerie's trouble enough, without going out looking for more.

'Here, what's been happening today? Any new developments?'

'Look, Tam, the boss has told you, I've told you, you're sitting this one out. Do you not think you've done enough damage?'

'What harm would a wee chat over a pint do?' MacNee coaxed. 'We're old mates, just happened to run into each other in the Cutty Sark, say, or the Salutation, whichever you prefer—'

'No, Tam. That's it. Get better quick, and then you can buy me all the drinks you like.'

'Dream on!' Then MacNee's tone changed. 'Well, Andy, it saddens me to have to do this, but I think I'm going to have to tell Big Marge about all the information you've been giving me. It's my conscience, see – I don't like to feel I'm deceiving her, and with you being her sergeant I think she should know how you've treated her instructions with contempt.'

'For God's sake! Blackmail, even!' Macdonald gave an exasperated sigh. 'Oh well – I suppose so. MacNee, you're a bastard.'

He could hear the smile in the man's voice. 'Oh aye, right enough. But I'm a *cunning* bastard.'

Catriona Fleming let herself into the house, dragging her feet. She felt terribly tired, as if someone had attached lead weights to her hands and feet.

There had been a dreadful atmosphere in school today, with the teachers shocked and solemn and the girls in tears half the time. She'd had the embarrassment of having everyone looking at her when Will Wilson and Tansy Kerr were doing interviews because she knew them, and she'd been a bit rude when they were questioning her. She didn't know anything, anyway.

Then there had been one of these awful form sessions where they were meant to give healthy expression to what they thought, which was, like, totally embarrassing. Eventually someone had gone, 'But they were bullies, weren't they? That's really bad,' and then there'd been, 'Yeah, but she shouldn't . . .' and, 'Well, if they hadn't . . .' until the bell went.

Cat had taken no part in it. It had reflected, all too clearly, the struggle she was having in her own mind. What they had done to the old lady was cruel and horrible, but they were her friends and she was by nature loyal. The teacher had noticed her silence and stopped her afterwards to say there were counsellors in school if she wanted to talk to somebody. She'd said no, she was fine – everyone knew counsellors were rubbish – but she felt awful inside.

She dumped her bag in the mud-room. She'd seen her father in the distance, out on the quad bike, and Cammie had a squad practice, so the house would be empty.

But when she opened the kitchen door, the warm, clean smell of laundered linen greeted her. Karolina was there, standing at the ironing board with a neat pile of ironed clothes on the table in front of her and a rather larger unironed pile in a basket at her feet.

Karolina was small, with neat, short fair hair, blue eyes and a pink-and-white complexion. She wasn't pretty, but she looked as if she'd be a nice person. Her English, though it wasn't quite fluent yet, seemed to be improving by the day. She greeted Cat with a shy smile.

'I am sorry – today I am late. Janek had to see doctor for his cold. I make tea for you, Cat?'

At the mention of her name, a toddler poked his curly blond head out from under the table. He had blue eyes like his mother and a very runny nose. 'Cat! Cat!' He scampered towards her on all fours.

She knew the routine. 'Miaow,' she said, though without enthusiasm. 'No thanks, Karolina. I'll grab a Coke.'

She fetched it from the fridge as Karolina pounced on her son and subjected him to a ruthless clean-up. Cat was heading for her own room when Karolina said diffidently, 'I think you are sad, Cat? Something is wrong?'

Cat began to cry. 'Horrible!' she wailed, and sat down at the table, sobbing. Karolina unplugged the iron, put it safely on a shelf and sat down beside her. Janek, distressed by Cat's tears, was hugging her legs and ready to cry in sympathy. His mother gently detached him and sat him on her knee where he put his thumb in his mouth and looked on, wide-eyed and solemn as Cat poured out her misery.

Karolina didn't speak until she had talked herself out. Then she said, 'This is very, very sad. So – careless, is this right? To throw away—'

'Wasteful,' Cat supplied. Yes, that was exactly what it was. 'Unnecessary,' she said, adding as Karolina looked enquiring, 'It just means it didn't have to happen.'

'They did a not-nice thing, but he was nice – this boy who died?'

'Yes.' Cat stopped. 'Well – no, he wasn't, actually.'

Karolina's brow creased. 'But – you like him?'

Had she liked Barney Kyle? *Liked* him? He was cool, he was daring, he had a wild reputation. And he had fancied her, fourteen-year-old Cat Fleming. Her friends had been awed. That was what she'd liked, really, not the person whom she'd often seen being casually cruel when he felt like it.

'He liked me,' she said slowly. 'And I suppose – I suppose I was flattered.'

Karolina's mouth twitched. 'Ah! I know. I like a bad boy, once. He is very exciting. But – no good.'

Cat was intrigued. 'What happened to him?'

'Is very rich! Black market in Poland, you could make very much money. But one day perhaps the police come—' She shrugged. 'Is better here.'

'Doing our ironing?' Cat always felt a little embarrassed, even though what Karolina did was just a job like any other.

'Is a good place, here – good for children. And Rafael, he loves the farm. We have nice house and they are so nice, good people, your mum and dad.'

'Oh, *Mum*!' Cat was reminded of her grievances. 'She's had it in for Barney and the others, right from the start. I got real grief because I was out with them when I shouldn't have been. She said they were bad news.'

Even as the words came out of her mouth, she realised what she was saying. 'Yeah, I know. But . . .'

'You do not like that your mother is right? I know. I am the same, then. I . . .' she groped for the word, 'forgive, I think – is right? Later.'

Karolina set Janek on his feet and got up. 'But I must do ironing, or no tea for Rafael tonight!'

With considerable misgiving, Fleming had settled for the non-committal statement. She couldn't say the major charge had been dropped until the fiscal had dropped it. By tomorrow he'd have had time to vary the complaint, and perhaps they might even have laid hands on Pete Spencer, or at least found hard evidence of his involvement. Or preferably both.

The risk was, of course, that the press would assume Christina Munro's guilt and write solemn whole-page articles about householders' rights and the problem of the modern ned. They'd be baying for revenge when they realised they'd been on the wrong track.

Damned if you did, damned if you didn't, really – as with

all dealings with the Fourth Estate. It was done now; no point in going over it again when there were reports by the dozen waiting to be read and it was after five already.

It would have been good to get home in time to try to build bridges with Cat, but there wasn't a chance. She phoned Bill, who was unsurprised at being told she'd be late.

'Making progress?' he asked.

'Hard to say. One step forward, two steps back, probably. It usually is. How's – how's Cat?'

From his guarded 'All right', Fleming guessed she was in the room.

'That's good,' Marjory said lightly. 'I'll maybe see her if she's still awake when I get home.'

That was all she could do for the moment. So, leave that for now. There were more pressing matters to deal with, like the reports.

It was almost seven o'clock when she had got through them, and she sat back to think about it. She just had to hope her misgivings about Spencer were wrong, because otherwise there were too many plausible suspects.

Giles Farquharson had a whole twenty-five minutes unaccounted for. What was he doing during that time, and why had he lied about it? But Norman Gloag had lied too, and tried to convince his son to confirm that lie. Ossian Forbes-Graham – well, he seemed to have serious problems, and no very satisfactory account of his movements. And Salaman, who had a lot to gain from his grandfather's death, had been less than frank and open about the detective he had employed. His alibi would no doubt stand up, but the Colonel's killing, at least, had borne the hallmark of efficiency which characterised a professional killing. Could she imagine him hiring a hit man, to avoid sullying his own hands? Yes, she thought, she could. Without any difficulty at all.

It just had to be Spencer – the tidy, logical solution. She liked that – because if she was left with the others, she still wasn't sure who her prime suspect would be.

If there was one thing Fiona Farquharson hated more than any other, it was being the hired help at a party where she knew the guests. This one would be particularly galling because Giles, along with some of the others employed on the estate, would be a guest too. The Forbes-Grahams liked to invite their employees occasionally, when they had a big party: Deirdre always said it was to thank them for all their hard work, but Fiona cynically suspected that it was to show off to their county friends about the number of staff they had.

But she couldn't refuse. It was all money, and she'd be doing it for the rest of her life now. She didn't even have the comfort of dreaming about the parties she'd give at Fauldburn House one day, when she could settle old scores by blacklisting the hostesses who had been particularly patronising to her – Deirdre Forbes-Graham, for a start.

She spooned chicken liver pâté into pastry cases, lined up on a tray ready for transportation to the Forbes-Grahams' along with the cheese straws, tiny squares of quiche, vol-au-vents and cocktail sausages, told Gemma, who was already changed into her black-and-white waitress's outfit, to start loading them into the car, then ran upstairs to change herself. There was no way Fiona would demean herself by wearing a uniform, but she always wore the Little Black Dress which suggested almost that she was one of the guests who was helping to hand things round, without provoking an accusation from the paying client that she was inappropriately attired.

Giles should be here changing too, unless he had done so already. She didn't think he had: there was no untidy pile of discarded clothes all over the floor that she would have to nag him about. She finished doing her hair, put on her make-up – though who, she thought bitterly, would even notice? – then went out and called down the stairs, 'Giles! We'll have to be leaving in five minutes.'

She'd insisted that he look after the wine. Making himself useful was the least he could do, frankly, since he'd spend the evening drinking and then expect to be given a lift back. Being a cook was bad enough; she was damned if she'd be a chauffeur as well.

There was no answer. Fiona ran downstairs to the office at the back of the house. 'Giles, you're going to be late!' she scolded as she opened the door.

Giles was sitting at his desk. As his wife came in, he made a clumsy attempt to hide the half-bottle of Famous Grouse and the glass he was holding. 'Just – just on my way, old girl.'

He got up, a little unsteadily, and Fiona's lips tightened. It was the first time she'd caught him red-handed, but she'd known this was happening. He'd been reeking of the stuff ever since Uncle Andrew's death – before it, in fact, now she came to think of it.

'You're going to have to see a doctor about your drinking,' she said brutally. 'If you lose your licence, you'll lose your job, and you've done enough damage to this family's prospects already.'

'Nonsense! Just a sharpener, that's all.' Drink always made him more ready to stand up to his wife. 'I'll go up now.'

As he passed his wife, she said unkindly, 'Hurry if you can. You may have difficulty putting in your cuff-links. I'll give you a clue – you'll find the holes for them at the end of the arms of the shirt.'

Andy Macdonald had chosen the lesser evil of the Cutty Sark. He'd be less likely to be spotted there than at the Salutation, where the lads tended to gather – not that they would run and clype to Big Marge, and they'd certainly sympathise with him if he explained, since Tam's varied methods of coercion were the stuff of legend. But after the reminders he had passed on, being seen having a cosy chat wouldn't improve his reputation for professional integrity.

The bar tonight was fairly quiet. He could hear voices and laughter from the room on the farther side of the central fireplace and was just about to go round to see if MacNee was there when the man himself came strutting in the door, with that familiar cocky set to his shoulders under the battered black leather jacket, a smug smile on his acne-pitted face.

'Time you were back at work, MacNee,' Macdonald greeted him. 'You've too much energy and you're spending it all making life difficult for a man trying to do an honest day's law enforcement.'

The smile faltered slightly. 'Never been better. Now I've just got to convince that stupid gomeril of a doctor when I see him tomorrow.'

'He'll let you back, I'm sure.' Macdonald saw an opportunity here. 'Tam, you'll be round the nick tomorrow, ready to sort us all out.'

'Certainly should be,' MacNee growled.

'So why don't we leave it there for now? You'll get all the information you want tomorrow—'

'What a chancer! Forget it, Andy. Suppose I didn't get back? And it hasn't been one way, mind. I've given you a lot of useful information – and I bet you took the credit for it with Big Marge,' he added shrewdly.

In view of recent developments, Macdonald couldn't deny it. Resigned to his fate, he looked around for a table.

'I'll set them up,' MacNee went on. 'And I've had a thought about Christina – tell you when we sit down.'

'Never mind about Christina.' Macdonald enjoyed the surprised look MacNee gave over his shoulder.

There was a table free in one of the darker corners of the bar where they were less likely to be conspicuous, and Macdonald had claimed it when MacNee came back with their pints.

'Christina?' he demanded, even before he took his first mouthful.

Grinning, Macdonald took his own very deliberately, prolonging the suspense. 'Didn't do it,' he said at last.

'The Colonel? Well, I could have told you that.' MacNee was scornful. 'She's not the type to go killing dumb animals, and you mark my words – whoever killed that sheep killed the Colonel too. And I always reckoned it was an accident with the boy, right from the start.'

Provocatively, Macdonald took another pull at his pint. 'No. She didn't do that either,' he said, and watched MacNee's smug expression being replaced by astonishment. He was going to enjoy telling the lads about the day he saw MacNee at a loss for words.

'Struck dumb, Tam?'

'I – I don't get it.'

'She'd a gun that couldn't have fired the shot. And Pete Spencer's done a runner. Panicked last night when he saw the uniforms at his door. Romy Kyle came back to find he'd packed up all his things and gone. She's no idea where he is and neither do we, as yet.'

'Ireland, probably.' MacNee spoke absently, his mind obviously elsewhere. Then he clicked his fingers. 'Of course – the Colonel causing trouble for him, young Kyle causing problems too, more than likely—'

'That's the connection. Can't see we've got anyone else in the frame at all with a link to them both.'

Suddenly MacNee said, 'But hang about! Police at the door, to tell her about Barney? But then—'

'Yes,' Macdonald admitted. 'The boss picked up on that too. If he'd killed Barney, she couldn't see why he should panic when he'd be expecting them to come. She'd one or two other problems with it as well, but you have to admit—'

'What did she say?' MacNee had hardly touched his pint: he was leaning across the table, fixing his dark eyes on Macdonald with such intensity that the younger man almost felt pinned to his chair.

'Didn't think he'd have scarpered just at that time. Inviting suspicion.'

'Might have been sure he'd get clean away, if he left early enough,' MacNee pointed out. 'And the police arriving might not have been what prompted it. He could just have been packing up anyway.'

Macdonald liked that. 'I should have thought of that! Big Marge always sounds convincing and I don't see what's wrong with it. Thanks, Tam.'

But MacNee was frowning. 'There's still the sheep, though. How would the sheep fit in? That's what made me sure Christina couldn't have done it.'

That effing sheep again! Macdonald was getting sick of the problematic animal, and seized on the chance to turn the conversation. 'Did you take the dog back? How was Christina?'

'Aye, went up this afternoon. Bewildered mostly – well, given what you just told me, she would be, wouldn't she? She still thinks she's somehow on a murder charge, but I don't think she's anything like as scared as she was when she thought those toerags might attack her.'

'We're waiting on the fiscal varying the charge. If we pick up Spencer, it'll put a boot up his backside. You can't charge two separate people with the same offence.'

'Sounds to me as if you've a way to go before you charge anyone,' MacNee pointed out.

'We're working on it.' Macdonald had finished his pint. 'Drink up, Tam, and I'll get you the other half. Same again?'

Absent-mindedly, MacNee downed the two-thirds of a pint

he had left and handed the empty glass to Macdonald. 'Thanks, lad.'

When Macdonald came back, MacNee said, 'I've been thinking about it. I'm with the boss on the problem of the sheep. Cheers!'

Macdonald was getting exasperated. 'What's with the sheep?' he demanded. 'It's all Campbell's fault – he started her on that. But for God's sake! One of the neds we know and love took a fancy to pot a sheep – so?'

'And he had a shotgun? And a vehicle, capable of picking it up and carting it from the field where they shot it, to drop it in the Craft Centre – and why?'

Having silenced Macdonald, MacNee went on, 'It has to be linked. Far too similar – too close in time and too close in connection with people involved – for it to be coincidence.

'There's two possibilities. The sheep's a message, saying something to someone, and as a starting-point we need to know who it was for and what it said.'

'OK, OK. With you so far. The other one?'

'The other is that it's all unconnected. There's no reason for it at all – someone playing weird games out there, taking pot shots at anything he fancies because he's sick in the head. Can't think why the boss can't see that.'

Macdonald was silent for a moment. 'Oh, she sees it all right. It's just that she's refusing to recognise it.'

The party was quite as ghastly as Fiona had expected it to be. In fact, she found herself feeling thankful to have the excuse of circulating with the plates so that she couldn't stop and talk to pitying friends. They said things like, 'Oh, Fiona, you are so clever – such delicious things, for so many of us greedy people! You must give me your card for our next party.' Which, for commercial reasons, she'd have to do, smiling and looking grateful for their patronage.

She wasn't sure whether it was better or worse than being treated by Dan Simpson, who ran the clay-pigeon shoot, and Johnny Black, who organised the motocross events and ran a shop selling motorbikes, for heaven's sake, as if they were all erks together. With a frozen smile on her face, she had moved on as quickly as she could.

Giles had done a few dutiful rounds with the wine, but now, she noticed, Gemma seemed to have taken over. Fiona looked round for her husband and found him propped in a corner with a couple of men she didn't recognise. He wasn't taking much part in the conversation and his eyes were glassy.

Her lips tightened. There was no point in making a scene; if she insisted that he return to his duties, he'd probably fall over, which wouldn't help anything. She'd have to tell Gemma not to give him any more. She'd yell at him later – probably tomorrow. Tonight he'd be feeling no pain but by tomorrow when the hangover had kicked in he'd be feeling terrible even before she started.

Wilfrid Vernor-Miles hailed her. 'Fiona! How's my favourite professional lady?'

She beamed at him as he came across to kiss her on both cheeks. Wilf was always so charming! 'For that, you may have a vol-au-vent,' she said gaily. 'Two, even, if you like.'

'And what will that do for my spreading waistline? You're a wicked woman!' He shook his head at her.

Just as he was helping himself, the drawing-room door opened and Murdoch Forbes-Graham appeared, ushering in a young man. He was slight and creamy-skinned, with dark oriental eyes, and he was wearing a suit which to Fiona shrieked Savile Row.

Heads had turned, as they do at a new arrival, and then, though they were politely turned away again at once, a little ripple passed through the company.

'Who on earth is that?' Fiona asked.

Vernor-Miles barely glanced at her. 'That's our newest neighbour, Zack Salaman – I must go and introduce myself, make him welcome to the neighbourhood.'

'Neighbour? Where?' She was intrigued. You didn't often see such an exotic creature, here in the sticks.

'Fauldburn, of course.' Then he stopped, suddenly realising who he was talking to. 'Oh – I'm frightfully sorry. Think I may have put my foot in it. You don't know him?'

'*Fauldburn!*' Fiona really thought she might faint. 'Who is he?'

Vernor-Miles looked round desperately for support, but everyone round about was engrossed in conversation.

'It's all round the neighbourhood – you don't mean you haven't heard? Oh . . . look, this is most terribly awkward, but I suppose you'll have to know sometime. I'd have thought the lawyer would have told you. He's Andrew Carmichael's grandson. Wrong side of the blanket, of course.'

'Grandson . . . ? Sorry – could you take this? I'm – I'm not feeling well.'

She thrust the platter into Vernor-Miles's hands and half-ran out of the room. He took it and made his way, with some relief, into the nearest group. 'Vol-au-vent, anyone? Shocking business just now, poor Fiona Farquharson, didn't know a thing about it . . .'

How very ugly they all were, these women – bulky, badly dressed, coarse-featured! Even the young among them, in what should be the bloom of youth, were totally unappealing: in their faces and figures you could already see the seeds of destruction which would turn them into their mothers in a few years' time. And no wonder, the way they were grazing on these greasy pastries, so clumsily presented. Zack Salaman waved away a waitress who was presenting a tray.

He was well aware of the sensation he was causing, and

the surprise and gratification of his host and hostess. They had sent an invitation via the lawyers, and with nothing better to do he had come tonight on a whim, prompted by a mild curiosity about the society which had produced his ancestors. He was regretting it now as he began to ache with boredom.

Though perhaps it was laying one or two ghosts for him, at that. He'd wondered, a little painfully sometimes, about the other side of his heritage, but the blood of his Scottish forebears was not stirring now. There was nothing here that spoke to him, nothing at all. His own background was one of simple elegance in food, in clothes, in architecture and decor, and this overblown Victorian style, with the heads of dead animals in the hall and elaborate carving and blowsy chintzes here in the upstairs drawing-room, was an affront to his aesthetic sense.

The only interesting thing in the room was a very striking, very clever large abstract, and he kept looking at it even as he nodded, smiled and made polite responses to people who so oozed curiosity that it was surprising they didn't leave a slimy trail behind them on the floor. The painting was good, very good.

When Deirdre Forbes-Graham came up to him with yet another local grande dame demanding to be introduced, he took the first opportunity the other woman allowed to ask about them.

'I very much admire your taste in art. May I ask who is the artist?'

'It's her son,' the large lady supplied before Deirdre could speak. She was wearing a tartan silk blouse with a frilled piecrust collar, bought, he reckoned, at the time the late Princess of Wales had made it fashionable. She had obviously put on weight since then and the pearl buttons down the front were fighting a brave but losing battle against her imposing bosom.

'Not here tonight, is he, Deirdre? Playing hooky!' She gave a bellowing laugh, and Salaman noticed one of the buttons quietly give up the unequal struggle.

Colour rose in Deirdre's face. 'He's been a little under the weather lately,' she said defensively. 'Great artists put so much of themselves into their work that they become totally exhausted by it. It's hard for mere mortals such as us to understand.'

Salaman was not in the habit of considering himself a 'mere' mortal, but he was interested enough to pursue his enquiries. 'I'm sorry not to meet him. Does he exhibit in London – or would he perhaps consider a commission?'

Deirdre looked hunted. 'He's doing very well in London, of course. His last exhibition was a sell-out, but I'm not sure he's accepting commissions at the moment. Still, you'll have plenty of time to discuss it. With you as a near neighbour now, we'll be seeing lots of each other, I'm sure.'

Salaman made a deprecating gesture. 'There could be nothing more charming. But alas, I have my legal practice in London—'

The large lady snorted disapproval. 'Never a good thing, an absentee landlord. Your grandfather wouldn't have liked it, you know.'

Salaman did not like impertinence and his mouth tightened. 'I barely knew him,' he said coldly. 'I'm afraid I feel no obligation to try to imagine what he might have liked.' Indeed, au contraire, but that was another matter.

The woman recoiled. 'Well, really!' she said as Salaman, with a slight bow, moved away. He heard her go on, '*Not* a very nice young man,' and Deirdre's flustered reply, 'We felt it was only polite to send an invitation but I never thought for a minute that he would come. I hope there isn't trouble.'

The sooner he left the better. He was making his way towards the door and was disconcerted to find Johnny Black appearing at his side.

'Good evening, Mr Salaman! Being made welcome by your new neighbours, I see.'

'In their own way, I daresay. I wouldn't have expected to find you among them.'

The implication was offensive, but Black said cheerfully, 'Oh, a cut above my level. I do some work for Mr Forbes-Graham. He has a motocross circuit here and I run the meetings for him.'

'As part of your new career?' Salaman had been irritated by what felt like trespass on his territory, when Black had announced he was giving up the detective agency and staying here; he'd fallen in love with the place, he'd said, though Salaman suspected a woman was involved. Still, it had all worked out quite well, with Black on the spot and ready to take on any job that needed doing.

'Career?' Black laughed and shrugged his shoulders. 'I don't aspire to that sort of thing. But I'm happy here, got what I want.'

'Excellent!' Salaman said, with a smile meant as dismissal.

But Black went on, 'I hope you were satisfied, sir, with what I did—'

Salaman cut him short. 'I told you to send me your account. All right?' He turned away, his mouth a thin line of displeasure.

A woman was standing behind him, so close that he almost bumped into her, a stout woman with badly dyed blonde hair. Her cheeks were mottled puce and her eyes, red-rimmed, looked wild.

'You don't know who I am, do you?' she said so loudly that despite the baying din of well-bred voices, heads began to turn.

Salaman loathed being made to feel conspicuous. 'No,' he said acidly. 'I don't. Should I?'

'Should you? Oh yes, you should. I am the wife of Andrew

Carmichael's legitimate heir, and you'd better come and be introduced before we meet in court. You can explain how you weaselled your way into an old man's favour, made him cut out the nephew who has been his support all these years, being groomed to take over Fauldburn and run it the way it should be run.'

Fiona grabbed his elbow. Rigid with embarrassment, his face a mask of cold fury, Salaman removed her hand. 'If you insist, I will follow you. But oblige me by keeping your hands to yourself.'

She glared at him, then turned and marched across to the corner where Giles was still standing, alone now and glassy-eyed, his jaw dropping slightly.

The room had gone very quiet. Murdoch Forbes-Graham was elbowing his way urgently through his guests. 'Excuse me – excuse me—'

Fiona turned to her husband. 'This, Giles, is Uncle Andrew's bastard grandson. I thought you two should meet.'

'Bloody hell – a wog!' Giles said blankly, took a step away from the wall, swayed, then passed out on the carpet at Salaman's feet.

It was after half-past seven when Sandy Langlands knocked on Fleming's door. She had a desk piled with papers and was staring at the computer screen when he went in. She looked weary and rubbed at her eyes as she leaned back.

'Sandy. What can I do for you?' She looked at her watch. 'Just knocking off?'

'That's right, ma'am. But I've been chatting to DS Wilson and he said I ought to come and tell you something right away.'

He saw Fleming's eyes narrow and she sat up in her chair. 'Useful?'

Feeling unhappy, Langlands said, 'Don't think he thought you'd be pleased.'

'Oh. Hit me with it, anyway.'

'You know there's an APB out for Pete Spencer, in connection with the murders? Well, I know Dan Simpson who's a pal of his – used to live here, then went to London for a while and came back not long ago.

'I was walking home last night and Dan came along with Spencer. He introduced me and we were standing talking when two motorbikes went past, so fast we turned to look at them, and Dan made a joke about me running after them to book them. I've checked the times, and that was when Barney Kyle and his mate were on their way up to the farm, and it was only twenty minutes later they found his body.

'Pete Spencer couldn't have killed Kyle, at least. Dan Simpson could corroborate that.'

Dismayed, he saw that Fleming was looking as if he'd punched her in the face. But she only said, 'Thanks, Sandy. Will's right – it's not what I was hoping to hear, but it's good sound evidence.

'Get a statement from Simpson tomorrow, and have someone take yours, and we'll feed that in and see where we are.'

The door shut behind Langlands. Fleming put her head down on the desk and groaned, feeling sick. That was the obvious, logical suspect eliminated. She'd been proved right in the doubts she'd had, but this time she'd have settled for being wrong.

It was only four days, of course, since the Colonel's death, twenty-four hours since Barney Kyle's, so not having it all wrapped up was hardly surprising. What had she expected? A revelation direct from on high? Police work was reading, and sifting, and collating, and she had plenty of ideas for follow-up investigations. Christina and Spencer were both eliminated, so that had to narrow the field.

Yes, but . . . She knew the feeling she got when things were starting to fall into place, and she didn't have it. Suppose they were, as had been suggested several times already, in the realms of unreason. Where did you start? And when might the next victim appear?

16

The headline in the *Scottish Sun*, 'Sniper Strikes Galloway Town?', had provoked a media frenzy, just as if the question mark in the title hadn't been there. To DI Fleming, at her desk with a constantly ringing phone, it felt almost difficult to breathe, as if the air had been sucked out by the firestorm it had created. She was trying not to look again at the double-page spread, open in front of her, which featured snipers who had conducted reigns of terror in other, mainly American, towns.

She was waiting for a summons from Superintendent Bailey, who had been thrown by the Chief Constable to the lions of the press, armed only with a statement which condemned irresponsible speculation, pointed out that the investigations were still in their very early stages, with fresh evidence coming in all the time, and rounded off with the usual appeal to the public for information, in particular any activity near Wester Seton farm.

It was intended to assure the population that there was no need for alarm and to dampen down the wildest of the rumours, but Fleming suspected that even Bailey – a man not given to underestimating his capabilities – had few illusions about the outcome.

He sounded fraught on the phone when he returned and she set off for his office with the sinking feeling she remembered from schoolgirl encounters with higher authority. She had to keep telling herself she hadn't done anything wrong. It just felt that way.

Bailey was slumped back in his chair, mopping at perspiration on his bald head with a red spotted handkerchief. His complaints began as she opened the door.

'It was a bear garden out there, Marjory – a bear garden! Jostling, shoving, shouting – I could hardly make myself heard. All they were interested in was yelling questions without listening to the answers.'

Fleming sat down. 'Did you manage to give your statement?'

'Oh, eventually. But they weren't interested. I wasn't telling them what they wanted to hear. They've all made up their minds that we're going to be gunned down in the streets. Asked if we were bringing in troops to protect the public, for God's sake!

'That was the point at which I said I had made my statement and had no further comment to make. Then I left in a dignified manner, which I hope will go down well on TV – if they even show it.'

'TV as well?' Fleming asked hollowly.

'Four camera crews.'

They sat silent for a moment, contemplating the scale of the problem, then Bailey asked savagely, 'Who leaked it, anyway? It obviously came from here, from the details given. I want them on a charge.'

Fleming looked weary. 'We've been here before, Donald. Tell me who it is, and I'll nail them to the wall by their ears. But it could be anyone – more than one, even. The tabloids pay good money for tip-offs like that.

'I've tried to find out who knew about Langlands's alibi for Spencer last night, but the answer is basically everyone in the station. You know what it's like with gossip, and you can imagine how quickly that particular story got legs.'

'Marjory, this is intolerable! Can *nothing* be done?'

She sighed. 'I'll start a witch hunt, warn that careless talk costs careers – that's about all we can do.'

'Hmmph!' Bailey made his usual sound of frustrated disapproval. 'I suppose so. Monitor the situation anyway.

'But more importantly, is the *Sun* right? Do we have a sniper?'

'That's the doomsday scenario. Once you start doubting that there's any reason behind it, you've nowhere to go. If they're acting on a whim, you can't deduce from their actions why they did it, or where they may strike next time. Anyone and everyone is at risk.'

Trying to sound more upbeat than she felt, she went on, 'But we're not there yet, Donald. We've a list of suspects with straightforward reasons for wanting Carmichael dead, and it's perfectly possible that Barney Kyle somehow got in the way – may even have tried to make capital out of what he knew.

'For obvious reasons we haven't yet questioned anyone on that list about Kyle's murder. I've called everyone in today to get started. With a precise time of death, we may be able to do quite a bit on alibi, as happened with Spencer, and that could whittle down our suspects.'

'Then get on with it, Marjory.' His tetchy response was an indicator of his anxiety. 'No point in sitting here wringing our hands.' As she got up, he said, 'No word of Tam MacNee being passed fit, I suppose?'

'Not as yet. I think you can take it that the ink won't be dry on the doctor's signature before he's round here.'

Bailey nodded glumly. 'The way our luck's running, he won't be back for a month, and he's a useful man, very useful.

'Anyway, what am I going to tell the media tonight?'

'The same as you told them this morning, but in different words, I suppose.' Fleming was unhelpful.

He gave her a frosty look. 'I would really have thought it was much more appropriate for the press officer to do it – or you, Marjory, for that matter – but the CC insists that I have to be out there to show how seriously we are taking this.'

'I'm absolutely sure he's right,' she said heartily, only adding, 'It's your job and you wanted it,' under her breath once she was safely out of the room.

'Are the police coming back again?' Maureen Gloag, a cigarette in the corner of her mouth, stood in the doorway of her husband's study.

Gloag looked up, waving ostentatiously to waft away the smoke. 'Oh, I thought you weren't speaking to me?'

'Jeez, you're so childish! I want to know where I am. If you're going to be arrested, I'm taking the kids to my mother's.'

'For God's sake, woman, do you think I'm a murderer?' His roar of rage shook the glasses in the wall unit drinks cabinet.

Maureen's mouth tightened. 'Gordon told me how you wanted him to lie to the police. I'm not wanting them to see you taken away in handcuffs.'

Her cold hostility shook him. 'Maureen, you've seen the news. It's a sniper, someone who's off his head, with a grudge against society.'

'Load of rubbish,' she said flatly. 'You don't believe it any more than I do. The Colonel's death was pretty damn convenient, right? And I'll bet you've been chatting up the grandson too, now you know Farquharson's no use to you.'

Gloag's fleshy face turned purple. 'And – and what if I have? He doesn't know the neighbourhood, I can be useful to him. And what about Barney? Bumped him off in the interests of business too, did I?'

'You were raging about your car,' she pointed out. 'And always yammering on about him being a bad influence on Gordon.'

His eyes were bulging now. 'You're being even more of a

fool than usual, woman,' he yelled. 'And if you repeat any of this to the police—'

'Threatening me now? That does it.' She was perfectly calm. 'I'm away to phone my mother and start packing.'

'And don't come back!' As she shut the door, he took up a heavy glass paperweight from his desk and hurled it after her, in a fury. Hitting the door, it broke into four pieces.

Moments later, Maureen reappeared. She was carrying a digital camera.

'What was that you threw at me? Oh, I see. You could have done me a real mischief with that.' She focused on the shards and before he could stop her had clicked the shutter several times. 'Thanks. That'll look good in court,' she said as she went out.

The streets of Kirkluce, when Tam MacNee drove along to the doctor's surgery, were almost deserted. He was puzzled: it was never this quiet in the middle of a weekday morning.

There were fewer cars on the road than usual too, and though the shops were open there was none of the normal pedestrian traffic, no hurrying shoppers or chatting pensioners. It was eerie, alarming, like finding yourself in some sci-fi film where something terrible has happened and you're the only one who doesn't know.

He was tempted to stop and find out, but a look at the dashboard clock showed that he'd be late for his appointment if he did, and he wasn't going to risk being told he had to come back another day. He tuned into the local radio station, but there was only the sort of music that sounded like fifty cats with their tails in a mangle. He snapped it off again and parked by the surgery.

It was quiet too. 'We've had a lot of cancellations of routine appointments,' the receptionist said. 'Well, it's natural, isn't it? They're not wanting to come out if they don't have to.'

'Natural?' MacNee stared at her. 'Sandra, what the hell's going on?'

She stared back. 'You mean you don't know? It's been on the telly and everything.'

'Never watch it in the morning. That early, my stomach's not strong enough to take those grinning numpties on a sofa.'

'There's a sniper in Kirkluce, just picking people off like flies! No one's safe.' She shuddered in pleasurable horror.

MacNee was shaken. 'Are you sure? How do you know?'

'It's all in the papers. They said you lot are baffled, because it's just random.'

'The papers!' He spat his disgust. 'They make these things up, just so daft folk like you will buy them.'

Over months of appointments, she had got used to Tam and they were old sparring partners by now. 'Not as daft as your pals in the polis, running round not knowing what to do.

'Anyway, you can go straight in to see Dr Rutherford. He's twiddling his thumbs this morning.'

'Just as long as he doesn't decide to have me coming back, just to keep him busy,' MacNee said gloomily, and headed for the surgery, hoping that anxiety wasn't going to raise his blood pressure. Surely this time . . .

Stoop-shouldered and heavy-eyed, Ossian Forbes-Graham, with his mother fluttering anxiously at his side, walked towards Dr Rutherford's consulting room, not noticing the short, hard-faced man in a black leather jacket who was coming back along the corridor, turning his head to look after them as he passed. Deirdre glared her irritation at such intrusive behaviour, then opened the door to usher her son in ahead of her.

Rutherford rose to greet them. 'Ossian, do come and sit here.' He indicated the vacant chair beside his desk.

Indifferently, the young man slumped down. Deirdre looked around; the only other seating in the room was the examination couch. 'We need another chair. Would you like me to fetch one?'

'No, Mrs Forbes-Graham.' Rutherford's voice was kind but firm. 'I'll need to talk to Ossian alone.'

'But you don't understand! He won't tell you properly – he needs me to explain! I can give you all the background, and then we can discuss what it would be most appropriate to do.'

'That would mean you were my patient, not him, wouldn't it? I'm sure that's not what you want.' He went to the door and held it open, smiling reassuringly. 'Don't worry, Mrs Forbes-Graham. I've blocked out time in my appointment book so Ossian and I can have a proper chat, to see where we are. That's all – nothing threatening.'

Deirdre glanced towards her son but he didn't seem to have heard what was said. 'Well, I suppose . . . I'll be in the waiting-room.' With a last, reluctant glance over her shoulder, she went.

Rutherford returned to his seat. Ossian didn't look up. He waited for a moment, then said gently, 'I gather you've been having one or two problems, Ossian.'

At last he raised his head. 'You're going to start *probing*, aren't you? That's what people like you do – poke me like boys poke an animal that's all curled up, to make it do something?'

'Is that how you feel?'

'Yes. No. How do I know? I don't *feel* anything. Not now.'

'You used to?'

A light flickered briefly in his eyes. 'Oh yes. Then, I felt – everything! I could do anything. I could move mountains, make things happen, have whatever I wanted. I had power. I could paint the greatest pictures in the world. I could even make her fall in love with me. But what am I now? "*Eyeless in Gaza at the mill with slaves*".'

A little startled, Rutherford recognised the reference. It was Milton describing Samson, bound and powerless, shorn of his famous strength, who used the last of it to pull down everything around him into utter destruction. It was an alarming image.

'You feel trapped?'

'Betrayed. In chains. Blinded. I can't see what to paint. If I can't paint, if I can't have her, there is nothing.'

'Her?'

It was the last question that needed to be put to him. He talked, in a monotone, until his mouth was so dry that the doctor fetched water for him. Much of what he said was rambling, some of it seriously worrying. It was almost an hour before he stopped talking.

Rutherford said carefully, 'Ossian, I think it's hard for you at the moment to understand what's happening in your brain. There is help available that will make all the difference. I can refer you—'

For the first time he showed animation. 'No!' he said fiercely. 'I know what you're talking about – they'll drug me, and then I'll be like everyone else, all you poor, boring, *sad* people. I'm an artist. I need – whatever it is.' He subsided into listlessness. 'If I find it again . . . If not—' His shrug was a movement of utter despair.

With a spring in his step, Tam MacNee walked into the Galloway Constabulary Headquarters, announced to the desk sergeant, 'I'm back!' then set off up the stairs, two at a time. With only the most perfunctory of knocks, he bounced into DI Fleming's office. He'd been looking forward to seeing her reaction – exclamations of delight, relief, even . . .

She was sitting hunched over her desk with one of those scribbles she did with names and arrows connecting them in front of her – mind-maps, she called them, though MacNee had never seen the point of them himself. Just as he came in, she swore, crumpled it up and shied it in the direction of the waste-paper basket. She missed. He couldn't remember when he'd seen her looking so stressed.

When she saw him, a brief flicker of pleasure came to her eyes. 'Tam – has he signed you off at last?' she said, then, when he nodded, went on, 'Thank heaven for small mercies. Take a seat.'

It wasn't quite the welcome MacNee had been expecting. Things were obviously bad. 'A sniper, is it? That's what they're saying in the town.'

'Tell me about it! In the town, in the papers, on the telly – I swear they have the whole place staked out with photographers hoping to be in place to snap the next random victim as he crumples to the ground.

'Of course it isn't a sniper! But I've spent the morning trying to make some sense of it and the more I think, the worse it gets. Carmichael's death – that could be anyone, if you think about it. We don't even know whether the man was going to agree to sell or not.

'If he was, all the High Street shops would be affected – not just the ones on the site itself. There are farmers and suppliers of all kinds who have contracts with local firms that might go to the wall, and if there's no alternative but to sell to the superstores they know they'll be screwed into the ground on price.

'And that sheep – a farmer has all the means to do it, gun and transport readily available. When everything still seems to be going ahead despite that, he kills Carmichael—'

'Then Barney Kyle? What would he do that for?'

'I know, Tam, I know! Maybe he knew something that

compromised the killer, but we've no indication that he did. And supposing that's right, it leaves us with a crippling list of suspects.'

'If it was one of the locals, why the hell would they want to kill the Colonel? The main theory going round was that he was holding out against it. You'd have to be daft to kill him if you wanted to scupper it. Everyone knew what would happen if the Farquharsons inherited, them being the kind that would skin a mouse for its hide.'

The look of relief he had hoped to see appeared. Fleming even laughed and relaxed back in her chair.

'You're right, Tam, of course. I've been needing to be pulled up short. Everyone else just agrees with me and I've been chasing my tail round and round this morning till I was ready to disappear up my own backside.'

She picked up her phone. 'I'm going to tell them to hold all calls. I'll pay for it later, so you'd better make this worth it. Switch on the kettle over there.'

With mugs of strong black coffee before them, Fleming kicked off. 'Ideas? You start. I'm tired of mine.'

'Could be a sniper. Practised on the sheep, then took what came his way.'

'Let's pretend you didn't say that. If, God forbid, this is haphazard, there's nothing to talk about. All we could do would be to hope we caught him in the act as he lined up his next victim. Or a photographer does.'

'It's not nice to be bitter. Gives you acid indigestion.'

'And let's drop the dead sheep.'

MacNee grinned, but Fleming hadn't been joking. 'How much do you know at the moment, Tam?'

With studied vagueness, he said, 'Oh, quite a bit, one way and another. I hear this and that – you know what this place is like.'

'Oh yeah? Andy Mac, I suppose. Don't worry – I'm not

planning to follow it up. I hate to think what hold you've got on him.'

MacNee gave his gap-tooth grin. 'Good lad,' he said fondly.

'Indeed. So can I take it that if he knows, you know?'

'More or less.'

'Right. Whether or not Barney was killed because he knew too much, let's look at him first, instead of second. Pete Spencer's in the clear – rock-solid alibi from Sandy Langlands, of all people. The team's checking out the whereabouts of the others that were in the frame for Carmichael. At least we have the timing for Kyle's killing so precisely that we ought to be able to rule people out on alibi. And that's where I think we should focus – we're up against the clock now, with the whole town getting panicky.'

MacNee shifted in his seat. 'Andy and me – we were on the spot within minutes. The gunman must still have been around.'

'Yes.' Fleming pulled some papers towards her. 'I printed this out – the report from the SOCOs. They've found trampled grass and broken twigs behind the run of bushes along the side of the track, which is suggestive, though they can't say when that happened and there are no footprints. There's the possibility that he didn't fall off his bike instantly, but I think we have to proceed on the assumption that the shot came from there.'

'Could still have been there when we arrived, then?'

'Probably was. It's open fields either side of the track. You'd have been more likely to spot him if he'd tried to make off.'

He grimaced. 'I thought that. Makes you feel bad, that he was there for the taking – but of course, at the time we thought we knew who'd done it.'

'Must have given him a hell of a fright, you poling up,' Fleming said absently, then, 'But listen – that's not sniper behaviour, is it? Point-blank range, a stake-out, waiting for a precise individual . . .'

'And he had to know the boys would be coming!'

They looked at each other. 'That's the handle,' Fleming said. 'Who knew what they were planning? Now we're getting somewhere.'

'You know your problem? Your problem's been wanting to know why. What are you needing motive for anyway? Means, opportunity and hard evidence'll get you a conviction. The rest is fancy-pants stuff.'

'Rude bugger!' she said without animosity. 'Andy Mac never says anything like that.'

'That's because he's feart.'

'Never! Of me, with my famously sweet nature and patience? Anyway, as I was saying when I was so rudely interrupted, who knew?

'Will and Tansy interviewed Gordon Gloag and some kids at school – including Cat, I may say, which wouldn't please her. Apparently they announced their intentions in the motorbike shop after you left.'

'Mmm. There were a lot of kids there. If they went around gossiping, anyone might know. Black was there, of course, and Dan Simpson too.'

'I know that Gordon Gloag told his father. And Gloag Senior was trying to cover up the fact that he knew before they went out to Wester Seton, to the point where he asked his son to lie about it. That puts him in the frame – and now I think about it, when Macdonald interviewed him, he accused Kyle of damaging his car. There's a connection there.'

Fleming got up. 'I've spent too long between these four walls. I need to get out there and talk to people – get a feel for this.'

'Anyone on the suspect list who wouldn't have known about Kyle's nasty little plan, do you reckon?'

She considered. 'The Farquharsons have lied too, about when they came into Kirkluce for the meeting, but it's hard to see how they could have known where Barney would be – their kids are away at school. Ossian Forbes-Graham – who knows? Might have talked to Dylan Burnett, or Ellie, even, who might easily have heard from Dylan. Apart from that – hard to say.'

She picked up her coffee mug and put it back on the tray beside the kettle. As MacNee followed suit, he said hesitantly, 'By the way, that business about me knowing Christina Munro had a loaded gun . . . ?'

'So far, so good. With her being cleared it's not the problem it was, and Gloag's the only one that's mentioned it so far. With any luck he'll be nervous enough to be reluctant to cause trouble.'

'So well he might be. And I'm the wee boy to keep him that way.'

'Let's make a start on him, then.'

MacNee followed her out. He felt like himself again, comfortable in his skin, confidence restored. A happy man, '*o'er a' the ills o' life victorious*'.

17

'I've been thinking.' DC Campbell spoke suddenly as DS Macdonald drove them away from the school, where they had been taking a formal statement from Dylan Burnett.

Macdonald gave an exaggerated start of surprise. 'Well, stone the crows! Here's me thinking you were just sitting there counting the lamp-posts as we drove past, like you usually do.'

Campbell ignored that. 'We've been told to forget the sniper theory, right?'

'Don't even mention the word, or Big Marge'll take you by the ear and wash your mouth out with soap. And you'll probably be drummed out of the force as well under suspicion of talking to the *Sun*.'

'So if it's not that, there had to be a reason why Barney Kyle was killed.'

'Wow! That's, like, seriously impressive reasoning. You'll have to give me time to catch up with your lightning brain.'

'We've all been hunting for connections. Spencer's out of it. To everyone else, Kyle was just another kid, right?'

His laconic statements always tended to prompt Macdonald to foolish facetiousness. 'You mean, like he wasn't an alien from outer space? Oh, hang about – he was a teenager, and they all are, anyway.'

Doggedly, Campbell continued, 'So it has to be that Kyle knew something that was dangerous.'

'Just happened to be in the wrong place at the wrong time

– yes, we discussed that.' Macdonald was getting impatient now. 'He may have seen something and tried a spot of blackmail, or he may not even have recognised what he saw, but had to be wiped out in case something emerged. It's a theory, but there isn't any proof.'

'But where was he?'

'Where was he, when?'

'When he was in the wrong place at the wrong time.'

'How do you mean?'

'Carmichael was shot on his doorstep. Kyle would have to have been going past at the time and seen something.'

'Right enough,' Macdonald said slowly. 'It was a clean killing – point the gun, bang! Being seen really was the only danger. If the gunman got in and got out again without being spotted, he was free and clear. So what you're saying is, where was Kyle at that time on Saturday afternoon?'

Having made his point, Campbell only nodded.

Macdonald thought for a moment. 'If we can catch Big Marge at lunchtime I think we should run that past her. We'll need to talk to Mrs Kyle about it and it's a bit delicate, after serving the warrant yesterday to search the house, all for nothing. So we've time to do the Farquharson interview before that.'

'Will,' Tansy Kerr said hesitantly, as she and Wilson drove away from failing to find Ossian Forbes-Graham at home, 'what did you do last night, after you left the station?'

Wilson frowned. 'What do you mean?'

It was tempting to say, 'Did you read up the interview notes?' and pretend that was what she'd meant all along, but something was niggling away at her. She swallowed hard.

'The thing is, you said you had to hurry straight on home, but when I passed your house five minutes later, your car wasn't there.'

Wilson's frown grew blacker. 'Tansy, are you spying on me?'

She was indignant. 'Of course not! You may remember I said I'd go and see one of my mates instead, if you'd to go home immediately? She lives in Lauder Road, so I had to drive down your street or take a massive detour, which seemed elaborate. All right?'

There was an edge to her voice which made Wilson say hastily, 'Sorry, love, I didn't mean it to sound like that. It's just that Aileen always grills me about where I've been and what I was doing. Sorry again.'

Kerr didn't reply. He'd assured her again and again that he and his wife had agreed to lead entirely separate lives. She was beginning to feel acutely uncomfortable.

He went on, 'She phoned and I had to go to the Spar to pick up some stuff for her. Toilet rolls – isn't it always?' He flashed a smile at her. 'If you'd passed ten minutes later, you'd have seen me lugging in the grocery bags.'

She spent her professional life listening to people telling lies in response to accusation. She could probably write a 'How-to' manual on the subject, and if she did, this was an example she could quote. Anger, swiftly concealed, a play for time, a rapidly constructed story to cover the known facts and a neat little detail to make it sound authentic.

Sick at heart, she said, 'Oh, I see.'

Changing the subject, Wilson made an anodyne comment about the Forbes-Grahams, then a few minutes later said, 'Look, there's a pub. Shall we pop in for a bite? I'm starving.'

'No. We're on statement-reading and checking stuff this afternoon, remember, presumably as a punishment for being late yesterday. I think we ought to put in an appearance at the canteen, or someone's going to notice we're never there.'

He didn't argue. Reaching across to take her hand, he said, 'Good thinking, love. We don't want to have Big Marge on our case.'

He put her hand to his lips, then released it. She folded her arms across her body, tucking her hands into her armpits.

'Could we have a word?' DS MacNee held up his warrant card.

Norman Gloag looked from the small man to the tall woman with disfavour. 'I suppose you'd better come in.' He stood aside.

'Thank you, councillor.' Fleming stepped forward and followed him into the house. They had tried his office, but been told he was working from home today.

MacNee shut the door behind them. The house was very quiet, and Fleming had noticed that only one car stood in the driveway. 'Home alone?' she said lightly, and saw him scowl.

'My family is away – out,' he corrected himself.

The stumble caught her attention. 'Out – or away?' she asked as she sat down in one of the chairs by the coffee table in Gloag's study.

'I don't see that as being any of your business,' he said coldly.

MacNee, sitting down opposite the inspector, had taken out a notebook. 'Refused to answer,' he murmured, writing it down.

'I didn't say that!' Gloag was immediately agitated. 'I demand that you score that out! I only indicated that this was a personal matter. If it's important, my wife was talking of paying a visit to her mother, and I'm not entirely sure whether she has gone yet, or is planning to return to do some packing.'

'Thank you for clearing that up, sir. Strike it from the record, sergeant,' Fleming said gravely, with a look at MacNee which dared him to smirk.

'That's all right, then.' Gloag had to take the chair which

stood between them, which meant he must turn his head to field the questions from either side.

The inspector went on, 'I don't intend wasting your time or mine, councillor. You told me that your son Gordon had come to tell you of the plan to pay another intimidating visit to Wester Seton farm before it took place. You may remember our conversation?'

She fixed her eyes on him in a way she knew to be unsettling. MacNee, on Gloag's other side, did the same, and she watched with satisfaction as Gloag licked his lips.

'Yes – well, we were talking on a vague timescale when we spoke, weren't we? I had no clear idea of the time involved.'

He had a point there, and she saw with annoyance that he knew he did. 'I can appreciate that. But I have a report which states that you asked your son to change his story about what time it was when he told you.'

'You asked him to lie,' MacNee put in helpfully.

Gloag ignored MacNee, addressing himself to Fleming. 'I know you have a teenage daughter, inspector. You will understand, all too well, how stubborn teenagers can be. When I discussed the evening in detail with Gordon, after I had spoken to you, and heard when the tragedy had actually taken place, I realised that he was confused in his impression about when he had actually given me the information.

'Having had recent, and unpleasant, experience of police tactics – like, if I may say so, your sergeant's recent implication that I was asking my son to lie – I was very reluctant to let Gordon sow seeds of doubt in your minds about what happened because of a misunderstanding and a teenager's determination not to admit he was wrong.'

That was dead-horse territory, and Fleming wasn't dumb enough to go on flogging it. 'So, after this – misunderstanding, did you spend the rest of the evening in the bosom of your family?'

Gloag shifted in his seat. 'No, I had work to do and I drove back to the office after supper.'

Like a dog scenting a rabbit, MacNee was suddenly alert. 'What time would that be?'

'Oh, come, sergeant!' Gloag gave an uneasy laugh. 'Do you make a note of the time when you go back to do some work of an evening?'

With a quelling glance at MacNee, who looked set to explain to him the principles of overtime, Fleming said, 'In the circumstances, sir, you will of course understand that we have to be as precise as possible.'

'Of course, of course.' Gloag looked suitably grave. 'We finished family supper around – what? Perhaps eight o'clock, eight-thirty . . .'

'That's awful late to finish your tea,' MacNee suggested.

'We don't have "tea",' Gloag said acidly. 'We have supper, and it could even have been later than that. As I said, I really didn't notice the time.'

'For a busy man, who has work to do in his office,' Fleming said mildly, 'it does seem curiously late for your evening meal. However,' she went on over his attempted interjection, 'let's accept that – for the moment. Can anyone confirm when you returned to your office?'

'I shouldn't think so. I was there on my own.'

He was definitely uneasy now. 'Presumably your wife could confirm when you finished supper and left?' Fleming suggested.

'I doubt it.' There was sweat appearing on his brow. 'Let me be frank with you, inspector. My wife and I, for some time now – well, our relationship has not been good. We didn't eat at the same time, and though I don't like to say this, anything she tells you about me would have to be taken with a pinch of salt.'

'Rather like what your son says?' She watched, with clinical satisfaction, as the shaft went home, then went on, 'But am I right in saying you have other children who can confirm when you actually left the house?'

'The others?' He got out a handkerchief and wiped his brow. 'I shouldn't think they'd have the first idea. They wander to and fro, grazing like cows. It's all about TV programmes, with them. Hardly sit down at the table at all.'

'Ah! Then presumably they will have a good idea when you went out, in line with the TV schedules?'

'How do I know what they'll remember?' he said wildly. 'Most of the time they don't seem to notice my existence, except when they want money.'

'Yes, a growing family is pretty expensive, these days, isn't it?' Fleming said sympathetically. 'The cost of trainers alone . . .'

'Indeed.' He picked up eagerly on that. 'And nothing but the best will do. They seem to get more and more expensive by the week.'

'So money's pretty important, then,' MacNee said, snapping the trap shut.

Brought up short, Gloag paused, then said coolly, 'Fortunately, I have a good business. I often wonder how families in less comfortable circumstances manage with all the demands made on them.'

There was no doubt about it, he was tough. His voice sounded as if he was making polite conversation; only the sweat which obliged him to dab at his forehead again gave him away.

'You stood to gain a great deal from handling property transactions if the superstore deal went through, didn't you?' Fleming's voice grew harder and Gloag bristled.

'What are you implying, inspector?'

'How far would you have gone to make sure it didn't fall through?'

Gloag took a deep breath. 'I am trying to keep my temper. It is not easy. I demand that you clarify my status in this investigation.'

'Your status is as a suspect, the same as a number of other people. In your case, we believe that you might have benefited financially from Colonel Carmichael's death and we also have on record a complaint you made against the second victim, Barney Kyle.'

Gloag got to his feet. 'If the interview is going to continue in this vein, I wish my lawyer to be present. You have just misrepresented my position for a second time: my "complaint", as you term it, was the action of a concerned citizen, an informal warning to the police who can't seem to see what's going on under their noses – or if they can, are reluctant to deal with it. Perhaps, if action had been taken at the time, this second tragedy could have been averted.

'So, if you will excuse me . . .' He went towards the telephone on his desk.

Fleming, with a glance at MacNee, rose as well. 'I think we've covered the ground for the moment, apart from one thing. I understand you have a licence for a shotgun. Would you have any objection to telling us what kind?'

'It's a matter of record,' he said stiffly. 'A Browning 12-bore.'

'Thank you, sir. We won't take up any more of your time.'

As he showed them out, MacNee turned on the doorstep. 'Just a wee bit of friendly advice. You should really try and find witnesses who can speak to exactly what you did on Monday night. You'd sleep easier in your bed, that way.'

When he had shut the door behind them, Gloag went back into his study and headed for the drinks cabinet. He filled a tumbler with Scotch, his hands shaking so badly that he spilled some as he poured. He sat down, and swallowed almost half of it in two gulps.

When the phone rang, he was feeling so shaky he almost ignored it, but it was most likely the office and he'd be as well dealing with it now as later. Better, probably, given his immediate plans. He was still clutching his glass as he answered it.

It wasn't the office. When he heard the voice at the other end, he tried to sound upbeat, dynamic. Then he listened, with increasing consternation, to what it had to say.

'You're not serious, are you? But – can't you do anything? Surely—'

Gloag took little part in the rest of the conversation, only saying glumly, 'I see,' and, 'I suppose I'll have to, won't I?'

He put down the phone and slumped into his chair. He banged the glass on the desk, put his head in his hands and groaned. Then he yelled, 'Damn! Damn! Damn!' and in a blind rage brought both fists down hard, knocking over his drink. He didn't even notice as whisky soaked through the papers spread out in front of him.

'What did you make of that?' Fleming asked MacNee as they went back to the car.

'Not sure. He's lying, of course, but I wouldn't like to say why.'

'He obviously doesn't have an alibi, and he was smart enough to have worked out that knowing about Kyle's whereabouts before the time he was killed is dangerous. Given the distances, he could have walked either from his house or from his office to Wester Seton in – what, twenty minutes? And he's got that direct link to both victims too, which is more than we've established for anyone else.

'But—'

'Aye, but . . .' MacNee agreed, as they got into the car. 'Seems kinda flimsy, somehow. Would you kill one of your son's pals just because he's messed up your car?'

'He was worried about his influence on Gordon as well, and like they say, it's the first killing that's hardest. And we don't know what Barney may have happened to know. But I'm putting him down on the list of suspects.

'So what next? I want to get a grip on this, Tam – I need to feel we're making progress, at least on the elimination front if nothing else. The Farquharsons? They've a lot of questions to answer.'

'I tell you who I'm wanting to see. Ellie Burnett. I was talking to Alanna Paterson who does pottery in the Craft Centre on Monday,' MacNee said, then at a look from Fleming added hastily, 'just a wee unofficial chat in the shop, same as any customer might have. Anyway, she said Ellie and the Colonel were just like this.' He crossed his fingers to demonstrate.

'Ellie Burnett,' Fleming said thoughtfully. 'She's the invisible woman in this. No one's managed to interview her – we tried on Monday, but she wasn't answering the door after the Colonel was killed, and it wasn't as if she was a suspect – after all, she'd everything to lose by Carmichael's death.

'She was there on Monday night when they took Dylan home, of course, but it was hardly the time to ask her questions, and anyway by then the investigation had swung on to Christina. Then yesterday it was Pete Spencer, of course.

'But she could have something useful to tell us. She's in the middle of it all – close to the Colonel, Ossian's obsessed with her, her son's Kyle's best friend. And I tell you the other thing. She's shacked up, apparently, with Johnny Black. Now he's someone I really am interested in.'

'Black?' MacNee raised his eyebrows. 'Motive? Jealousy of Ellie's relationship with the Colonel? Seems far-fetched to me.'

'No, not that. Zack Salaman – the heir, you know?'

'Oh aye. It's the talk of the town.'

'He was seen going into the motorbike showroom.'

'By me,' MacNee said smugly.

'Oh? For some odd reason, Andy Mac didn't mention that. But I think we can assume that the detective Salaman hired to find his father was Johnny Black. He was running an agency in Glasgow, and I'd like to know why he threw it up and came to settle here.'

'Saw Ellie.' MacNee's response was prompt.

'*Saw* her?'

'You've never seen Ellie, have you? She sings in some of the pubs – the Cutty Sark, quite often. There's just – I don't know. Something about her.'

Fleming was amused. 'Tam, you've gone all misty-eyed.'

'Don't be daft!' he said gruffly. 'She's bonny, right enough, and she's a voice that would charm the birds out the trees – but there's something else . . .'

'She's got "It"?' she suggested sardonically. 'You're going quite pink!'

'I'm trying to explain,' he said with dignity. 'But I'm not sure I can. It's like Rabbie's Bonnie Lesley – "*To see her is to love her*". You'll understand once you meet her.'

'Or maybe not. Sounds to me like a guy thing. But you're saying this could be enough to make him throw up a business in Glasgow, and come here to work in a shop?'

'Well, maybe it wasn't such a great job, being a private eye in Glasgow, spying for jealous wives. There's plenty folk come here and think it's a great place to stay. And he's daft about motorbikes – does the motocross and stuff. Could be his dream ticket.'

Fleming was unconvinced. 'If you ask me, Ellie and the lifestyle are a bonus. My bet is that Salaman has been retaining him to stay down here, and it has crossed my mind to wonder exactly what he might have been paying him to do. There's a huge amount of anger against his grandfather there, rigidly suppressed. I could see it when he said that his mother had never been acknowledged because Carmichael "wanted to spare his wife" – and you can understand that. It's humiliating, and he's a proud man, proud and I should think ruthless when he needs to be. You'd want revenge, wouldn't you?'

'Black as a hit man?' MacNee was startled. 'Did you check his record?'

'Hasn't got one. Tansy ran a computer check. The agency's listed as being licensed too, with nothing recorded against it till it closed down.

'Anyway, we'd better get out of here before Gloag comes out and decides to complain that we're harassing him.' She started the engine. 'We'll go to the Craft Centre this afternoon. But meantime, we're heading back to the canteen.'

'I'm not—' protested MacNee, but she cut across him.

'I don't care whether you're hungry or not. You're only just back to work and you're going to eat properly. And I'll tell you the other thing – you're going home when the shift finishes, and I'm going to phone Bunty and tell her to expect you.'

With MacNee grumbling beside her, she drove back to the station.

He really was in a worse state than she'd ever seen him in before – grey-skinned and sweaty, shaky on his legs. In the quarter of an hour he'd been downstairs he'd twice had to head off for another session in the loo.

Fiona Farquharson looked in revulsion at her husband, sitting at the kitchen table staring glassily at the mug of black coffee she had dumped in front of him. That was her best offer: he could stagger to the bathroom cabinet to fetch his own Alka-Seltzer.

Without Giles as an awful warning, she'd have been tempted to hit the bottle herself this morning. Every so often, little waves of horror would engulf her as scenes from last night replayed over and over in her head: the shocked embarrassment of everyone round about; Black and Simpson carrying her husband out like a sack of potatoes; Deirdre Forbes-Graham saying in that terrible, *kind* voice that Fiona must just go home and not worry about her responsibilities; herself with her face aflame marching out as the ranks of guests separated silently to let her through; the swell of excited voices behind her as she shut the door.

Worst of all had been the superior expression of pained disgust on the face of the little sod who had stolen Giles's inheritance. For a wild moment Fiona had even considered wiping it off with a couple of slaps, but from somewhere she'd found the strength to control herself and leave with the pitiful shreds of her dignity still wrapped about her.

She'd been on tenterhooks all morning, expecting the phone call from Murdoch which would terminate Giles's employment. And then what would they do? People would hardly be queuing up to engage her to cater their parties – humiliating disasters a speciality – and even if they did, all she could make out of it was pin money, and not very adequate pin money at that.

Giles looked up at her pathetically. The whites of his eyes were muddy, streaked with tiny red veins. 'I feel ghastly,' he said.

'So you bloody ought to,' Fiona snapped. 'Do you even remember what happened last night?'

'Not – not clearly.' It sounded as if his tongue was sticking to the roof of his mouth. 'Not really at all, actually.'

The next five minutes were quite enjoyable, in a sick sort of way, and Fiona spared him nothing. She would have said his colour was as bad as it could possibly be, but she was wrong. By the time she had reached the point in the recital where he had called Salaman a wog, it had gone from being the colour of Farrow and Ball 'String' to something more like 'Cooking Apple Green'.

'I called him a *wog*?'

'And passed out in front of everyone,' she repeated unnecessarily. 'Black and Simpson had to carry you out.'

'Excuse me.' He pushed back his chair and rushed out again.

Oh, for heaven's sake! Calling the man a wog was the very least of their problems. The thought police were unlikely to be in attendance and Fiona had a shrewd suspicion that quite a number of people there would have sniggered quietly. She couldn't see Salaman going down well in local society.

This felt as if she was living in a nightmare, with her whole life disintegrating round about her. After all she'd done! She couldn't bear to think about it. Her heart was racing.

This wouldn't do. She simply must not go there. There were plenty more immediate problems.

After a moment's thought, she went to the cupboard where she kept the cooking brandy and when Giles came back, shakily wiping his mouth, she indicated the tumbler she had put on the table, filled with a dubious dark gold liquid.

'Hair of the dog. I know it's meant to be the start of the slippery slope, but in my reckoning you're well down it already. Get that inside you,' she said brutally.

Giles sat down and obediently took a sip, then spluttered. 'This is absolutely disgusting!'

'Don't think I'm going to waste decent brandy on you in your present state. Think of it as medicine – and the more unpleasant it is, the more I'm going to enjoy watching you drink it.'

He grimaced, but worked his way through it, and she saw his colour gradually improve. When he picked up his coffee mug and took a mouthful, and then another, without it provoking an immediate rush for the door, Fiona said, 'Giles, if you're in a fit condition to think, we've a lot of important things to discuss.'

'Oh God, I suppose we do. What – now?'

She was opening her mouth to say, 'When else?' when the door-bell rang. It was an old-fashioned pull-bell which clanged throughout the house and Giles moaned, clutching his head in his hands.

For a moment Fiona didn't move. She didn't know who had rung the bell, but she knew it meant trouble.

Macdonald was a little taken aback by Fiona Farquharson's appearance. When he'd met her last, she'd been looking stressed, certainly, but . . . well preserved, that was the unkind way of putting it. Now it looked as if she hadn't so much as glanced in a mirror this morning; her skin was dingy and sallow and her hair uncombed, showing dark roots.

'May we come in? Just a couple of questions . . .'

'If you must. My husband's in the kitchen.'

The previous interview had taken place in the chintzy drawing-room and she'd been very much on her high horse. Maybe, Macdonald thought, the kitchen setting would produce less studied answers.

If she looked bad, her husband looked worse. As he and Campbell came in, Farquharson turned his head to look at them with bleary eyes, then recoiled visibly, muttering, 'Oh God!' He was reeking of alcohol.

'Would you like coffee? I'm just making some more for myself.'

It was a routine offer of hospitality, but as Fiona busied herself setting out the mugs, milk and sugar, then fetched tins to put home-made biscuits on a plate, Macdonald began to wonder if it might not have been to give herself time to prepare for whatever she might be asked.

When at last they were supplied and she sat down herself,

she leaned forward confidentially. 'I'm afraid you find us both a little shaken this morning, sergeant. We had a rather – well, a very unpleasant experience last night.'

Judging by Farquharson's appearance this morning, 'shaken' must be the new 'tired and emotional'. 'I'm sorry to hear that,' Macdonald said with appropriate gravity.

'We were attending a party and were suddenly confronted with my husband's uncle's heir. We had no idea of his existence, let alone his,' she paused, 'nationality.'

Macdonald was startled. His auntie had known all about it, the day after Salaman hit Kirkluce, which presumably meant that everyone else did too. Everyone except, apparently, those most directly affected. 'I'd have thought the lawyer would have informed you.'

'You would assume that, wouldn't you?' She gave a bright, brittle smile. 'But no. Presumably he is too embarrassed to meet us face to face, having been party to all this.'

'It must have been very difficult for you.'

'It was.'

From the set of her mouth, that was the end of the conversation. Macdonald went on, 'We really called to ask you some questions about Monday night – when Barney Kyle was killed.'

Campbell put down his second piece of shortbread and took out his notebook, a formal move which, Macdonald acknowledged, created a more alarmingly official atmosphere.

She looked dismayed, and her hands gripped the edge of the table. 'But – but it was on the news – it's a sniper! I could understand last time this sort of question having to be asked, with Giles being Uncle Andrew's heir – as we thought – but this is inexcusable! To suggest that we might have had anything to do with this other death – a boy we didn't even know!'

'Well . . .' Farquharson spoke for the first time. 'I knew him. He and his friends used to come to the motocross trials, hanging around Johnny Black.'

'You never told me that!' Fiona cried, looking at him in consternation.

'Why would I?' he said simply.

Macdonald could see her working hard at pulling herself together. 'Anyway,' she managed at last, 'shouldn't you be looking for some unbalanced loner? You're not suggesting that either of us goes out with a gun and picks people off at random?'

'I'm afraid you shouldn't believe everything the media tells you, Mrs Farquharson. We are still pursuing our enquiries, and if you and your husband would be kind enough to detail your movements, the night before last . . . ?'

Fiona got up and carried her mug to the sink, though she hadn't finished her coffee. 'Simple enough,' she said, her back turned as she rinsed the mug under the tap. 'I was doing the catering for the Forbes-Grahams' party last night so I was here in the kitchen, preparing food – as usual – and my husband was in his office, doing the accounts. Weren't you, darling?'

His look of surprise might only have been in reaction to the endearment, so out of keeping with his wife's tone of voice. But he said, 'Yes, that's right,' and lapsed again into silence.

'So I'm afraid that's all there is to it – another exciting evening chez Farquharson.' She seemed more confident now, picking up their coffee mugs and putting them in the sink as a signal that she expected them to leave.

At a nod from Macdonald, Campbell stood up, still munching. 'Great shortbread,' he said.

Macdonald gave him an exasperated look. 'Thank you, Mrs Farquharson. We've noted that, and someone may come back to you to take a formal statement.'

She inclined her head, then said suddenly, 'Wait a minute. I've just remembered something. If you're still investigating Uncle Andrew's murder, I think you should know this.'

* * *

After they had gone, Farquharson looked at his wife. 'You must be mad,' he said quietly. 'What if they check up?'

She tossed her head. 'They won't bother. Not now I've given them something else to think about. No thanks to you, though. If it was left to you, we'd be their prime suspects.'

18

The canteen was busy today. With so much activity centred on Kirkluce and its near surroundings, and the addition of a number of officers seconded from the neighbouring Dumfries force, there was standing room only when Fleming and MacNee arrived.

MacNee's appearance was greeted with shouts and even a smattering of applause, and colleagues took turns to shake his hand and slap him on the back with cheerful insults.

'Lucky it was only your head, eh, Tam?'

'Auld Nick looks after his own, right enough!'

'It's been rare and peaceful without you – now the trouble starts.'

Fleming looked on, amused. Tam was popular, certainly, but the news channel running on the TV in the corner was a perpetual reminder of the pressure they were under, and contributing to his welcome was an almost superstitious belief that Tam's return would signal some improvement in their fortunes. She wasn't immune to the feeling herself.

Tansy Kerr and Will Wilson, who had been sitting at the far end of a table for eight, got up and elbowed their way through. Tansy, moist-eyed, gave him a hug: she'd always been close to Tam, and Fleming promised herself that once this was over she'd see to it that the dangerous partnership of Wilson and Kerr was broken up.

'There's a seat there, boss, if you want one,' Wilson said to her, but she shook her head.

'I'm just having a sandwich. I only came in to make sure Tam didn't run himself into the ground on his first day back.'

MacNee was saying teasingly, 'Dearie me, Tansy, what's happened to your hair? It's all the one colour – that's not like you!'

With a sinking heart Fleming observed the telling look that passed between Wilson and Kerr, the slight smile on Wilson's face and the colour that came into Kerr's cheeks. She'd been going to have a word with Tam about her worries over the pair of them, but she saw now, as he eyed them shrewdly, that she wouldn't have to.

Kerr patted her hair self-consciously. 'Well – thought I'd try monochrome for a change. More sophisticated, you know.'

'Going for the femme fatale look, aren't you, Tansy?' Wilson, not a sensitive man, gave her a broad wink.

'How's that young man of yours?' MacNee asked innocently. 'Seemed a nice lad, when I bumped into the two of you that time. If you'd just convince him to take up the Beautiful Game instead of the ugly one, he'd be all right.'

'He's history,' Kerr said shortly.

'Now, that's a real shame. Still, there'll be another one along in a minute, I've no doubt.' He turned to Wilson. 'Good to see you, Will. And how's the family? The boys'll be getting big now.'

Wilson shifted uncomfortably. 'Fine, Tam. And it's nice to see you've decided to stop skiving. You're looking good.'

As a diversionary tactic it failed. 'Bunty was saying she'd met Aileen the other day – expecting again, I hear. Congratulations – you're gluttons for punishment, you two.'

Wilson turned crimson. Kerr recoiled, as if someone had slapped her face. 'Is – is she, Will?'

'Yes, I suppose so,' he muttered.

There were only a few people close enough to hear but among them there was foot-shifting and an awkward silence.

Kerr said, 'Excuse me,' and hurried out. Wilson made to go after her, but MacNee's hand shot out and grabbed his wrist in a brutal grip.

'Don't think I'd do that, if I was you.' Then, very quietly, he added, 'And don't think you won't pay for this, you little bastard.'

Wilson, looking sick, wrenched his hand away and went back to his seat. MacNee turned round. 'Now, someone said there was haggis on the slate today. Lead me to it – "*great chieftain o' the puddin' race!*"'

'Oh, someone stop him giving the full "Address", for any favour!' someone pleaded, and the laughter that followed dispelled the tension.

When Murdoch Forbes-Graham came in for lunch, his wife was stirring soup on the stove. He looked round the kitchen. 'Where is he?'

'He went up to his room after we got back from the doctor's. I promised I'd call him when lunch was ready.'

'How did it go, then?'

She turned away from the stove, her delicate features contorted with anxiety. 'Oh, Murdoch, I'm so worried! The doctor wouldn't let me stay while he talked to him, and Ossian seemed quite disturbed when he came out. All he would say was that the doctor wants him to see someone else, so he obviously thinks there's something wrong – you know, mentally, but he simply doesn't understand!'

Her husband put his arm round her shoulder, patting consolingly, but he didn't say anything.

She went on fiercely, 'It's that woman, Ellie – that's the problem. He's obsessed. It's the only word for it. He said yesterday that she was sleeping with Andrew Carmichael, and now with Black – I don't know whether it's true or not, but he sounded really angry, and – Murdoch, I'm scared!'

He made her sit down at the table, with its cheerful blue-and-white floral tablecloth and the places set for lunch. His voice was gentle. 'Don't you think it might be an idea to get further treatment? We can both see that Ossian's very unhappy, and they might be able to make things better for him. There's no disgrace in mental illness, my dear. Your own father—'

Deirdre covered her ears. 'Don't say that! He was only . . . volatile, like Ossian is. But what frightens me is that she could bend him to her will. He'd do anything she wanted, anything!' She began to cry.

He hated to see her so troubled. 'My dearest, if you're talking about these dreadful murders, you need to look at it more calmly.' He sat down beside her, taking her hands in his. 'Even if she could control him – which I would question – why ever would she want Carmichael killed? I've no idea what their relationship was, but my reading of the situation is that she'd have been a lot worse off without him to stop the Craft Centre being sold—'

Deirdre was shaking her head. 'I'm not talking about the first one. She wouldn't have told Ossian to kill Andrew, but he hated him anyway. It's the other boy – I shouldn't think Ossian even knew him, but he told me *she* couldn't stand him, blamed him for leading her son astray, getting him into trouble with the police—'

Forbes-Graham stared at her, shocked. 'You're telling me you think our son would be capable of killing twice, in cold blood?'

She was crying in earnest now. 'You have shotguns, Murdoch. It would be easy for him just to get one from the cupboard, and if she brainwashed him—'

'Hush, darling. You're distressing yourself quite unnecessarily. I can set your mind at rest on that anyway.

'To be honest, I've been worried about Ossian for some

time. Not that it crossed my mind that he would harm another person but . . .' He paused, reluctant to say the word 'suicide'. 'He gets so excited sometimes, so strange, that I thought it would be best to keep the keys to the gun cupboard on me so that there was no question of him finding them. He hasn't been on a shoot for months now, and on the odd occasion when he wanted to shoot clays, I just told him to get a gun from Danny.

'So I can assure you it's impossible for him to be implicated in any of this.' He produced a handkerchief from his top pocket and wiped her cheeks tenderly, as if she was a child. 'There you are. Now, blow!'

He smiled at her and she laughed, a little shakily. 'Oh, Murdoch, what a relief! You are my rock! I should have told you all this sooner, instead of worrying and worrying by myself.'

'Indeed you should. But there is one thing. I don't often lay down the law, but I'm going to insist that we get help for him. His behaviour at the moment simply isn't normal, and it can't go on like this – apart from anything else, it's distressing you too much.'

She gave him the smile that had bewitched him from the moment he met her at a dinner party, a slender divorcee in a pale blue dress which exactly matched her eyes, and as unlike the sturdy, sensible woman he was then married to as it was possible to be.

'Of course we must, darling, if that's what you feel,' she said soothingly. 'He can go and have another chat with Dr Rutherford and I'm sure we'll find he can help him get things straight.'

'But,' he protested with the feeling of helplessness he so often experienced in dealing with his wife, 'we must take the professional advice he gives us.'

'Of course we shall,' she said, patting his hand and getting up. 'Now, I'll just finish making the soup, if you'd like to go up and tell Ossian that lunch is ready.'

Forbes-Graham left the kitchen with something close to despair. She always agreed with him, without argument, but somehow what she didn't want to happen never did.

Three minutes later, he came back in. 'He's not there,' he said. 'There's no sign of him.'

Deirdre sighed. 'Probably gone back to his studio to moon over that wretched woman. Murdoch, what are we going to do about that?'

With a sinking heart, Murdoch recognised the marital 'we' – denoted in normal speech by the pronoun 'you'.

The only sandwiches left in the canteen were cheese and pickle, not what Fleming would have chosen, and she was finishing one gloomily when Macdonald and Campbell came in. Macdonald was looking around and, spotting her, came over.

'How's it going?' she asked.

'I hoped we'd catch you, boss. There's a couple of things—'

She made a quick decision. Going back to her office was risky, since she was trying to avoid being trapped at her desk, but on the other hand this was a good opportunity. 'There's the briefing tonight, of course, but the team's all here at the moment and with Tam back it would be useful to meet and share what we've got. Round up Will and Tansy, can you, and I'll prise Tam away. He's on his second helping of haggis and enough's enough.'

As Fleming and MacNee walked upstairs to her office, she said ruefully, 'That was an awkward little scene earlier. You were quick off the mark in spotting it, Tam. I was going to have a word with you about doing something before it got nasty.'

'Bunty said Aileen was a bit tearful when she saw her.

Three kids under six was putting a strain on their marriage already, she said, and she was scared this would finish it completely. Then when I saw the look between the two of them . . .'

'Yes. I'd have thought better of Tansy, though.' Fleming sighed. 'Still, at least that will have stopped it before it became a disciplinary matter. I've scheduled them for routine stuff this afternoon, but I suppose we'll have to rejig the partnerships tomorrow.'

'You could keep him on routine. Just ground him – no one likes doing the basic maintenance.'

'Good thinking.'

They reached her office and she looked with distaste at the blinking light on her phone. 'I'll run through those, see if there's anything urgent. I'm not even going to look at the emails, though.'

Fortunately there was nothing that couldn't wait, and she was ready to start the meeting by the time the others appeared. Wilson, looking shamefaced, took the seat furthest away from MacNee, and Kerr had clearly spent some time working on her make-up, though it didn't conceal her swollen eyelids.

Ignoring the atmosphere, Fleming said, 'You kick off, Andy. You'd something to say.'

'Two things, actually. We interviewed the Farquharsons this morning. Ewan's just longing to write up the report for you, of course.'

Campbell looked resigned. Macdonald went on, 'But there was just this and that about what was said – hard to pin down, but I'm sure we weren't getting the truth from them—'

'From her,' Campbell corrected him.

'Fair enough, from her. She told him what to say, and he said it, not very convincingly. Right little Lady Macbeth, she is.

'But then, at the end, she suddenly came out with something

she'd heard the night before, when Zack Salaman turned up unexpectedly at a party at the Forbes-Grahams'. Turns out the Farquharsons didn't know a thing about him – must be the only people in the whole of Galloway who didn't – and it threw them completely. You have to keep in mind that Mrs Farquharson has an axe to grind, but she told us she'd overheard this conversation between Salaman and Johnny Black. Black was talking about some job he'd done for him, and what caught her attention was that Salaman was seriously annoyed with him for mentioning it. She just wondered, she said, what sort of "job" they were talking about.'

'Black,' Fleming said with considerable satisfaction. 'I've had my eye on him. He was in a pretty seedy business, and coming here from Glasgow—'

'Thanks!' MacNee said dryly. 'But I have to say, I think that one's got legs, Andy. The only thing is, I can see him killing off Carmichael – revenge, profit, particularly if Carmichael was determined to reject ALCO's offer. But Kyle?'

'If you're still claiming it wasn't a sniper, that's hardly rocket science,' Wilson chipped in aggressively. 'Salaman didn't order that one. That was Black's private initiative, because Kyle caught him in the act.'

'Certainly, that's the theory we've been running with,' Fleming said hastily, seeing MacNee's hackles rise.

'Actually,' Macdonald said, 'Ewan's had an idea about that.' He looked at Campbell, then as Campbell made no move to pick up his cue, outlined the point he had made: that it would be useful to find out exactly where Kyle had been when the Colonel was killed.

'That's good,' MacNee approved. 'You've quite a talent for hitting the nail on the head, haven't you, laddie?'

Campbell looked pleased.

'Is it OK to speak to Mrs Kyle again?' Macdonald asked. 'I thought I'd better check with you – she was pretty strung-up about the warrant yesterday and we don't want complaints about being heavy-handed.'

'Why not try his pals first?' MacNee suggested. 'Saturday afternoon – he's more likely to have been with Burnett and Gloag than sitting at home with his mammy.'

Fleming approved that. 'Get back to the school, Andy, and see what you can come up with.

'Now, what else? Tam and I spoke to Gloag this morning and got a pack of lies. I don't really have him in the frame at the moment, but he's definitely a sharp operator. Figured out that we were keen to establish if he'd have had time to get to Wester Seton to lie in wait for Kyle to arrive, and he put up a smoke screen about Gordon being confused about the time and not prepared to admit he was wrong. Unless his wife or one of the other kids was around at the time, it would come down to his word against the boy's, and there's not a lot we can do about that.'

'Oh yes there is.' Kerr had been very subdued; Fleming was pleased to see her suddenly alert and interested. 'I've made a start to reading statements, and I went over the interview with Gordon Gloag that Will and I did, Andy. He said after he told his father what Kyle was planning, and that he hadn't gone along with it, his father was so pleased he said Gordon could order pizza. If we can find out where it came from, they might well have a record of the delivery.'

'Andy, get that from Gordon and pass it back to Tansy for checking. I don't want to waste too much time on him right now, but it's a loose end we might as well tie up. Anything emerge from other visits this morning?'

Wilson didn't seem interested in contributing, and Kerr said hastily, 'No. The main objective was to interview Ossian Forbes-Graham, but he was out.'

MacNee nodded. 'That's right, he was. He and his mother

were at the Medical Centre this morning. He was going in when I was coming out from my appointment.'

Wilson said coarsely, 'Gone to see the doc because the wheels are coming off his wagon, no doubt.'

Without looking at him, Kerr said to Fleming, 'I do think we have a problem with him. He seems dangerous to me – certainly not normal.'

Fleming scribbled a note. 'Point taken. We'll be looking into that. Now – anything else before we wrap up?'

Campbell stirred. It was, somehow, a portentous movement, and the others turned to look at him. 'Er – I was just thinking. Could it maybe have been meant to be Dylan Burnett? They were both wearing helmets – it wouldn't be easy to tell the difference, if you didn't know already.'

There was a brief silence, then Fleming said, 'You're right, of course, but I'm not sure it gets us anywhere. The same arguments, more or less, would apply. Thoughts on that, anyone?'

'We could keep it in mind,' Kerr suggested, 'and see if there are connections he might have had that Barney Kyle didn't. Ask him if anyone had a grudge against him, say.'

'We can do that this afternoon,' Macdonald said.

'Fine. I think we've covered the ground. Tam, I want you to come with me to see Ellie Burnett. We could look in on Ossian Forbes-Graham after that. Will, could you wait a moment too, but the rest of you carry on. Keep me in the picture; I'll want everything you have in time for the general briefing.'

Kerr went out with her eyes lowered. Wilson didn't move, but his face took on an expression of surly defiance.

Fleming ignored that. 'Will, it's getting to the point where there's a huge amount of stuff coming through, and it would be helpful to have one of the team here at headquarters designated to monitor what comes in. With Tam back now,

I want you to take that on. You could trawl especially for anything that could possibly link either Dylan Burnett or Barney Kyle with the Colonel.'

He looked as if he would have liked to argue, then thought the better of it and shrugged. 'If that's an order,' he said, and left.

MacNee grinned. 'Didn't like that, did he? Just scared to complain.'

'Wisely. Right, Tam—'

The phone rang. It had been blessedly silent during the meeting, and she looked at it with resignation. 'I suppose I'd better take that. Too many people know I'm in the building.

'Yes?' She listened, then said, 'All right – put him through.' She just had time to say to MacNee, 'That's a piece of luck. Salaman's on the line,' before she heard his voice at the other end.

'Yes, Mr Salaman? What can I do for you?'

'I'm getting very tired of staying in an extremely inadequate hotel, inspector. I wondered whether there was any reason to protract my stay?'

'We have your London address, of course, so I don't see that there would be any difficulty, unless you were thinking of leaving the country.'

'Not at the moment, no.'

'Then I think, on that understanding, there should be no reason to ask you to stay. There's just one small matter I would like you to clear up for us.

'I gather that you had a conversation with Johnny Black at the Forbes-Grahams' party last night, in which there was discussion of some "job" he had done for you.'

The voice went very cold. 'And?'

'Would you have any objection to telling us what that job was?'

'Yes, I think I would. It was my own private business. I

can assure you that this was nothing whatsoever to do with the case you are investigating.'

'I can appreciate your feelings, but I would prefer to be the judge of its relevance.'

'I'm sure you would.'

That was all he said. Pulling a face at MacNee, Fleming went on, 'I understand that his mention of this "job" caused you serious annoyance. Why?'

'I don't know how familiar you are with the customs of polite society,' Salaman said acidly, 'but I am not in the habit of discussing business matters with my employees at parties.'

Fleming seized on that. 'He was employed by you? I recall that you were reluctant to give me this information when last we spoke.'

She could tell from his voice that his slip had annoyed him, but he said only, 'That, too, was a complete irrelevance.'

'I must press you.'

'And I must decline.' It was a steely reply. 'I would remind you that I am a lawyer, inspector. The information I have given you so far was on an entirely voluntary basis. If you wish to force answers, you will, as you are no doubt entirely aware, have to put this on a different footing.

'I shall be returning to London immediately, unless you detain me.'

'We have no plans to do that at the moment.'

'Good.' The line went dead.

Fleming slammed down her receiver. 'Damn, damn, damn! Got absolutely nowhere with him.'

'Lawyers!' MacNee rolled his eyes.

'Get most of that, did you? Now, no doubt, he'll phone Black on his way to the airport, instructing him not to say anything. We'd have to arrest Salaman to compel him to answer, and we haven't a leg to stand on, as he very well knows. And if we put a toe out of line, we'll be mince. He'd sue at the drop of a hat.'

'Maybe it's a pointer, though,' MacNee suggested. 'Why would you be reluctant to be open about something like that, unless there was something you were trying to hide?'

'You'd have to allow for sheer cussedness,' Fleming said gloomily. 'And a lawyer's reluctance to give the police any help at all. But put it into the melting pot, with the other theories.'

'It's certainly still wide open. Can't say I think we've got a glimpse of a logic behind this. To be honest, I'm beginning to doubt that there is any.'

Fleming felt herself tense up, as she always did, at the suggestion of irrationality. 'Of course it's still early days,' she was reminding him, and herself, when the phone rang. She groaned. 'I suppose I'd better take that too.'

'I was wanting a word with Tansy,' MacNee said. 'Let me know when you're ready to go.'

She nodded. 'Yes, Donald?' she said wearily into the phone.

Kerr was sitting at a desk in one corner of the CID room, staring at a screen, when MacNee went in. There were half-a-dozen other officers working there too, but, he established with a quick look round, Wilson was not among them. He sat down on the edge of the desk.

'How are you doing, then, Tansy?'

She bit her lip. 'Ashamed, Tam. Really, really, ashamed.'

'So well you might be,' he said, but his voice was not unkind. 'What did that rotten bastard tell you?'

'Said they were getting divorced, that he and Aileen had been living separate lives for a year now. I shouldn't have believed him, though, I know. It was just – well, it happened at a bad time . . .'

'What went wrong with young Rory, then?'

'Took me home to meet his parents, didn't he? His dad's a sir, and it's this great big house. He didn't tell me, or I'd never have gone. I made a fool of myself, wearing the wrong things, and I'm sure his mother thought I was garbage but she was "awf'ly nice" about it,' she said with savage mimicry.

'And then at the meal at night they'd all these knives and forks, and I didn't know what to use, and it was awful. I told him I was leaving the next morning and we'd this huge row – him standing up for them and saying they liked me, as if I couldn't tell they totally despised me—' She broke off. 'Sorry. It doesn't matter now, anyway. It's finished.'

'Shame,' MacNee said unemotionally. 'But maybe you wouldn't have adjusted, even if they did. Anyway, no more nonsense with Wilson. Big Marge knows, of course, but she's pretending she doesn't.'

'Thank God for that!' It was a heartfelt exclamation. 'I was terrified. But Tam – I can't go around with him professionally.'

'No, she's thought of that. He's going to be stuck at a desk for the next bit. That'll teach him!'

He got the faintest of faint smiles. Then she said hesitantly, 'There's something else, Tam. Maybe I shouldn't say it, because I could be wrong—'

'Say it anyway,' MacNee urged. 'If you're wrong, I'll forgive you.'

'It's not you that would have to forgive. But anyway – you know the story about the sniper in the paper, after we heard about Pete Spencer being in the clear?'

'I heard everyone went crazy about it.'

'There was a real witch hunt, yes. The thing is, I was with Will when the news about Spencer came. We were all exclaiming, and suddenly he goes, "So it really could be a sniper then, right?" And basically we all agreed it was looking more likely.

'Then about five minutes later, he suddenly said he had

to get off home. The thing was,' she paused again, looking acutely uncomfortable, 'we'd – we'd been going to go back to my place, just for a bit. And he hadn't had a phone call, or anything, though he said he did when I asked him about it today.

'So he left, and then I rang a girlfriend and said I'd go round there instead. But when I went past his house, he wasn't there. So I – I just began to wonder if he'd been taking the time to contact somebody – you know, with that story appearing this morning.'

MacNee was intrigued. 'So you think he's our grass?'

'He even talked about what the papers paid, once – then laughed about it and said of course you'd be crazy to do it. But Tam, I don't see how we can prove it. The paper will never give away a source.'

'I'll have a think about it. Leave it with me, anyway.' He smiled at her doleful face. 'And cheer up, hen! You never died a winter yet!'

'What's that supposed to mean?' Kerr demanded, but he only winked and left her to her task.

Ossian Forbes-Graham stood in his studio, looking out across the courtyard. There was no sign of Ellie. She hadn't been in her shop since he told her about Colonel Carmichael's death and he'd only seen her occasionally at a window of the flat, like a fairytale princess locked in a tower. He'd always run out into the courtyard when she appeared, but she had consistently ignored his pleas to let him rescue her.

But now she had chosen her protector prince, and it was Black, not him. How could she choose a man like that?

He looked round the studio at the pictures he had created. Once, he had been proud of them. Once, they had value. Now, what were they worth? What was he worth? Nothing.

Slowly, deliberately, he fetched a Stanley knife from his

tool drawer. Slowly, deliberately, he scored the canvases across and across, then down and down. He threw the knife on the floor and then, with another look at the blank windows of Ellie's flat, he sat down and put his head in his hands.

Fleming appeared in the CID room looking harassed. 'OK, Tam, we can get away now,' she said, then, as they walked down the corridor together, wiped imaginary sweat from her brow.

'Donald's in a state about the press conference this evening. He wanted me to find something new for him to say, but there isn't anything. And I can't see that there's likely to be anything more to report tomorrow.'

'Unless something else happens,' MacNee said thoughtlessly, and she shuddered.

'Just – just *dont*! Let's get on with the routine. We have to believe that sooner or later some sort of rationale will emerge.'

'Maybe it's some sort of sick game, that's all.'

Fleming wasn't prepared to acknowledge that. 'Maybe our interview with Ellie Burnett will unlock the whole thing,' she was saying as they went out into the reception area. A man standing by the desk turned his head as they appeared.

She stopped dead. 'Good gracious, Bill, what on earth are you doing here?'

The desk officer said, 'Oh, there you are, ma'am. I've just been buzzing your office,' but she didn't hear him. At the look on Bill's face her heart had started to race.

'What is it? Oh, Bill – the children . . .'

'No, no, they're fine.' He came over to put his arms round her. 'I'm sorry, love, I'm afraid it's your father. He's dead.'

19

Normally, DS MacNee would have walked the short distance from Galloway Constabulary HQ to the Craft Centre, but just at the moment walking along in the open street gave him an uneasy feeling, somewhere round the back of his neck, and he didn't want to prove the sniper theory the hard way. He went to fetch his car.

He wasn't the only one feeling like that, obviously. The High Street, when he reached it, was unnaturally quiet. Such shoppers as were about were hurrying in and out of shops, and there were none of the usual groups of pensioners in casual conversation with friends. How quickly even a rubbish rumour in a gutter rag could destroy the cheery confidence of this couthy wee town! Bastards!

He drove along, thinking now about Marjory Fleming, and her father. When Tam had joined the force, Angus Laird had been a sergeant: a rigid, old-fashioned policeman who wasn't regarded with much affection by either his subordinates or his superiors. But no one had ever said he wasn't dedicated to the job and straight as a die, and if his training of younger officers had been harsh, it had also been effective. His daughter was entirely different, in methods as in personality, but sometimes you could see the same steeliness of purpose, the same belief in justice and the rule of law.

Tam and Marjory had never gone in for deeply personal conversations, but you couldn't work with someone for as long as that without getting to know them pretty well. However much Marjory might believe she had rebelled against him, it was Angus Laird, and not her sweet-natured mother, who had undoubtedly been the major influence in her life. Tam suspected she might be taken aback by her own reaction to his death.

Still, that was none of his business – any more than Tansy and Will Wilson were, but thinking about that brought a scowl to his face. Tansy hadn't behaved well, certainly, but she hadn't set out to be a home-breaker and, as Rabbie Burns knew all too well, '*to step aside is human*'. She'd just let herself be deceived, but there was no excuse for Wilson. In Tam's book, if you'd been blessed with kids it was your job to give them the best possible chance in life, which didn't mean walking out on them when it suited you. And Tam had no difficulty at all in believing that Wilson was the one who'd been leaking to the press. If he could see a chance to put the boot into the little bastard, he'd take it.

In the meantime, he'd more pressing matters to think about. Bailey had agreed that he should stand in: Marjory wasn't likely to take much time off, things being as they were, though they'd cancelled her evening briefing.

When he reached the Craft Centre, it had a deserted air. Macdonald's auntie's coffee shop was closed, and with the chairs all piled up on the tables, looked as if it might well not open up again. There were no display lights on in the other units, but as Tam walked across towards Ellie Burnett's shop, he thought he caught sight of a movement in Ossian Forbes-Graham's studio, though he couldn't be sure.

There didn't seem to be much sign of life in the flat above either and he wondered if Ellie Burnett might again prove elusive. But a minute later, in response to his knock, the door opened and Johnny Black stood there. That was handy – two birds with one stone.

'Sergeant MacNee!' He greeted him politely but without enthusiasm.

'Is Ms Burnett in? I was hoping for a chat with you both.'

'You'd better come in then, I suppose.'

As MacNee was following him up the steep staircase, he stopped and said in a lowered voice, 'Look, can you try not to upset her? She's been in pieces over this. She was fond of the Colonel, and then Barney too – well, you can imagine. It could just as easily have been Dylan, with someone going round taking pot shots at people. You're not any nearer laying hands on him, I suppose?'

That suggestion about Dylan again! MacNee filed it away as he handed out the standard line, 'We're pursuing several active lines of enquiry.'

Black opened the door to the living-room kitchen. It was quite small and sparsely furnished, with kitchen units down one side and a table in the middle. Ellie was sitting in a rocking-chair in the farther corner of the room, slowly moving back and forth, and he went over to her and took her hand.

'It's the police, sweetheart. This is Sergeant MacNee. They're trying to find out who's done these terrible things.'

The last time MacNee had seen her, she was singing in the pub, so lovely and with that heart-catching air of vulnerability about her. Now, her smoky, grey-blue eyes seemed too large for her face and the shadows below them were almost black. With her slight frame, she looked like a frightened child. No wonder the man was so protective! He kind of felt that way himself.

Black perched on the edge of the table while MacNee sat down on a corner seating unit opposite. He said gently, 'Ms Burnett – Ellie – I know this is difficult for you, but I'm needing to ask you some questions. They're just routine. We're trying to get a picture of where everyone was at the time the crimes took place, and what they might have noticed. Can you help us?'

She licked dry lips. 'I'll try.' Her low-pitched voice was faint and reedy.

'Last Saturday afternoon – what did you do?'

Ellie looked towards Black, as if for support. 'I went to the meeting.'

'The meeting about the superstore? What time would that have been?'

She looked vague. 'I don't know. It started at half-past six, so I suppose I went a little before that.'

'And earlier – what were you doing?'

'I – I don't really remember. I was here, I expect. Or maybe I went out shopping.'

'You'd have been here, in the shop,' Black prompted.

'What time does it shut, then?' MacNee found himself getting impatient. It wasn't that long since Saturday – even if the woman was upset, surely she must have some idea of her movements.

'Five – five o'clock, or so.'

'So between five and, say, six-fifteen, you were either here or along the High Street?' Ellie nodded. 'Did you notice anything that now, knowing about Colonel Carmichael's death, seems suspicious?'

She shook her head. 'Nothing. I'd probably just have been going along to the shops. I wouldn't have noticed.'

It would have been too much to hope that she had. He moved on. 'Now – Monday night. Where were you when Barney Kyle was shot?'

She shrank back as if he had struck her and the chair began to rock faster. 'I was here. Where else would I be?'

'Alone, while Dylan was out?'

Black had begun shifting uneasily. Now he said, 'I phoned you, remember? And I even know what time it was, because I'd been watching a league game and I rang when it finished – just around half-past nine.'

'Yes,' she said expressionlessly.

It would be simple enough to check that out from phone records, if the need arose, but he couldn't get his mind round the frail-looking woman in front of him managing to handle a shotgun, let alone aim it accurately. Black, on the other hand – that could as easily be setting up an alibi for him as for her, and MacNee rather thought the boss's money was on him. But that could wait till he'd finished questioning Ellie.

'You knew both the Colonel and Barney. Do you have any idea why the two of them should have been killed? Any link between them? You must have wondered.'

The rocking became even more agitated. 'I – I try not to. I can't bear to think about it.'

'If it had been your son instead—'

'No! No! I can't, I can't!' She jumped up and ran across the room.

Black went after her but she turned. 'Leave me!' she said fiercely and went through the door leading to the bedrooms.

He came back and sat down again. The chair was still swaying, as if the ghost of her presence lingered, and the two men stared at it for a moment in silence. Then Black said, 'Sorry. She's in a total state – can't deal with what's happened at all.'

'I can see that. What has she said to you about it?'

'She won't discuss it. I'm worried sick about her. I think I've persuaded her that she and Dylan ought to move in with me. I'll have to open up the business tomorrow, but I don't want to leave her alone here. The neighbours are – difficult.'

'Mrs Kyle?'

'Oh, poor Romy! No, that's awkward, but she's not a problem. But Ossian – well, you saw yourself how he was behaving the other day. He's all but stalking her and Ellie's not strong enough to deal with that at the moment.

'He's over there now, you know, watching the place, and if she was on her own I wouldn't trust him not to break in, or something. And to be honest with you, I think he could be dangerous.'

Tansy Kerr had said that too. MacNee got up and went to the window which overlooked the courtyard. He could just make out a figure sitting in the unlit studio in a chair facing towards them. 'Mmm. So when is the move to take place? Is her son all right with it?'

'I'd like it to be tonight, but probably tomorrow. Oh, Dylan's fine. Keen, actually – well, living above a motorbike workshop's every teenage boy's dream. And in fact, he's dead worried about Ellie – doesn't know what to do.'

'I can imagine that.' MacNee sat down again, and when he spoke his voice had a harder edge. 'Now, if you don't mind, there's a few things I wanted to ask you too—'

Black gave a crooked half-smile. 'Oddly enough, I was expecting that. Before you ask, Saturday – I'm not quite sure what time you're looking at, but I'd some kids round at the flat in the afternoon watching Sky Sport. I guess it was maybe eight, eight-thirty they left, and after that I'm afraid you'd have to take my word for it that I was there on my own till they came back for a beer – half-ten, maybe? Couldn't be sure.'

'You get on well with them?'

'We've the same interests – bikes and football – and you can have a bit of a laugh. I suppose you'd put me down as a sad middle-aged biker, trying to recapture my youth. And I don't have mates around here yet – one or two blokes I meet down the pub, but that's all.'

'So why did you move here? You'd a good business in Glasgow, mates there, presumably. Seems a lot to give up.'

Black grimaced. 'You might think so. But it's not such a great job, raking through other people's dirty linen.' He paused, frowning. 'You – er – know why I came here at first? It's just . . .'

'Mr Salaman doesn't like his business being discussed,' MacNee supplied, and Black's face cleared.

'You've come across him? Scary kind of guy. It always seems a good idea to do what he wants, sharpish.

'But one of the things I like about the bike job, apart from the fact that I've been daft about bikes all my life, is that I don't have to take instructions from people about what I'm to do today. Oh, there's an owner, of course, with half-a-dozen businesses like this, but his big idea is to make profits without being bothered by details, which suits me fine. Stumbling across it was a lucky break.'

'As was finding Ellie?'

'Ellie? Oh yes.' His eyes went to the door she had left by, as if he could see her by staring at it.

The man had it bad, there was no doubt about it. Well, Tam couldn't blame him for that. 'Anyway,' he said, getting back to business, 'what did Salaman employ you to do for him?'

'Wasn't difficult – and more interesting than sitting outside rundown flats with a notebook and a camera. He wanted to trace an army officer who'd been in the right place at the right time. He could give me the name of the regiment and a couple of other minor details and after a couple of false starts Carmichael's name emerged. Didn't take long – and he pays well.'

'Did you break the news to Carmichael yourself?'

'God, no! Not my place. Job for the lawyers, I'd guess. Then Mr Salaman asked me to stay on a retainer, just do the odd thing for him. With ALCO in the picture, he wanted to keep up with what was going on.'

He did, did he? Now, that was interesting. 'And "the odd thing" you did for him?'

'Wasn't that much. He wanted to know about his grandfather, what sort of man he was, before he contacted him.

Then after they'd met, he wanted a lot of local information, about the property, that sort of thing. Once ALCO came into it, he got me to report back about the situation. I arranged accommodation for him when he came, just for a look, discreetly. I was able to show him round without him having to ask and have it getting back to his grandfather that he was poking around.'

MacNee's gaze sharpened and unconsciously he moved forward to the edge of his seat, catching for the first time the scent of a trail. 'Now, why would he be wanting to do all that?'

'You'd better ask him. I didn't.' Black looked entirely relaxed.

Mr Cool, that one. But MacNee had a trump card, and it was time to play it. He gave his menacing smile. 'You see, Johnny, we're interested in this "job" you were talking about having done for him, at the Forbes-Grahams' party. Salaman seemed pretty angry about having it mentioned.'

The reaction wasn't what he had expected. Black stared at him, then roared with laughter. 'You don't think I'm a hit man, do you? And even if you did – why would Salaman want the man dead? He's money coming out of his ears – absolutely loaded.'

'Revenge,' MacNee suggested, hanging on grimly to his theory. 'And there's no such thing as enough when it comes to money. He stood to lose substantially if ALCO's offer was turned down.'

That set Black laughing again. MacNee eyed him with frustration. 'Care to share the joke?' he said acidly.

'Yes, well – that party. I should have known better. He's a raving snob for a start – was a bit put out to find me at the same party he was at, even. And then to him private's private, and this was – well, sensitive, you could say.

'The thing was, he hadn't got back to me about this "job"

I'd done for him, and you always feel edgy with him until you know he's satisfied. I blew it – it wasn't the time or the place, and he was livid. Phoned me this morning and gave me a bollocking and sacked me, not that I care. I suppose he was worried I'd blurt out something about what he'd asked me to do.'

'Which was?' MacNee wasn't enjoying this. It didn't sound as if Salaman had contacted Black to tell him to keep his mouth shut, but it didn't sound, either, as if it was going to matter much.

Black grinned. 'He wanted to know which were the charities his grandfather would be most likely to disapprove of. The value of the property wasn't big money to him – he just wanted to get shot of it with the least trouble to himself, and put up two fingers doing it. And when it's all gone through I'm to send a statement to the newspapers, so everyone can see how much he despised everything his grandfather stood for.

'I'd had to dig around the Colonel's background already and he was the old-fashioned type, all for the Countryside Alliance and the old regiment and that, you know the kind of thing, so making a list was dead easy – Amnesty International, Greenpeace, anything in favour of gays or nuclear disarmament, the League Against Cruel Sports, Animal Rights. He wanted a list prepared so that he could have his people get in touch with their people – he really does talk like that.

'He's a chip on his shoulder a mile wide about the way his family was treated, so you were right about revenge, sergeant, but his was a bit more subtle than gunning down his grandfather.'

It had the ring of truth, that was the terrible thing. MacNee took down a few details – names of the kids Black claimed had been at the house on Saturday afternoon

(Dylan, Barney and Gordon – the usual suspects), asked if he owned a shotgun and was told no, then took his leave, feeling dispirited.

Marjory Fleming drove home behind Bill in the old jeep, feeling sad but perfectly calm. Angus's death came into the category that is usually described as 'a merciful release': it had been painful to watch a proud man become, in his needs, an oversized infant. If it had hurt her, how must her mother have felt?

Janet was principally on her mind. Angus had been her life: even this past year, when he showed no sign of recognising her and indeed, on a bad day, was likely to abuse her along with everyone else, she had spent hours at the home, bringing in his favourite home-baking, talking to him as if he could understand, chatting to other residents, who did. 'She's as good as an extra member of staff, dear soul,' the matron had said affectionately to Marjory on one of her visits.

How would Janet cope? It worried her terribly; her mother had the habit of strength and Marjory had felt woefully inadequate on the occasions when comfort was needed.

As long as Angus was alive, Janet had a purpose to her life, and even latterly she could tell herself that, however little he might show it, he needed her. Her life would be empty, and once the shell of the man she had loved so faithfully all these years was no longer there, surely the memories of the man he had been before, the young man she had married, would engulf her in grief?

And Marjory began remembering herself. Angus's speech at her own wedding, when he'd actually said, in public, that she was a 'good lass' and Bill was a lucky man. Her eyes began to sting. He'd been so thrilled when Cammie was born, too – 'another man in the family' – and so proud of his grandson's rugby prowess. He hadn't been much interested in Cat, of course – hard to forgive him for that – but, but . . . that was just the way he was.

He'd been hard to please, but when she had managed to win his praise – like when she'd won the medal for the best athlete at the school sports – it always felt as if she'd been given a very special present. And would she be as she was now, without him challenging her?

Whatever he had been, he'd been her dad. Marjory felt tears start to gather, and she swallowed them back. She mustn't think of herself. Janet would be waiting at the farm, and she had to be ready to be strong for her.

She reached the farm and drew up in the yard beside the jeep. Bill was waiting for her; he put his arm round her shoulder as they went into the mud-room. 'How are you doing?'

Marjory managed a tight smile. 'Fine. Is Mum on her own?'

'Karolina's with her. She'll be all right.'

He held the kitchen door open. Karolina, sitting at one end of the kitchen table, looked up with a sympathetic smile. Janet, who had her back to the door, turned her head, and got up. She looked drained, but calm, and there was no sign that she had been crying. At the sight of Marjory, her face twisted in anxiety. 'Oh, my bairn! Are you all right, dearie?'

And Marjory, bursting into tears, flung herself into her mother's arms.

'The police would like to see you again, Dylan.' The maths teacher had just been handed a note by the school secretary. 'You OK with that?' he asked sympathetically.

Dylan shrugged. 'No problem,' he said, and went out with his hands in the pockets of his jeans, feeling the other kids watching him in a silence unusual in Sad Shane's maths class.

It was terrible about Barney, of course it was, and last night he'd had the sort of dreams he didn't like to think about, even in broad daylight, but in a way being a victim was quite cool. A girl he fancied who'd always frozen him out had come up and given him a big sloppy kiss. 'It could have been you, Dylan! You could have been, like, *dead*.' It would have been gross to make a move on her then, of course, but he reckoned he'd have a good chance later.

The cops in the waiting-room weren't the ones who'd been there this morning. One was a ginger and the other was a big guy with a buzzcut who seemed to be in charge.

Buzzcut said, 'Sorry to pull you out of class again, Dylan. What was it?'

'Maths.' He sat down in one of the chairs and leaned back, stretching out his legs. 'It's a doss anyway. No one does any work.'

'I'll try and spin this out a bit for you, shall I?'

It was tragic when they tried to get all chummy and jokey. Dylan ignored the attempt, and Buzzcut got the message.

'Right, I'll tell you what we wanted to know. Did you see Barney last Saturday afternoon?'

Well, doh! 'I told you already he was my best mate. What else?'

'Fine. So what did you do?'

'I'd a problem with the throttle of my bike, so I went round to Johnny's so he could fix it for me. He said me and Barney and Gordon could stay and watch football with him – he's got Sky.'

'Johnny Black? How long were you there?'

'Dunno. Till we went for chips, later. Gordon went home for his tea.'

He saw the two men glance at each other. 'Did Barney stay too?'

By now, he'd had quite a lot of experience of the polis, one way or another. This was obviously the big question, though he couldn't quite see why. 'Yeah. Till we went out to the Square. That's where we hang out.'

'We've noticed.' Buzzcut was being sarky now. 'So, what time was that?'

Dylan scowled. 'Dunno. Look, how was I to know anyone would care? Don't even wear a watch.'

'That's OK,' Buzzcut said hastily. 'Just roughly – after seven, say?'

'Later, probably. Eight, maybe – I dunno.'

'And then—?'

Dylan remembered, suddenly, what they had done that evening and coloured. 'We kind of mucked about. Then a bunch of us went back to Johnny's for a couple of beers and we were there till one o'clock, half-one maybe?'

'Johnny's a mate of yours too, is he?'

'We-ell, not exactly – like, he's old, isn't he? But he's pretty cool. And . . .' Dylan hesitated, feeling awkward about saying it out loud, 'he's with my mum now. So it'll be sort of like he's my dad. We'll be staying at his place.' It gave him a good feeling, saying that.

'Sounds all right. Now, do you know if anyone had a grudge against Barney? Any reason why anyone would have wanted to kill him?'

Dylan looked blank. 'Apart from her at the farm, you mean? Well – no.' He didn't try to hide his contempt at the stupid question. Everyone knew snipers just did it for kicks – except the dumb cops.

'Or you?'

Where did they get these guys? Straight out of Form 3, remedial? ' 'Course not. That's just daft.'

'That's all we needed, right?' Buzzcut glanced at Ginger. He didn't say anything, just went on scribbling in a notebook. 'We'll be having a chat with your pal Gordon now, but that's all we need from you. Thanks, son.'

Afterwards, Dylan drifted off outside. The bell hadn't gone for the end of the period yet and he didn't fancy another session with Sad Shane. Feeling in his pocket for his fags, he headed for the waste ground at the back of the boiler-house.

MacNee glanced at his watch as he came out of Ellie Burnett's flat. He'd hoped to go across and have a word with Ossian, warn him off Ellie, but Bailey wanted him back at the station to brief him on any developments before the press conference at four. The Super would go ballistic if he was kept waiting, so he'd better get back with the unwelcome news that another theory had run into the sand.

Pity. Black's background made the contract killing theory less fanciful than it might otherwise have seemed, and Salaman fitted the part – cold, clinical and with the kind of money that made guys think whatever you wanted could be bought. Black was wary of crossing him, and even the boss had been pretty keen to be sure they got it right where he was concerned.

Suddenly, an idea came to him. It was an unscrupulous, wicked, dangerous idea. He certainly shouldn't do it, and if Fleming had been around he wouldn't even have considered it. Could he get away with it? Trying to think of all the angles, he drove back to the station.

DC Kerr sat back in her chair and closed the computer document she'd been reading. She'd had a rotten afternoon; all she wanted to do was go home, fling herself on the bed and howl. The sort of pounding headache she had would have been a legitimate excuse, but working on through it was a sort of penance. She hadn't even taken painkillers. She deserved to suffer.

The humiliation was bad enough, as was the knowledge that she'd lost the boss's respect, and Tam's too, though he'd been kind. But the shame was worse. You could live down humiliation, but shame ate away at your inmost being.

All she could do to blot out her wretched thoughts was to work flat out. Will was around; he'd gone past her a couple of times but she hadn't looked up and she knew he hadn't looked at her either.

Still, her frantic onslaught had other uses too. She'd always prided herself on her attention to detail and a couple of nuggets of information had come to light that she could usefully follow up.

From their order book, the pizza place had been able to give Kerr a time fix – seven o'clock, which showed that Norman Gloag was being at the very least economical with the truth. Big Marge had all but ruled him out, but the fact remained that he'd have had more than enough time to get himself out to Wester Seton before the boys arrived, even if he'd walked. He might well have done that, given it was less than half-a-mile out of Kirkluce, and he certainly wouldn't have wanted to advertise his presence with a parked car. An appeal had already gone out to the public, asking for reports of any suspicious activity near the farm, but without results; maybe if they asked specifically about anyone on foot, cutting across the fields, say, something more might come in.

Kerr had found, too, the report from the uniform who'd checked the CCTV footage for Saturday. It hadn't been cross-checked against the statements yet, but what it told her was interesting – very interesting. Giles Farquharson, who had claimed he had driven in from Ravenshill in convoy with his wife to the superstore meeting, had appeared at 17.45 from a totally different direction.

Now what she needed to do was run through the film from Monday evening. She phoned to get it sent through.

It was a tedious job, but just at the moment punishment made her feel better, in an odd sort of way. The problem about the cameras, of course, was that they covered such a small area. You could see when people went to and fro along the High Street and in the Square, but not where they were going to or what they were doing, except right there in the centre of town. Their movements told a story in themselves, but if you were taking trouble to avoid being seen there were plenty of back streets. It was no secret where the cameras were placed.

Kerr skimmed through, slowing down when she saw MacNee going into the Cutty Sark and again, rather later, when Macdonald appeared and went inside. Walked right into it there, hadn't he? she thought with a wry smile.

Then, at last, she spotted something. She froze the frame, checked the number plate, and wrote down the time. She called up Saturday's footage, fast-forwarding to the appropriate time, and had a look at that, too. Yes, this was definitely interesting. Very interesting.

She logged off, then went in search of MacNee. Wilson was working at a desk at the other end of the room, his head bent in ostentatious concentration.

It took her some time to run the sergeant to earth, but she finally found him in the control room, leaving instructions for the telephone operators with the Force Civilian Assistant who was in charge.

'Nothing's to be said to the press, whatever the query, except that Superintendent Bailey will be making a statement in the morning. DI Fleming isn't to be disturbed – you heard about her father?'

The woman nodded, and he went on, 'And there's no point in putting them through to me or to the Super, because that's all we'll say. OK?'

Seeing Kerr, he turned. 'Got something for me?'

'Might have. Couple of things.'

They walked out of the control room together. There were several interview rooms further on down the corridor, but she was surprised that MacNee said, 'We'll just go into one of these, shall we?' instead of heading back to the CID room. Still, it suited her. The less she saw of Will just at the moment, the better.

She told him about the pizza delivery, and he grinned. 'Nailed the bastard on that one, anyway. He'll have some explaining to do, at the very least. And?'

'This is the interesting one. The Farquharsons' statement claimed that on Saturday they'd left the farm in convoy to go straight to the superstore meeting. But the CCTV footage shows him coming into Kirkluce at quarter to six. She came in at around ten past. She came from the Ravenshill direction but he didn't.'

MacNee's eyes gleamed. 'So what was he doing, for three-quarters of an hour before the meeting started? I like that – I like it a lot.'

'I can do better than that. On Monday evening, when they claimed neither of them left the house, she's on tape coming into Kirkluce, about twenty minutes before Barney was shot, driving towards the Wester Seton end of town and coming back again after all our cars started going out there.'

'No sign of Farquharson himself, though?'

She shook her head.

'Conspiracy,' MacNee said thoughtfully. 'Seriously plausible motive; they both had everything to gain – or thought they did. Leaves big question marks, mind. How could she have found out that the boys would be there at that time? Not to mention why he had to be killed. Kyle didn't happen to go past Fauldburn House at a time when he could have seen something incriminating – Black told me the boys were with him in the afternoon, and when Macdonald and Campbell spoke to them this afternoon they confirmed it.'

'We need to have a go at the Farquharsons, though. I don't mind working late tonight,' she urged, but MacNee wasn't up for it.

'I'd rather have a word with the boss first. I'm sure she'll be back tomorrow, and we can pull them in then.'

She was a little surprised – it wasn't like Tam to hold back. But it was his first day back at work, after all; maybe he wasn't feeling great and didn't want to admit it. 'Fine,' she said. 'If that's all, I'll just go back and tidy up before the end of the shift.'

MacNee looked at his watch. 'Is that the time? For goodness' sake – hadn't realised it was so late. Is Will still here, do you know?'

She tried not to cringe at the mention of his name. 'As far as I know. He was in the CID room when I left it.'

It had sounded as if MacNee wanted a word with him, so she was surprised when he didn't follow her to the CID room, heading instead for the reception hall.

None of her business anyway. She headed there herself to finish off and prepare for a long, miserable evening. She hadn't even the heart to phone one of her girlfriends.

MacNee looked anxiously round the reception area. It was quiet at the moment; there was a man waiting at the far end, patiently reading a newspaper. The evening shift was coming on, and his brow cleared when he saw that the desk sergeant, Linda Bruce, was handing over to Jock Naismith.

He greeted the two officers, then asked whether Will Wilson had gone home yet.

'Don't think so. Hasn't passed here, anyway. Have a good evening, boys!' She slung her bag over her shoulder. 'I'm just off to aerobics. The things we do for so-called pleasure! Ta-ra!' She went off with a grin and a wave.

Naismith grinned after her. 'Nice lassie,' he said to MacNee.

'Yes,' MacNee agreed absent-mindedly. 'Listen, Jock, I'm going to do something awful. It's going to cause trouble.'

'Oh God! And you only back today!' Naismith was resigned.

'Listen.' MacNee outlined his plan. At the end, he said, 'Are you with me?'

Naismith groaned. 'You're aff your heid!'

'Not as much as you think. I can cope. Are you in?'

Naismith said guardedly, 'Well, I won't say anything to contradict what you say.'

'And you'll say that one line I told you?'

Naismith gave a heavy sigh. 'I'll say that one line you told me. But I must be as daft as you are.'

It was only minutes later that Wilson appeared, going off shift. His face was set in hard lines, and though he nodded to the others as he passed, he didn't speak or smile. Then MacNee called, 'Will, I just wanted to warn you – there's press sniffing around. Watch what you say about it if they approach you.'

Wilson looked surprised, but came across. 'About what?'

'Have you not heard? We've made an arrest.'

'I'm surprised you haven't heard,' Naismith said a little woodenly. 'Everyone's buzzing with it downstairs.'

'Who is it, then?' Wilson's expression had changed to one of avid interest.

'Salaman. He's being charged with Carmichael's murder.'

'Really? Thought he was miles away at the time.'

'That's what we all thought,' MacNee said solemnly. 'But—' He shrugged.

'That's amazing. And what about Kyle?'

'Hasn't been charged with that yet – there's a bit more work needed. But look, Will, I was wanting to warn you – we've to be careful. The *Daily Record* seems to have picked up on it – one hint of confirmation and they'll run the story. And the Super's dead keen to announce it at his conference tomorrow.'

'Sure, sure,' Wilson said eagerly. 'I'm on my way home anyway, and I'm not stopping to talk to anyone.'

'Good lad,' MacNee said, and he and Naismith watched in silence as Wilson went out, looking rather better pleased with life.

'I hope you know what you're doing,' Naismith said heavily.

'I know what I'm doing, all right.' MacNee grinned. 'I'm just not absolutely sure what will happen now I've done it. But you can get a long way with flat denial.'

The editor was doubtful. 'No official confirmation of this, though?'

'No,' the reporter admitted. 'They're stalling. Couldn't get hold of anyone in authority and all they're saying is there's to be a statement tomorrow – don't want their thunder stolen is my guess. But my source is a good one – given us some great leads, one hundred per cent reliable in the past.'

'It's a huge risk. Anything else at all to back it up?'

'The hotel says he left unexpectedly this afternoon, which would fit the facts. And apparently the *Daily Record*'s snooping around. They've obviously got wind of it too somehow. If we don't run it, they'll dig it out and get the scoop. And it's a great story.'

The editor chewed his lip, between the devils of the deadline and the deep blue sea. 'OK,' he said at last. 'We'll run it. But I hope to God you're right.'

20

DC Will Wilson came into the CID room with a spring in his step. Avoiding Tansy Kerr, who was hard at work at one of the desks, he made for the group of detectives standing over by the window, talking about football. That surprised him a little: usually when stuff was happening, there was a hum of excitement.

'Hey! What about Salaman, then?' he said jauntily as he joined them. 'Any more news this morning?'

They looked at him blankly. 'Salaman?' one said.

'The arrest. You know,' he prompted.

'Has he been arrested? Who said?'

They were all staring at him and he felt the first prickle of unease. 'He was arrested yesterday afternoon – they were going to charge him with Carmichael's murder at least. Tam MacNee told me.'

'Maybe they're keeping it quiet,' someone else said doubtfully. 'But I booked someone in on a drink-driving charge early evening yesterday and they didn't say a word down at the charge desk.'

'*Everyone's buzzing with it downstairs . . .*' Wilson could hear Naismith's voice saying it. Someone else said unkindly, 'Probably Tam having you on. You're not flavour of the month around here, you know.'

Wilson could feel the blood draining from his face. His head felt light, as if it might detach itself and float away. 'Where's – where's MacNee?'

No one seemed to know; there was a bit of tittering. He set off to find him, his stomach starting to churn. If this was one of MacNee's little games he'd – well, he'd make him pay. Somehow.

He saw his quarry coming towards him along the corridor, with his usual cocky stride. Seeing him, MacNee broke into a grin and it was all Wilson could do not to seize him by the throat and wipe it off with his fist.

'Is it true, MacNee?' he said thickly. 'What you told me last night – is it true?'

'What did I tell you last night, Will?'

'You know perfectly well – that Salaman had been arrested for Carmichael's murder.'

'Arrested? Dear me, no! Now Will, you should listen more carefully to what people say or there could be a serious misunderstanding. I said he had a powerful motive and it would be good if we had found anything to arrest him for.'

'You set me up, you bastard! You know you said no such thing!' Wilson howled.

'Oh, I think you'll find I did. Ask Jock Naismith – he was there at the time. That's a dangerous habit of yours – jumping to conclusions.' Then MacNee's playful tone changed. 'But I can't see that it's really a problem, even if you did get hold of the wrong end of the stick. Why does it matter, Will?'

Wilson's eyes fell. 'You know why, don't you?' he muttered.

'Yes, of course I bloody do.' MacNee stepped closer until his face was only inches away from the other man's. 'And it answers a question that's been bugging us for years – who's the dirty bastard who's been tipping off the press? Must have been a nice little earner.'

Wilson shrank back, his legs feeling like rubber. He leaned against the wall, attracting a curious look from a passing FCA. 'What – what are you going to do?'

'Oh, I think it's more of a question of what you're going

to do. If you want a suggestion, put in your resignation right away. Tell them you want to spend more time with your family – that's the usual line.' The sergeant's tone was caustic.

Wilson hardly heard him. 'They've run the story. What'll they do to me?'

'Your pals in the gutter press? You know them a lot better than I do, I'm happy to say. But Salaman will sue, of course, and he'll be looking for big bucks – he's a hot-shot London lawyer, after all, isn't he? And he'll have them over a barrel. Let's put it this way – I doubt if they'll be putting you up for an award for services to journalism.'

Cold fear brought rage. 'I'll dump you in it too, MacNee!' Wilson blustered.

MacNee's lip curled. 'You think they'll be interested? This is between you and them. You can always come and make a complaint to your ex-colleagues when they send someone round to break your legs.' He started to walk away, then turned back.

'You'd be best to take up that job Aileen's dad offered you in his firm. You'll need a wage to support Aileen and all those bairns. Not that he's going to make it easy for you. You're one of these folks Burns talks about – "*Who know them best, despise them most.*" '

With a look of utter contempt, MacNee walked away.

Making the coffee so strong had been a bad idea. It had been meant to clear her woozy head, but it was disgusting. Marjory Fleming took another sip, grimaced, then pushed it aside. She was feeling terrible this morning, with aching bones and heavy eyes, almost as if she had flu or something.

For hours she'd been unable to sleep except in brief snatches, when she would wake with wet cheeks. Then in the early morning she'd dropped off at last and woke in a panic to find it was eight o'clock.

When she got downstairs, the children, on their way to school, hovered round her with unnatural solicitude. Cammie had done the hens for her and Cat – all grudges apparently forgotten – had cleared up breakfast and even washed Bill's porridge pan. She'd given her mother a bear-hug before she left, too. Marjory was touched by the affectionate gesture, but it all contributed to the feeling of unreality she was struggling with.

Janet had insisted on going back to her own house where she had old friends all about her, so Bill had driven her back after a supper when they had found good memories to talk about. Janet had shed a few gentle tears, but Marjory dared not let herself start. Her mother's control was amazing.

As Janet left, Marjory had said to her anxiously, 'You've been so calm – you're not going to go back and cry all by yourself, are you?'

'I lost your father long ago, pet. I did my grieving for him then, and now I'm just glad he's not bewildered and unhappy any more.'

Pressing her lips together, Marjory nodded, and her mother went on, 'It wasn't his way to show it, but you know he was real proud of his clever lass.'

Marjory had managed not to cry until she waved the car away, but it was these words which had haunted her dreams.

Bill had less than hopefully suggested she take a day off, but accepted that working, when she had no time to think of anything else, would give her respite from the exhaustion of a grief that had so totally taken her by surprise.

Work had taken her mind off it, all right. The fuss over Salaman had had time to build by the time she'd got in, and she'd hardly caught her breath before she'd Bailey on the phone. It really was the last thing she needed; she'd done her best to calm him down with assurances that it was nothing they had said and then sent for MacNee to try to get to the bottom of it.

MacNee arrived in a cheerful mood. 'Och well, at least it gave the Super something to say at the press conference,' he said cheerily.

She gave him a jaundiced look. 'I can't imagine where this story can have come from,' she fretted. 'No one seems to know anything about it, but the editor got on the phone, claiming the information came from a police source. I told Donald to point out that unofficial police sources are not our responsibility.'

'Right enough,' MacNee approved. 'Serves them right, sneaky sods.'

'But where can anyone have got that idea?' she persisted.

'Somebody must have got hold of the wrong end of the stick. Probably.'

There was something about the way he said it . . . 'Tam,' she said sharply, 'you didn't have anything to do with this, did you?'

'How could I have?' He was trying to look hurt at the suggestion.

She wasn't amused. 'I asked you a question, and you didn't answer.'

'There are some things,' MacNee said sententiously, 'that it's better not to know.'

Fleming was tired, worried, wrung out by emotion. She lost it.

'MacNee, if this is your doing, I'll have you on a charge!' she yelled. 'You can tell me all about it, or I pick up that phone to set up an internal investigation. And you can consider yourself suspended.'

'Marjory—'

'Ma'am,' she snapped. 'Is there permanent damage to your brain or something? It's the only charitable explanation.'

She saw that she had got him on the raw, but she didn't care. 'We've got a murder investigation – *two* murder investigations, that are going nowhere. Every time the phone rings, I'm expecting it to be to tell me someone's been gunned down in the High Street, and now I've got a doolally sergeant.'

MacNee's face had gone rigid with anger but then she saw something else too, something worse – uncertainty. Her fury evaporated and she put a hand to her aching head.

'Sorry,' she said tiredly. 'Sorry, Tam, I didn't mean it. Forget what I said.'

'I'm prepared to make allowances, ma'am,' he said stiffly.

It was clear she wasn't altogether forgiven, but she wasn't about to grovel. 'I shouldn't have spoken like that. But if you've landed us in this mess, you should apologise too.'

'I didn't say I had,' MacNee pointed out, but he wasn't about to push it, adding hastily, 'I think you'll find Will Wilson will be putting in his resignation, though. And after that you won't have to worry so much about leaks to the press.'

Fleming gaped. 'Will – he's been behind them?'

'Well, let's just call it a hunch I've got.'

She pursed her lips in a silent whistle. 'Salaman's going berserk, got his lawyers on to it already, and libel comes expensive. I wouldn't like to be in Will's shoes this morning.'

'Couldn't happen to a nicer fellow,' MacNee said callously. 'But here – there are one or two things Tansy came up with yesterday . . .'

It was a blatant attempt to change an uncomfortable subject, but she let him get away with it. He seemed pretty confident that whatever he'd done wasn't going to backfire, and he was right – the less she knew about it, the better.

She listened with considerable interest to what he was telling her. 'Let's bring the Farquharsons in for questioning, separately. We've clear evidence they've been comprehensively lying to us, and formal questioning might shake them enough to get at the truth. Though it's hard to see what link they could have had with Kyle—'

Her desk phone rang. 'If that's more on the Salaman business,' she said, looking daggers at MacNee, 'I'll have your guts for garters.'

He grinned at the familiar threat.

But it wasn't about Salaman. It was a message from the control room that there was an on-going incident at the Craft Centre; a car had been sent, but they had thought she would want to be informed.

'Thanks,' Fleming said. 'I'll be right there.'

She felt hollow inside. Another victim? 'On-going incident,' she said to MacNee as they hurried downstairs. 'Could that mean they've caught someone in the act?'

'If it's firearms, you'd better not go rushing in,' MacNee cautioned. 'You haven't got body armour, and neither have I. And I obviously can't afford to lose any more brain cells to a stray shot pellet.'

It was a barbed comment, but there were more important matters to attend to at the moment than MacNee's hurt feelings and insecurities.

The scene at the Craft Centre when they arrived was rather less dramatic than the one Fleming had constructed in her imagination.

There was a police car in the centre of the courtyard which looked as if it had been abandoned rather than parked as officers jumped out in a hurry. There was a small blue van with its back doors open, with a rocking chair, a sound system and a couple of suitcases visible inside. It was parked outside Ellie Burnett's shop; the door to the flat upstairs was standing open, and Johnny Black was standing in front of it with his hands on his hips, surveying the scene.

At the other side, two officers were talking to Ossian

Forbes-Graham. He was standing beside them quietly, every line of his body proclaiming dejection: head down, shoulders drooping, hands hanging by his sides.

Seeing Fleming and MacNee arrive, the woman officer turned and Fleming saw that it was Sergeant Linda Bruce. 'Bit of a storm in a teacup, ma'am,' she said in a lowered voice as she reached them. 'Ms Burnett's apparently moving in with Black and Forbes-Graham took exception. Says the lady's being forced against her will but I've spoken to her myself and it's nonsense. Frankly, she looks to me as if she's badly needing someone to look after her.

'But anyway, young Ossian sees himself as her knight in shining armour and has a go at Black there. Seems to have come off worst – he'll have a fine shiner to show for it tomorrow. But he was going on shouting and carrying on, trying to pull things out of the van when Black went upstairs to fetch more stuff, and in the end he called us.

'With all that's gone on, it got top priority, but quite honestly . . .' She gestured towards Forbes-Graham and shrugged her shoulders.

Fleming nodded. 'Looks like a case of giving him a flea in his ear and leaving it at that, especially since Burnett's moving out. We'd been planning to have a chat with him anyway, so no need for you to hang around. Tell him to go back to his studio or whatever he calls it and wait there for us.'

'Ma'am.'

As she returned to her colleague, Black came towards them. 'Sergeant MacNee. And—?' He looked enquiringly at Fleming.

'DI Fleming,' she supplied. 'I gather you've had a spot of bother.'

'Yes, we bloody have. See here, inspector, I know this looks trivial, and in a sense it is – I can handle a lad like that with my eyes shut and one hand tied behind my back, without bringing the law into it.

'But I'll be straight with you. I'm worried. The guy's obsessional about Ellie and after all that's been going on I'm afraid of what might happen. You have to ask yourself, what has he done already? He's not normal – you've only to look at him.'

He certainly had a point there. The constable was escorting Forbes-Graham across the yard, the young man walking with exaggerated, dragging steps, as if he hadn't the energy to lift his feet clear of the ground.

Fleming said only, 'We have noted your concern, Mr Black. As I understand it, with Ms Burnett moving in with you today, there won't be the same opportunity for harassment.'

'There certainly won't. I have gates to my yard below the flat and I plan to keep them locked. But even so, inspector, I feel there's more to it than that.'

'Any reason?' MacNee asked bluntly.

'If I had, I'd have come to you with it long ago. It's just . . . well, I've told you what I think. Over to you.' He turned away and went back up the stairs.

MacNee looked after him, his eyebrows raised. 'Could be right, you know. Jealous of the Colonel, and if Kyle got across him somehow—'

'To tell you the truth, I'd be a lot more worried about suicide, given the way that boy's looking. Let's see what he has to say for himself.'

Fleming gasped as she entered the studio. The contrast between the starkly white walls and the dramatic colours of the paintings on the walls was startling, but more startling was the fact that each of them had been slashed, again and again, so that the canvas hung down in streamers. For all she knew about modern art, this could have been deliberate, but the Stanley knife lying on the floor in front of them suggested otherwise. She and MacNee exchanged troubled glances.

The artist was sitting in a chair facing out into the courtyard and he was crying quietly. There was no other chair in the room; Fleming went over and crouched beside him.

'You seem very unhappy, Ossian.' Her voice was low, attractive, inviting confidences.

He turned his head as if only now registering the police presence. There was bruising coming out already round one of the light blue eyes and the thick, dark lashes round them were wet and clumped into spikes like a crying child's.

'I'm losing her,' he said. 'He's taking her away and there's nothing I can do.'

'She's made her choice,' Fleming said gently. 'You have to accept that.'

'But I can't, I can't! What does it say about me? If she preferred that – that oaf, to someone who creates – created these,' he corrected himself with a whirling gesture towards the damaged paintings, 'then I'm nothing.'

It was very pathetic. 'Look, lad,' MacNee said with gruff kindness, 'what you're worth isn't to do with what anyone else thinks. I know you're seeing Dr Rutherford. You go and talk to him. That'll help.'

Forbes-Graham only shook his head, still staring hopelessly out of the window. Fleming noticed that his nails were not only bitten to the quick, but raw. His problems, though, weren't really their business. She wasn't sure she'd get any sense out of him at all, but she might as well try.

'Did you know Barney Kyle, Ossian?'

He turned his head slowly. 'She hated him. He was bad for Dylan, a bad influence, and Dylan's her world. Or he was – till now.' His face darkened. 'I wouldn't have minded sharing her with him – but *Black*—' He spat the name.

That degree of loathing was, in the circumstances, worrying. 'And the Colonel?' Fleming went on. 'What about him?'

Forbes-Graham scowled. 'She needed him, that was the

thing. She told me, if it wasn't for him, she'd be on the scrap heap. She'd have done anything he wanted.'

'And what did he want, Ossian?' She made her voice softer again, coaxing him to talk.

'What would any man want from Ellie?' he said, then jumped up so suddenly that Fleming almost overbalanced. 'Look! There she is! See for yourself!'

She straightened up, looking with considerable curiosity at the woman she had heard so much about, and saw a slight woman with silvery-fair hair which came down to her shoulders in pre-Raphaelite waves. She had the sort of delicate beauty which is unfashionable in this brasher age, with fine features and porcelain skin, but she looked tired and thin, and her grey-blue eyes, as she looked up at Black helping her into the van, had an expression which Fleming could only describe as haunting. She could see just what MacNee meant, and when she glanced at them both men were gawping at Ellie with identical expressions on their faces.

Fleming cleared her throat loudly, and MacNee jumped. 'What are you going to do now, Ossian?' she asked.

He didn't speak, watching intently as Black slammed the doors of the van shut and drove away. Then he collapsed back into his chair. 'Gone,' he said dully. 'Gone.'

MacNee was prowling round the studio, possibly, Fleming thought, to cover his own embarrassment. Suddenly he said, 'Boss!' with urgency in his tone.

At the back of the studio a corner had been blocked off to provide a small lavatory and a basic kitchen area, with a sink and a microwave. Propped against one of the storage cabinets was a double-barrelled, over-and-under shotgun.

Tansy Kerr's spirits had lifted when MacNee summoned her to accompany him out to Ravenshill while Fleming interviewed Ossian. She'd hoped to be given a more interesting detail this morning but nothing had happened, what with the boss being in late, and all the fuss about Salaman . . . She had a dreadful feeling that it had something to do with what she'd told Tam about Will, but she'd made a deliberate decision not to go there.

She'd made a point of occupying herself with trawling through every report she could lay hands on, hoping to redeem herself by finding some wow-factor evidence, which so far hadn't appeared, but she reckoned that by now she knew more about the details of the case than anyone else did, up to and including Big Marge.

Still, it looked as if penetrating insights wouldn't be called for. Everyone was playing it cool, but there was a mood of excitement – and, of course, she had fancied Ossian Forbes-Graham for it from the start.

He hadn't been arrested, just agreed to 'help the police with their enquiries'; he was at the station now. And she and MacNee were heading off to ask Daniel Simpson at the clay-pigeon range some very pointed questions.

MacNee had been upbeat. 'Ossian's got the motives, you see – weird ones, but no one ever said he wasn't weird. And by his own admission, he nicked the gun out of one of the lockers. Claimed he hadn't managed to get any ammunition for it, and that if he got some he was only going to use it on himself, but then—'

'He would, wouldn't he?' Kerr finished for him. 'So where does that leave us?'

'Tricky situation. His father owns the clay-pigeon business, so by extension the guns, and they're all properly licensed. If he claims his son had it with his permission, given that it wasn't loaded and there wasn't a single cartridge in the studio, we haven't a leg to stand on.'

'So where do we go from here?'

'Lean on Simpson, for a start. Find out if he's as casual

about ammunition as he is about the guns. I came up here earlier, and I could have helped myself to a gun myself if he was distracted for a few minutes, after he let me see where the keys were and watch him while he tapped in the code.'

The place was very quiet when they arrived, with only one car, presumably Simpson's, parked outside. When they went into the converted steading, he was sitting reading a shooting magazine.

As MacNee showed his warrant card and mentioned their names, Kerr saw unease in Simpson's eyes.

'I know who you are,' he said roughly. 'What are you wanting?'

'Just a word about security,' MacNee said.

'You saw it all last time, when you were wasting my time, pretending to be a punter.' His tone was unfriendly. 'Is this an official inspection, then?'

'Let's call it that. Are all your guns accounted for?'

'Of course they effing are. You don't think we let the clients take them away as a party bag, do you?'

'You count them out, and you count them all back in again, you might say?'

MacNee, Kerr thought, was enjoying this, like a cat finding a mouse whose self-preservation skills were seriously under-developed.

Simpson got up. 'Yes, all twelve of them, though I can't remember when we last used more than four. People bring their own guns. But I suppose you want to see for yourself.' Looking elaborately bored, he led the way through to the back office, fetched a key from a drawer, then went to a security pad by a doorway and keyed in a number.

'You don't change the code, then? That's the same as it was when I came out last time,' MacNee pointed out unhelpfully.

'So? There's always one of us here when the place isn't locked up, and there's an alarm system, of course.'

He showed them into the windowless room with three steel cabinets against one wall. He unlocked the nearest.

'These are the guns we use mostly.'

There was a rack to hold four guns, with a gun in each slot. Simpson looked at MacNee. 'Satisfied?'

'And the next one.'

His shrug indicated how pointless he thought all this was, but he did as he was told, gesturing to the four guns inside.

'And the last one.'

He was looking towards MacNee as he opened it, rather than into the cupboard, hoping, Kerr guessed, to see a look of chagrin. When, instead, MacNee's gap-tooth smile appeared, Simpson's face changed and he whipped round to see three guns, and a space where the fourth should have been.

'But – but—' he spluttered. 'It can't be missing! We haven't had a break-in or anything.'

'We're not suggesting you have. When was the last time you opened this cabinet?'

Simpson had turned very pale. 'I couldn't tell you. Months ago.'

'I see. Where do you keep the ammunition?'

'We have to keep it separate.' He locked the cupboards, saw them out of the room and closed the door. Catching MacNee looking at the keypad, he said defensively, 'I'll change the code later.'

'Right, right. Smart thinking, locking the stable door like that. You wouldn't want the horse getting back in, or anything.'

Trying to ignore MacNee's sarcasm, Simpson went to a cupboard on the far side of the room, pulled some keys on a chain out of his pocket and opened the door. It was stacked with boxes of cartridges, marked with numbers which meant nothing to Kerr.

MacNee jerked his head towards the keys. 'Is that the only one for this cupboard?'

'Giles has his set on a chain like this. Makes it easier to have it handy along with the others we use a lot.'

MacNee went on, asking if there was a log recording how many were used, but it seemed that this was another area where the casual attitude prevailed too and it seemed unlikely that anyone would have any idea whether some had gone missing or not. Simpson was looking less and less happy.

Still studying the boxes in the cupboard, Kerr asked, 'Which are the ones that hold buckshot?'

'None of them. We never keep it. You'd only need it if you were going to shoot deer, or something like that.'

MacNee looked at her quizzically as she asked, 'How would you get it, if you wanted it?'

'Easiest off the internet, probably. Or a gun shop, if you wanted to go and get it yourself.' He named the only one locally, a country store about ten miles away.

Kerr got out a notebook and scribbled down the name. MacNee was clearly intrigued, even a little irritated, by his own ignorance of the line she was taking. Well, she'd felt that often enough working with him. Time for a bit of role reversal.

'I think that's all I wanted to know. What about you, sarge?'

Torn between annoyance and curiosity, MacNee agreed and they left. 'What was all that about?' he demanded as they got back into the car.

'I've read the post-mortem report. It was buckshot that was used.'

'Right,' he said slowly. 'So wherever he got it, he didn't get it here. Damn. Opens up a whole new set of enquiries.'

'At least it opens up something,' Kerr pointed out. 'Our problem so far has been every line we've followed shutting down. I suppose it's the gun shop, next.'

21

DI Fleming left the interview room with DS Macdonald, nodding to the constable at the door as she went out. She wasn't happy.

'What did you make of that, Andy?'

'Nothing to go on, really, was there?'

She groaned. 'I was hoping you'd spotted something that had passed me by. He's got access to a shotgun, he's got motives, of a tenuous sort, and he's vague about where he was when Carmichael was killed. That's all, and I can think of a dozen people that applies to, and he claims he was home with his parents on Monday evening. We've no case, have we?'

'Not so far. I could go out and check with the Forbes-Grahams, though.'

'Might be an idea to do that before we turn him loose and they know what they need to say to back him.'

She was frowning as they walked along the corridor. 'I just don't know about Ossian. Maybe he's guilty, maybe he isn't. He has such weird reactions anyway that I can't get any feel for it.

'I don't think we need worry too much about Ellie Burnett's safety, though, whatever Black says. If anything, I'd think Black would be a likelier target, and I reckon he can look after himself, now we've removed the gun.'

They were just reaching the bottom of the stairs. 'OK, Andy, you head off then,' she was saying, when a policewoman came hurrying down.

'Oh, ma'am, I've been looking for you. Mr and Mrs Forbes-Graham are at the desk, wanting information. They're – well, she's very persistent. I think PC Brodie's getting a bit frantic, if you know what I mean.' She delivered her message and went off with a small smile that indicated a reprehensible, if human, enjoyment of another's misfortune.

Fleming went across to the glass door which led into the entrance hall and saw a solidly built dark man and a woman with greying fair hair and wearing drifting draperies, at the reception desk. The woman seemed to be having what might diplomatically be described as an animated discussion with the duty officer.

'Ah,' Fleming said. 'Trouble.'

'Looks like it.'

'Might as well take it on the chin. It'll save you a journey, anyway.'

'I'm right behind you, boss.'

'Behind me, I notice, not in front,' she said tartly as she opened the door and walked across to the desk.

Murdoch Forbes-Graham, standing a little back from his wife and looking uncomfortable, turned as they approached, but Deirdre, in full flow, paid no attention.

'I demand to speak to the person in charge. I ask you again, where is my son?' She had a plaintive but penetrating voice.

PC Brodie was a probationer, a somewhat chinless young man who, as the inspector approached, was opening and shutting his mouth, trying to get a word in, and failing. As the detectives reached him, he cast Fleming a pitiful look, his round blue eyes glassy with alarm.

Trying hard to put codfish out of her mind, Fleming said, 'It's all right, constable, I'll take over,' and was almost blown away by his sigh of relief.

'Mr and Mrs Forbes-Graham? I'm DI Fleming. This is DS Macdonald. Shall we go into the waiting-room?'

She led the way, ignoring Deirdre's querulous litany of complaint. 'And I learn of my own son's detention in a phone call from a neighbour – a neighbour who had seen him being driven along the High Street in a police car! I demand to know where he is, and what right you have to treat him in this way . . .'

Getting her to sit down by means of hand-signals wasn't easy, but eventually Deirdre subsided into a chair, still complaining. 'I have had no satisfactory explanation, none at all. Is this what we have come to – the police state?'

Fleming said nothing, simply studying her hands, and taking his cue from her Macdonald, too, showed no reaction. Sooner or later surely the woman would realise that when you wanted information you had to stop talking in order to get it.

Murdoch was looking acutely embarrassed. At last he interrupted, with a tentativeness at variance with his appearance and bearing, 'My dear, I think you should give the officers time to answer our questions.'

She gave him a wounded look. 'I'm sorry. I am, quite naturally, overwrought. My son was exhausted when he came home last night – exhausted! And now this! However—' With a sweeping gesture she indicated that the officers could now begin their apology.

Fleming was in no mood to play games. She let the pause lengthen, then said, 'Right. Shall we start again? I understand you want to know what has happened to your son. Since he is not a minor, you have no entitlement to information, but in the interests of good relations I am happy to talk to you.

'Your son has not been arrested. He agreed to come here to answer some questions, and you may be able to help us here. My sergeant and I would like to question you both, separately. This may help us to eliminate him from enquiries, but of course it is entirely up to you.'

Deirdre clasped her hands and bowed her head. She had

very dramatic body language: Fleming interpreted this as relief, perhaps, that there had been no arrest along with a prayer for a successful outcome.

'I will do anything, inspector, anything, to help you clear my son's name.' She gave Fleming a tremulous smile.

Murdoch, however, was unimpressed. 'I'm somewhat uneasy about this, inspector. You mean, you want to check our stories against one another – and against what Ossian has already told you?'

It was, of course, exactly what they wanted to do, but it was supremely unhelpful to have it spelled out. Deirdre's face changed and her hand went to her heart.

'You mean – you are going to use us to try to trap him? How – how despicable!'

'Not trap him, madam,' Macdonald put in earnestly. 'We only want the simple truth – that's easy enough, surely?'

There were, Fleming reckoned, at least three people in the room who felt that simple truth was a difficult if not impossible demand, and that was to give Macdonald's sincerity the benefit of the doubt.

Murdoch said frigidly, 'Of course it is our duty to answer your questions. But there is no way I would permit my wife to be taken away and interrogated on her own. She is extremely sensitive, and she is quite distressed enough already.'

Deirdre's eyes obligingly filled with tears. 'My husband is right. I shall certainly refuse to say anything, unless he is present.'

'Very well,' Fleming said, in some irritation. Her patience was in short supply today, and this pair would have made Job curse God and die. 'Mr Forbes-Graham, your son was found today in possession of a shotgun which he tells us he took from the lockers at your clay-pigeon range. Did he have it with your permission?'

Deirdre gasped. 'Oh, Murdoch, you told me he had no access to a gun—'

'Be quiet, Deirdre!' he snapped. She gaped at him in hurt astonishment as he said in measured tones, 'Naturally, my son has my permission to use anything that is my property. Including these guns.'

He'd cottoned on to the implications quickly, she'd give him that. Fleming tried again. 'Is that altogether wise? If he is having treatment for medical problems—'

Deirdre sat bolt upright in her chair. 'Who told you that? Did Ossian say he was?'

'No,' Fleming admitted. She couldn't actually recall how they knew; MacNee had mentioned it and Ossian certainly hadn't denied it.

'Then you shouldn't know anything about it!' his mother said fiercely. 'Medical confidentiality – I shall have to consider making a complaint.'

Oh, awa' and bile yer heid! She had to bite back the coarse phrase, only saying flatly, 'That's a matter for you. Mr Forbes-Graham, had Ossian access to ammunition?'

'God, I hope not!' the man burst out. The strain was beginning to show. 'Certainly not at home. I've taken particular care to keep it under lock and key in the estate office, and secure the premises whenever I leave.'

'Because—?' Fleming prompted.

'Because I was afraid he would harm himself. I still am.'

Deirdre gave a cry of fright. 'Oh no, no, Murdoch!'

'I can understand your concern.' Fleming came in quickly. 'But surely he could get it on the internet – buy it in a shop—'

Murdoch was shaking his head. 'The only computer is in the office. Technology has never interested Ossian. And he doesn't drive – walks the five miles to the studio and back. Says he likes the exercise. If – if he got hold of ammunition, it must have been at the time he took the gun. Simpson's been negligent, quite clearly. He'll be looking for a job tomorrow.'

Deirdre's tears were real enough now. 'You said he couldn't have got ammunition, you told me—'

He turned on her. 'I said I was sure that my son hadn't killed anyone, whatever anyone else might think. And I believe that.'

'You've never spoken to me like that before – never!'

'I'm sorry.' It was a perfunctory apology. Murdoch turned to Fleming. 'I think we've both had as much as we can take. Was there anything else?'

Unsettled was just how she liked her victims. Hastily she said, 'Just one thing more. Where were you on Monday night – both of you?'

They looked at each other. 'Monday,' Murdoch said, frowning.

'What did Ossian say?' Deirdre asked innocently, but got no reply. She bit her lip, then suddenly her face brightened. 'Oh, I remember! There was that documentary about Rothko on BBC2 that Ossian wanted to see. He and I watched it together, and you were in and out, Murdoch.'

'That's right!' he exclaimed. 'I had a phone call – there was a problem with cattle on the road and I had to dig out Farquharson to get them rounded up. We'd all had supper together before that, a nice family evening. Then there was the programme – two hours, wasn't it? – and after that we all went to bed.

'Is that what you wanted, inspector?'

'Yes,' said Fleming, but she lied. She hadn't wanted that at all. Another line of enquiry had just petered out.

She escorted them out of the room, leaving them in the reception area with the promise that Ossian would be with them shortly. She and Macdonald went back through the glass door.

'So where do we go from here, then?' She felt bone-weary, barely able to put one foot in front of the other.

'If you'll forgive me for being blunt, boss, I reckon the short answer for you is, home.' He hesitated, then said diffidently, 'Sorry about your father.'

'Thanks, Andy. I am too. Rather more than I expected to be, to tell you the truth, given his condition this last bit.' She cleared her throat. 'Anyway, I've been meaning to pull in the Farquharsons – discrepancies in their statements . . .'

'Look, it's your call, obviously. But if he did it, or if she did it, they're not going to knock someone else off between now and tomorrow morning. And if it wasn't one of them – well . . .'

He didn't need to finish the sentence, and she didn't want to finish it herself. And he was right; she'd found it hard to behave professionally during that last interview and it was after seven o'clock now. She was hungry and she was very, very tired. She wanted home, and Bill, and comfort.

'OK, sarge, you win!' she said, and saw that Macdonald's smile held something of relief that, having stuck his neck out, she hadn't torn his head off. What a monster she must be!

Norman Gloag woke in his chair with a start, confused for a moment. His tongue was stuck to the roof of his mouth, he felt queasy and his head was thumping; he had gone into work, but left early and started hitting the whisky on an empty stomach – a recipe for disaster. Blinking at his watch, he saw it was half-past seven. Somehow, the whole afternoon had vanished. He staggered to his feet, moaning, and headed for the kitchen.

The house was uncharacteristically silent. It made him feel disorientated, as if all that was familiar to him had vanished during a Rip van Winkle slumber. He filled a jug with water from the tap, fetched a tumbler and sat down at the table. He looked around him as he drank thirstily.

It was Maureen's domain, the kitchen. It had been expensive enough, heaven knew, but it was untidy, with dirty dishes dumped on the surface waiting to go into the dishwasher. He looked round him with distaste. There was a greasy pan steeping in the sink and the laminate floor needed washing.

His world was falling apart around him. He'd had a vision of success which would take him to a different level, open up whole new avenues for him – a new life, indeed – and the cup had been dashed from his eager lips. And in addition to that, he was facing serious trouble.

He'd been arrogant. Bullying and bluster had always worked before as intimidation, but he had seriously underestimated the police. He'd got himself into a hole and hadn't been smart enough to know when to stop digging.

Gloag rubbed his brow, as if he could wipe away the fog within. There must be something he could do, on that front at least. A long evening stretched ahead with nothing but miserable thoughts to occupy his mind, an evening when, if he wanted a clear head, he couldn't even have recourse to the whisky bottle. A long, long evening, with the prospect of a troubled night ahead.

Surely there was something he could do? He looked at his watch again, then got up and went to the phone.

'Good evening. This is Councillor Gloag. Is DI Fleming available? Oh, I see. Then could I make an appointment with her for first thing tomorrow morning?'

The kitchen, when Marjory Fleming reached it, was empty. Even Meg, the collie, wasn't curled up by the stove, so Bill must be out doing his rounds, or perhaps there had been one of the regular farm emergencies. She opened the door to the hall, but she couldn't hear any sound of life. Ever since the kids got iPods they had listened to their music through headphones; she'd never thought she'd miss the infuriating sound of a thumping bass percolating downstairs, but now the silence made her feel very alone. She could hardly go up to her children's rooms and beg for company.

Marjory went back into the kitchen, picked up the phone and dialled Janet's number, anxious to hear how she was, but the phone rang until the answering service cut in. She must have been scooped up by friends to have supper. Marjory left a loving message, then went to fetch supper for herself.

She was looking bleakly into the freezer – why did she go on buying macaroni cheese when no one really liked it? – when there was a tap on the door and Karolina came in. She was carrying a tray with a dish on it from which came a delicious, savoury smell. Marjory's mouth was watering before she even said, 'Oh, Karolina! How lovely!'

'I watch for your car. You have hard job and you are very sad – you need good food.'

Marjory was very touched. 'And kindness. And a glass of wine – but I don't want to drink alone. Can I get one for you?'

Karolina smiled. 'Why not? Rafael is there. I look after Janek all day – he has a cold, and tonight he is – bloody awful. Is that right?'

Marjory laughed. 'Spot on, I should say.' She found glasses and a wine box while Karolina dished up the stew. 'That looks wonderful. What is it?' She sat down and began to eat.

'*Bigos*. I can tell you how to make—'

'It's delicious, but don't bother. I could make caviar taste like fish paste, just spooning it out of the jar. Cheers! I really am grateful – it all just felt a bit bleak when I came home and there was no one around. Do you know where Bill is?'

'He is going out as Rafael is coming home from feeding stirks. He says there is "cowpit yowe" but I don't what this is.'

'A sheep on its back somewhere. He shouldn't be long,

unless it's managed to harm itself in the process, which is the average sheep's main aim in life.

'Have you seen my mother today?'

'No. Bill, he goes in to do the things you must, you know?'

Marjory nodded. 'Yes, register the death, speak to the undertaker, probably.' Bill, as usual, had taken on the family duties that would have fallen on her shoulders: did she really appreciate him enough?

'She is with her friends, he says. Is best, I think.'

'Yes, is best.' Basic English was catching. 'I suppose. But really I should be with her, making all the arrangements, shouldn't I?'

Karolina gave her a surprisingly straight look. 'Why? You have important job, like a man. Bill likes this – he is happy to do these things. He is good – good for Rafael, too, to see this in him.'

This was almost the longest conversation she'd ever had with Karolina, and Marjory was interested. 'You feel it won't do Rafael any harm to have to cope with your son this evening, without you hurrying back?'

She'd never really thought she'd actually see someone doing this, but Karolina definitely dimpled. 'Is good start,' she said demurely.

Marjory burst out laughing, just as the kitchen door opened and Bill came in with Meg, who pranced over to greet her mistress. He had been looking anxious; now his face cleared.

'That's a good sound to come home to! How are you, love?' He came over to kiss her and smiled at Karolina. Then he looked at Marjory's almost empty plate. 'Hey! What's that you've got? It looks a lot better than what we had – pizza and oven chips.'

'If it weren't for Karolina, I'd have been stuck with macaroni cheese again. No, don't go—' Marjory exclaimed, as Karolina got up, her wine unfinished.

'I think is long enough, at first. I don't want to—' She hesitated, groping for the words.

'Push your luck?' Marjory suggested, and then they both laughed.

'What was that about?' Bill demanded as Karolina left.

'Oh, just girl-talk,' Marjory said. 'I don't get enough of it.'

Unlike Karolina, she had drunk her wine; she finished off what was on her plate and got up. 'Come on, Meg. It's my bet Karolina's laid the fire in the sitting-room. I'll put a match to it while you bring the Bladnoch, Bill.'

There was a disappointed silence in the car as DC Kerr drove MacNee back to Kirkluce after an abortive visit to the gun shop. They had both been hoping to return with confirmation from the owner that Ossian Forbes-Graham had gone there to buy buckshot. He hadn't, and nor had anyone else recently. The man was quite definite. He knew the Forbes-Grahams, sold very little buckshot, and none of it to Ossian.

It wasn't conclusive, of course, but the disappointing outcome of their enquiry meant everything would be much more difficult, checking out mail order and the internet. They drove away in gloomy silence.

'So where does that leave us?' Kerr said at last.

'Unless the boss has taken Ossian round the back and got him to confess, we need to keep the other options open.'

'What other options? As far as I can see, we're running out of them.'

'I was just thinking we should do a bit more on Barney Kyle – or Dylan Burnett, even, if you go along with Ewan's idea about mistaken identity.

'I've never spoken to Romy Kyle. I'll maybe away round first thing tomorrow and just have a word with her. I've spoken to Ellie already, but you can't get any sense out of her – the woman's away with the fairies most of the time.' He sighed. 'Bonny, though, and sings like a wee lintie.'

Kerr, about to make a caustic remark, thought the better of it. If you were going to do a 'me-too', mocking the man wasn't a smart way to begin.

'I could give you backup – a woman's touch and all that,' she offered, trying to sound offhand.

MacNee wasn't fooled. 'Och, I'm in a generous mood. You're needing to be in on the big breakthrough when it comes, if you're to get yourself back in the boss's good books, and you're not going to get that doing paperwork, are you?'

'Thanks, Tam,' Kerr said, squirming only a little. Eventually, she supposed, they'd all forget what she'd done. Even if she didn't herself.

Dylan and Johnny were in the front room with the door shut. Ellie Burnett could hear the familiar sounds of a football match in progress – the roaring of the crowd, the synthetic excitement of the commentator, a groan from the men as a decision didn't go their way.

She shut the front door of the flat with exaggerated caution, though it was very unlikely they could hear it, then went down the stairs to the yard below. Johnny's workshop was locked up and the big gates across the entrance were closed. She could see the padlock he had attached today to the bar across them, but she had taken the bunch of keys he kept on a hook upstairs.

Ellie unlocked the padlock and swung the bar away; it clanked, and she shot an anxious glance at the curtained windows above. They didn't move and she heard a shout of triumph from inside as she swung open the gate, then pulled it to behind her and went out into the High Street.

Usually at this time, half-past eight, it would be if not exactly busy, then well populated with folk going to pubs and restaurants and youngsters 'hanging out', as they always said. Tonight, you'd have guessed it was one o'clock in the morning, apart from the lights in the houses where frightened people had stayed indoors.

Ellie had two choices. It was almost like tossing a coin, though she knew it was heavily weighted in favour of one of them. What were the chances, at this time of night, that the other would be available? Still, with everything – or almost everything – stripped away, she had reached bedrock. What was somehow still part of her, bred in the bone, meant she had to allow that option its chance to dispel the darkness that was gathering round her with some sort of miracle.

The Roman Catholic church was a small, low, whitewashed building just off the High Street. It didn't have a large congregation and she hadn't added to it, except at Christmas or Easter, and not always even then. Ellie couldn't remember the last time she had been to confession, didn't know the hours for it. Perhaps, just perhaps, it was this evening. She rehearsed the words in her head: *Bless me, father, for I have sinned* . . . Would she be able to go on, after that opening? Was there any point in trying? Could it change what she felt, in her heart of hearts, must happen next?

If the church was closed, if there was no priest there waiting to save her soul, she hadn't made the decision – God had.

As she approached the church, it was clear what that decision was. There were no lights on, no cars parked outside, but even so she went up to the heavy doors, rattled the unyielding handle and then, in a frenzy of despair, battered on them with her clenched fists.

When she stopped, the silence engulfed her. A breeze had sprung up, with a cutting edge to it, but she stood with her head bowed until she began to shiver. Then she shook herself like a dog and walked away. There was only one answer now.

Ellie felt in her pocket and the banknote crackled reassuringly in her fingers. If God wouldn't help her, there was someone she knew in a backstreet near here who would.

22

It was far too long since Marjory had sat with Bill, swirling her malt in the heavy crystal tumbler, here in the comfortable, shabby sitting-room. Under Karolina's care, the brass fender which bore the scars of age and family life was glittering in a way it never had before and the wood of the old-fashioned furniture, which had belonged to Bill's parents, and indeed grandparents, now had a patina which glowed in the soft light of the side lamps. The nights were drawing in and it had started raining: with the cheerful blaze of the fire and Meg blissfully stretched out on the rug, it seemed more than ever a haven of comfort.

They talked family business: the funeral was to be on Saturday, Janet was being cherished by friends who were helping her prepare the service, Cammie was fine, Cat was very subdued.

'She's had a lot to cope with,' Marjory sighed. 'She hasn't had anyone she knew die before, and two within days is shattering. Especially when one was someone her own age – you believe you're immortal, till one of your friends dies. I remember when that happened to this day, and I was eighteen at the time.'

'Are you any nearer to knowing who did it? Probably the last thing you want to think about tonight, but—'

'No,' she said. 'If you're in listening mood, it would help to talk.'

Bill leaned back in his chair and stretched out his legs.

'Nothing better to do, unless someone else finds another sheep with an ambition to practise somersaults.'

'The thing is, it just seems to be trickling through my fingers. Every time, it's promising, then it doesn't work out. We're not even close.'

'Early days,' Bill pointed out. 'It's not a week yet since Carmichael was killed.'

'I know, I know. But we've been working flat out, even brought in extra help to do it, and we've pretty much covered all the bases. They were both opportunistic crimes which have left us with very little in the way of hard evidence.

'Oh, plenty of people had good sound motives for killing Carmichael, but their links with Barney Kyle are casual or non-existent. We've established he didn't happen to walk past and see someone raising a shotgun, and any other motive we've managed to dredge up seems flimsy in the extreme. Nearly all our suspects have an alibi for one murder or the other – we're almost at a standstill.

'Councillor Gloag is still in the frame, being slippery as usual, but unless there's more to it than meets the eye, you have to ask – two murders on the basis of getting a big business contract?'

'And it's not going through anyway, I hear. Janet's friend Mrs Duncan was full of it – ALCO has decided that being associated with a double murder isn't good for PR, and they're looking elsewhere.'

'Really? Well, that's good news for the High Street, and for the farms too, but there would have been advantages on the domestic front. It might have offered a healthier selection than pizza and oven chips from Spar. I'm going to have to get a grip on that once all this is over. If it ever is. If it doesn't – get worse.'

Bill raised his eyebrows, but she went on, 'Tomorrow I'm going to pull in the Farquharsons – you know the story there?

Oh, need I ask – Mrs Duncan! Well, they at least thought they had good reason to want the Colonel out of the way before he refused ALCO's offer. They have definitely lied to us about their movements and if you assume conspiracy their alibis have gaps in them you could drive a tank through. But again, we hit the problem of a link with Kyle – doubt if they even knew him, and it's hard to see how they'd be sufficiently aware of his movements to set up an ambush.

'I'm getting desperate, Bill. If this *is* rational, it's a logic I don't understand. I don't know where else to go. Any suggestions?'

He looked at her empty glass. 'What about another dram, for a start?' He brought over the bottle and topped them both up, then sat down again, his brow furrowed in thought.

Marjory waited patiently, listening to the peaceful sound of rain pattering on the windows. A burning log sent up a flurry of sparks and Meg stirred in her sleep, giving a muffled 'wuff'at something in her dream.

At last he said, 'You want to believe there's a reason, don't you?'

Marjory stiffened. She had asked him, but now she wasn't sure she wanted to hear what he had to say.

He went on, 'You've looked for links between the people, connections, their motives for choosing those victims. What if it isn't like that?'

'A sniper,' she said dully. She had been relaxing; now she found herself tensing up again, almost expecting that at the use of the dreadful word the phone might ring with news of another victim.

'Not necessarily – but suppose it was? What do you do then?'

'*I don't know!*' There was desperation in her tone. 'I don't even begin to know where to start. I've read stuff about it when it's happened in the States and they haven't any answers either. You check out the known loners and weirdos, but more often than not it's someone they describe afterwards as quiet and ordinary.

'It happens again – and again, possibly, then either someone sees something and gives you a lead, or they confess or kill themselves. That's how most crimes get solved – information or confession. And I can't see any sign of either at the moment.'

'The only thing is,' Bill said, 'when you read about it, they just pick off a passer-by. Here, he's gone out of his way to choose someone – in Kyle's case, very carefully.'

Marjory brightened. 'Someone else said that. And it's true, isn't it?'

'But from what you say you're in some doubt as to whether there's reason behind it at all. The crimes seem random.'

'So where do I go from there?'

There was another of Bill's long silences, then he said, 'Look at the crimes, not the person. See if the answer's there.'

'The crime, not the person,' she repeated slowly. 'I think I see what you mean. It's a new angle, anyway, and I was desperate for one. Thanks, Bill.' A gawping yawn took her by surprise. 'Oh – sorry.'

Bill got up. 'Time you were in bed, anyway. You get on upstairs. I'll take the glasses through and lock up.'

'Thanks.' She yawned again. 'I think I'll sleep tonight.'

'You certainly should, after two doubles and goodness knows how many glasses of wine with Karolina,' he said drily. 'And you never told me what the joke was.'

Marjory smiled. 'There are some things,' she said, 'that it's better for a man not to know.'

It was kind of early for an official visit but, as MacNee had pointed out to Kerr, they could always check that the curtains were open and there were signs of life downstairs before they actually rang the bell.

He was desperate for a lead, any lead. This morning he had found himself more tired than he should have been, and evading Bunty's watchful eye he'd taken his pills to ward off the headache that was brewing. He might not have the stamina for day after day of this. Andy Mac had said that Marjory too had been low last night after the information about Ossian, and she wasn't herself either – touchy, impatient and suffering sense of humour failure. And with the threat that the killer might strike again, they were up against the clock.

Hence the early visit. But when they reached the house, they realised it was not early but too late. Curtains were open, certainly, but no one answered the door and there was no car outside.

'Maybe she's gone away to stay with her family or something,' Kerr was suggesting, when MacNee had the uncomfortable sensation of being watched. He swung round.

A sour-looking woman had appeared from next door, bent with age but with darting eyes behind the thick glasses she wore.

'Looking for her, are you?' she called.

MacNee walked over to the dividing fence. 'That's right. Has she gone away?'

'You reporters, then?' she asked with a hopeful expression. 'There'd be a charge, mind, but I could tell you—'

He cut short the sales pitch. 'Police.'

'Right,' she said, with obvious disappointment, making to go back inside.

'Hang on. Do you know where Mrs Kyle is?'

She looked as if she was framing the words, 'What's in it for me?' but the glare he gave her changed her mind. 'Try where she works,' she said grudgingly. 'She goes there funny times. Half-past five she left this morning, in her working clothes. That's all I know.' She hobbled back in and shut the door with a resounding slam.

'Wow, respect!' Kerr was impressed. 'Could we employ her to do surveillance? On the job round the clock, obviously.'

'Everybody's ideal neighbour. Why half-past five, do you reckon?'

'Poor woman probably can't sleep,' Kerr said soberly. 'Son's body still in the morgue waiting for release to bury him, partner on the run – no wonder she needs work to take her mind off it.'

They drove round to the Craft Centre. Today it looked more desolate than ever, with the other shops shut and Romy's car the only one in the courtyard. The shelves in the shop part of her unit were bare but the lights were on and they could see her facing the back wall, standing in front of a fiery glow.

The door, when MacNee tried it, wasn't locked, but he banged on it as he opened it to alert her to their presence. There was a hot smell in the air and a roaring sound from the compressor for the powerful blowtorch she was operating in a sort of three-sided chamber, but she heard them and looked round. She cut off the gas supply to the blue flame and went to set down the dull silver piece she had been working with on the solid wood bench which ran along the back wall. It was deeply scarred with burns and gouges, untidy with tools of every description – mallets, saws, drills, shears, hammers, files.

Romy was wearing a dark red fisherman's smock which, like the bench, had suffered from her professional activities, and she was looking dreadful: gaunt and dull-eyed, with lank hair and red blotches round her mouth and chin. Their intrusion was clearly unwelcome, but when she spoke it was as if she hadn't the energy to sound hostile.

'Who are you? What do you want?'

Kerr flashed the cards and introduced them and saw her unbend a little. 'I thought you were more bloody journalists. I was considering using the blowtorch if you were.'

'Had a lot of trouble?' MacNee said with ready sympathy.

'All the time, the first couple of days. Thought I'd go mad. Mercifully only one thought of coming here, so it's been my bolt-hole.'

'It must be so very hard for you. Your only son . . . I can't imagine what you must have suffered.' Kerr, having offered the woman's touch, seemed keen to supply it – overkeen, perhaps.

Romy looked at her coldly. 'You can't even begin. Look, if you've got questions, get on with it and ask them. Spare me the mushy stuff.'

Crestfallen, Kerr subsided and MacNee did as he was told.

'I'll be honest with you, Mrs Kyle. We're working flat out, but so far there are no definite leads to point to your son's killer. Is there anything – anything at all, that you know about Barney that might make someone decide to kill him?'

'Don't think I haven't thought about it. I've gone over and over it, hour after hour, day and night since it happened. How do I know what he did, who he got across? He's – he *was* . . .' For the first time her voice faltered, but she went on, 'a teenager, and it was the usual thing – "Where did you go?" "Out." "What did you do?" "Nothing." You know?

'There isn't anything I can tell you. The only person who had a reason to hold a grudge was that old woman and she didn't do it – so . . .' She gave a helpless shrug.

If she hadn't come up with something, after all that, what hope was there that this wasn't a dead end? MacNee continued, a little desperately, 'What about Dylan Burnett? It's been suggested that they were wearing helmets, so it could be mistaken identity. I don't suppose you can think of anyone with a reason for wanting him dead?'

Romy gave a humourless smile. 'Apart from me, do you mean? He was a bad apple – Barney would be alive today if it wasn't for that boy.

'But no, same answer, I'm afraid. The old woman – no one else I know of.'

Not noticing MacNee's sudden silence, Kerr asked, 'Did Barney and Colonel Carmichael know each other, Mrs Kyle?'

MacNee hardly heard the reply, that they might possibly have spoken on the odd occasion but as far as Romy was aware had no further contact. His head was buzzing with questions and he had a cold feeling in the pit of his stomach.

Suppose Christina Munro wasn't just a poor, helpless, beleaguered old soul? Suppose the dead sheep, which had made him believe she couldn't have done it, actually had nothing to do with the case? Suppose she had, not the wisdom, but the cunning of age? Suppose, as the pathologist had said, it couldn't be ruled out that the momentum of the bike had carried Barney on, after he'd taken the fatal wound? What were the chances that anyone had done a thorough search of the outbuildings at the time? None, or less than that? What if somewhere on her farm, or buried now in the fields around it, was another gun, a bigger gun, loaded with buckshot?

'I've come to make a confession, inspector.'

DI Fleming looked at Norman Gloag with an unfriendly eye. Somehow she didn't think that this remark, delivered in a frank, open, one-reasonable-chap-to-another manner, was the prelude to the sort of conversation which meant she could produce the handcuffs. And unless her expectations were overly pessimistic, this early appointment with one of her bêtes noires was not a good start to a day which she feared was only likely to get worse. The Chief Constable had been at a conference in London; he would return tomorrow expecting serious progress and Bailey was getting his knickers in a preparatory twist.

She raised her eyebrows coolly. 'Yes, councillor?'

My goodness, the man sweated easily! He had his handkerchief out already, patting at his jowls, but he went on smoothly, 'I have been very foolish. No, that is being too lenient. What I did was simply wrong.'

His small eyes, in that pinkish, porcine countenance, were studying her closely. She didn't react, looking at him steadily in return.

The response which didn't come provoked another outburst of patting. Then he said, 'You see, you pointed out that as someone who had prior knowledge that a crime was planned, I should have contacted the police. I am ashamed to say, in my relief that my son was not again involved, it didn't cross my mind. As a councillor particularly, it was my duty and I was afraid that this might come out.'

'Your knowledge, rather more importantly, made you a suspect.'

'Yes, yes!' He waved his hand in a dismissive gesture. 'Of course I know that. Which is why, as I now realise, what I did was extremely foolish as well as wrong.

'Inspector, I assure you, on my honour—'

Fleming permitted herself a small, satirical smile, and he said defensively, 'Yes, I realise that my behaviour entitles you to treat that with scorn, but I will attempt to outline—'

She had had enough. 'Councillor Gloag, you are not in the council chamber now and I have no time to listen to speeches. You said you had come to make a confession. Perhaps you could just get on with it.'

She wondered if this would provoke aggression, but he only gulped. 'I'm sorry. In my second conversation with you, I claimed I was told later than I had been, quite falsely. But I wasn't lying to cover up guilt.

'It was vitally important that you would rule me out of your enquiries at the very start. In a place like this, gossip travels like wildfire. If you'd started questioning people about my movements and told them that I was aware an attack was due to take place on an elderly and vulnerable constituent, and had done nothing about it, I would have been punished at the ballot-box. As you no doubt realise, success in local elections is a matter of just a handful of votes, and I would be in line to be leader of the council next year, a position which will – would have,' he corrected himself bitterly, 'allowed me to bring the great benefit of modern shopping to the folk of Kirkluce.'

'Ah yes. I understand the ALCO deal has fallen through.' Seeing him wince was the only part of the interview she had enjoyed.

'Yes. Most unfortunately. And nothing, it appears, can be done about it now.' He gave a gusty sigh. 'But to return to the problem that brought me here. I can see, inspector, that I have placed myself in a most invidious position.

'You probably consider me a serious suspect. I had, I admit, hoped I could simply convince you that I had nothing whatsoever to do with these dreadful acts, since if you demanded corroboration you would have turned to a source who would not supply it. My wife, seeing me in difficulties, has left the family home – the luxurious home she was quite content to have me supply for her – taking the children with her, and I could hope for no loyalty from her.'

'Perhaps she felt she should be loyal to the son you attempted to suborn,' Fleming said cruelly. 'Or even, dare I say it, to the truth? In any case, it is hardly relevant. We already have evidence that shows the account you gave us – the second account, that is, contradicting the first – was untrue.'

'Yes,' he said, unconsciously twisting the handkerchief he had in his hands. 'I was afraid you would. What I have told you now is the absolute truth, but it now comes down to this – do you believe me?'

On balance, and to her own annoyance, Fleming thought

she probably did. The squalid little man was quite stupid enough to behave as he had for just such stupid reasons, and arrogant enough to think he'd get away with it. If he hadn't lied, would he have been a serious suspect? Unlikely.

Not that she was going to tell him. She wanted him left to twist in the wind a little longer. She got up.

'Thank you for the information. We will take into account what you have said.'

At the failure of his confession to produce immediate absolution, Gloag looked almost comically dismayed. 'But – but now you've heard what I have to say, couldn't you at least tell me unofficially what you yourself believe?'

'Believe, councillor?' She gave him a wintry smile. 'I'm a police officer, not a theologian. Now, I'm afraid you must excuse me . . .'

When MacNee came into Fleming's office, she was frowning over one of those 'mind-maps' she was so keen on. She looked up, then, a little self-consciously, folded it over. He'd expressed himself fairly freely in the past about what he saw as a pointless exercise.

'Tam. Anything come up?' The words were hopeful, but the voice was flat.

He wasn't ready yet to explain his latest idea. He wanted to sniff around, talk to Christina, talk to Annie again, perhaps. When he'd played gin rummy, too, he'd always preferred to gather his winning cards so that he could put them down at the same time and say, 'Gin!' It was one of his weaknesses, and even what had happened last time he'd tried it hadn't discouraged him. Christina Munro wasn't tall enough to hit him over the head.

'Not a lot,' he said. 'Bit of a bummer about Ossian having a solid alibi – Andy Mac was telling me. So what's next – the Farquharsons?'

'Yes.' Fleming glanced at her watch. 'They're bringing them in shortly. She was unamused, I hear.'

'Given their statements were as full of holes as a fishing net, they're lucky not to be under arrest.'

'Certainly are. But we've given the press enough sensation lately.' Fleming gave him a pointed look.

He parried it effortlessly. 'Don't know what you mean, "we". Changing the subject completely, they're saying downstairs that Will's resigned. He's not even in today.'

It had the desired effect. 'He has? Oh – I'm sorry about that lad. He had real promise. And Tansy – what's the situation? Should I have a word with her?'

'Only if you're thinking of cruel and unusual punishment. She's black burning ashamed, as my mammy was always saying I should be about something I'd done.'

'Not sure she doesn't deserve to be.'

'Aye, she does. But "*gently scan your brother man . . .*"' he suggested.

She'd slated the patronising follow-on, '*Still gentler sister woman*', before now and he was prepared for some scathing comment. None came: Fleming looked as if some uncomfortable thought had occurred to her and he suddenly wondered whether, unlikely as it seemed, she too had known what it was to be tempted.

But all she said was, 'Is she coping?'

'Och, yes. Keeping her head down and hoping we'll all forget about it.'

MacNee saw her eyes go back to the folded-over paper on her desk. 'Tam,' she said slowly, 'how much thought have you given to the dead sheep?'

As she spoke, the phone on the desk in front of her rang and she picked it up. 'Yes?'

She listened, said, 'Thanks,' and put the phone down again. 'That's the Farquharsons arrived downstairs. I want them questioned separately, obviously, and we don't take no for an answer. Which do you fancy?'

'Lady Macbeth,' MacNee said immediately. 'That's what Andy Mac calls her. He reckons it's a conspiracy that she's master-minded. Interview under caution?'

Fleming considered. 'See how it goes. I reckon this is probably a preliminary skirmish, so softly-softly to start with. We've frightened the horses enough lately.

'Who's around? If Tansy's downstairs, she can pair up with you. I think Andy Mac's in the building so I'll draft him in. I don't think I want Campbell – he has the odd impressive insight but it unnerves me having to check in the course of the interview that he's still breathing.'

MacNee went off in search of Kerr. He was turning into the corridor leading to the CID room when Sergeant Bruce hailed him.

'Tam! Big Marge asked me to find you. I've just buzzed her again to say that the Farquharsons have been taken to the interview rooms and everything's set up for you to start.'

'Right.' Tam turned back. 'I'd better go straight there. Can you tell Tansy – in the CID room, I think. She's to sit in.'

'OK.'

Bruce headed off and MacNee went along to the interview rooms. He'd been hoping he might have been able to slide off quietly to check out this latest theory, but it wasn't on. And was he absolutely sure, anyway, that Fiona Farquharson didn't fit the role Andy Mac had assigned to her?

When Sergeant Bruce reached the CID room, DC Kerr was sitting at one of the desks with a sheet of paper in her hand and a thoughtful look on her face.

'Hi, Tansy!' Linda Bruce said brightly. 'Tam wants you for an interview. They're going to grill Colonel Carmichael's nephew and his wife – them that thought they'd a big windfall coming.'

Without looking up, Kerr said, 'Yes,' almost as if she hadn't taken in what had been said. Then, 'Is the boss in, do you know?'

'She's interviewing too. You'll see her along there.'

Kerr nodded and left, still with the paper in her hand. When she reached the interview rooms, there was no one around apart from a constable on duty outside.

'They're waiting for you. Better move it,' he advised as she approached. 'Big Marge and Andy Mac have started already. Tam's in there with the wifie.'

'Oh.' Kerr thought for a moment, then put her head round the door he had indicated.

'Could I have a word with you, sarge?' she asked.

It wasn't MacNee who answered. The woman sitting opposite him across the table, a stout middle-aged woman with high colour and straw-like blonde hair, looked up and glared. In the cut-glass tones that brought Kerr out in a rash, she demanded, 'What is this? Are we to be further delayed in getting this ridiculous situation sorted out?'

It was perhaps an indication that MacNee's recovery wasn't complete that instead of taking the woman on, he only said wearily, 'Is it urgent, DC Kerr?'

She hesitated. 'Not exactly urgent, no. But—'

MacNee didn't wait for the rest of her sentence. 'Then let's get this dealt with first.'

And Kerr, reckoning that in the grand scheme of things it probably didn't matter that much, went in, identified herself for the tapes and sat down.

23

If you could convict someone on demeanour alone, Giles Farquharson would right now have been on his way to Peterhead to start a life sentence. Shifty-eyed and ashen-faced, he was stumbling over his words. Holding up a notice saying in block capitals, 'I am a guilty man' would, DI Fleming thought, probably have been less revealing.

But guilty about what? The man was saying one thing, apologising, saying another, contradicting himself, then apologising again. As it had been Macdonald who had taken his earlier statements, he was leading the interview, putting them to Farquharson and challenging the version of events he had given.

Suspects who stuck to an improbable story in the teeth of evidence disproving it were common enough, and the ones who rolled up immediately and confessed weren't unusual. But Fleming had never known one who, while apparently sober, so quickly degenerated into spouting a sort of gibberish in which admission and denial seemed to come randomly and 'sorry' was the only coherent word.

The wildness of the man's replies was beginning to draw Macdonald into the morass of confusion too. Farquharson was breathing faster and faster and Fleming judged that he was starting to hyperventilate. They'd have him passing out on them if they weren't careful.

She had taken no part in the questioning so far but now she leaned forward. At the sudden movement, Farquharson jumped in alarm and she thought for a moment he was going to make a run for it. As Macdonald at her side tensed for action, she spoke with stern authority.

'Mr Farquharson, stay where you are and be quiet. You are becoming extremely confused and you need to calm down and take stock of what you are saying.

'Listen to me. You and your wife have given each other alibis for the times when both murders took place. It is evident that these are false from the CCTV footage we have checked. Now, I am going to tell you exactly what it shows, and you are going to tell me what your movements actually were, in accordance with that.

'You aren't going to explain, or apologise, or try to tell me anything about what your wife was doing. You are going to give me straight answers to direct questions.

'You and your wife did not drive into Kirkluce on Saturday evening in convoy. You came in some twenty-five minutes earlier. Yes or no?'

Farquharson's breathing had steadied. He hesitated only for a second, then said, 'Yes.'

'You were driving in the direction of your uncle's house. Did you go there?'

'Yes.'

Fleming and Macdonald exchanged startled glances. They had expected some story which, however flimsy, could be hard to disprove, and this frank and ready admission took them totally by surprise. She said hastily, 'Giles Farquharson, I am now going to caution you. You are not obliged to say anything, but anything you do say will be noted and may be used in evidence. Do you understand what that means?'

At least the caution in use in Scotland had the advantage of clarity over the newer English version, and he nodded.

'Could you say, "Yes," please, for the record?'

'Yes.' He seemed to have relaxed, as if a sort of fatalism possessed him now.

'What happened when you went to see your uncle?'

'I was going to plead with him to change his mind. I had gone there in the afternoon, you see, to talk about the superstore. Fiona was desperate that the chance shouldn't be missed and she wanted me to make it an issue of family duty.

'I didn't want to do it. But the thing is, I've been such a failure, a total failure, ever since leaving the army – and to be honest, I wasn't a terrific success even there. Being Uncle Andrew's heir was all I had to offer Fiona and the boys, and she was right – I owed it to them to stop him throwing away what should have been theirs in the future.'

There was something deeply pathetic about Farquharson's utter dejection. He might once have cut a fine figure in his uniform, but now the big man, with muscle run to fat, looked like a sagging sack as he slumped in the chair.

'I got there around four o'clock. Uncle Andrew didn't look pleased to see me, but he asked me in. He seemed very awkward, but I thought it was just because he was going to say no to ALCO and hated having to tell me. He'd do anything to avoid unpleasantness, Uncle Andrew.

'But then he told me he had a grandson and that he owed it to him to change his will, to set right the wrong he had done all those years ago. I was – well, struck dumb, really. Couldn't say anything. That was our future, gone. I'd failed again – and how was I to tell Fiona? Never a day went by without her planning what she'd do when we moved to Fauldburn House.'

Farquharson was talking now as if he were in the confessional. Fleming sat still and silent, willing Macdonald to do the same.

'Of course, he'd never actually promised me. It wasn't the sort of thing you discuss, after all – what you're going to get once a chap's dead. But my late mother was his only sister and he had no children so she'd always told me it would all be left to me. So this was – well, I felt as if he'd punched me. I was dazed.' He stopped, as if contemplating his own bemusement.

'I can see that,' Fleming murmured encouragingly.

'Yes. I was so devastated, I couldn't stay. I didn't wait to hear the details. I just turned and walked out without saying anything and drove around for a good while, trying to decide what to do. In the end, I thought, well, there's still time. He was pretty fit; I could work on him and persuade him to see it in a different light, see that as his closest legitimate relative I was due a sizeable share, at the very least.

'The grandson could be a fraudster, could be anyone. I didn't know anything about him – certainly not his nationality – but I could dig around a bit, check him out. Without telling Uncle Andrew, of course – no point in offending him. But then I thought that I could use all this to persuade him that to be fair, he ought to accept ALCO's offer so there would be plenty in the kitty to divide between us. If Fiona heard he'd agreed to sell, it would have got her off my back, and even if this grandson was genuine, it could be years before she found out what the situation was.'

'So you had told her nothing of this?'

'Couldn't face it.'

Fleming was interested. Like uncle, like nephew – keen to dodge unpleasantness. 'So you went there before the meeting, at quarter to six—' she prompted.

'Yes. Yes. It was – horrible!' He was becoming agitated again. 'I didn't know what to do, what would happen. I was – I was – he was dead, you see.'

'Dead when you got there?'

'Dead. Lying in the doorway. Shot. I went – thought, a heart attack, but – then I could see. Terrible. And if he was dead –

well, it was all over for me, for us. Finished. Ruined. What would Fiona say? My fault – not really – but what could I do?'

Fleming cut across him. 'Did you touch him?'

He shuddered. 'Couldn't – couldn't—'

'Was there anyone else around? Anyone passing the house when you drove up?'

'No – don't know. Didn't see – just me, by myself.' His breathing was getting shallower again until he was almost panting.

Macdonald poured some water from a jug on the table into a glass and gave it to him. 'Drink that. Take your time. You're doing fine.'

They waited while he sipped at the glass. When he seemed to be steadier, Fleming took up the thread again.

'You saw your uncle, realised he was dead. But you didn't summon help or phone the police—'

'You'd – you'd have thought it was me. Revenge – something. I was scared.'

'So what did you do?'

'Got back in the car. Drove away. Tried to think – well, pretend I hadn't been there. Then came back to park in town and go to the meeting.'

'And you said nothing to Mrs Farquharson?' Macdonald was sceptical.

'Nothing. No. It was going to be – well, hellish, frankly, when she found out. Couldn't face it,' he said again.

Macdonald pressed him. 'But she concocted an alibi for you? Why would she do that?'

'She just said I'd be suspected, being his heir. I hadn't done it, so it wasn't wrong. Easier, she said.'

Fleming closed her eyes in exasperation. The trouble that was caused by people who thought lying to the police would make things easier! 'And she didn't question what you were doing before you turned up at the meeting?'

'Didn't know. She'd no idea when I left home.'

'Right,' Fleming said slowly. There was a lot to assimilate; when Macdonald looked at her enquiringly she nodded to him to take on the next stage of questioning.

'When we spoke before, you said you knew Barney Kyle,' he said.

'He was at the motocross a couple of times in a group that hung about with Simpson and Black.' He sounded much more confident now that they were away from the subject of his uncle. 'Never had what you'd call a conversation with him.'

'And on Monday evening, when Barney was killed? What were you doing?'

'Don't know what time you're talking about. But I was at home till about eight when I got a phone call from Murdoch Forbes-Graham about some stirks that were loose on the road. I called the stockman, and we were trying to get them rounded up till after ten.'

It was, Fleming had to admit, a good alibi, checking out with what Forbes-Graham had told her earlier. Macdonald made a note of the stockman's name and address, but that pretty much wrapped it up.

Fleming looked directly at Giles Farquharson. 'Did you kill your uncle?'

He met her eyes without hesitation. 'Why would I? Him living long enough to change his will was our only hope.'

And you couldn't argue with that.

The interview with Fiona Farquharson was less protracted.

Confronted by the CCTV evidence and accused by DS MacNee of concocting a false alibi for her husband on Saturday, she was totally unfazed. 'You should be grateful,' she said brazenly. 'I knew he'd never have killed Andrew. To put it bluntly, he hasn't got the guts, but I knew how your plods' minds would work.

'He was the heir – or thought he was, thanks to Andrew Carmichael's despicable duplicity – so you'd have him clapped in irons before he could say, "I didn't do it." And then you'd have manipulated him, because he's not the sharpest knife in the drawer and there would have been a miscarriage of justice. So yes, I told you that we were together.'

Controlling himself with some difficulty, MacNee said, 'That's quite an admission, Mrs Farquharson. It's wasting police time, and it's a criminal offence.'

Fiona was scornful. 'Oh, prosecute me if you like. You'd be throwing away the tax-payers' money, since they'd just tell me I was a naughty girl and not to do it again. If it ever reached court, which it probably wouldn't.'

The woman was right about that. With mounting frustration, MacNee said, 'Let's turn to Monday evening, then. Again, you claimed that you were both together.'

'You said you were working in the kitchen and your husband was in his office,' Kerr put in, anxious to show some of the encyclopaedic knowledge of reports which she now possessed.

'Same reason – I told you. He was out for a while rounding up straying cattle or something, but you probably wouldn't have believed him.'

'Leave his movements out of it. It's yours we're interested in.' MacNee took a vicious satisfaction in making the point. 'You drove into Kirkluce very shortly before Barney Kyle was killed and back again afterwards.'

Fiona gaped at him with what appeared to be genuine astonishment. 'You don't mean – you can't think that I . . . oh really, this is just *too* ridiculous! I've never set eyes on the boy.'

Her total self-assurance, MacNee thought gloomily, was either the sort of acting that would make Dame Helen Mirren look as if she belonged in the Kirkluce Amateur Dramatic Society, or the bloody woman was right, and could most likely prove it.

'For the record,' she was saying now, 'I had my assistant Gemma Duncan working with me for the first part of the evening. I then drove her home and went in to check with her husband that he would be able to drive her to the Forbes-Grahams' the following night to save me having to come into Kirkluce, since she doesn't drive. I stayed talking, making final arrangements about the party for some little time – I couldn't be precise, but they will bear me out. Is that clear enough, even for you?'

Fiona looked at them disparagingly. Neither spoke, and with a triumphant smirk she grabbed another handful of salt to rub in the wound.

'Oh, and before you ask, on Saturday, when your cameras no doubt picked me up on my way to the meeting, I was on the telephone to a client about a lunch party she wanted to arrange, until I left. It was on the landline, so that can be easily verified, but I can give you her name as well if you like. Spell it out slowly, if your constable struggles with unfamiliar words.

'Earlier, Deirdre Forbes-Graham had come in to check that everything was in hand for their drinks party, and had a cup of tea. After lunch, which I had with my husband, I was working in the garden. Several people passed who would have seen me there – if you think you can take in several names at once, some of them quite long and hard to spell, I can give you them—'

MacNee got up. He could almost hear Tansy Kerr grinding her teeth and his blood pressure was going to shoot up to the top of the column and go 'Ding!' like one of those try-your-strength fairground machines, if he didn't get rid of this unpleasant bitch.

'That won't be necessary.' Officially, he ought to thank her for her cooperation, but they'd have to tear his throat open to get those words out. 'You're free to go.'

Fiona Farquharson swept out with one final contemptuous smile. Not trusting himself to speak, MacNee followed her.

He jerked his head towards the door of the other interview room. 'Husband's still in there with the boss, is he?' and when the duty constable nodded, said acidly, 'Probably enjoying it more than being at home with his wife.'

Coming out behind him after collecting the tapes, Kerr said, 'Tam—' but he was already on his way down the corridor.

'Something I have to do,' he said over his shoulder. 'Back shortly.'

Kerr stopped, frowning. Oh well, she'd better just get back to her reports – more stuff would no doubt have come in since this morning. She'd speak to him later.

Fleming was feeling thoroughly annoyed with MacNee. His interview with Fiona Farquharson had been brief, apparently, so there had clearly been no major breakthrough there either, but that didn't mean he should dash off without reporting.

She wanted him, mainly, to throw around the idea which had been stirring in her brain since on her latest mind-maps the arrows had all started pointing to one person, and for the first time she had felt the small shiver of excitement suggesting that she might, at last, have caught a glimpse of the trail to follow, as if she was at last at least a player in the mind game. It still wasn't definite, just a hint of a warped rationale . . .

Why a dead sheep, a man well on in years, a boy with his life before him – escalating crimes? She was still a long way from working out the implications, which was where Tam's thoughts on it would be welcome. But it felt right, somehow.

So where the hell *was* Tam? He'd been more bother than he was worth recently, what with the business about Christina Munro's shotgun, and whatever he'd been up to with Wilson (and that she *really* didn't want to know). Now he'd gone AWOL exactly when he was needed.

Had he got some lead on the murderer that he'd decided to follow up on his own, despite the disastrous consequences of his last attempt at individual enterprise? If he didn't get hit on the head this time, she'd be tempted to do it herself when he deigned to return.

MacNee parked the car in the yard outside Christina Munro's cottage. The front door was open; he banged on it, called, then stepped inside. The main room was empty, but there was a pot simmering gently on the old range. A brace of rabbits, strung by their hind legs from a hook in the ceiling over a newspaper placed to catch bloody drips, was attracting attention from two frustrated cats.

He went back outside. After the heavy rain last night, it was a golden day, with just a slight breeze to ruffle the hedgerow bushes, whose tired green leaves looked ready to take on their autumn livery with the first frost. The three donkeys were out in the paddock beside the house and when he looked over the fence he could see Christina at the farther end, in her funny crocheted hat, tweeds and heavy-duty waterproof boots which looked too big for her skinny legs. She was heaving at a fence-post which had tilted and he saw her push it vertical with surprising strength, then straighten her back painfully.

It was the dog that noticed him first, coming lowping across with those great deer-like bounds, ears pricked. It seemed to recognise him; the thin tail tucked between its legs twitched and it put its nose into his outstretched hand when it reached him, studying him with mild, intelligent eyes.

Then one of the donkeys raised its head. Curious about the stranger, it started towards him, followed by the others, and Christina too had seen him now. She made no gesture of recognition, only began plodding across the field. As she approached, one donkey turned to nudge her and she rubbed its soft muzzle absent-mindedly. The greyhound stepped daintily to her side and the other donkeys were gathering round her too, demanding their share of attention.

'Well, Tam MacNee, what are you after today?'

MacNee hesitated. On the five-minute drive out to Wester Seton, he hadn't really had time to plan out his angle of questioning. What came to him now was, 'I just wanted to tell you a story, Christina.'

She looked at him blankly, then the weather-beaten, nutcracker face split into a smile and she gave a cackle of amusement. 'It's been a long, long time since anyone told me a story. I haven't time to sit and listen so you can take that jacket off, MacNee, and come and give me a hand.'

Somehow, he found himself doing as he was told and climbing over the fence. His shoes weren't designed for squelching through mud and there were puddles from last night's rain to avoid as well as what the donkeys had lavishly deposited. Despite her hobbling gait, Christina moved faster than he did and was waiting for him when he reached the far end with sodden shoes and mud-spattered jeans.

'Hold that steady,' she ordered, indicating the post, 'while I shore it up.' She seized a spade which had been propped against the fence.

He felt moved to protest.

'Christina, that's heavy work. Give me the spade—'

She gave him a scornful look, then began digging with a practised economy of effort he knew he couldn't match. 'What about my story, then?'

Had there ever been a dafter interview with a murder suspect? Still, there was nothing for it now but to get on with it.

'There was once a woman who had a secret affair with a

man when she was very young. He used her, then dumped her, and all her life she held a grudge against him. Then years and years later, something happened – I couldn't quite say what—'

Christina was growing breathless from her efforts, but she managed to say, 'Not much of a story if you don't know what happened.'

'Maybe she found that all these years later he was at it again, taking advantage of a lassie she knew and cared about.' His eyes lingered on the crocheted hat. 'Anyway, whatever it was, it set her off. She'd been angry for years. She took a gun – she was a good shot – and she killed him.

'Could be she wasn't seeing things quite straight at the time. She was being persecuted by some boys and they were scaring her badly. She'd killed once and got away with it so maybe it wasn't so hard to do it again, and it would be the answer to her problems.

'But she was cunning. She'd two guns, the one she used to fire a harmless shot, the other, bigger one that she'd used already on the Colonel, to kill one of the boys – didn't matter which. That gun wasn't found. And she'd got her revenge at last, and the donkeys were safe and she wasn't scared any more because the boys wouldn't be back. A story with a happy ending, you could say – if you didn't mind about a couple of murders on the way through.'

Christina had stopped digging and straightened up. Now she put down the spade and looked at him squarely.

'Now I'll tell you a story, Tam. It's about an old wifie who looked just like me, who lived in a forest in a gingerbread house and one day a boy and girl called Hansel and Gretel came to see her. It's a fairy story, but it's a damn' sight more true to life than the one you've just told me.

'You stupid bugger! Oh, arrest me if you like – I was here right enough when that boy was killed and I've no one to say I was here too when the Colonel was shot, but it's God's truth.

'I never spoke to Andrew Carmichael in my life, didn't know about any current – activities.' She sniffed. 'Always supposing there were any. And you can't prove I'd another gun, because I didn't. You can search the place right now. Go on, take it apart if you like, dig up every square inch of the fields – I've nothing to hide. But you're wasting your time, MacNee, and even if you've the time to waste, I haven't. If I don't get this post set in, the donkeys'll be out.

'Now, are you going to help me or not?'

And MacNee, with his heady feeling that he could be on the verge of a breakthrough disappearing like snow off a dyke, held the post meekly while she finished her digging, then helped her stamp it firm, before retreating to his car with his tail as markedly between his legs as any greyhound's.

'Boss?' DC Kerr put her head tentatively round the door of DI Fleming's office. 'Have you a minute?'

Kerr, too, was feeling irritated with MacNee. She'd been trying to lie low, afraid of what Big Marge might have to say about her own behaviour. She'd suffered a mauling on occasion before, and it was an experience she would go a long way to avoid repeating. She'd hoped to give Tam the information that had come her way and have him relay it to the boss, but she'd no idea when he'd reappear, and getting stick for not passing this on as soon as possible wouldn't be any fun either.

To her relief, Fleming didn't seem to be planning to raise the subject of her behaviour. All she said was, 'Yes, Tansy?' but she wasn't looking severe.

Kerr went over to the desk. 'I found this with the latest batch of stuff that came through this morning. I thought you'd want to see it as soon as possible.'

Fleming took the papers she was holding out and glanced at the heading. 'Oh, a copy of Carmichael's will – that's interesting.' She began flicking through the pages, scanning them.

'There's one bequest,' Kerr was saying, when Fleming found it for herself, and her eyebrows shot up. 'Well, well, well!'

The bell rang for the period before break. Dylan Burnett slouched out with the rest of the class, then paused in the corridor.

One of his mates stopped too. 'Coming for a fag?'

'Nuh. Not just now.' He didn't feel like company. The other shrugged, and left him.

Come to that, he didn't really feel like school. He'd maybe slide when no one was looking, go back to the shop and have a talk to Johnny.

It wasn't difficult. There were loads of kids milling around and he just walked out like he'd permission. Not that he wouldn't have got it at the moment, if he'd said he wanted to go home, but he didn't need the hassle. Chances were no one would notice he'd gone.

Dylan was dead worried about his mother. She'd looked seriously weird this morning – well, she'd looked weird since this whole thing started, but this morning she was weird weird. She'd drifted round as if she was, like, out of it, and he'd seen that Johnny had noticed too.

He had a nasty cold feeling in the pit of his stomach, telling him it was drugs again. He'd been willing to swear she hadn't touched them for years and years but he could remember all too well how it had been when he was a kid, with her being scary and no food in their yucky flat. Apart from the odd puff on a spliff, he'd never done them himself, but there were guys he knew who did, and they were like that sometimes.

Johnny wouldn't fancy her if she got like that again – how

could he? He'd walk, wouldn't he, and then Dylan would have to stay with her while everything fell apart, or else go back to his dad and spend his life being trailed round manky wee towns, minding the shooting gallery and spinning the cars on the waltzer. Who wanted to live like that?

Watching TV last night with Johnny had been so cool, like they were a regular family. He'd never really had a proper father. Barney hadn't either, which was probably why they'd both hung out with Johnny. But he'd been trying not to think about Barney. Barney being dead – that spooked him.

If he told Johnny what was happening with his mother, spelled it out so he could make her stop before it all went bad – he was sure Johnny could fix it, get her help or something. She was just really stressed, that was all.

Dylan reached the showroom and tried the door, but it was locked, and there was no sign of Johnny inside. He frowned. Johnny'd said he was going to open up today, couldn't stay shut for ever.

Maybe there hadn't been any point. All the kids had been yakking on about how their parents weren't letting them go out on the streets because of the sniper, and there was hardly anyone around. Johnny had probably decided to do stuff in the workshop instead.

Dylan walked past the front of the building, then turned the corner towards the yard at the back.

24

'And where the hell have you been?'

MacNee, finding the eyes of two women fixed on him accusingly, and uncomfortably aware that he hadn't made much of a fist at getting the mud off his shoes and jeans, contemplated bolting. But that wouldn't solve anything; he said, 'Should I maybe go out and come back in again?'

'Don't bother. Just answer my question.' Fleming was in no mood to be trifled with.

'Fiona Farquharson has alibis for both murders,' was his next bid.

'Tansy told me. And Giles has an alibi for one and is most unlikely for the other. And?'

He shifted uncomfortably. He'd looked a fool in front of one woman this morning already. 'Well, I had this idea. Didn't come to anything.'

'You didn't think to share it with the team? Do you remember what happened last time?'

MacNee put his hand melodramatically to his head. 'Not – not clearly. In fact, I've sort of been walking round in a dwam, all confused, ever since, or else I'd have told you all about it – whoever you are.'

With Big Marge in her present frame of mind, it was a high-risk strategy, but to his relief her mouth began to twitch and she burst out laughing. Better still, she allowed herself to be distracted.

'MacNee, you're a pain in the backside! But look, something's come up. Tansy brought it in, and we've been working around it.'

For a moment, relief at being off the hook was replaced by a pang of jealousy. 'Oh yes?'

'She's been doing a good job, keeping on top of the paperwork. And this morning, we were sent a copy of Andrew Carmichael's will. There are some minor bequests, but the bulk of the estate goes to Salaman, with fifty thousand and the kids' school fees to Farquharson—'

That cheered MacNee up considerably. Fifty thousand might be serious money to him, but he guessed Fiona would be mightily pissed off.

'– and what is really interesting is, twenty thousand to Ellie Burnett.'

He blinked. 'Ellie Burnett,' he said slowly. Then, 'Did she know?'

'I phoned the solicitor. According to him, Carmichael was the type who'd have thought discussing money was vulgar. In the circumstances, though, if he'd decided to agree the sale with ALCO – and we don't know that he hadn't – he might have told her about it to reassure her about the future.'

MacNee's whole being revolted at the implication. Beautiful, fragile Ellie, who made him want to shield her from any rough wind, killing first for money and then, with cunning and utter ruthlessness, shooting a boy she disapproved of as a friend for her son? 'I shouldn't think she even knows how to fire a gun,' he said flatly.

Kerr sprang into the argument. 'It's hardly difficult. The upper classes, with barely a brain cell between them, seem to manage it, considering how much wildlife they massacre each year.'

Fleming was clearly irritated at this outing for Kerr's recently acquired hobby horse. 'What's that about, Tansy?

Knock the chip off your shoulder and we can get back to more important things.'

Kerr went red, and Fleming continued, 'This all sort of fits, in a way, with what I was wanting to run through with you, Tam. Always supposing you'd been here.'

She gave him a beady glare. He said hastily, 'I'm here now. What was it?'

'It starts with the dead sheep.'

Dylan Burnett opened the gate into the workshop yard. He'd been sure he'd find Johnny here, but the place was empty. He hesitated.

If Johnny had gone off somewhere, he didn't want to have to deal with his mother alone. He'd be better off at school. But he didn't want to go back there either, and the big Suzuki bike and the blue van were both there, so perhaps Johnny'd realised his mother had problems and stayed to look after her.

He opened the door to the flat and went up the stairs.

'I started looking at what had actually happened, instead of who had a reason for doing what. We'd been snatching at straws – conspiracy theories, blackmail, possible links that showed no signs of actually existing. But I still couldn't believe it was completely random.'

Didn't want to believe, more likely, MacNee thought rebelliously. He didn't like where this latest theory seemed to be heading, but since he'd used up most of his credit this morning, it would be smarter to wait till she'd finished before rubbishing it.

'The dead sheep,' she said again.

The woman was getting a bee in her bonnet about the animal. He was tired of thinking about it – the way folks were these days, it was probably just someone's idea of a sick joke.

'I thought it could have been a sort of graphic illustration of what could happen, if . . . And then, Carmichael's death—'

With the most perfunctory tap on the door, Sergeant Naismith burst into the room.

'Sorry, ma'am,' he said breathlessly. 'I think you'd better come.'

There had been no sound of voices when Dylan reached the top of the entrance stairs. 'Johnny?' he called hopefully, but he didn't get a reply.

The door to the sitting-room was ajar, though, and from it came the faint creak-creak of his mother's rocking-chair. He didn't really want to see his mother. There could be awkward questions about why he wasn't at school, for a start – if she still had her head together enough to notice. If she didn't, well, that would be bad too. On the other hand, she'd have heard him coming in and anyway she might know where Johnny was. He pushed open the door.

It was as if he'd stepped into a different reality, something from a bad film, maybe, or a too realistic computer game. At the far end of the long room, his mother was sitting, pushing the rocking-chair Johnny had brought from their own flat to and fro, to and fro. Creak-creak, creak-creak – time seemed to stand still.

Between them, lying spreadeagled on the carpet, was what was probably Johnny, though it was hard to tell. There was blood everywhere, on the walls, on the floor, on his mother's clothes. The smell—

Dylan gagged, then screamed and screamed again. He couldn't move, he was paralysed—

It was only at that point that Ellie seemed to notice him. Her eyes were blank and staring, but she blinked, then focused on him. 'Oh, Dylan, I've waited for you.' She sounded quite calm. 'I had to see you, to explain, so you'd understand—' She got out of her chair.

The power of movement came back to him. 'Don't – don't come near me,' he croaked, backing away.

'It's all right. You don't know, you see—'

All right? When Johnny was lying there—? She was coming towards him and he turned to run. He saw a gun, propped against a wall near the door, seized it and ran down the stairs.

He thought it might be loaded still. He held it carefully as he ran, ran and ran along the High Street till he came to the Kirkluce Police Headquarters. In his wake, two passers-by were reaching for their mobile phones.

'Drugs,' MacNee said heavily. 'Didn't realise. Wonder how long that's been going on? Don't really need to work out a motive, do you, if she's off her head?'

They were all shocked. He, Fleming and Kerr stood in the workshop yard as Ellie was taken away and uniformed officers set about securing the scene.

'You'd have to say she knew how to fire a gun, all right,' Kerr said with what MacNee felt was tasteless point-scoring.

'OK, OK. But that bonny girl – can't believe it, really.'

Fleming had been very quiet. 'Yes,' was all she said, then, 'Sorry. I'd better get back. Phone calls to make . . .' She moved away.

'Men!' Kerr was saying scornfully. ' "Bonny girl"! Even after all this time, you still think we're poor, pathetic, feeble creatures. But we're not.'

And MacNee, thinking of Fiona Farquharson, Romy Kyle and Christina Munro – and, indeed, Marjory Fleming and Bunty MacNee – couldn't find anything to say.

* * *

Fleming was on the phone to Superintendent Bailey when Dr Rutherford came in. 'Sorry, can I call you back? Police doctor's just arrived from seeing Burnett.'

She set down the phone. 'Dr Rutherford, do sit down. What is the situation with Ellie Burnett?'

Rutherford looked grave. 'In my judgement she ought to wait until tomorrow morning at the very earliest before she says anything, but she's adamant that she wants to do it as soon as possible.'

'Is she under the influence of drugs?'

'Without running tests I'm not prepared to make a judgement on that. But she should certainly have a lawyer present before she makes any sort of statement.'

'No,' Fleming said flatly. 'She has said that she is ready to speak to us, and as I understand it you are not claiming that she is medically incapable of giving informed consent. She cannot see a lawyer until we have had six hours to question her.'

Rutherford was definitely put out. 'Is that legal?'

'Yes.' Fleming was getting irritated in her turn; surely he should know that most basic rule?

'I see. Then I can only say she would be much wiser to wait but I can't state that she doesn't know what she's saying.'

It had become an adversarial situation, which she hadn't expected. 'Can I be quite clear about this? If asked later, you will confirm that you agreed she could be questioned?'

'Yes.' The word 'regretfully' hung on the air.

'Thank you, doctor.' They both stood up, and he left, clearly unhappy.

As the door shut behind him, Fleming pulled a face at it. It was probably something to do with the Hippocratic oath, and all very admirable, but she had a job to do. Ellie wasn't his patient; he was the police doctor and they were meant to be on the same side.

She looked at the time. She'd better phone the fiscal, before she called Bailey back for what was likely to be quite a lengthy discussion. With the phone calls that had come in about a deranged youth rampaging through the streets with a gun, rumours would be rife, and it would never do if the fiscal heard a garbled story from someone else, when he was technically in charge of the enquiry.

It was a surprise, when she was put through, to hear a female voice at the other end of the line saying, 'DI Fleming? This is Sheila Milne.'

One of the deputies, Fleming assumed, but she needed to speak to the fiscal himself. 'I'm sorry, I wanted Duncan Mackay.'

'I'm afraid that won't be possible. Mr Mackay is in hospital after a heart attack. I've been brought in as acting Procurator Fiscal.'

It was unreasonable to take against someone's voice, just because she was making an unconvincing attempt at a posh accent. Hiding her feelings, Fleming said, 'I'm very sorry to hear he's ill. Is he going to be all right?'

'I understand they're optimistic. They're having to do a triple bypass, though, so he will be off for some considerable time. So for the foreseeable future I shall be in charge.

'I've been reading your reports, naturally, but I would prefer to be briefed more directly. I want to know exactly what is being done in my name.'

Fleming's heart sank. The portly Duncan Mackay's reluctance to get directly involved had made her life a lot easier; she knew from colleagues in other forces what a nightmare it could be when you had a fiscal who fancied starring in high-profile cases.

'Of course, if that's what you want,' she said. 'In fact, I was phoning to alert you to the latest development . . .'

At the mention of another shooting, she heard a sharp

intake of breath at the other end of the line, but she hastily explained that the woman was in custody and seemed likely to enter a guilty plea, at least to the most recent killing.

'That's very satisfactory. Confessions are what we want – saves our time and the tax-payers' money.'

'I accept that,' Fleming said carefully. 'Provided we are sure of corroboration.'

'Inspector, do you imagine I am unfamiliar with Scots law?' The accent had slipped a little. 'Look, you do your job, which is getting the evidence, and I'll do mine, which is getting convictions. I hope we understand each other?'

'I'm sure we do.'

'I shall, of course, wish to visit the scene of the crime. Can you arrange for that, please?'

Fleming assured her this would be done, then put down the phone with serious misgivings. Somehow she didn't think Sheila Milne would be easy to work with, and with all her heart she wished poor Duncan a speedy recovery.

She wondered what Milne would make of the crime scene, which was one of the most unpleasant she herself had ever had to attend. The state of the body and the room – and Ellie Burnett, blood-spattered and dazed-looking . . .

MacNee was right, of course, that drugs were involved in this somewhere. But as she had been taken out past them, Ellie had looked full into her own eyes and there Fleming had seen such a depth of agony and despair that she felt shaken by it still.

It seemed, as the fiscal clearly thought, a satisfactory solution to it all – but Fleming wasn't satisfied. She pulled out the mind-map again and studied it, tapping her finger on her front tooth.

She was playing with ideas, twisting and turning them in her mind, when, with the suddenness of the tumblers of a combination lock falling into place, she understood. There was, as she had always a little desperately believed, a rationale behind all this, but it was one so warped, so shocking, that she gasped, then shivered. It was as if she had looked into a pit of darkness, and saw the deadly game at last for what it was. She still didn't know everything, but if she was right, there was a quality of purest evil here that she had never, in all her professional life, encountered before.

'Is there someone you can stay with meantime, Dylan?' Dr Rutherford asked gently. 'Your father—'

The boy's teeth were chattering so that he could hardly speak. The motherly Sergeant Bruce, who had only recently managed to get him calm enough to speak at all, said, 'I've contacted the mother of one of his schoolfriends. She's coming right over.'

'Good. You'll be all right then, Dylan, and I'm going to give you something that will make you feel a bit better. How are you about injections? OK? Good lad.'

He turned to take a syringe out of his case. 'Have we contact details for the father?' he asked Bruce as he rolled up the boy's sleeve.

'He's been reached by mobile phone. The funfair's up in Elgin at the moment – five, six hours' drive, maybe? I guess it'll be tomorrow before he gets here.'

Rutherford nodded. He rubbed Dylan's arm with a swab and injected the sedative. The boy hardly seemed to notice.

'You'll feel a bit better shortly. Just sit back and try to relax.'

Dylan did what he was told, like a zombie. As Rutherford went to the door he said to Bruce, 'I know he's not under age, but I want to make it clear that he is totally unfit to cope with police questioning, at least before his father gets here in the morning.'

He spoke sternly, and Bruce gave him a cool look. 'No

one's considering anything except his welfare at the moment. He'll talk to us when he's ready.'

Dylan looked up sharply. 'She killed Johnny. I'll do anything you want if it helps to make her pay. It was – it was like he was my real dad. And she killed him, her with her rotten drugs.'

Bruce sat down beside him and put her arm round his shoulders. 'Shush, shush. Time enough to think about it later.'

But she couldn't stop him. He had been in shock before; now, perhaps with the calming effect of the quick-acting drug, he was starting to think about it. 'And – and Barney, and that old guy too. Oh God, I want to die!'

Neither adult spoke. What was there to say? Soon, the chemical comfort would ease his agony, but only until tomorrow morning.

Fleming had detailed MacNee to join in Ellie Burnett's interview, though she wasn't entirely sure it was wise. Tam had been so disillusioned by the toppling of this icon of beauty and vulnerability that she was afraid he might go in too hard on a woman who must by now be teetering on the brink of mental disintegration.

She hadn't told him what she herself thought. It was, after all, still only a theory, and MacNee had the sharpest mind of any of her team. It would be better to let him come with a fresh mind to Ellie's evidence – always supposing it was coherent. Which would, presumably, depend on what drugs she had taken, and when.

'Yeah, sure.' MacNee gave his usual laconic response to the summons to Ellie Burnett's interview. He'd have been offended if Fleming had detailed anyone else, but he wasn't sure how much he wanted to do it.

His romantic soul, the part of him that responded to love poetry and patriotism, was well concealed, or so he liked to think, and overlaid in real life with healthy cynicism. Yet somehow Ellie Burnett had got under his skin and he found that hard to forgive.

And the drugs. He took a hard line on drugs – too hard, Fleming told him sometimes, but then she hadn't had his experience. They always trotted out the excuses about poverty and deprivation – well, been there, done that, got the T-shirt and the scars. And when it came right down to it, you'd a choice. A tough choice, if you'd been stupid enough to make the wrong one in the first place, but not making it was your decision and you should take the consequences. He was living proof that being a victim wasn't compulsory and he wasn't about to make allowances for her.

He was angry with himself for being gullible, and angry with Ellie for what she had made him feel, even if all she'd done was be what she was and sing like an angel. Added to that, what she'd done had left her son in pieces, according to Linda Bruce.

So he was taking quite a bit of baggage with him into this interview – not the best professional attitude, maybe, but that was just the way it was. Anyway, this was an open-and-shut case, and the boss had a talent for talking even the more reluctant ones through it. He could just tuck in behind.

But when he reached the interview rooms, Tansy Kerr was waiting in the corridor with Fleming.

'I'm going to get you and Tansy to take this one, Tam,' Fleming said. 'I want to observe, at least for a bit.'

'You're the boss,' MacNee said, but he wasn't happy. He could do keeping his mouth shut, but he wasn't good at disguising his feelings if he had to speak and he didn't want to scare the woman into silence.

'You kick off, Tansy,' he said. 'Get the story out of her, get her softened up before I start.'

* * *

Fleming leaned against the wall, watching quietly. MacNee had taken no part in it so far, letting Kerr ask the opening questions.

Ellie Burnett was sitting very still, her hands in her lap. She gave an occasional shiver, and yawned twice, but showed no other signs of suffering withdrawal symptoms. The clothing she had been wearing had been taken away for forensic examination and what she was dressed in now – a pink flowered skirt and a home-made heavy navy sweater – showed signs of having been grabbed at random from her wardrobe by someone else. Her fair skin, drained of all colour except for the blue-purple shadows round eyes that looked too large for her pinched face, appeared almost translucent, and the ill-assorted clothes seemed to swamp her thin body. Only her hair, with its rippling, silvery-blonde waves and tendrils, had life and energy.

Ellie seemed quite collected, sitting calmly with her hands folded in her lap, though Fleming suspected she had removed herself from what was happening to some safer place, either deliberately or as the result of profound shock. She was speaking in a level, lifeless voice.

'Last night,' she said in answer to Kerr's question about her drug use. 'H. I took it last night and then again this morning.'

'Not before?' Kerr was clearly sceptical.

'No. Not for years and years.'

'Why last night?'

'I needed it – for what I had to do. I was afraid, otherwise, that I wouldn't be able to do it.'

'What did you have to do, Ellie?'

'Kill Johnny.'

Fleming caught her breath. She could sense the tension in MacNee and Kerr too, but Kerr said without inflexion, 'You are admitting that you killed Johnny Black?'

'Yes. You saw him.' It was an unnervingly emotionless reply.

It was MacNee who spoke first. 'Did you know how to handle a shotgun?'

'Of course. I'm a good shot. I even used to do a bit of trick shooting when I was travelling with Dylan's father at the funfair.'

Fleming shut her eyes in despair. She thought she knew much of the truth already, but the way this was going, Ellie would never be believed. Perhaps it was time to intervene – but how could she blatantly lead a self-confessed murderer into justification?

'And did you get in some target practice with Barney Kyle and Andrew Carmichael first?' MacNee was demanding with a savagery inappropriate to a cooperative witness. Kerr shot him a warning glance but Fleming could see he was paying no attention.

The sudden accusation threw her. 'No – no, of course not!' she stammered. 'I didn't, I wouldn't—'

'Come on!' MacNee sneered. 'Who do you think you're fooling?'

He had disrupted the narrative and Kerr, who had been drawing out these damaging admissions, was looking understandably annoyed. Fleming stepped forward. 'Let's leave that for now. Ellie, why did you kill Johnny?'

She had barely noticed Fleming. Now she turned those great tragic eyes on her and said, 'I – I had to. You see—' She stopped and took a long, deep breath.

Fleming glanced at MacNee, daring him to speak, but he was listening with a cynical expression.

'I was – I was a sort of hostage, I suppose. Once he had me, as long as he had me, he wouldn't do anything. He warned me what would happen when I refused to sleep with him, showed me, even, with a sheep he'd killed, but I didn't believe he would do it.' She was becoming visibly calmer as she told this part of the story, as if she had rehearsed what she would say. 'And then when he killed Andrew – I was so shocked, I couldn't even think straight. I needed time – but he didn't give me time. Then it was Barney. So I had to give in. He'd have gone on, you know.'

'And you couldn't, I suppose, have called the police, to tell us what was happening, like a normal person?' MacNee hadn't changed his aggressive tone and she shrank back in her seat.

'He told me if I did, he'd have killed Dylan long before you could have got to him.'

The last, missing piece of the pattern fell into place. The arrows on her mind-map had focused Fleming's attention on Black. This morning she had understood the message of the shootings, each one more callous than the last and, she could now see, each one getting closer and closer to Ellie; Fleming had even, after Black's death, worked out what she believed had been their purpose. What had eluded her was the threat which had kept Ellie silent about murder and enduring repeated rape by a psychopath without even trying to escape, allowing him to play his terrible power game. The thought of it made Fleming feel physically sick, but the way Ellie was telling this, it sounded pat and unconvincing . . .

'Surely you could just have sent Dylan away somewhere?' Kerr was clearly unmoved.

'Dylan didn't want to go. And anyway somehow, he'd have reached him. Even if I killed myself, he'd have killed him afterwards. He told me. He'd have found him, tracked him down. A car accident – something. He was clever – he was a detective, you know.'

'And what did he find out about you?' MacNee said. 'What did he discover, that meant you had to kill him?'

'He didn't! It wasn't *like* that!' She glanced at Fleming, as if sensing she was in some way an ally, but Fleming could say nothing. Ellie would have to speak for herself.

'Let's see. You're suggesting that your victim – who, incidentally, was described by your son to one of our officers as being "like a real dad" – was some sort of sadistic psychopath?'

At the mention of her son, tears came to Ellie's eyes but she still spoke in the same steady, emotionless voice. A chilling voice, unless you believed what she was saying. 'Yes. Oh yes. And he could be charming, so charming! He'd worked on Dylan deliberately, so he thought Johnny was his best friend. If Johnny had pointed a gun at him, he'd have thought it was a joke.

'So you see, to save Dylan, the only thing to do was to kill Johnny.' She sounded almost matter-of-fact. 'I hoped there might have been another way – something – a miracle,' she shrugged, 'but there wasn't. That's why I got the drugs – so it wouldn't be so difficult. It makes things – less real, somehow.' She gave a convulsive shiver, as if, perhaps, that effect was wearing off, but she didn't stop.

'He had to have the gun somewhere, you see, and I thought probably in the workshop, so when he and Dylan were watching TV last night I took Johnny's keys and slipped out and . . .' she hesitated, 'went for a walk. Then when I came back, I let myself into the workshop. There was only one locked cupboard and I found it there, so I loaded it and took it upstairs to hide under the bed.'

'You planned this, then?' MacNee said sharply. It was the vital question: premeditation was evidence of murder. If he hadn't, Fleming would have had to ask it herself, however little she might like doing it.

Ellie didn't seem to understand the significance of her reply. 'I had to. It was the only way. When Dylan had gone to school I fetched the gun. Johnny turned and saw it, and came for me, but I got the shot in. I'd have killed myself then too – I had the other barrel for that – but I had to wait to see Dylan, to explain why. I couldn't have him think his mother . . .'

For the first time, she showed real emotion. Silent tears began to pour down her face. 'He wouldn't listen. Can I speak to him now? Tell him how it was? Where is he?'

'That won't be possible. He's being looked after,' Kerr said without sympathy.

'From what my colleague says, he'll refuse to speak to you anyway,' MacNee said cruelly.

Ellie gasped, then collapsed on to the table, sobbing.

Fleming had had enough. 'We'll break there,' she said, and went out, with a nod to Kerr to complete the formalities for the tape. MacNee followed her, and as the door shut she turned on him. 'What the hell are you trying to do, MacNee? Get the woman to top herself?'

'Oh, I doubt it. Cool as a cucumber, that one. And she wouldn't be much of a loss, would she?'

Fleming looked at him coldly. 'I'll have to have her put on suicide watch. And did you listen to what she had to say?'

'Yes, of course I did. She was claiming rape, but she would, wouldn't she? Didn't have a lot to back up her claims with, though. I've seen them together, and when I was questioning her, he was clucking round her like a mother hen, kept making excuses for her. Then, remember, when Linda Bruce asked her if there was a problem, she said no, didn't she? If she'd told Linda the story she told us just now, we'd have had the handcuffs on him before he could do a thing.'

'But in her situation, you could be far too afraid to work that out,' Fleming argued.

Kerr came out, and Fleming turned to her hopefully. 'What did you think, Tansy?'

Kerr pursed her lips. 'Quite a piece of work that one, isn't she? Had it all figured out. Could have sounded quite convincing, if Black didn't have such a solid alibi for Carmichael's killing.'

He had, of course. Somehow, Fleming had forgotten that, but what Ellie had said chimed so exactly with her own theory that she wasn't about to give it up. Solid alibis weren't always as solid as they at first appeared.

But if Ellie hadn't been convincing in there, how would she appear to a jury?

The Procurator Fiscal was clearly disappointed that confessions had not been forthcoming for the other two murders. Still, she said, at least there was no problem about the murder charge for Black's killing. Manslaughter as an alternative charge, a tentative suggestion from Fleming, was instantly dismissed.

'The lawyers can have their fun with that one,' Milne said flatly. 'And we can state that we are not looking for anyone else in connection with the other cases.'

'I'm going to have another look at Black's alibi for Carmichael's murder,' Fleming said. 'I feel there may be holes in it.'

'No, you are not, inspector. That's the job of the defence, and they are not going to have it done for them in police time. Your job is to look for evidence against her in the other two cases, though given the high level of success you have enjoyed so far,' Milne said with biting sarcasm, 'we may never get it. It may have to be enough that we know the woman's behind bars.'

The conversation finished with procedural arrangements, then Fleming put the phone down, deeply depressed.

She'd argued the point with MacNee and Kerr – 'Why would she kill the sheep? Why Barney Kyle?' – and met a stonewall as they united against her.

'Could have been vandals that killed the sheep, for all we

know,' MacNee had said, and Kerr added, 'And Ossian told us she hated Barney because he was getting Dylan in trouble. If she could shoot Black in cold blood—' She shrugged.

Fleming pointed out how well Ellie's account had fitted with her own hypothesis, but that had merely increased their scepticism. 'She'd dreamed up a story to fit the facts so the same story occurring to you doesn't mean a lot,' MacNee had said, and Kerr plainly agreed with him.

Fleming made a heated defence, but they only listened in silence until she recognised the futility of the argument and let them go.

All she could do was detail Macdonald and Campbell to finish the interview, checking details of times and places, and hope that something to support Ellie's version might emerge, but since she hadn't heard from them after they'd finished, she could only assume that there was nothing significant.

She could always defy the fiscal and push on Black's alibi. If he'd gone to Carmichael's house by way of one of the backstreets, for instance, avoiding the cameras, he would only have needed fifteen minutes at the most; the boys watching football might well have assumed he was below, in the workshop. But even if she did prove it could be shaken, the fiscal's office had wide powers in deciding what it would and would not lead as evidence, or even disclose to the defence.

Sick at heart, Fleming decided to pack it in for the night. It was ten o'clock, and tomorrow she was burying her father.

For Angus Laird's funeral service the parish church, where he and Janet had been married and their daughter had been christened, was almost full. As the minister announced the last hymn, Fleming glanced round. She had never been under the illusion that her father was popular, but the number of officers past and present among their family and friends suggested professional respect, at least. The Chief Constable had actually asked Donald Bailey to be his official representative in making a tribute, an unexpected honour. Marjory was pleased for herself, but even more for Janet.

Today, as the final farewell drew near, Janet's composure had deserted her. She had needed Bill's arm to help her down the aisle, and was sitting now, head bowed, as the congregation sang the twenty-third psalm, to the tune 'Crimond'. It had been sung at their wedding too; was she, perhaps, seeing a tall young man, standing waiting for her at the top of the aisle where his coffin now stood?

Marjory herself was calm today: she felt as if she had cried herself out – or perhaps yesterday's events had somehow blunted the raw edge of her grief. Cat, upset by her grandmother's distress, was blowing her nose, but Cammie, tall and solemn at his father's side, was steady enough. He looked like a young man, not a child, Marjory thought with a stab of pain. The years passed so quickly, one generation going and the next coming up to take its place.

She looked anxiously at her mother as they stood waiting for Angus's coffin to pass, but she had got shakily to her feet with Bill's arm round her. Marjory breathed a prayer of gratitude that at least, following the old Scottish tradition, the women would not be going to the graveside.

The walk down the aisle seemed very long. Marjory smiled at the sympathetic faces turned her way, but Janet's head was bent and her daughter wondered if she even saw them. She didn't stop at the door either and Marjory, with a glance at Bill, stepped forward to support her mother, while he and Cammie waited to line up at the door with the minister. With Cat on Janet's other side, they went slowly down to the car waiting to take them home.

They were putting the coffin into the hearse now, laying on top of it the two wreaths – the Flemings' one, of autumnal flowers, and Janet's own, a wreath of red roses so dark they were almost black.

Janet stopped, then stepped forward from her daughter's protective arm as the undertakers respectfully fell back. She touched her trembling fingers to her lips, and then to the coffin. And Marjory found that, after all, she still had tears left to shed.

25

It was a dreich Edinburgh day, with leaden skies and a sharp east wind driving the rain which was putting a shining slick on the grey cobbled setts and flagstones of Parliament Square. The severe front of Parliament House and the looming bulk of St Giles Cathedral were uncompromisingly bleak, with their stone rain-sodden until it looked almost black. The only colour around came from the garish souvenir shops of the Royal Mile, flying bedraggled Saltires and Lion Rampant flags, with windows full of tartan dolls and thistle tea-towels and T-shirts demanding, 'Wha's like us?'

Coming out of the High Court of the Justiciary, where Ellie Burnett's trial for murder was in progress, DI Fleming made a disgusted face at the weather and put up an umbrella. DS MacNee, behind her, hunched his shoulders and turned up the collar of his black leather jacket.

'Calls itself May!' he said bitterly. 'I'm perished with cold. See Edinburgh? East-windy, West-endy – you can keep it.'

'Mmm.' Fleming plunged her free hand into the pocket of her trench coat. She was feeling deeply depressed.

Neither she nor MacNee had been needed as witnesses, and this was the first day they had come to the court. The trial was in its closing stages, with Ellie Burnett in the witness box.

From what Fleming had gleaned from officers who had been called to give evidence, and from the media coverage, she gathered it wasn't going well for the defence. The prosecution had managed to suggest that Black had been killed because he'd discovered Ellie's previous crimes, highlighting her monetary reasons for killing Carmichael and her expressed dislike of Kyle as a bad influence. Dylan's testimony, talking about Johnny's care and kindness with a genuine sense of loss, taken together with outright condemnation of his mother, had been damning indeed.

Ellie had no alibi to offer and the QC for the defence seemed to have found nothing in Black's background, either, to support what Ellie had said about him. Fleming had wanted to do a bit more digging herself, but the fiscal, supported by Superintendent Bailey with his eye on the budget, wouldn't hear of it. And, Fleming had to acknowledge, it wasn't unreasonable: they hadn't found any record of criminal activity, either by him or the agency, and it wasn't the job of the police to try to punch holes in the prosecution case.

She still stubbornly refused to believe that Ellie's story was a tissue of lies. Despite intensive work on the murders of Carmichael and Kyle, both by themselves and by the team from Stirling drafted in as assessors of the investigation, no evidence implicating Ellie had come to light over these past months, even with all the forensic reports in. There was nowhere else to go, either to convict her or to confirm the accusations about Black, and that wasn't for want of trying on Fleming's part.

The gun Ellie had used was loaded with the type of cartridge which had killed all three victims, though Fleming had made the point that the fingerprints of the dead man had been found on it as well as hers. Ownership of the gun, MacNee retorted, wasn't in dispute. He'd kept an unlicensed gun. So? And the cartridges used to kill Carmichael and Kyle had no prints at all.

Just as stubbornly, MacNee persisted in his belief that Ellie was guilty. Whatever Fleming said, his reply was, 'Depends how you look at it.' Even mentioning the dead sheep became provocative.

'You might as well be a sheep yourself, bleating on about it,' he said in a frank exchange of views over an early evening pint in the Salutation one night when Fleming had joined the others to raise a glass to an officer's retirement. 'You don't know for a fact that the beast was shot. Sandy Langlands is not just what you'd call an expert and Linda told me she never even looked at it, it was so messy. Maybe it was run down in the road and someone dragged it there out of the way.'

She had nothing to say to counter that, and in the end they had agreed further argument was pointless.

So today, Ellie Burnett was on the stand, fighting not for her freedom, but for a verdict of manslaughter rather than murder, and a lighter sentence – even a very light sentence, if her version of events was accepted. She had been ready to plead guilty to the lesser crime, but the prosecution had no interest in a deal. The hidden agenda was the assumption of her guilt for two murders which seemed unlikely ever to yield enough evidence for a prosecution.

As Fleming and MacNee walked off down the Royal Mile – looking, in Fleming's case, for a café which didn't only serve pies, and in MacNee's, for one that didn't fail to offer them – she said, 'She's not doing well, is she? And this is the easy part, with her own advocate taking her through the story. Wait till the prosecution gets started.'

'Didn't do herself any favours, anyway,' MacNee agreed.

Ellie had looked almost extinguished after her nine months on remand. The exuberant hair had been scraped into an unbecoming bunch at the back and her face was without colour or animation. The magnetism she had somehow possessed had vanished and her answers sounded as if she had them by heart – as indeed, having gone over them so many times, she probably did.

'You know her problem?' Fleming said. 'It all hinges on her claim that he was so utterly obsessed with her that he would kill twice to possess her. And I could see the men on the jury thinking, "You're joking!" and the women going, "If she's Helen of Troy, I'm Cleopatra." I think she's finished.

'And who knows, Tam? Maybe you were right after all.'

'Aye.'

There was something in his tone that made her look at him sharply. 'You're not changing your mind, are you?'

'We-e-ell,' he said, and stopped suddenly. 'Look – what about this place? I can get a pie and a pint and you can be high-minded and have coffee and a sandwich if you like.'

The pub looked decent enough. Fleming compromised on a sandwich and a half, and they found a table.

'Go on, Tam,' Fleming urged. 'Well?'

'She had to be smart as well as tough to work out all that to cover up what she had done. And today – well, that wasn't a smart lady. That was a victim, maybe a victim of the prison service, OK, but it got me wondering . . .'

Fleming smiled at him. 'You and Bunty,' she said affectionately. 'Dog with three legs, cat with one eye, a broken woman – it's all the same.' MacNee glowered at her over the rim of his glass, but she went on, 'The trouble is, Tam, wondering isn't any good. I've been wondering for months, and it hasn't made any difference. All you can hope is that there's a stubborn member of the jury who looks at it that way too and can convince the others.'

'How's the trial going, boss?'

DC Kerr came along the corridor from the CID room to find Fleming and MacNee, just back from Edinburgh, talking at the foot of the stairs.

Fleming grimaced. 'Not good for Ellie. The afternoon was worse than the morning, and in the morning she didn't come over well. It's his lordship's summing up tomorrow, and if you want a bet I'll give you a pound to a dud penny that it's unfavourable.'

'Poor woman,' Kerr said, but without real feeling. 'Tam, there was a message for you from your pal Sheuggie in Glasgow. Got some good news for you, he said.'

'Always ready to hear good news,' MacNee said. 'Makes a change.'

He went on to the CID room, and Fleming slowly and unhappily climbed the stairs.

'Here, Tam – just thought I'd tell you what happened about Ronnie Lafferty. You know, the guy whose fingerprints you got when he cheeked your Big Marge last year.'

'Oh aye – gutter scrapings, him. Well?'

'Ten years. How about that?'

'That'll teach him to mind his manners. Good result. As it happens, I'm just back from the High Court myself. You maybe read about the case – there was a lot of rubbish in the press about it being a sniper.'

Sheuggie was vague, and MacNee tried to jog his memory. 'The victim was a guy from your patch – had a detective agency. Johnny Black.'

'Black?' Sheuggie was puzzled. 'You've got it wrong there. Black was killed, oh, must have been well over a year ago. We still haven't laid hands on the killer, but we know who he was.'

'You're kidding,' MacNee said hoarsely.

'Kidding? Listen and learn, my son. Sad case, was poor old Johnny. Getting a bit past it, then his only son who'd been with him in the business died, he'd no other family, and he started drinking till he never knew if he was coming or going. As far as we could piece it together afterwards, he took on an assistant without making the usual checks, and picked a right one – Joe Connolly, with a record for GBH and stalking. We had him on a rape charge too, but we couldn't make it stick. He did it, though, right enough. I'd dealings with him – psychopath, if you ask me.

'Persuaded Johnny to let him take charge of everything, managed the business and was operating under Johnny's name, till he cleared out the office bank account, shot Johnny and disappeared around last March sometime. Poor old Johnny – lay there a couple of weeks before someone found him. And we'd never have known who'd done it if Connolly's prints hadn't been all over the place. Not that it did us any good – got clean away with it.'

MacNee found himself, for a moment, lost for words. Then he said, 'Not quite clean, maybe, Sheuggie. Send me the mugshot. If it matches, we've cracked another case for you. We'll be sending in the bill.'

'Good God!' Fleming said, when a breathless MacNee appeared in her room and spilled out the story. 'Of course, we never took fingerprints from Black except once he was dead, to establish that they were his on the gun, and naturally no one ran them through the computer. If you'd spoken to one of your pals in Glasgow to find out about the agency, his death would have come out then, of course, but Tansy just checked the computer records.'

'And John Black's a common enough name. When Ellie killed him the media just described him as working in a motorbike showroom, so no one in Glasgow made the connection. And Sheuggie said they'd circulated pictures of Connolly as being wanted, so no doubt they'll be in a file somewhere, but another shooting in Glasgow doesn't really make the front pages.

'So where do we go from here?'

'I call the fiscal. It's late, but I've got an emergency number.'

Fleming was reaching for the phone as she spoke. 'Get her to contact Edinburgh first thing and explain that new evidence has emerged, ask for an adjournment.'

'Aye, you could.' MacNee was looking sceptical as he listened to the conversation and watched Fleming's face get darker and darker.

'But it's a matter of justice,' she said desperately at one point, and eventually, 'I shall be taking it up with my superintendent,' before she slammed down the phone.

'She flatly refuses to lift a finger. Anecdote and speculation, she says. Nothing to do with us. If the defence can come up with the evidence, they can lodge an appeal. I'm going to see the Super, at home if he's left for the day.' She got up.

'And you think that'll do any good?' MacNee said drily. 'Oh, he won't have the same attitude as she does – we're going to have real trouble with that one – but he'll talk about taking your time, letting Glasgow use their budget for any further investigation . . . I can write the script.'

Fleming, already on her way to the door, stopped and came back. 'Yes, of course he will. There's no hurry, is there? Ellie will go down tomorrow for murder, and Dylan will think his mother is a serial killer and the psychopathic bastard who took a sadistic joy in destroying lives was a saint.

'I believe her when she said she would have killed herself, if it hadn't been for the threat to her child. She did it all for him. But will it change what he's in the habit of thinking, if the truth does come out eventually? The majesty of the law will proceed at its usual dignified pace – they won't speed things up.'

'Could take years,' MacNee said. 'Years and years.'

When Marjory Fleming arrived home the next evening, tired and depressed, Bill was just going up to walk the hill to check on the sheep. It was a bright spring evening and after a couple of wet days the colours were particularly fresh and bright.

'I'll come with you,' Marjory said, kicking off her shoes in the mud-room and putting on wellies instead. 'I need the exercise. Where are the kids?'

'Cat brought Jenny home. They're allegedly working on a project, but unless it's on pop music I don't think much is getting done. I've sent Cammie off to do his homework, but he was helping me drench some of the sheep after school today – he's getting to be a real help around the farm.

'I phoned the plumber about that leak from the sink in the utility room—'

They set off through the fields with Meg racing in excited circles round them, talking domestic trivia as Bill scanned the sheep they passed with a practised eye, until they reached the top of the hill where they could look down to the farm and across the valley. The sky was a soft eggshell blue with slow-drifting fluffy clouds, and in the still air birds were winging their way back to roost. Below them, the old orchard was foaming with pink blossom and the low sun was silvering the slates of the farmhouse roof. Marjory turned to admire the view, taking a deep, deep breath, and Bill watched her sympathetically.

'Hard day?' he said. 'What was the verdict?'

'Murder, of course. You could see in the jury's faces that they all believed she did the other two killings as well – you would, wouldn't you? But she didn't, Bill – we've got proof that what Tam found out was right. They faxed through the mugshot, and it's definitely him. But the fiscal's only interested in her conviction record – she'll be happy now.'

Marjory's lip curled in distaste as she went on, 'And the worst of it is that now Glasgow knows that Connolly's dead, Black's murder will go on the back burner. Tam reckons it could be years.'

'And you can't tip her off yourself?'

Fleming pulled a rueful face. 'Not if I want to keep my job, no. And of course, she's not technically been tried for anything except killing Connolly, which she did. All this would just have been mitigating evidence, so the jury might bring in manslaughter.'

'For which she'd go to jail anyway,' Bill pointed out. 'Nothing you could do about that.'

'I know. It's just – I can't bear to feel that Connolly somehow won, after all. That he managed to drive her to kill him, that he poisoned the relationship with her son . . . The world shouldn't be like that!' she cried passionately.

Bill looked down at her fondly. 'Still the idealist, in spite of everything!'

'And when you think about it, it all stemmed from kind, amiable Andrew Carmichael. If he hadn't been too cowardly to face up to his wife and acknowledge his daughter, his grandson would never have had to hire a detective to find him and none of this would have happened to poor, hapless Ellie.

'Sometimes you can convince yourself that good has come out of something like this, that the shock has changed the lives of the people who became involved for the better, but this time I can't believe it has. The Craft Centre has been sold off, the Gloags are in the throes of an acrimonious divorce, Fiona Farquharson will go on feeling bitter about her poor, downtrodden husband and Ossian will repeat the cycles of manic ups-and-downs unless that silly mother of his makes him get psychiatric help. All you can hope is that he may produce some more masterpieces on the way through.'

'Plenty of artists have,' Bill pointed out. 'Creative people often seem to have that sort of temperament. Just like us farmers are all stolid, unimaginative, lacking in the finer feelings . . .'

'People who fish for compliments don't get them,' Marjory said, but she tucked her hand through her husband's arm as they plodded down across the next field to where some of the flock were grabbing the last few mouthfuls of grass before they settled for the night. Her mind, though, was still on Ellie Burnett, sedated, perhaps, or sleepless tonight as she lay in her cell.

The next morning, there were headlines in the *Daily Mail.* 'Was Ellie's victim a killer himself?' Beneath it, an exclusive report from the crime correspondent speculated about a link between the murder of a private detective in Glasgow and the man who had lived under his name in Kirkluce, Galloway, only to die at the hands of his partner.

'The fiscal's fit to be tied,' Fleming said with relish. 'There's pressure building strongly for an immediate appeal. She was all ready to accuse me of leaking it, but of course I pointed out that the Glasgow force, having found out, would be keen to get as much publicity as possible for having tracked him down.'

'Right enough,' MacNee said solemnly.

She looked at him sharply, a terrible suspicion dawning. 'Tam – it wasn't you, was it?'

'Me?' He was indignant. 'The *Daily Mail*? That fascist rag? I wouldn't touch it with a clothes peg on my nose and a ten-foot pole.'

He wasn't even minimally convincing, but she didn't push him. There were, indeed, certain things it was better for an inspector not to know.